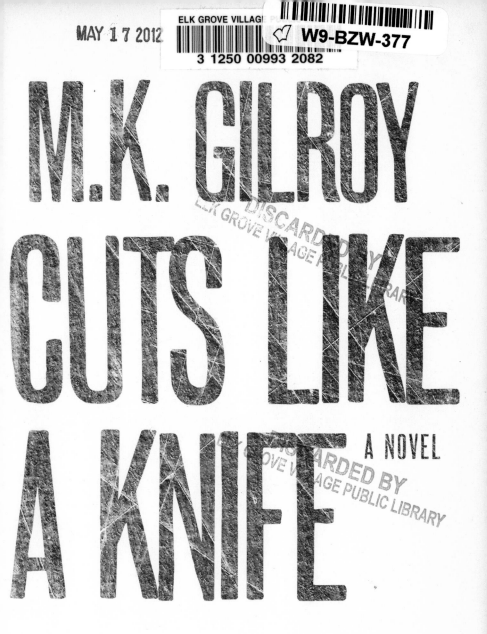

M.K. GILROY

CUTS LIKE A KNIFE

A NOVEL

WORTHY
PUBLISHING

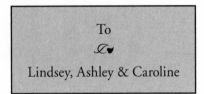

To

L♥

Lindsey, Ashley & Caroline

© 2012 by Mark Gilroy Creative LLC
www.markgilroy.com

Published by Worthy Publishing, a division of Worthy Media, Inc., 134 Franklin Road, Suite 200, Brentwood, Tennessee 37027.

HELPING PEOPLE EXPERIENCE THE HEART OF GOD

eBook available at www.worthypublishing.com

Audio distributed through Oasis Audio; visit www.oasisaudio.com

Library of Congress Control Number: 2012931878

This novel is a work of fiction. Any references to real events, businesses, celebrities, or locales are used only for a sense of authenticity. Any resemblance to actual persons is entirely coincidental.

For foreign and subsidiary rights, contact Riggins International Rights Services, Inc.; www.rigginsrights.com

978-1-936034-69-7 (trade paper)

Cover Design: Faceout Studio, Tim Green
Cover Photography: Tyler Gould
Interior Design: Inside Out Design & Typesetting

Printed in the United States of America
12 13 14 15 16 17 18   LBM   9 8 7 6 5 4 3 2 1

THE END OF MARCH

It was one of those March days
when the sun shines hot
and the wind blows cold:
when it is summer in the light,
and winter in the shade.

Charles Dickens

1

March 31, 9:59 p.m.

I should have stayed in California. It was seventy degrees in San Diego yesterday. Almost orange on the weather map. It snowed here last week. And then the DePaul University kids showed up in swimsuits at Wrigley for the Cubs game today. I was stuck next to a screaming troop of baboons. They distracted me from a good game. One yammering monkey spilled beer on my scorecard. I hate it when my scorecard gets smudged. I like a neat scorecard. If I sit near that profane waste of human life again—and he howls at drunk girls in bikinis the whole game—I will kill him. I wonder if he's bright or ever sober enough to realize that's not a figure of speech when I use it.

Maybe I'll teach him what the word exsanguination *means. A slice to the femoral artery would be a simple and effective lesson— much too kind for him, really. He spilled beer on my scorecard.*

I can't figure out what to wear in this wasteland of broken asphalt. I left my jacket at home when I went to the art museum two days ago. I froze on the walk over. It almost hurt as much as suffering through the Mark Rothko exhibit. I think I know why he killed himself. That's not art; that's misery with a straight edge. Then I put my jacket on the same afternoon and was sweating. I don't like to sweat when I'm not in my workout clothes.

Chicago weather. Why would anyone want to live here? I should be able to help a few of the city's denizens find ultimate relief.

My days of living in self-imposed limbo are coming to an end.

Six months of restraint and anticipation. Painful. Excruciatingly painful. Being denied of what is rightfully mine—not being able to experience my life in full. It has been torture to my soul. But you don't do what I do without a precise and careful system. And personal discipline. I am rich in both. That's what makes me unique. Special. A force above all others.

They don't have a clue as to who I am and all I've accomplished yet. That's good. But that makes me feel sad, too. My signature artistry will never be on exhibit for the world to marvel at. I suspect certain law enforcement agencies know I exist by now. I would certainly hope so. But what can they do about it? Nothing. I'm too careful, too meticulous, too good. Someone is sitting behind a computer right now looking for me and wondering where I'll show up next. I bet I'm driving him crazy. Maybe it's a her.

Tomorrow is April Fools' Day. Fools indeed.

Here I am. Sitting at the precipice of my next great work. Ready. I am back.

THE MONTH OF APRIL

April is the cruelest month.
T.S. ELIOT

Mom, I told you this isn't a good time. I've got to go."

"Honey, it's never a good time."

"I know, Mom, but it really isn't a good time this time. I have to go. Now."

My partner looks at me with utter incredulity. He's just bounced our car through a couple potholes, slammed the gearshift into park, and unbuttoned his sports jacket. I see him flip the snap on his holster for easy access to his Glock. I shouldn't have picked up Mom's call, but I thought I could get off the phone fast. She keeps nagging that I never pick up. Now I'm going to hear how I'm always the first to hang up. I can't win.

"Mom, I'll call you back. I'm getting off right now. I have—"

"You'll be at Jimmy and Kaylen's Sunday?"

"Yes, Mom. I have—"

"And church?"

I don't get to answer because Don reaches over, snatches my cell phone from my hand, and hits the red "end call" button. I wonder if it's possible to make the sound of slamming the phone down by hitting the button with force. If so, Don just did it.

"Momma's going to have to wait, Kristen. He isn't going to hang around all day waiting for us to say hi. Let's get in there. Now."

A surge of adrenaline courses through my body as I step out of the car, touch the gun that's holstered on my side one more time—just to make sure it hasn't mysteriously disappeared—snap and unsnap the top strap, and head into the Gas & Grub, game face on.

As we walk through the door the two guys working the cash register nervously look up at us, probably wondering if they're about

M. K. GILROY

to get busted for selling cigarettes to minors again. We pulled into the parking lot in our unmarked, mud-brown Crown Victoria—not the world's greatest disguise when you want to approach a suspect under the radar. The extra antennae on the trunk lid don't help either. Might as well put a Chicago Police Department billboard on the roof in neon letters.

My partner, Don Squires, gives a nod as he heads down one aisle and I take the one next to it. I quickly round the corner to cut off our suspect's line of escape. Don is four or five feet away from him on one side and I position myself an equal distance away.

"Don't move. Leave your hands where we can see them," Don says with the throat-rumbling snarl he saves for special occasions like this.

Lloyd, a friend and a 300-pound EMT from one of the ambulance services, recognized the punk's description from an APA bulletin and put the call straight to my cell phone. I know what Lloyd was doing there and need to kick his butt for eating those quarter-pound hot dogs they serve. I called Dispatch for backup while Don hung a U-turn in heavy traffic and stomped on the accelerator.

The punk, late teens or early twenties, is a retro-'80s piece of work. He's wearing a black T-shirt with a skull and the name of a group that I don't recognize in jagged, blood-red letters dripping off a computer screen. TwistedTweeters. Clever—almost. He's got a thick heavy chain hanging from the front pocket of his black jeans, connected to what I assume is a wallet that he doesn't like to use, based on his current crime spree. All he needs is those black boots with the metal and leather straps to finish his ensemble. But surprisingly he has on a pair of comfort shoes that look like what we used to rent at the bowling alley; all black, of course, but you can see the stitching. Footwear isn't going to slow him down if he makes a run for it. But it's not going to be an issue; he has nowhere to go.

Neither Don nor I have pulled guns because the convenience store

6

is packed. Doesn't mean our hands aren't touching the brushed metal grips, however. There must be twenty gas pumps out front on a busy street. And people from the blue-collar, working-class urban neighborhood are using the back door too. So we've got people coming and going from every direction. No sense starting a panic. We have a CPD mandate that prohibits us from taking risks that are likely to result in collateral damage—even if it means allowing a suspect to escape. Not that that's happening today.

I'm staring at the punk's hands. If he even twitches anywhere near a pocket, my Beretta 96 is coming out in a hurry.

The kid looks up to see Don holding up his detective shield. Even with the punk in near profile, I can see his glare of hatred. He mouths something to Don that I can't make out, but I'm guessing he's not complimenting him on his choice of ties this morning. Don bristles and they face off. I want to jam the kid's arm behind his back right now, but protocol says I wait for Don to issue verbal instructions. If the punk doesn't obey, then the leash comes off. *Relax. Follow the rules.*

The punk is probably six foot one and less than 170 pounds, soaking wet. Did I mention the tattoos and slouch? Even if he wasn't into armed robbery, which turned just short of lethal for the seventy-seven-year-old victim who fought back, I still wouldn't like this kid on sight. We're obviously not supposed to profile, but my daddy didn't raise a fool. This is a kid who screams anger and rebellion at the world without having to move his lips.

My money is on Don if this takedown gets physical. Heck, my money is on me if Don decides to turn around, pour himself a cup of coffee with two creamers, and leave the heavy lifting to me. I can take this punk. I'm not the greatest shot, but I've taken every hand-to-hand combat course the Chicago Police Department offers.

The punk breaks eye contact with Don and then turns toward where I block the other end of the aisle. He slowly looks me up and down and smiles. I'll give the jerk credit for being cool under pressure. He rolls his eyes and blows me a kiss. He will pay for that. Suddenly he slings a spinner rack filled with chips in Don's direction. As Don pushes the rack aside, the punk vaults over the condiment counter between us. Nacho cheese sauce and pickle relish fly everywhere. He knocks two people down by the dairy cooler and crashes through the back door in a frantic sprint. I wonder if I can hit a moving target with the Beretta while running. Just a flesh wound.

I'm half hoping he wants to play rough, because I'm more than ready. He nearly beat a senior citizen to death—and he just made us look foolish with his escape. Temporary escape. This won't be the first time I ask God to forgive me for wanting to smash someone bad's face in today—or tomorrow—but I badly want to be the one who cuffs him. Tightly.

Don and I bump shoulders in the doorway to the back lot, but don't lose a step. Don's wearing his shiny black leather wingtip shoes, which are not good for speed. I have no sympathy. I've told Don forty times to get some Rockports or Eccos with a soft, flexible, comfortable sole. He just looks at me in abject horror. *Focus, Kristen.*

The kid is surprisingly fast. Real fast. I wish some nice high school track coach could have gotten a hold of him before he got into all this trouble. He clears the lot behind the Gas & Grub and turns right on a residential street of classic Chicago row houses. Don is sprinter fast—he was a running back in college, he likes to remind us—but if the kid makes us run more than half a mile, he'll be sucking air and puking. I was a college soccer player and ran distance back in high school. I may still complete a marathon someday. Depends on if my surgically repaired knee will hold up.

I already hear Don's labored breathing as we near the street. I've barely broken a sweat. I make a hard right on the sidewalk two or three steps ahead of Don. A kid on a bike swerves to miss me and plows into my partner. I slow to see the two of them sprawled out on the sidewalk. I look the other way and can see the punk's at least fifty yards ahead, not a good thing, so it's time to turn it up a notch. My macho-man partner won't like it, but this is no time to make sure his male ego gets proper care and feeding. Don's on his feet and helping the kid up as I give chase on my own. He shouts, "Fall back and regroup. Too dangerous. Kristen! Hey, KC, hold up!"

"You fall back," I yell over my shoulder, which isn't very mature. I hate when people call me KC. I don't think I have a major anger issue, even if I do have a temper. Despite what my mom says. But lately, I admit, I get mad at people pretty easily. Too easily. Dad said I'd grow out of it, but I wonder if it's an occupational hazard. *Focus, Kristen. Pick up the pace. Fast hands!*

I let my track training take over, speeding up my hand movements but keeping my arms low.

My feet follow my hands' lead and I am closing the gap on the punk. I can't believe he's run this hard, this far. But that adrenaline is going to burn out soon. I'm not going full speed but I've lengthened my stride and am on pace to run a sub-six-minute mile. My energy tank is not close to empty.

The punk turns into an alley and I'm less than half a basketball court away. Top of the circle and taking it to the hoop, baby. I barely slow down as I round the corner, and now he's in my sights. He rolls two metal trashcans in my path. Amateur. Did I mention that I did hurdles for my high school track team too? The effort has slowed him down, but not me. I am going to catch him soon, any way you look at it. He'll have to make a decision really soon. Fight or flight.

The punk turns to face me and he has a knife in his hand. So it's fight. Not only is he fast enough to make any high school track team in the city; he can just as easily get a part as a Shark or Jet in the school's rendition of *West Side Story*.

I'm mad he's managed to surprise me. Stupid. The knife has been his MO in all three of his known robberies. I put on the brakes fast before I run right into his range of attack and reach toward the small of my back for my Beretta, but the punk is already rushing at me. He's red in the face and sucking air, but he lunges quickly to close the gap before I can de-holster my weapon.

On cop shows and in the movies all you have to do to deflect slashing metal is employ some serious martial arts moves. Even if you were trained to fight by Jackie Chan, it doesn't work that way. When two people fight and one has a razor-honed blade, the person without the weapon is going to lose some blood.

His first slash catches the sleeve of my suit coat and pops the button off as I dance away. No problem. Mom will sew it back on—and it was a half-off of a half-off sale at Macy's anyway. I feel just a trickle of blood soaking my sleeve. Okay, he got more than a button. So much for Mom rescuing it with her Singer. I barely felt it, so I don't think he got deep—hopefully not enough to scar. I don't want another scar. I have enough from ACL surgeries.

I am on my toes and jump back and dance to the left. He circles and gives a head fake in my direction like he's going to charge. I jump again and he smiles. He's way too cool about this; he's done it before. His next move is a step left and then right. I lean the wrong way and he slashes at my face with a wide sweep of the knife. My head jerks back and he misses, but I swear I felt the air on my cheek. His feints and parries make reaching for my gun next to impossible. For the first time, I wonder if I should've waited for Don.

Simply evading the knife isn't working. If the punk can go on the offensive, so can I. I stutter to my left and he mirrors it. I quickly spin right this time and let loose a round-house kick that I bet is beautiful to behold. Not as fine as a Jackie Chan move, but well executed.

But the punk ducks under my kick and I miss his head. I catch some shoulder and he stumbles. I pounce with a combination jab to his ribs and jaw. I thought I had him nailed, but this dude knows how to slip a punch. He staggers back, instantly recovers, and kicks at me. I rotate sideways so his shoe scuffs my hip with no damage. He takes a step back but lunges straight at me, steel in hand leading the way. This punk is fast. And sneaky. I move to block his knife thrust. He anticipates that perfectly and throws a tight left hook that clips the edge of my chin. Way too close. I try to hook his foot and trip him. He jumps and spins, slashing at me again. I catch his wrist and use his momentum to half-turn him. I finally connect with all my weight behind a punch to his kidneys. It doesn't put him down, but from the sound he makes, I know I hurt him. Suddenly he throws an elbow that catches me square in the side of the head. My ears ring. But I hold on to his arm and jam a knuckle into his upper back, digging for the suprascapular nerve, which should put him on the ground and slow his arm movement.

He's a fighter. He almost catches me with a back head snap and when I flinch he is free again, but not without me getting a nice kick to his right quad just above the knee. A little lower and he'd be down for the count. A foot and a half higher and he'd sing soprano in the choir. We face each other. Both of us are in fighting position and looking for an opening to attack. He is limping, but I've learned not to trust appearances with him—he's sly and resourceful. I dart in and get a combination to his torso but miss the solar plexus. I am back out as his knife slashes through air. Slower than before. I've got him. I'm crouched and ready to spin in either direction. Our eyes meet and lock.

His eyes dilate. He drops the knife and raises his arms.

Don walks past me calmly, his gun aimed at the center of the punk's chest.

"Keep your hands where I can see them, kick the knife to the side, and get down on your knees." There's a nanosecond of hesitation and Don shouts, "Now!"

"Make it easy for us and I'll make it easy for you," I add as I push him flat on his face, maybe with a little extra nudge, and cuff his hands behind him. I see blood splatters on the shiny metal.

Don keeps the gun trained on the punk as he hits a speed button on his cell phone to tell the uniforms where we are.

"We got him," he says to me as he snaps his flip phone shut.

"We?" I ask him, but not loud enough or with enough conviction to start a fight.

Then he says, "You need to listen to your partner and stand down next time."

"One of us needs to catch bad guys," I storm back. "And by the way, it's only a flesh wound, so I'm fine. Thanks for asking how I'm doing."

We glare at each other until his phone chirps again.

Don's a great partner and I won't stay mad. Neither will he. I don't think he will. I like that he is a big time family guy. He's got an almost stay-at-home wife and a girl and a *boy*—bless my poor dad's jealous heart, he just had me and my two sisters. Talk about a committed guy, Don doesn't smoke, drink, cuss—at least not much, which is saying a lot in our line of work. And great for me as a partner, he doesn't flirt and would never think about fooling around on his wife. I'm not trying to be presumptuous, but let's be honest: when you're a female in a male-dominated work environment, inappropriate things get hinted at. And sometimes not hinted, just said outright. What is it with some guys always testing the waters? Sometimes the married ones are the worst.

Don has a finger stuck in his free ear and is growling directions to someone. He glances over where I lean against a big green trash dumpster, a blood-soaked sleeve. Is that guilt in his eyes? I hope so. I hear sirens heading our way. No time to fight with the partner. I roll back my sleeve to see how deep the cut is.

It's 7:00 on a Saturday morning. There are no cars in line at the JavaStar drive-through, but I refuse to pay almost five bucks for a cup of steamed java and not get at least a little ambience to go with my caffeine. I have to be at the soccer fields in thirty minutes, so at most, I've got ten minutes to sit in an orange vinyl chair, savor the image of coffee beans overflowing from burlap sacks on terra cotta wallpaper, watch sleepy people in sweatshirts read their papers, and listen to a soundtrack with number-one hits by the Beatles, sung by people like Bono, Carrie Underwood, Mick Jagger, Sheryl Crow, and John Mayer. John Mayer doing "Revolution"? I like his music but it's not the right song for a crooner. Someone in Seattle has very weird taste in music.

"What can I get for you this morning?" a guy with a tongue stud and a green apron asks me with a little too much enthusiasm for a Saturday morning. He should know I haven't had my coffee yet.

"Quad-shot, one Splenda, grande soy latte," I answer carefully and clearly. If you don't say things in the right order, for the next five minutes you'll be explaining that, no, it's only one Splenda, not four, and yes, four shots of espresso, not one.

He writes my order on the cup and asks if he can get my name. There is no one behind me in line nor currently awaiting an order. I am about to ask him how hard it's really going to be to identify me and make sure I get the right drink when it's finished, but I'm working on my attitude, so I answer nicely, "Kristen."

He asks if Kristen is spelled with a *K* or a *C,* and it's all I can do not to threaten him bodily harm if he doesn't have someone start grinding beans and pushing buttons on the spaceship console they use to make coffee. Taking a breath, I answer, "K."

Then he tries to entice me with a pastry.

"No, thank you," I answer with all the matching polite earnestness I can muster. Can he tell I'm faking it?

It's been a tiring week. We arrested Jared Incaviglia, the punk, but Don ruined a $300 pair of shoes, which the department is not going to reimburse him for, and he was in a foul mood all day Friday. I looked it up online and told him that Allen Edmonds will refurbish his shoes for free if he'll pay for the shipping each direction. That useful information didn't help his mood a bit.

"Those bad boys were brand-new," he told me. "I don't want refurbished."

"Can you tell a difference?" I asked him.

"Yes, I can."

Okay. A wrinkle on the front of a dress shirt is traumatic for Don, so I'm not convinced any of the rest of us will be able to notice a small scuff on one of his shoes hidden by freshly applied shiny black polish.

I ended up doing all the paperwork for the arrest, which is only slightly more appealing than jumping into a tank of sharks with a bloody nose, but Don did brighten up in time to smile widely and vigorously shake hands with the deputy commissioner of the CPD, who wanted to personally congratulate us for our fine work. Commander Czaka thanked me too, but my handshake was a lot shorter and less enthusiastic. Did that have anything to do with our recent heated email exchanges? Being the ace detective I am, I suspect yes. I think he gave me a dirty look with the handshake. I think I returned the favor. *Dumb.*

I'll give Don credit. He carefully pointed out that I was first on scene and that I was the one who got the tip in the first place. He pointed out my bandaged left wrist, which was embarrassing. Doc doesn't think it will leave much of a scar. What's "much of"? I still accused Don of being a glory hog afterward. His mind was still on his shoes—and he was worried the dry cleaner wouldn't be able to get the nacho cheese sauce off a silk tie he really likes—so he hasn't taken the bait and fought with me. Sissy.

Then, twenty minutes before end of shift, my boss, Captain Karl Zaworski, head of detectives for the Second Precinct, called me into his office. He let me know that Jared, the punk, felt his civil rights were violated by the "excessive force" of my grinding his face into the ground.

Excessive force? Jared better hope I don't get to spend time alone with him in an interview room.

Once the phrase "excessive force" is added to your personnel files, the CO has the option to immediately suspend you with or without pay pending further review, which Zaworski didn't do. But my work on the case just got a whole lot tougher. Some defense attorney is going to have a heyday with this to try and tie a jury up in knots. After a terse meeting with the captain, I logged back onto my computer and went back over the paperwork, making sure I dotted every *i* and crossed every *t* twice.

Internal Affairs will be called in to investigate me, Zaworski informed me, and as every cop in America will tell you, IA is not your best friend under such circumstances. Meetings with them are rarely pleasant. Of course, I'd be in a bad mood if I spent all day trying to fire cops, too. Okay, I'm not being fair. There are bad cops who need to get the boot.

The timing for this kind of scrutiny is never good, but based on a few conflicts I've had—namely with Commander Czaka—this couldn't come at a worse time.

"Kirsten," my barista announces loudly enough for the crowd across the street at Dunkin' Donuts to hear. I am five feet away from him and he is looking right at me. Is there the start of a smug smile on his face? Since he got my name wrong, Kirsten instead of Kristen, I hope he at least said it with a *K*.

I ask for a java jacket to keep my fingers from burning off, which for the price, should have been slipped on the paper cup without my asking. Java jackets are now in the same category as having a clean new towel each day of an extended stay in a hotel. You can have it but not without feeling a little guilty for destroying the planet. I'm not feeling guilty today. I consider sitting a minute in the funky chair they might have bought from the Jetsons' garage sale, but look at my watch and head for the door instead.

I wonder again why I am not sleeping in. That would, of course, be because I'm the coach of my niece's soccer team. Her name is Kendra. All the girls' names in my family start with the letter *K*. My sisters are Klarissa and Kaylen. I guess we're just special that way. A guy friend from my high school days called us the Special K girls. I don't think he meant it as a compliment since he would usually add that Special K girls deserve special education.

Kendra is seven. My older sister, Kaylen, thought it'd be great for Kendra if Aunt Kristen was her coach. I played competitive soccer after all, and neither she nor Jimmy ever played the sport. To satisfy his own competitive impulses, Jimmy said he played on the chess team and was a regular at the science fair. Tell me he was joking.

I wanted to ask Kaylen if seven-year-olds need someone with my playing experience as coach, or if having a parent, preferably one with infinite patience and a low-stress job, wouldn't be better. I congratulated myself on keeping those thoughts unspoken; Kaylen would have just spent an hour explaining to me—in that annoyingly sweet and patient way she has—that being a full-time mom has its own stressors.

"How much time is required to coach?" I asked.

"The girls are only allowed one practice a week and then Saturday games," she answered, while trying not to smile triumphantly.

Our team name is the Snowflakes—Coach Kristen wasn't consulted—and our uniforms are naturally, uh, yellow. Wasn't there an old song that warned us about yellow snow?

The zinger was when Kaylen asked if it would be too much for me to pick up Kendra for pre-game warm-ups when we were scheduled for early games. That way she could sleep in a few extra minutes.

"We'll be there before the game starts," she said. "We'll never miss."

Of course not. And since their house is only a few miles out of the way, it really wouldn't be any extra work for me. Did someone tape a sign on my forehead that spells s-u-c-k-e-r?

I said yes, of course. Kaylen and Jimmy are the nicest people in the world. He's a pastor. They're really busy and need a little help with their two kids. Mom told Klarissa and me that Jimmy and Kaylen are working on number three. Should I ask how much work is really involved?

Since I spend my days chasing thugs like Jared in back alleys, I need to be with a group of Snowflakes, I guess. Despite my expert training—and being the only coach of seven-year-olds who insists that the team show up thirty minutes early for warm-ups and drills—we've lost all our games so far. But it's a new day. The girls don't seem to mind the losses as much as the parents. Or me. I wonder if I would get reported to the commissioner for doing some extra practice sessions the next couple of weeks.

The girls are actually having a lot of fun, and I've only had one run-in with a parent. Tiffany's dad would like to see more scoring—especially from Tiffany—and was getting quite loud from the sidelines the first couple of games. He explained to me he was just encouraging the girls. When I explained that screaming at seven-year-olds wasn't encouragement in my book, he tried to intimidate me with the knowledge that he had played soccer. I just pulled a concept from my cop training on him: repeat if necessary, but never explain. He backed off.

I look at my watch. I'm going to get Kendra and me to the fields on time for warm-ups, thank God, without having to do more than ten miles over the speed limit. I'm five minutes away from Kaylen's and switch to a news station. A young woman has been murdered. I wonder which precinct has the case. If it's ours, I wonder who Zaworski and Czaka will give the lead assignment to. Zaworski knows Don and I get the job done. But Czaka doesn't like me and his commander rank wins tiebreakers.

Then I again recall the punk we collared and Internal Affairs. It's conceivable I won't be working for the next month or so. Then I think there's no way I'm going to be in serious trouble for it. Incaviglia has a couple of misdemeanors on his record—and now he is facing major assault charges and resisting arrest. I have a bruise on the end of my chin and a couple butterfly stitches on my wrist, which should give allowance for me cuffing him with, ah, enthusiasm. But you never know when IA gets involved. I didn't push his face down that hard, did I?

As I pull in the driveway to get Kendra, I hit another preset button on my radio. The murder story is getting a mention on the classic hits station, too. The last thing I hear before I turn off my engine is, "Police are reporting that Sandra Reed has been found dead in her Washington Park apartment, the result of a dispute with her boyfriend . . ."

Good old domestic violence. We'd be out of a job without it.

April 3, 8:19 a.m.

I couldn't sleep last night. Even popping that little blue pill from her cabinet couldn't temper my happiness. I'm still wired this morning. My pulse rate must be at 120 sitting still. Oh, how I've missed this. I feel . . . euphoric.

I like that word. Euphoria. Wish it would never wear off. But it always does. That's when the thoughts, the cravings, the all-consuming need starts up again. It'll be time to find a new girlfriend, then. Maybe blonde this time. One I saw at the coffee shop was quite attractive. But her tattoos were repulsive. What kind of mental illness would make someone mar what is supposed to be pure? I like skin that is smooth, without barbaric markings and piercings. It's the clean slate I require for my art.

The media has it all wrong. Par for the course. Sandra was killed by her live-in boyfriend in a case of domestic violence? Is it any wonder so many newspapers are going out of business? They apparently hire only the lazy and inept. I would call them idiots but that would be an insult to idiots everywhere.

My work is my legacy and I dislike seeing such shoddy reporting on it. It's been that way everywhere I've gone. To know that my accomplishments might be lost forever makes me feel sad . . . wistful.

When I was a teen, my assigned therapist said I should start keeping a journal. I had problems with self-aggrandizement and self-delusion, he said, and perhaps writing it all down would help me "sort it out." But is what you believe and say about yourself really self-aggrandizing if you're truly better than everyone else? My deeds prove it.

What did that therapist know, anyway? He wanted to keep me a prisoner of the state forever. Probably just to make sure he had a full caseload and job security.

But the thought of keeping a journal appeals to me now. Maybe I'll pick one up and start writing my story. That way it will never be lost.

I could even send a copy to the FBI when the time is right.

They don't have a clue. Literally.

5

No, Kendra! The other way! That way! Kendra! Dribble the ball that way!"

I bellow and wave my arms like a crazy woman. Tiffany's dad is watching me, his arms folded and a smug look on his already smug face. Better take the volume down a notch. Or three.

The score is tied, 3-3. According to my stopwatch, we have only two minutes before the ref blows his whistle to end the game. We need a win. I need a win. I could deal with a tie, but a win would be so much sweeter.

Kendra has scored two of our goals. Since then she's been getting mugged. The other team is tugging on her jersey even now. She's been tripped four times. These are sweet little seven-year-old girls, so the other coach has got to be instructing them to foul. No way are they thinking of this on their own.

I'm giving the coach a piece of my mind in my imagination when Kendra, who has lost the ball, steals it back and becomes a yellow streak set to score a breakaway goal. She's not old enough to keep dribbles close to her feet, and the other coach—Attila the Hun—is screaming for his goalie to leave the box and charge the ball. Apparently her name is Olivia, as anyone within a mile of the soccer complex can attest.

"Charge the ball, Oliviaaaaaa."

I might charge Attilaaaaaa.

It's going to be close. Kendra isn't quite in control of the ball. It's about equal distance between her and the goalie with the speed of the roll. I'm praying, really praying for a miracle, for a win. Does

God hear the prayers of sports fans? What if two people rooting for opposing teams are praying equally hard? I'm not a theologian, so I just keep praying—even if God is laughing at me or just not listening.

Please, God, help her to be first to the ball.

Maybe it was my prayer that did it. Kendra redirects the ball with the outside of her left foot—and any coach of seven-year-olds will confirm that this is a miracle, especially when you consider she is right-footed—leaving her all by herself in front of the goal. She taps the ball in for the winning score just as an opposing player tackles her from behind.

The goal counts. I feel a tingle in my surgically repaired knee as I start to run out to check if Kendra is hurt. She bounces up instantly and appears to be fine. The girls high-five her and jump in the air and attempt to do butt bumps as they head back for the other side of the field. As the Snowflakes line up for one more kickoff, the ref, with everything his ample pot belly can muster, blows the whistle to end the game. We get the win, but I'm still furious with the other coach. After the girls form a line, hold their arms out and slap hands with the other team, run through the tunnel formed by two lines of parents who have linked outstretched hands into an arbor, and then head toward the cooler for juice pouches—the highlight of the game for many of my girls—I am in the other coach's face.

"Hey, pal, you better get your girls under control before someone gets hurt," I say as I poke his chest with my finger. *Not smart. Kristen. Don't touch.*

"What are you talking about, little lady?" he storms back, taking a step into my personal space.

Little lady? Who calls anyone that these days? Maybe his license plate is expired and I'll arrest him in the parking lot and cuff him.

"You know exactly what I'm talking about, *big guy*," I answer, not backing off an inch. "I'm making sure my girls don't get injured because some Neanderthal is teaching seven-year-olds to trip and push."

"Teaching girls to push and trip?" he nearly sputters. "How would I do that? You're out of your mind. Is this your first time coaching youth soccer? They all trip each other without any coaching help."

Do they? I don't know if that's true. It is my first year to coach little girls. I do know I've blown it again. What gets into me? Sometimes I excuse myself as the victim of an occupational hazard.

The ref, who has no sense of the drama unfolding right before his eyes—almost as oblivious as he was in the game—walks up and we both back up to let him stand between us. He sticks a game card in my face.

"Need your 'John Hancock' on the bottom line," he says.

I sign. Attila signs.

"Good game, coaches," he says as he trots toward the referee hut.

I look over at my Snowflakes. They are contentedly slurping juice and munching on granola bars. Jimmy's arms are folded and he is unhappy, though he won't make eye contact with me. Kaylen does. And she is scowling.

I know it happens in professional sports all the time, but I wonder how often volunteer soccer coaches get fired mid-season.

Kristen, you've got to get your temper under control," Kaylen says to me. We have our own table at Pizza Palace for the Snowflakes' celebration lunch. It is only late morning, so I guess we're having pizza brunch.

Eleven girls are munching greedily at a long table we've created by pushing several tables together. The parents, including Jimmy, have morphed into groups of four or five at surrounding tables.

I guess I'm at the time-out table because it's just Kaylen and me. I have an untouched piece of pizza in front of me and have taken just a couple of sips of my Diet Coke as I get chewed out by my older sister.

"Kendra could have been hurt," I protest. "That guy is ruining things for the girls."

"Maybe so, but he wasn't the one trying to start a fight with you, and the girls seem no worse for wear," Kaylen says. She points to the Snowflakes who are laughing and shoveling food into their mouths. Kendra is now standing on her chair and is rotating her hips like she is twirling a hula hoop. I hope that's what she's doing at least. She is explaining to the other Snowflakes how she scored the winning goal. I guess that's her celebration dance.

"Kendra!" her dad barks and she is immediately back in her seat, a sheepish expression on her face. I can tell she's trying not to smile. I'm doing the same thing because I know how she feels. I'm in trouble, too. No smiling allowed.

"Where did she learn to do that?" I ask Kaylen, hoping to change the subject. Doesn't work.

"Kristen, I'm serious. You're thirty and this in-your-face anger has got to stop. You were almost as bad as Tiffany's dad today." She looks over her shoulder to make sure he didn't hear her. "Check that, worse," she continues in a lower tone. "He was very well behaved and only cheered today, per the coach's order."

Ouch. I'd argue some more, but the problem is, she is right. I've always had a temper. I've always been in your face. But it's never been so relentless and as personal until now. *For a while now, actually,* I admit to myself. And I've never lost it in front of the kids. Never before. I'm a good girl. I don't smoke and I don't chew, and I don't go with guys that do. What's happening to me?

I start to apologize when my phone begins playing Tchaikovsky's "1812 Overture." I am going to ignore the call, but I recognize Captain Zaworski's number. The boss rarely calls on the weekend. I'm hoping this doesn't have anything to do with Internal Affairs and the punk.

"Conner," I answer, turning away from Kaylen and putting a finger in my free ear to buffer the noise. She is watching me with suspicion. She obviously thinks I'm trying to escape this conversation by slinking away. And she would be right most days. I listen for half a minute, tell him it will take me twenty—my eyebrows furrowed enough to cause permanent wrinkles—and hang up.

"Kristen, you can't get away this easily; we need to finish this conversation," Kaylen begins. I knew that was what she was thinking.

I cut her off. "But not now. There's been a murder and I'm on the case." I'm on the case? My language skills sound like a B movie.

I'm already standing up and pulling car keys from my purse. I'm about to leave without a word, but I stop myself. "I'm sorry," I say as I turn and hug Kaylen close. "I am. Honestly. Just say a prayer for me and don't be mad. I've got to go right now."

"'Bye, Coach!" eleven voices chirp in near-unison. I turn and smile. I tell them they played a fabulous game and circle around the table to give a little love to each one. Kendra hugs my neck hard as I bend down to kiss her. Kids can be very forgiving.

There is almost a tear in the corner of one of my eyes as I walk out the door and into the sunlight. Man, it's bright today. I blink it away.

Did my sister say I was thirty? She'll pay for that.

I flip stations the whole way over to the Second Precinct. I know more about who to call for all my insurance needs to save money, but don't catch a peep about our murder case or the score of the Cubs game last night, the only two items of vital interest to me. Bulls might make the playoffs but since the day Jordan retired, I was never as interested in the NBA. On the murder case, the media usually gets it screwed up anyway, so better to start with a clean slate and no false information embedded in my mind.

I consider stopping by my place to grab a sixty-second shower and a change of clothes. No time.

I'm still the last person to the conference room after parking, entering the back door with my electronic key, and pounding up five flights of stairs to Homicide in the Second Precinct, too impatient to wait for an elevator. I look around and realize this could be about a hundred different rooms in our precinct. Gray table and chairs. Gray walls. The white ceiling must have been the interior designer's idea of a contrast. A couple of the ceiling tiles are cracked and chipped at the corners. Several tiles are rust-stained from a leak on the floor above and look

like they are ready to cave in. I used to drink water from our anti-
quated porcelain fountains when I first joined the force. I shudder and
thank God for bottled water. Who knows where that leak came from.

"Grab a seat," Zaworski says, barely nodding at me. I sit next to Don.
He looks dapper in designer jeans and a white mock turtleneck. Summer
weight. Loafers with no socks. You've got to be kidding me. Does he not
have to clean the garage or mow the lawn on a Saturday morning?

Four other men are at the table besides Zaworski and Don. One
is in uniform with sergeant stripes; I think his name is Kincaid.
Then there are two detectives from another precinct that I recognize,
both wearing jeans with one in a cotton pullover and the other in a
couple layers of T-shirts. I don't know either by name. Finally, there
is a very nice-looking man, maybe early thirties, wearing a suit way
too fine for local law enforcement. Except for Don, of course. Navy
blue with a light blue stripe, white oxford shirt with button-down
collar and monogram on the chest pocket and sleeves—AER—and
a pale yellow tie with a diagonal blue stripe. This guy has got to be
a federal agent or a salesman for IBM. I am suddenly self-conscious
of my worn-out soccer shorts and ratty NIU sweatshirt. I wore my
cleats to the game but have switched into a pair of Crocs with Mickey
Mouse smiling on one and Minnie Mouse on the other. Christmas
present from Kendra.

I don't catch myself in time to not take a quick glance at the Fed's
ring finger, which is naked. I think he catches me looking, which is
very embarrassing. I kick myself for even wondering because I have a
sort-of boyfriend who is madly in love with me—at least that's what
he tells me. The problem is I'm not crazy in love with him. So I don't
reciprocate with the words he longs to hear. Every time I try to break
things off completely, he assures me that he's very comfortable just

being very good friends and that he is willing to wait for me to feel the same way for him that he feels for me. I have got to put him out of his misery and end this thing.

Captain Zaworski makes the introductions.

Nice suit guy is FBI, like I guessed, and his name is Austin Reynolds. The sergeant's name is Konkade, not Kincaid, so I was close. If he has a first name other than Sergeant, he's not giving it out. The detectives are Bob Blackshear and Antonio Martinez from Third Precinct. We all shake hands, say our "heys," and nod.

The mood is somber and I resist any temptation to crack a joke. Don't know why I would think to do so in the first place. We're talking about murder—and no one laughs at my jokes anyway. Except for Kendra. She thinks I'm hilarious. *Focus.*

Captain Zaworski passes crime scene photos around the room. A very pretty girl in the alive photos; a very disfigured girl in the dead shots. No details were given on the radio. Good thing. She died at the hands of someone very nasty and very good with a knife. Nope, no jokes today.

"How long have we been on the scene?" Konkade asks.

"Detectives from the Third got there at five or so," Zaworski answers, nodding at Blackshear and Martinez. Don and I look at each other in surprise. Konkade purses his lips and runs a hand over his bald scalp.

"Why aren't we all there now?" Don asks for both of us. "Time's wasting and the bugs are eating our clues."

For detectives, rule number one in investigating a murder is that you get to the scene of the crime as quickly as possible to see things as they really are with your own eyes. Even though you can practically guarantee the first officer on the scene will be diligent in protecting evidence—everything from segregating witnesses to establishing a non-invasive traffic pattern to the victim—you know there is going to be corruption. If every criminal leaves a trace of his activity—so does every investigator looking for him. Or her.

"Soon enough," Zaworski answers. "Everything will still be in place, including the body, when you get there. I know that on one hand, we're not doing this exactly by the book, but on the other hand, we're going to make sure the book is followed to the letter of the law. So we've decided to go slow on this one. Blackshear and Martinez got the first call and they got to look around a couple minutes before we pulled them out for this briefing. They'll share initial impressions in a moment. The deed was done right on jurisdictional lines." Zaworski pauses and continues, "We're not sure if the Second or Third Precinct owns it, so you'll be working together."

Uh oh. Sharing and police work rarely go hand in hand.

"We're not sweating the politics," he adds, looking pointedly at me. "This one gets even more complicated." He looks around to make sure he has our undivided attention. "The second our initial report hit the data ports, a red flag went up in DC at FBI headquarters. They've tagged a guy with a very sophisticated and extensive crime pattern. He's been killing lots of people and moving to new cities for a number of years now. They think he's been a member of our community for the past six months, getting ready for his first victim in Chicago and a good number to follow. Sandra Reed may have been first, not last."

Oh man. What's a "good number"?

The captain goes on. "Major Reynolds was flown in specially by the US Army this morning in order to assist us in our investigation. He's going to fill you in on what the FBI knows about our perp and help us apprehend him. Not only are we going to work well between the Second and Third precincts but also across agency lines. That order has been jointly issued from the director of the FBI and the CPD commissioner. Mayor Doyle's office strongly endorses it. I do too."

He nods to Reynolds.

"Actually, I wish we knew more about who the perp is and how we're going to apprehend him, but we don't," Reynolds begins, clearing his throat. "About six years ago we received some software programming money from the Department of Homeland Security. We hired some geniuses from Silicon Valley to create a specialized search engine to cross-collateralize and correlate a number of local, state, and federal databases. The purpose was tracking terrorist activity, but some other good things came out of Project Vigilance."

Reynolds pauses dramatically for a sip of water and I whisper to Don, "Wow, it's got a name—Project Vigilance, just like a spy novel." Don leans away, frowns, and arches his eyebrows to let me know I need to keep my mouth shut, and let anyone else know with his body language we are not a team.

We all wait as Reynolds sets his water bottle down slowly and picks up his papers again. I can't pull off a similar "pregnant pause" because I live in a constant state of fear that I'm putting people to sleep when I talk. There's precedence to support me on this one.

"PV is one of the biggest breakthroughs in profiling unsolved crimes," he continues. "Obviously, it connects the dots between federal, state, and local investigations. It gets computers talking to one another—and that leads to people talking to one another. One of the key ideas was to make information available whereby other law enforcement agents and analysts could study and make suggestions on a case, even if there was no solid line of connection with something they were working on. PV stole a page from a business textbook and has become a kind of 'best practices' online symposium."

"I bet that goes over real good with the guys working the case," Martinez chimes in. "Sounds like one more way everybody in the world wants to second-guess you and look over your shoulder if you're a cop."

"You'd be surprised at how well it works and how well it's been received, Detective Martinez," Reynolds answers. He's good at remembering names. "I guess ideas and advice don't offend as much when someone's nose is in your case from a thousand miles away. But the unexpected positive outcome from Project Vigilance is that it has revealed to us almost 1,000 connected cases. PV has correlated crime events that were once treated as singular and jurisdiction-specific crimes into non-isolated crime streams."

What did he just say? Jurisdiction-specific? Non-isolated crime streams? I'm writing this stuff down. I think I'm back at NIU in an advanced level criminal justice seminar.

"So, Boss, how come we aren't on Project Vigilance, if it's so good?" Martinez asks, turning to face Zaworski.

"It's still under review," the captain answers curtly. His steely look suggests further comments and interruptions are not welcome.

I look straight down at my notebook. No way am I going to snicker. Don must have been worried about me because he kicks me under the table. *Ouch.* That one I didn't deserve.

"So did you start this Project Vigilance? Do you run it?" Blackshear asks Reynolds.

"I wish," he snorts. "No, I'm a single investigator who has benefited from someone else's vision and work."

I'm impressed. Handsome and dutifully humble.

"I do have the distinction, however," he continues, "of identifying thirty-seven streams; more than any other investigator. I've spearheaded seventeen busts nationwide."

So much for being humble.

"But I've had my eye on one stream from the first day PV started connecting dots for us. This particular stream pulled together six unsolved crime factors. And by factor, I mean each of the cities that have experienced multiple murders at the hands of the same perp, who I'm about to tell you about."

"How many murders in all?" Konkade asks.

"As I said, we've identified six factors, which means six cities," he answers. After a pause he continues, "There are now forty-seven known murders. We aren't counting Chicago as a factor yet. It's also possible PV has missed some of his handiwork, so there could be more."

Everyone is still. Blackshear gives a low whistle. Don whispers, "Sweet Jesus," under his breath. Martinez crosses himself and mumbles, "*Santa madre de Dios, apiádate de nosotros!*"

"If we're right about who the killer is, today's murder is just the first he has planned for your city," Reynolds continues. "We believe Sandra Reed is victim number forty-eight."

I can't help myself—I gulp. An hour ago I was poking my finger in a coach's chest for encouraging rough play. Or maybe girls just trip each other. Now I am saying a prayer for help with something that really matters. Someone has committed forty-eight murders and is planning more. How can that be?

"We haven't seen our friend for almost seven months, so we were afraid he had changed his modus operandi and disappeared from PV's ability to detect patterns. Honestly, I was starting to go a little crazy with the thought that I wouldn't get another shot at him. But last night tells us—or at least strongly suggests—he's back."

Reynolds lays out details of forty-seven murders in six cities and why last night's murder in my city looks like a fresh start and factor number seven.

"This guy sounds smart," Blackshear interrupts. "He's going to be tough to catch. Have you all gotten close to him yet?"

"Catching him is going to be tough," Reynolds responds. "He is smart. And we haven't gotten close yet. But he's a sociopath. And sociopaths are delusional—especially about themselves. So they leave clues."

"But you said this one doesn't," Don says.

"I said he hasn't, but believe me, he will. Sociopaths love narratives. As long as they are the star of the story, of course. They start believing they can dictate life by force of will. We all know the Burns' line, 'the best-laid schemes of mice and men often go awry.' Even though everyone in this room gets frustrated when plans go awry, most of us know that's part of life. Sociopaths are not quite as understanding and get a lot more frustrated. That's when they make mistakes. I'll admit this guy is on one incredible roll. But not every break is going to go his way."

Handsome and literate. He goes on to tell us what they guess they know about the perpetrator's childhood and adolescence, about what makes him tick.

Forty-seven murders in six previous cities. Murder number forty-eight has happened in my precinct—or at least right next to it. Holy cow. He's back.

I hate when bad people go free. My younger sister, Klarissa—already a star news reporter on a local TV station—says I get too uptight and worry about things I can't control. Dad would have said that makes me a good cop. And now I'm on the primary investigative squad tracking a serial killer. That means I do have some control.

If I can keep my temper under control—and Internal Affairs doesn't bust my chops.

I turn the ignition on my Miata; it starts right up. That's a good thing because it's been acting real funny for the past couple of months. I keep meaning to get it in the shop tomorrow, but tomorrow becomes today. I end up looking for parking spaces located on inclines, so if it won't start, I roll it backward and pop the clutch in reverse. I'm glad I couldn't afford an automatic transmission when I bought the thing slightly used. There would've been no clutch to pop. And it would've been a lot more expensive to repair.

Don looked up my car online and said a salvaged starter will cost about 200 bucks. I could actually afford the starter if that was the total bill. But that doesn't cover labor, which will be the same amount. I almost had enough put aside when I decided to switch from a standard-issue Glock service handgun to a Beretta. *For 900 bucks, I better shoot straighter.*

I look at the cracked leather passenger seat and think about how hot this thing used to look. No major body damage but a small dent in the back left corner. There's a little rust there now. Something else I don't have money to fix.

I look down at my cell, which I left in the front passenger seat. Six missed calls. Great. Only one person that can be. I've been at the crime scene for four hours, still decked out in my torn, paint-stained sweatshirt. I realize now that I forgot to call Dell, my sort-of boy-friend, to let him know something had come up. He's been after me to drive out of town about a hundred and fifty miles to see a historic Amish village. I've been putting him off. I think my new case qualifies as a good excuse; a great excuse, in fact. But after having used several lame excuses in previous weekends, he'll just feel put off again. I could be honest and just tell him I'm not interested in eighteenth-century customs and furniture, even if they managed to make it all without metal nails or the aid of electricity. Mom keeps telling me that this sounds like a lot of fun. I think my point is made.

Dell gets offended pretty easily, even if he fights hard not to show it. He's easy to read. Of course, I am a detective. Wonder if he feels put off because I always put him off? I met him at church six months ago, which I've been told—by my mom, of course—is a great place for single adults to meet members of the opposite sex with shared values and beliefs. I agree with all that, but it certainly doesn't mean I'm morally obligated to fall for him, just because he's good-looking, has a great job, drives an expensive car, and is very spiritual.

Maybe it's the pressure I feel from everyone, including my sisters. Maybe it's his name: Dell. I am thankful I haven't met his parents yet because there's a good chance I'd bring the name thing up. Maybe it is Dell's earnest patience with me that sabotages my feelings for him. He basically says he's there for me and is willing to wait until I feel the same about him. That's a turnoff.

Kaylen says his patience with me is incredibly romantic. Yeah, whatever. And what's with the Amish village thing? My mom says I always decide whether something will be fun or interesting before I give it a real chance—and that I'm often wrong. I don't remember the being wrong part as much as she does.

I've missed one call from Kaylen and five from Dell. Did he call her to tattle on me? Three voice messages. I just hit the call-back option for Dell. I'm not crazy about him, but I do think I should explain what's going on and why I'm missing our Saturday date. The ringtone bleats four times then clicks into voicemail: "You've reached the phone of Dell Woods . . ."

I jab the off button with my pointer finger. Better to listen to my voicemails from him first anyway. I do believe this is the first time Dell hasn't picked up my call within the first two rings. I guess I made him mad. Good for him. It should make him mad. I don't treat him as well as he deserves. If I don't feel guilty, it's because I've been honest with him all along, except for the Amish village thing. Besides, six months isn't very long to really know who someone is. *Especially when you refuse to let someone get to know you.*

I'm on the entrance ramp to the cross-town expressway that will deliver me to my apartment and a hot shower in twenty minutes. I work through the gears quickly and have it in fifth before I've merged onto the highway. The Saturday night party crowd is still at home getting ready, so I have pretty light traffic to weave through.

Austin Reynolds of the FBI was pretty thorough on what we should expect when we got to the victim's trendy townhouse. But I don't think you can be thorough enough to prepare someone for the shock of what we saw.

I've been in homicide two years now. Got my promotion and gold detective shield a year earlier than my dad did. And plenty of people let me know that my dad is the reason I got bumped up so young. So I've seen my share of death and destruction. But whoever this guy is, he's a sicko. He's evil. I'm not positive the case is going to stay with Don and me, but I have some intense feelings coursing through my body and soul. I can physically feel something from the top of my head to the soles of my feet. I'm angry, but it doesn't feel like the lousy kind of anger I've been mired in the last couple months. Maybe I'm feeling a little of the holy anger Mom likes to brag about when talking about Democrats and the liberal bias in the media. All I know for sure is that I want to be the one to bring this guy in before he does any more damage. I won't push his nose in the pavement, though.

———

I wrap one towel around my body and one around my hair after a thirty-minute shower. Got every last ounce of hot water there was. I'm fading fast now. I want to do my nails—a ten-minute job for me and an afternoon for media star Klarissa—but may not have the energy. I plop on my couch and pick up the remote. I'm debating between watching a TV show I recorded and just hitting the sack. Haven't done a crossword in a week. My brain's gonna turn to mashed potatoes.

I grabbed an oven-roasted turkey sandwich at Subway on my way home and then did a workout in my living room on a foam mat to blow off steam. I started with eagle jumps, but they make too much noise and I didn't know if the old guy who lives below me was home or not—he has complained about me to management regularly since I moved here—so I only did one set of thirty. I shadowboxed with weighted gloves for ten minutes, keeping my fists at chin level the whole time—my arms were on fire the last two minutes. Then I did a core workout that had my abs screaming.

I look at the top of my left wrist. A thin line, dark rust down the middle and a few angry dots—from where the stitches got pulled—flank it on both sides. The doc said it will be almost impossible to see. My orthopod said the same thing about my right knee, which has a very noticeable road map of scars.

I look at my cell phone. No new messages. Dell still hasn't called back. I left him a pretty detailed explanation, leaving out crime scene details, of course, but I suspect he has had his fill of my explanations and is throwing some passive-aggressive payback in my direction.

Good for him.

Sometimes, no matter how long of a shower you take, you just can't feel clean. I toss the remote on my couch and head to the bedroom. I pick up a Lee Child novel I got at the library. I only make it through ten pages before my eyes get too heavy to continue. I turn off the light and pray, but sleep and prayer elude me.

He's back keeps echoing over and over in my mind.

THE CHITOWNVLOGGER

APRIL 2, 6:03 A.M.

He clicked replay one more time before posting the video on his YouTube channel. From there it would travel seamlessly to his vlog site and over to more than a hundred thousand RSS feeds plus another couple hundred thousand direct subscribers.

Axl Rose screeched out the words "Welcome to the jungle" as the title DEATH IN THE CITY: NEW IN A THEATER NEAR YOU! rolled on the screen.

He was well-known in Chicagoland, having been news anchor at the city's largest local TV station until he was fired. No reason was publically given, but a publicist for the station hinted that there had been "professional conduct issues." There were rumors of a sexual harassment suit being settled quietly for big bucks. He would admit he drank a little too much in public—and maybe in private—but he knew he had never harassed a woman. Leave that for presidents and senators. He knew very well the real reason for his dismissal. He had packed on an extra thirty pounds. That coupled with a receding hairline, and long story short, he wasn't as handsome as he used to be.

No matter. It turned out to be the best thing that ever happened to him. Now he had his own news show—a couple of two- or three-minute reports most days—and he could say whatever he wanted. With a million hits every twenty-four hours, he was making more money off of Google advertising dollars and a few small sponsors—well, the city's largest Harley dealer wasn't that small—than he did when he was with the mainstream media.

Go figure.

He watched himself carefully. He had leaned back in his battered office swivel chair, and looked right into the miniature digital camera he had set up on a tripod. He could have wetted down his white hair and run a comb through it, but no big deal. For his reports, he used no notes. He recorded them in one take, every time. He edited everything himself. Talk about low overhead. He watched himself. He wasn't the striking figure he had been when he dreamed of anchoring the *CBS Evening News*, but his trademark baritone voice was deep and clear as ever. His blue-gray eyes had not lost their ability to bore into the hearts and minds of his viewers.

"Welcome to my jungle, friends and family, fans and foes. You are watching the ChiTownVlogger—Chicago's number one source for news that matters. It's the wee hours of the night, so good thing for you, I never sleep.

"I started getting some calls and texts and email messages late last night. Some very interesting—and very disturbing—chatter. So I reached out to people who are in the know in the mayor's office and at Chicago Police headquarters—and no one wanted to talk to me. That hurt my feelings a little, but it made me even more curious about a potential story of blood and horror. You already know that when I get curious, it turns to suspicion. And when I get suspicious, I really go to work. Usually when people won't talk to me it means they have something they want to hide. It also means our very own führer, the one and only Mayor Doyle, is doing his best Joseph Goebbels impression and trying to suppress your access to important news. Particularly news that doesn't help his reelection campaign.

"After pulling strings for a couple hours, I learned that the mayor was awakened from his beauty sleep—not an easy task—and spent a long night on the phone with the director of the FBI in Washington, DC, and his favorite crony at the Chicago Police Department, Commissioner Fergosi.

"Good to know they'll put in at least a little overtime since crime and violent crime is up in Chicagoland for a third straight year. What caught the mayor's attention? No, they still haven't captured the old lady who keeps letting her dog do a nasty deed on the sidewalk in front of city hall without scooping it. That wasn't it.

"I did check with the big boys, the serious news sources, to see what they knew first. But when you've sold your soul to Chicago politicians and the Corporate States of America, you're content not to know much. Case in point, they didn't know what has caught the mayor's attention either. They're still asleep even as I speak.

"Let me make it simple, folks. You heard Sandra Reed was murdered. Maybe you weren't paying attention—and that's just what Mayor Doyle and Commissioner Fergosi hoped for. If you can remember her name and the report at all, you probably heard she was murdered in a dispute with her boyfriend. *Wrong.* She doesn't even have a boyfriend. What Commissioner Fergosi and the men in blue don't want you to know is this was no domestic dispute, no crime of passion, no simple shoot or stab murder.

"One of the fair maidens of our city was brutally cut up. Yeah. You heard me right. She was slashed and bled out in a gruesome death that might have been designed to last an entire night. Sadist? Satanist? Sicko? All of the above? Or a different kind of animal? You'll know when I know. I don't operate like Mayor Doyle. And I'll know before 'they' know. You know who 'they' are.

"I won't keep you any longer. So now you can go listen to the hacks from WGL, WCI, and the other *serious* news sources as they play catch-up with the ChiTownVlogger. Check back into my jungle soon. There's a predator on the prowl."

Satisfied, Allen Johnson hit the button to upload and publish his report.

I'm going to get a million hits before noon.

I look at the clock on my nightstand. How did it get to be 9:40 already? Did I just sleep ten hours? Since I tossed and turned all night and never really drifted off, I guess the better question is whether I've been in bed ten hours. Regardless, the answer is that I've overslept, big time. I jump out of bed with a start. I told Kaylen I would get to church early to help her with Kendra's Sunday school class. Soccer coach; class helper; what next? Weekend babysitter? Yeah, I've already done that gig, too. Not that I'm complaining. Not really.

I slide into the pew next to Kaylen. She's singing and barely acknowl-edges me. That means she is not happy with me. She finally looks over a stanza or two later and gives a half-hearted nod. I don't think her smile is totally sincere. Not very nice for a pastor's wife. In my typical contrarian pathology I immediately feel better. If the nicest woman in the world is being pouty, then I can't be that bad, right? I almost smile. I look over to see if there is any sign of a cute little baby bump. Not yet. Maybe she and Jimmy need to work harder. She feels my gaze and scowls at me. Now I do smile. My gorgeous, kind-hearted, forgiving older sister can never stay mad at me—unlike my younger sister who can stay mad at me for years and who isn't in church with us again this week, I notice.

I missed all of Sunday school and was fifteen minutes late for the worship service. That means another ten minutes of singing. All stand-ing up. The words are projected on a screen. I understand contemporary church services are designed to appeal to contemporary people like me, but it wouldn't kill us to sing a couple verses from the hymnal—prefer-ably sitting down. Ten minutes of announcements and the offering will follow. Jimmy will preach about thirty-five minutes.

We're usually out the door at 12:15. The Baptists, who are appar-ently more punctual, will have all the good restaurant tables tied up by then—the charismatics follow in waves at 1:30 or so. Our indepen-dent church is in the no-man's land of Sunday dinner scheduling, so we always eat at Jimmy and Kaylen's house. All of us are on a budget except for Klarissa anyway. We used to do it at Mom and Dad's house, but there is more room at Jimmy and Kaylen's. Tradition can be a good thing. Like I said, it wouldn't kill us to pick up a hymnal and sit down for a song or two. I think the hip and contemporary train left the station without me. My news reporter sister got in the first-class car.

She said she was just going to visit somewhere closer to her house for a week or two, but I think she has wanted a change, maybe something a little more formal and sophisticated—like her. No big deal. There has to be a reason there are so many different kinds of churches. At least I hope so. I'd criticize her for not just coming out and admitting that to Jimmy and Kaylen, but after not telling Dell that I did not want to visit an Amish village with him, it would be hypocritical.

I'm leaning hard with two hands on the chair in front of me. Kaylen's giving me sideways glances and decides to forgive me for slinking in late. I get a sideways hug. Maybe she has put on five pounds.

My mind sometimes wanders in church, but not today. It stays focused. Just not on church. I'm thinking about yesterday's meeting at headquarters. After Reynolds' presentation, Captain Zaworski recapped the FBI profile of our alleged perp. Male. White. Very methodical, maybe an accountant or engineer. He's intelligent. Watches TV, because he leaves next to no trace of his existence at the scene. All those shows on forensic evidence have seen to that, even though, technically, every human encounter does leave some physical record. He blends in well. Probably helps old ladies cross the street. Will say hi to new neighbors, but won't engage. His relationships won't be in his neighborhood. He's a good actor.

How the FBI has identified his bonding issues, his desire for narrativity—a fancy way of saying he likes to tell stories about himself—and a childhood filled with an alienating, abusive, and neglectful mother and an absent father—left the family? died?—is beyond me. And as I like to tell Don and anyone else who will listen, I'm not just muscle and good looks. I am a college graduate. Not *summa* or *magna cum laude*, but *cum laude* by the skin of my teeth, and that's still honors in my book. I'm on the slowest boat possible toward a master's degree in criminal justice. That means I sign up for three classes a year and usually drop one of them on the exact date that doesn't count against me grade-wise, but where I don't get much of my tuition money refunded. My mom gets after me for wasting money, but I'm on my own dime now and can be stupid with money any way I want.

I'm not sure how all this psycho data is going to help us actually find him. But Reynolds does have one clue we can actually work on. In five of the six known cities our murderer has worked, multiple victims attended Alcoholics Anonymous meetings. This apparently confused the FBI a lot at first because the profiling doesn't suggest someone who abuses alcohol or drugs. Someone suggested the obvious; he is pretending to have a drinking problem. *Duh.* All the pieces fell together.

Of course, we're putting a lot of confidence in a computer program called Project Vigilance. We're assuming Virgil—I've given the program a name of my own—hasn't missed other cities that would reflect a broader or emerging pattern of behavior. To be fair to good old Virgil, he's only going to be as good as the input he has to work with.

Reynolds is convinced that the connection of the forty-seven previous crime scenes is valid and that we are factor number seven. Why can't he just say we're the seventh city? Our perp has been hibernating for six months and is ready for serious business again.

Sandra Reed and many of the victims didn't attend AA, but twenty-nine did—more than half—so it's a major priority in our investigation.

Kendra, my niece, has switched spots with her mom and is at my side. She tugs on my sleeve. How long have I been the only one in the congregation standing? Kaylen looks over and stifles a laugh.

Very funny, big sis. I guess long enough to be noticeable. Is Jimmy giving me a dirty look from the pulpit? I'll remind him that pastors aren't supposed to do that. I'm sure his message will be scintillating as he starts off with a joke that people find very funny, but my mind wanders away again to yesterday.

———

We agreed that the four detectives in the room would start attending a couple AA meetings a week. I don't drink—okay, I've had a sip of Klarissa's white wine once or twice—but I've heard enough sob stories from winos when I walked a downtown beat that I can fake it well enough. For that matter, there are enough cops with drinking problems—self-medicating with alcohol is one of our occupational hazards—that everyone on the force likely has firsthand experience with someone who has been in, or should be in, AA. We considered putting out the word that any department employees already attending AA meetings need to keep their eyes open. But we couldn't quite figure out what they were to look for—or how to keep that kind of information from getting leaked to the press—so we scrapped the idea.

There was nothing else but the crime scene. We dispersed quickly and all seven of us headed for separate cars to caravan over to a small apartment house in Washington Park. I didn't even mess with the starter on my Miata. I rolled it back and popped the clutch.

———

Jimmy is winding things down up front. He asks a couple of questions about the current state of our soul when it comes to anger. That wakes me up. If I had paid attention I wouldn't have been so surprised that he wasn't talking about having too much bad anger—the kind I've been wrestling with—but rather not having enough godly anger.

Holy anger. Righteous anger. My mom's kind of anger. Things that make God mad are supposed to make us mad.

I can embrace that. First of all, I already feel lousy enough about myself right now, and it's nice to not feel judged, especially at church. And yesterday's crime scene made me feel a little of God's fury; it still was resonating in my chest today. I shook my head, remembering. It was unlike anything I've ever witnessed. Worse than any of the films they showed us at the academy. Slasher film bad. Torture more than murder. If seeing that doesn't stir some godly anger, I don't know what will.

We pray the benediction in unison as I stretch and arch my back; I think I sigh out loud because Kaylen leans over and gives me an elbow to the rib. Not very nice of her. Again.

Jimmy says "amen" and I turn into the aisle. I see Dell about six rows back. Our eyes lock. I squint and tilt my head to the side to give him a plaintive "I'm sorry" expression. He takes a step backward and half turns as a twentysomething puts her hand in the crook of his arm. He looks back at me, trying to stifle a look of triumph.

Okay. That was unexpected.

But you go, Dell. I had it coming.

I can't stop thinking about the crime scene.

We should have carpooled, but no one wanted to lose any more of a Saturday afternoon in the salt mine. But we all pulled into a narrow street in Washington Park about the same time. Three- and four-story houses, each two units wide—the classic Chicago row house neighborhood. There were a few double-wides here and there in the neighborhood, as well as some small apartment houses. It was one of those timeless kind of streets that looked like an elegant '50s film set but was now a contemporary, neo-bohemian enclave. The side yards weren't much more than the width of a sidewalk and maybe a row of tomato plants. A back alley serviced the small parking lots behind each house that could each accommodate one car each. That meant half the street's residents parked out front. Everything was well cared for, and a lot of high-ticket cars were on the street.

Even more than five hours after the crime scene had been established, there were still six or seven black-and-whites with rotating blue lights, a couple of dark brown Crown Vics and shiny black 300Ms, indicating more detectives and some brass had arrived, along with an ambulance and two crime scene tech vans. Both of the vans were wedged on the strip of grass and sidewalk in the front.

As we approached the apartment house's front steps, we could hear a neighbor complaining to a uniform that the vehicles would damage the lawn and somebody was going to have to pay for it. The kid, stoic in a starched blue, was looking right in the lady's eyes, but obviously not listening. Good man.

Two of the uniforms had set up sawhorse roadblocks a couple houses away in each direction. One of the guys had pulled the barrier aside to let our train of cars trail in. Our entourage officially finished filling in the center of the street. I thought I was last to pull up, which I figured was good because it would be easier to get out when we were done.

I had forgotten about Major Reynolds' car. He drove a rented

Cadillac in behind me. I didn't think the government approved luxury cars on expense reports. He's either more important in the Bureau than we already suspected or he got a free Hertz upgrade.

The seven of us huddled at the front steps, and we found out the Caddy was an upgrade courtesy of Enterprise. I was relieved to know he was a humble everyday officer of the peace, just like the rest of us. Not. He looked like he should be picking up a date for dinner rather than visiting a bloody crime scene.

A techie offered each of us a cotton ball dipped in a little ammonia mixture at the front door, in case we needed something to help us with the odor ahead. No one wanted to be the first to touch a drop beneath our nose because it looked weak. But when an EMT staggered through the front door, leaned over the rail, and sent his breakfast and lunch spewing—maybe even a midnight snack—we applied the ammonia in unison.

Martinez led us up the steps into the foyer. The security door was propped open. We walked past twelve white buttons underneath twelve dull brass-colored mail slots, each about four inches wide and eight inches tall. That meant four two-bedroom apartments per floor. I did a little calculation in my head and figured at least 2,000 square feet each. Probably storage cages and a laundry room in the basement. Twelve-foot ceilings on the first floor. A wide circular staircase and a small three- to four-person elevator dominated the lobby. Everything was in great shape, including the elevator with a checker-sized black button for each floor. I rejoined the circle of investigators in the foyer.

"According to the neighbors, our victim lived alone," Blackshear started. "Nice apartment and furniture. She appears to be a very tidy person. No sign of anyone breaking in. We've checked all ground-floor windows and front and back doors. For right now we're assuming the victim knew the perp and let him in voluntarily."

"Or her," I said. I thought it was a good point and worth noting. You know, not starting with any assumptions on anything, including gender. No one commented.

"Our victim—" Blackshear started again.

"What's Sandra's age?" Don asked, interrupting.

"Late twenties, early thirties," Blackshear said. He flipped back in his black notebook. "Thirty-two. Not that her attacker made it easy to tell." He paused until he caught his train of thought again. "She's single, an accountant in a big firm downtown. She's got a VP title on her card. Must've been smart, to be a VP this young."

"Divorced? Married?" Don asked.

"The human resources director from her firm has been helpful. She's divorced. No kids. And before you interrupt again, Don, we've already got a call in with the ex, but no answer yet. He doesn't live here anymore. He's in the L.A. area. Maybe he sleeps late. Local cops are checking in with him."

Don just nodded calmly at the rebuke. No big deal. Maybe I could learn how to handle such things from him. It was just the type of comment that would've sent me stewing for the rest of the day.

My mind went to the ex-husband. Family always ranks as the first suspects. Especially an ex. If he was sleeping in, he was about to get a wake-up call from the LAPD.

"The perp took her cell phone, just like every other case, so there's no phone log. No sign of forced entry in her third-floor door either," said Blackshear. "And before you ask, no one we've talked to remembers hitting the entry buzzer to let a stranger in yesterday."

That was the oldest trick in the book for burglars. Hit buzzers until someone answers. Tell them you're UPS delivering a package or you're dropping a cake off for your aunt on a different floor. People hit the entry button because they don't want to be hassled. Of course, after a murder, who admits they were the one who opened the door for a serial killer to get in the building?

"Time of death?" I asked.

"Not official, of course," Martinez chimed in. "But probably a six-hour window between 7 p.m. yesterday and 1:00 this morning. The techies got her temperature about ten this morning and it was down about fifteen degrees. Jerome was looking at dilation of her pupils and thinks time of death is closer to 1 a.m. Once the ME has her on the table, he'll be able to see how long the bugs have been nibbling on her."

"Didn't take long for someone to note that a person living alone is dead," Konkade said. "Is there a clue there? Who found her?"

"A neighbor on the second floor," Blackshear answered. "They run together most Saturday mornings. She confirmed with Ms. Reed that they'd meet at eight in the morning. That was at 6:30 last night. We think she is the last person in this building to see or speak to her."

"Except for the perp," Don added. Everyone nodded.

"Yeah, except for him," Martinez shrugged. *"Este tipo es un loco diablo."*

I don't speak Spanish, but I had a pretty good idea that Martinez wasn't being complimentary.

"Are we assuming that she died from the cutting wounds?" Don asked Blackshear.

Reynolds had just caught up with us and answered for Blackshear: "If the perp is who we think it is, then yes, he bled her to death. It'll take a little time for your ME to confirm, however, because there will be a list of pharmaceuticals to factor and rule out, and his binding method does suggest possible asphyxia."

"Yeah, what he just said," Blackshear said with a nod of his head at Reynolds and a little shrug of his shoulders. "We've got more to give you," he continued, "but let's get everybody upstairs for their own look before the body really starts going bad. It's been a nice cool March, but the perp turned up the thermostat all the way. That's why Jerome's being shy on his guess as to time of death."

"It's April," I said.

No one commented. Am I invisible? I turned and was first in the elevator.

"Let's do the stairs," Blackshear said with a nod away from the elevator. "Unless you've got all day. That thing is slow and we can't all fit in there."

We trudged up after him, me with my face burning red. Don wouldn't have given it a second thought.

As reported, Sandra's place was neat and stylish. Except for the pale corpse tied to the corner posts on a blood-soaked bed. Reynolds had reported in the profile session that the killer didn't have sex with his victims. Possibly some foreplay. But apparently he—or she—got jollies in inflicting pain and cutting up women, not having sex with them. He would drug them, secure them with duct tape, and spend a lot of slow, seemingly deliberate time with his knife; for most of that time they would be alive.

Cause of death: exsanguination.

Toxicology reports from the various cases could not definitively declare the extent to which the victims were conscious and aware of what was happening to them. On the majority of victims that followed the pattern we were looking at, there were signs of struggle on the wrists and above the ankles—the main areas where they were taped down. But this could simply be in keeping with someone who is drugged but not quite knocked out, and therefore putting up a last-minute fight. The abrasions were not so severe as to suggest the kind of frantic thrashing that someone in intense pain would exert. So there was no definite confirmation of torture. Back in the pre-crime scene meeting, Konkade had said that maybe our guy has a streak of mercy in him. Looking at Sandra Reed in the middle of her bed, I doubted he would say it again. Maybe our killer has some kind of code, but mercy wasn't in it.

We all took our time searching for clues, moving room to room and lingering in the main bedroom, while the two techies waited patiently to bag the body and get it down to the morgue. I did a solo version of a line search, starting in one corner of each room, moving to the far corner, and then taking one step to the right each time so that I was sure to cover every square inch visually. Furniture made it an inexact survey method, but with four detectives and a horde of other cops in the apartment, it was good to have any sort of system in the midst of the orchestrated chaos.

I did a total canvas of the apartment—I would love to have a place this big and roomy—and then went back to the primary crime scene, doing my best to imagine what might have happened. I went back through every room, just trying to get a sense of the world of the victim and what might have drawn a killer to her—or her to him. I didn't have to struggle too much with her draw. It was clear she was good-looking, successful, tidy, and had great taste in art and furniture.

I wondered if she had an interior designer help her decorate. The place was put together almost too well. But the indelible image burned into my mind during and after our crime scene review was the victim herself. Sandra. A real person with a real life, filled with joy and sorrow, dreams and disappointments. And she was gone.

We are a product of our upbringing and mine was very religious. There were signs of that scattered through the modest little Chicago row house I grew up in, from the picture of Jesus knocking on a door that hung by the thermostat in the hall leading to our three bedrooms, to the big, beat-up, black leather Bible that sat on Dad's nightstand. Sandra had no such imagery anywhere. My mind started wandering toward thoughts of the afterlife, but I forced myself back on task.

Konkade left first. When we exited the building, we saw him talking with the uniforms that were first on the scene, probably reviewing protocol on how potential witnesses were separated and the evidence protected.

We reported to Zaworski on the front lawn and then Blackshear barked out orders to a group of ten uniformed officers. The two youngest were put on garbage pull. Seniority does have a few rewards. The rest were given a few instructions and assigned to help us start canvassing the immediate and adjoining blocks. When we met together three hours later, all of us had the same story. Nobody remembered seeing anything unusual the night before. We didn't talk to anyone who actually knew Sandra Reed. Chicago is supposedly a city of neighborhoods, but this section of Washington Park wasn't being very neighborly right now.

I went home, did my makeshift workout, and took a long shower. I read through my notes. If you cry, this would be a good time cry. But I don't. If you yell and cuss and throw things, this would also be the time for that. I just yell and throw things. I did pray but I still didn't feel very spiritual.

I tried to get back into the Child novel but my mind was still racing around the crime scene, so I put the book on my nightstand and turned off the light. I fell asleep with light jazz playing in the background to soothe my frazzled psyche. I had put on an old Larry Carlton CD, *On Solid Ground*, which I like a lot for the tunes, but also because it is guitar- rather than sax-driven. But sleep didn't come even when Larry played "Josie."

Just thoughts of Sandra. I don't know what time I drifted off, but it wasn't that far away from time to wake up. No wonder I was late to church.

Kaylen didn't know that. I'm not mad at her. I love my sister, both of my sisters, fiercely. I just wish they understood me a little better.

So what's going on with Dell?" Kaylen asks.

I am chewing a large bite of grilled chicken, so I don't answer right away. I've already devoured the twice-baked potatoes, fruit salad, broccoli and cheese, three Sister Schubert's dinner rolls with plenty of butter, and a few bites of Kendra's macaroni and cheese.

I think that macaroni and cheese is all the kid eats. And not just any brand. It has to be Kraft or the noodles don't taste right, she claims. Her parents need to make Kendra eat green stuff—and not just lime jello. If I had to eat vegetables growing up, then Kendra should, too. If they'd make her eat more healthy foods, I'd eat healthier, especially when I sit next to her at Sunday dinner.

My news reporter sister, Klarissa, is carefully cutting another microscopic sliver of chicken, probably not big enough to choke a lab rat. She puts it silently in her mouth and chews slowly. She has to be just going through the motions; there's not enough meat to require more than two to three bites before swallowing. Most of her food is still on her plate and there wasn't much to start with. Kaylen should be grilling Klarissa about her producer pushing her to stay skinny for the camera, rather than bugging me about Dell.

Kaylen gets distracted by four-year-old James, who needs another glass of milk, so I'm off the hook for a second. I stick another bite of chicken in my mouth so I still have an excuse when she turns back to me. Why doesn't she ask Klarissa about Warren? That's a far more interesting question, as far as I'm concerned. Warren is Klarissa's on-again, off-again boyfriend. He's the sports guy at a rival television station. They met at a local media awards banquet. He's about ten years older than Klarissa, but fit and handsome. Great teeth. I'm a firm believer that all good gifts come from God, but not *those* teeth. Is it possible to have teeth that are too good? Too straight? Too white?

Apparently he was a good enough college quarterback at Western Illinois that he got drafted by the Redskins. He has told me numerous times that he stayed in "the league"—which means the NFL, he explained, in case as a mere woman I find sports lingo confusing—for three years. He doesn't mention the fact that he never took a single snap in a regulation game, but then I'm being snippy again. I remind myself that if you were good enough to get drafted in the NFL, then you were one heck of an athlete. He's been a sportscaster for thirteen years now, since his playing days ended at the ripe old retirement age of twenty-five.

"Well?" Kaylen asks me again. She isn't going to let this drop. "You were going to tell me about Dell?" Mom and Klarissa are focused on me now, too.

I chew extra slowly and finally answer her question after a fake cough and long drink of Diet Coke with a clever question of my own: "I was?"

"You were. At least I thought you were." She's trying not to get exasperated.

"What about him?"

"He was at church with someone else. I didn't know you two had broken up."

"I didn't know we two were together."

"Well, excuse me, but he's been coming to Sunday dinner for the last few months."

"Because my family invites him."

"And, if I'm not mistaken," Kaylen soldiers on, "you two were supposed to have a big day trip planned yesterday."

"I guess I forgot," I answer sarcastically. "Oh, and maybe a little murder case I'm officially working got in the way."

"Was there a murder at the Amish village?" my mother asks in horror. "What happened?"

I laugh out loud and spit Diet Coke on my now-empty plate. Mom, you have got to get your hearing checked. The kids, Kendra and James, think that's hilarious and screech in delight. Kaylen is not amused.

"Give it up," she demands. "What happened?"

Given her no-nonsense tone, everyone at the table looks at me soberly.

"Where's Mr. Dell?" James asks me earnestly. "I like him."

"That's because he gives you a dollar for your piggy bank whenever he comes over," I say.

"He does?" Kaylen asks, surprised. James's head bobs up and down, but he doesn't make eye contact with his mom due to an instinctual understanding that too much discussion could lead to the end of the gravy train he has set up.

56

I am hoping we are off on another subject, but now my brother-in-law, Jimmy, is curious. "Dell seems like a good guy. He's obviously crazy about you. What happened?"

What happened? What happened? Let it go, people!

Do I sense an undercurrent of recrimination in his tone? It's no secret that Dell has done all the work in our relationship. I'm just not crazy about him. I like him. But that's it. I've never been dishonest with him or led him on. So why are people trying to make me feel guilty? Everyone is looking at me, including Mom, so I guess I'm trapped and have to say something. But it's not like this has been a big deal to me. Bringing a revenge date to church was more than a bit of a surprise, but hey, maybe she likes learning about farm tools from another century.

"I wish I could give you guys the scoop," I say. "But there's no story. Everyone move along. Nothing to see here."

"So did the trip to the Amish village put you over the edge or what?" Kaylen asks. Is there a retro obsession with horse and buggy culture? Is the energy crisis that bad? Did no one hear me say I'm on a murder case?

"As I tried to communicate earlier, we didn't really take that drive at all."

"Oh?" Klarissa's eyebrows are arched upward. Should I tell her that will cause wrinkles? That would give her something more important to think about. Klarissa always complains that male newscasters are allowed to age but female newscasters have a short shelf life and spoil when the wrinkles start showing up.

Everyone is staring at me, including the kids.

"What?" I ask. "I just said we didn't go."

"Did Dell have to go in to work?" Mom asks. "Because I know he's really been looking forward to seeing it."

"Actually, I got called into work, Mom. Right after Kendra's soccer game. I have a job, too. And in case you weren't listening before, I was assigned the case that's on the front page of today's paper."

"You're doing security when the president comes to town?" Mom asks.

"No. I'm not guarding the president, Mom. I'm working the murder of the young woman in Washington Park."

"Yeah, I heard two of the producers talking back in the green room," Klarissa says. "Her boyfriend shot her."

"I didn't catch that story," Jimmy says. "That sounds awful."

"No guns were involved, Klarissa." That's all I'm saying.

"Well, that's good, I hate guns," Mom says, oblivious to the gap in her logic. "Now tell me again why you didn't take the drive with Dell? I think he's a sweetheart."

James saves me. He's been playing with a straw and suddenly spews milk in a fine mist all over the table. I knew he liked my little show with the Diet Coke so he decided to try it himself. It's my turn to crack up, trying to hide my laugh behind a hand. Kaylen is up in a flash and James' exultant smile turns to a plaintive wail to let her know it was all a big misunderstanding. She marches him from the room, encouraging him on with a swat to his rear. Kendra knows she's not supposed to smile, but does so anyway. Jimmy gives her a reproachful glance and she guiltily clamps her lips in a straight line. Smart girl. Mom looks at me from the corner of her eyes, without turning her head my way. I know she thinks I'm being a bad influence on the kids. I bite down on my lip, even though I feel like defending myself against a look. After an awkward moment, Jimmy gets the conversation rolling again. He's good at that.

Thankfully the table has lost interest in Dell and our torpedoed

Amish excursion. The Washington Park murder is forgotten, too. We talk about the Bulls and the Cubs and about the great spring weather, even though it has been all over the charts temperature-wise. For a few minutes we discuss why some people believe in predestination and why some don't believe in eternal security, which somehow segues to a new discussion on whether Klarissa should consider interviewing for the news anchor job with the number two television station in the Baltimore market, which could be one step closer to a national position. News *reporter* in a market like Chicago is doing very good for a twenty-eight-year old; news *anchor* puts her at the top of the food chain.

I want to have a serious discussion with Jimmy. He may be a bit naïve and sheltered, but he is a smart guy. I want to ask him why people do what they do. Especially evil people who cut up innocent women. I also want to ask him if he thinks it is ever okay to tell a lie, like when it is for a good cause or just by omission or part of the job description as a detective. I'm not sure Jimmy knows what to make of me, so he rarely engages and listens like he does with others. So once the conversation transitions to Klarissa's career and then back around for another go at the weather, I know I'm not going to get his attention and my mind drifts away. Maybe I should make an appointment to talk to him in his office. I do listen carefully to a joke Kendra tells me in a loud whisper when she loses interest in big people talk, too.

"Knock knock."

"Who's there?"

"Canoe."

"Canoe who?"

"Canoe come out and play?"

I laugh enthusiastically and interrupt something Jimmy was saying for just a second, but he soldiers on. I do fear Kendra has inherited the same gene I got for joke telling. Hopefully she'll have a better left foot in soccer than I ever did.

Kaylen and James return—and I'm glad my nephew looks no worse for the wear—as Jimmy tells everyone about Kendra's three goals. She beams. I beam. James is ready for some attention and insists that he plays soccer, too.

When no one pays attention he yells, "I scored a thousand," tired of his sister hogging the limelight.

I know how he feels about the limelight. When you have two beautiful sisters that have legs and smiles to stop traffic at the Indianapolis Brickyard on race day, you feel a little ignored sometimes. Klarissa is a princess's princess. And Kaylen is married to Jimmy King—Dad used to call him King James—so that makes her a queen. I guess I'm the court jester. But today I want to stay in the shadows.

I look around at my yammering clamoring family. We've had a tough couple of years and took another punch in the gut in the past month. There's an empty space at the table and maybe in each of our hearts. Not sure any of us feel whole right now. But we're strong enough to laugh together—and fight together. And maybe that's as good as it ever gets.

My mind moves to Sandra Reed and the family she left behind—a mom and dad in Columbus, Ohio, a brother in San Clemente, California, and a sister out in Lake County. Only one thing might help them a little over time . . . to know the monster who murdered their loved one is off the streets.

God, help us . . . help me tell them we caught her killer.

So you're telling me you did not push the back of the suspect's head toward the ground with force sufficient enough to cause multiple abrasions and bruising to his facial area?"

"No, sir, that's not what I said."

It's Monday morning and I wasn't in the greatest mood to start with. I'm not a Monday morning groaner as a rule. I don't go out partying over the weekend as a few of my colleagues are wont to do—and it shows on their faces on Monday mornings. I wasn't in a sour mood because I don't like my job. In fact, I love my job.

This particular Monday morning just started wrong. First of all, after not enough sleep on Saturday night and church and Sunday dinner with my family, I spent the rest of Sunday afternoon and early evening in the situation room back at the precinct. Ever since the advent of CNN and around-the-clock cable news, plus a new generation of cop shows, you have to name things with a little more flair. It's not good enough to go to a conference room. It's got be something dramatic, as in, a *situation* room.

I got home at eight, ready to do a light workout with my home exercise equipment, which consists of a floor, gravity, and the weight of my body. Then I was going to relax with my favorite TV show and get to bed early. But I procrastinated and by the time I was poised to do a set of one-legged squats, Dell stopped by to talk things out. What things? It was quarter to nine. He knows that at quarter to nine there are only fifteen minutes until the only show I watch every week comes on. I am the only person in America who doesn't know how to schedule a show on TiVo for the whole season and I'm not sure I pushed the record button for this week, so I probably won't get to see it later. He also knows I need some alone time after a typical Sunday with my family. I really needed some alone time last night.

I knew from his loud knocking and the way he entered my apartment that he was mad and going to vent. I'd never seen him mad before. And vent he did. Hey, I never pledged undying love and devotion. I never even gave a hint of reciprocity. I never let the guy steal a full hug or kiss—though that hadn't seemed to be on his agenda. I didn't know if it was refreshing or strange. I'm used to hand-to-hand combat to keep the wolves at bay. Is that why I've let this charade continue—because he's been so easy to control? And even if I did miss a Saturday drive in the country, for obvious good reasons—and admittedly, my effort to get a hold of him and explain was late—it wasn't me who brought a revenge date to church. Why am I the bad one?

After I had heard enough of the pain and suffering he's experienced at my hands and a little bit of analysis on my inability to bond, I came back with both guns blazing. I explained clearly that any pain and suffering he was feeling was self-induced. I let him know I liked him, but reiterated that I did not return the level of feelings he professes toward me. I let him know we had covered this territory before. And I let him know that I thought his church date was cute and that perhaps he needed to devote his considerable attentions to her.

"And we're not going out anymore."

That stopped him in his tracks. His response was interesting: "You know it's only you, babe. I was hurt and just wanted to get your attention. It was stupid to bring Carrie to church. Will you ever be able to forgive me?"

I thought I was going to puke. What would it take for him to get it? I pushed him out the door at eleven. He wanted a kiss. I obviously didn't. When I yanked my head back, he got the message and stomped down the stairs.

I was so tired I didn't brush my teeth or hang up my clothes. I just fell in bed and squirmed under the covers. When I woke seven hours later, it felt like my teeth had a film to rival barnacles on the underside of a cruise ship. When I stumbled to the bathroom and took a look at myself in the mirror, it was downright frightening. That's how I greeted Monday morning after my alarm went off like a tornado warning at six.

It didn't help that when I arrived at my cube, with just fifteen minutes to spare before my Internal Affairs interview—make that interrogation—there was a large Post-it note on the center of my computer screen with a message written in all caps:

DEAR DETECTIVE CONNER—HAVEN'T MEANT
TO LEAVE YOU OUT! JUST WANTED TO LET YOU
KNOW THAT YOU ARE ALWAYS WELCOME
TO BE A PART OF AARP! (ANGRY AND RAGING
POLICEPERSONS) WE FEEL YOU'VE GOT LOTS
OF PROMISE. YOU'RE EVEN BEING CONSIDERED
FOR A MENTORING ROLE. DETAILS TO COME!

That was bizarre. Who would write that? I looked around a couple times and then crumpled it up and threw it away. I wasn't going to give someone the satisfaction of seeing me get angry. For once.

———

I am in an interview room usually reserved for suspects. I guess that makes me a suspect. Tom Gray of Internal Affairs and I have been sparring in a twelve-by-ten room, sitting across a six-foot folding table centered in front of a large mirror—which anyone who's ever seen a cop show knows is one-way glass—for ninety minutes now.

If anyone from my detective squad—and the curiosity, and yes, embarrassment is killing me—has been watching, they've got to be close to nodding off. I'm not a cooperative suspect. Just as I was leaving my cubicle, Zaworski and Konkade stopped me and in hushed tones advised me to say as little as possible. That had me wondering if I should be worried. I'm still asking myself the same question at a time when the interview should have long been over.

After introducing himself just as Tom Gray, and giving no rank, which is atypical for an officer of the peace, he opened a thick manila file and leafed through it for almost ten minutes in complete silence. I knew he was trying to create an awkward silence where I would blurt out a confession of premeditated and unmitigated brutality. Exactly what I would do if I were in his shoes.

I wanted to say, *Hey, Tom, thanks for coming prepared and respecting my time.* Instead I forced myself to keep quiet. I guess that's why the boys stopped by and told me to keep it zipped—they knew it would be the hardest part for me.

I think we're coming to the end—maybe wishful thinking—of a pretty unproductive, ninety-minute interview, and I make myself refocus.

"I don't understand," he says. "You said that in cuffing the alleged perp, you pushed him to the ground while your partner covered you with a drawn weapon. If the threat was nullified, why push?"

"Tom, the punk may be an alleged smash-and-stash perp to you, from the comfort of your cushy IA office, but the knife he sliced me with was very real. Would you like to see my scar?"

"You know the legal rules, Detective Conner; we say 'alleged' until a perpetrator is convicted. Don't get off point."

"The bruise on my chin from a swing he took at me was pretty real too," I say, defiant and undeterred. "You've been studying the report like it's tomorrow's final chemistry exam, so I think you know a lethal weapon, brandished at a police officer by an alleged smash-and-stash perpetrator, was recovered, bagged, and sent in as evidence. And the punk's prints were positively identified. How many times do I have to repeat that?"

"I understand exactly what you're saying about the knife, Detective Conner," he says as if speaking to a child who is a slow learner. "But I don't understand the contradiction in your testimony."

"Tom, there is no contradiction in my testimony. If there's a contradiction, maybe it is in your questions."

My heart is starting to race. I'm feeling nauseated. Am I in trouble? Over a punk? Had I contradicted myself in something I said?

Another eternal pause. He looks up, closes the folder, places one hand atop the other on the table, and raises his left eyebrow with a polite, quizzical expression. I'm not going to answer an eyebrow, so he is going to have to ask it. We face off for thirty seconds, and I know that for a fact, because I count from one-Mississippi all the way up to thirty-Mississippi.

He breaks the silence, asking, "How so?"

Ever difficult and actually not understanding what he's asking, I respond, "How so, what?"

He stifles a sigh and asks politely, "How are my questions contradictory, Detective Conner?"

"I'm glad you asked, Tom. When you asked if I used excessive force, the answer was no. When you asked if I pushed my attacker to the ground, the answer was yes. So maybe the questions aren't technically contradictory, but neither are my answers. Yet you seem to find something contradictory there. I think your questions are ignoring an important qualifier. The qualifier is that the punk, someone who is suspected of beating a senior citizen half to death, wielded a weapon with deadly intent and needed to be restrained."

"And yet your training specifically prohibits using retaliatory force once an alleged perp is remanded. So pushing his face to the ground was unnecessary and extra."

"But he wasn't absolutely, 100 percent remanded. I pushed him to the ground in the process of remanding him."

"But why with the force to create contusions and abrasions? You said yourself that your partner had a gun trained on him."

"Well, Tom, when you're in the field, you learn a lot can happen between the time a dangerous criminal is initially subdued and when he is actually in handcuffs and contained in a safe space. With all the action of the previous few minutes, we didn't know if he had another weapon or would make a desperate play for freedom that might involve *additional* harm to my body. If he had chosen to make things rough again, there may very well have been a moment when my partner's gun was trained on me, not the punk."

Tom interrupts, "But he was flat on the ground. You had cuffed him. The hard push came afterward."

"Tom, let me repeat, the push was because (a) he was squirming and struggling, and (b) he was not yet cuffed."

"Are you sure? Because that's not what I'm reading."

"I'm positive that the cuffs were not secured and that I needed to keep him down to protect myself from a head butt or donkey kick. The punk was resourceful."

"Why do you keep calling the alleged perpetrator a 'punk'?"

I say nothing. We stare at each other to see who will break eye contact first. He looks down. Ha! My first win of the day.

He reopens the file and riffles through a number of papers until he finds what he is looking for. He reads it studiously.

"Well, maybe this explains my confusion," he says looking up, his eyes piercing into me. "The report, signed by you and detective Don Squires, doesn't mention the alleged perp squirming or struggling. In fact, it says he went down easy once Detective Squires entered the scene with drawn gun."

"It's a police report, Tom. Not a chapter from *War and Peace*. And easy is relative to our fight."

This is ridiculous. Am I going to get punished on a sequence of events that covered less than two or three seconds? Did I go too far with that push on the punk's head? I don't think so, so why in the heck am I getting grilled by my own department? If I hadn't run like a gazelle, he would have gotten away. I was attacked. Despite words like "abrasions" and "contusions," I didn't really hurt him. I should have emphasized that the punk was squirming, but I didn't think about it when I was typing. He was sly and dangerous and I did want physical distance, even if it meant only inches of additional separation. And yes, I was mad. I'm wondering if this will kick me off the biggest case in the city.

"Detective Conner?" Gray asks. "Is there something more you want to say?"

"I didn't know you asked another question," I answer defiantly. Probably time to read *How to Win Friends and Influence People* again, an assignment my dad gave me several times in my teen years, requiring a three-page report filled with life lessons I had learned each time.

Gray is apparently done. He carefully organizes the file and places it in his briefcase. He snaps the clasps and then places his case on the table. He takes off his glasses and wipes the lenses on his red tie with paisley amoebas. I'm not sure it's in style. That looks like one of my dad's ties. From before I was born.

He picks up the case and walks toward the door. I guess we're done and I stand, eager to stretch my back. I don't know whether to be relieved or worried. He opens the door halfway, pauses, pulls it shut, and turns back to me. I am suddenly wary.

He looks at me with his deep brown eyes and says, "Detective, I knew your father. Great cop. An even better man."

I freeze. Where's this going?

"I worked in the same office with him the last year or two he was on the force. I wasn't always in IA, so I know what you deal with on the streets."

I start to mumble something but he holds up his hand to stop me.

"Your father was one of the good guys." Gray is speaking softly. It's hard to hear him and I lean forward, despite a burning desire to get as far away from him as possible. "I never once heard him refer to any of his collars as a 'punk.' And not because he arrested a bunch of saints. It's just not how he went about his business. This thing with Incaviglia is done. But for your old man's sake, I'm telling you I don't like the vibe you're projecting. I don't have to tell you that you're not real popular with top brass right now. So why make people wonder if you have your act together? Unless you don't."

I want to say something. Maybe I want to say I'm sorry—sorry for pushing the perp's head into the pavement even if the APB described him as armed and dangerous; sorry for having such a crummy attitude; sorry for not respecting that he has a job to do, too; sorry that I don't care what the top brass thinks of me after what they did to my family. Or maybe I want to call him out for trying to lay a guilt trip on me.

I look up to say something, but he's gone.

I stand and stare at the door for a full minute. I look at my watch. It's almost 9:30. Time to work on catching a killer.

Time to get serious about my anger problem.

I picture myself in a support group.

Hi, I'm Kristen and I'm an angerholic.

April 3, 11:00 a.m.

The crime scene was certainly interesting. A simple murder and half the city's finest showed up. Has someone picked up my scent? I believe so.

The guy that got out of the Cadillac wasn't local. His suit was way too nice. From the cut, I'm guessing a Hugo Boss. I like a nice cut. Nice handsewn shoes too. I can tell handsewn a mile away. In this case I was only 300 yards from the scene, so not so hard to spot. The assymetrical laces aren't to my liking—I truly prefer symmetry—but I'm willing to recognize good craftsmanship. I am a craftsman myself. The suit was navy—boring. It might have had a light chalk stripe in it. Couldn't tell for sure. My Sunagor binoculars are supposed to be the best, but it's probably time to see if anyone is making a better lens.

The Italian suit guy has got to be Fed. FBI. Federal Bureau of Incompetence. No big deal. About time they showed up. His Caddy was a rental so he's not from the Midwest office. I do believe the boys and girls in Washington, D.C. finally know something about me and my manner of business. All I can say is, it's about time. I invited them out to play seven years ago. I'll take this seriously, but it's one thing to know I exist and entirely another to figure out how to find me.

The star of the show was none other than my dream girl, Detective Conner. Kristen Conner. The only word I can use to describe her is "exquisite." That chestnut hair; I can just imagine it cascading like pure silk between my fingers, right before I kill her.

She turned in my direction once. I know she couldn't see me, but I wonder if she sensed me. Somehow, our paths are destined to intertwine.

Little does Kristen know how much I know about her. And her family. Her niece is cute—the spitting image of her. The little guy could learn some manners.

I took some risks to increase the chances she would work this case. And voila, a little surveillance at the crime scene and there she was. Sometimes you get lucky. Sometimes you're just good. Sometimes you're both.

I know her—and she will know me some day, much more intimately. But I've got more work to do in this city first. For the record my intentions are purely platonic. I am, after all, always the consumate gentleman.

Kristen. I took my time, studying her through the binoculars again, daring her to find my window. Almost wanting her to find me. But she didn't, of course.

I love that she's tough, strong, and yet weak and insecure below the surface. Savvy. Naïve. Such a delicious mix of contrasting forces. If only she was neater. Her car is dirty; inside and out. I don't like that. And something has to be done with her wardrobe. Maybe I'll buy a nice outfit to dress her up in when we are finally together. She would look good in Vera Wang. Her coloring can handle the patterns.

Okay. Enough. Kristen's tantalizing to think about, but she's not the only beauty I have my eyes on. More importantly, I need to think through how I proceed with the Feds in town.

I need a diversion. I already lifted weights—chest and arm day. Think I'll head to the Cubs game.

Those DePaul primates better not show up.

I'm furiously scribbling notes from phone messages on my cell and office lines while trying to scan and delete email messages that don't require an immediate response. I fear my inbox is going to explode. But the last message on my cell makes me stop and just listen.

"Kristen, this is Dell. I know you're swamped. Don't worry about calling back. Just wanted to say . . . just wanted to say I'm sorry. I'm reading the *Trib* right now and can't imagine what you're having to deal with. I was just feeling sorry . . . just thinking of myself last night. You didn't . . . you don't need that burden right now. I also want you to know Carrie doesn't mean anything to me. Even if you don't feel the same way about me, you're the only one in my life. I'm here if you need someone to talk to. Whenever. Doesn't matter what time, day or night. I was miserable all day yesterday. Bringing Carrie to church was a bad idea. Well I guess it's not a bad idea to bring someone to church, but you know what I mean. She's in my office and we're just friends. I have to tell you, even if you don't want to see me again, I'm still going to invite myself to Sunday dinner with your family. I didn't grow up with that. You all are amazing. I really missed your weekly fight with Klarissa. Plus James is a buck short on his college fund now. Tell him I'll pay him double next week. Okay? Seriously, I've . . . I've never felt like this for anyone in my life. Don't cut me off because I was ugly to you yesterday. I just want to say—"

Dell never got to finish his sentence. He ran out of message time. I shake my head and laugh out loud. His life story with me; I have no time for him. He deserves better. And he's weirding me out.

Carrie's a very cute girl. I hope she'll treat him better than I do when Dell finally sees the light and breaks up with me. *Wishful thinking. You know you're going to have to do the deed yourself, Kristen. And it's going to get real ugly because he's not listening.* Treating him better is really not a tall order. Does he keep bringing her up in the hopes I'll get jealous? I might send Dell a text suggesting he find out if Carrie wants to tour an Amish village.

Stop. You don't have time to think about Dell.

I can't get my mind back where it belongs. I wonder how someone can just lay their emotions out on the table like Dell does. I mean, I think his phone message is a little embarrassing, for both of us. I know he does great in business, or so it appears, based on the brownstone he's renting—can't imagine what it costs—the Porsche Boxter he drives on weekends and the Lexus he drives during the week. He's explained to me that he is a freelance contract worker who specializes in supply-chain management. I don't have a business background, but I get the basic idea. Companies need materials to make products, but don't want to pay for them or store them in a warehouse until they actually need them. The key is to make someone else be the banker, is how he put it, which usually means the manufacturer or even the supplier of raw materials.

Since I work for government, I'm confident I don't understand all the nuances of his business specialty. I'm pretty certain, for example, we have a lifetime supply of paper clips at the CPD. Dell could do wonders for us—but I'm not sure he'd be safe if an armed workforce found out someone wanted to mess with their supply of Styrofoam cups and sticky notes. Come to think of it, someone keeps forgetting to order coffee filters.

Dell's told me he moves a lot. He has shown me pictures of a rustic home on about twenty acres he has out near Durango, Colorado. Nineteen acres of pine and one acre cleared for the gravel driveway and homesite. Only about thirty minutes from Wolf Creek Ski Area. He has been pestering me about a family trip during ski season. He wants Jimmy and Kaylen to bring the kids so he can teach them to ski. Mom, Klarissa, and Warren—or whichever guy she is dating seriously at the time—are invited, too. I think he's trying to use my family to get close to me. There I am, using my skills of detection again.

I asked him how he picked Durango. He loves to ski and liked Wolf Creek. I asked why buy a house you don't live in. He says it's too much hassle to buy and sell houses with as much moving as he does, so he bought the land and built the cabin—that's what he calls it, but it looks more like a home to me—to build real estate equity. I asked how bad he had been hit by the downturn in the economy. That seemed to impress him. So he explained his investment model—and even drew a graph on a napkin at Ed Debevic's one night—and where real estate fit into that, how he was protected by diversification and some market hedge tools, and how he'll bounce back even if there has been some valuation slippage before you know it. I sat there thinking about a savings bond I bought when I was about twelve.

He's told me he has never pursued anyone like this before, he has always liked the single life, and women usually chase him. I'm supposed to be impressed and flattered.

I'm not sure how Dell and I became such an item based on my explicit lack of affection for him, but I know there's a lot of assumption and presumption involved. We met at church. Why is it that when reasonably attractive, similarly aged people meet at church, people assume it could be a match? Here's how it went down: Reasonably attractive female detective doesn't have a boyfriend. Handsome stranger introduces himself. Out of the blue, sweet sister of reasonably attractive detective invites handsome stranger to family dinner. Handsome stranger is liked by everyone in the family, including the detective, though that same detective has considerably less ardor toward him than any other family member, including the four-year-old who is trying to get college paid for or buy a new Star Wars action figure, one buck at a time.

Handsome stranger and reasonably attractive detective go out for a meal and a movie. They show up at some church functions and sit together, and voila, they are declared a couple.

I can understand how it looks from the outside. But I can't understand his pacing. One month into a comfortable little pattern of getting to know each other, he tells me he loves me. I inadvertently spilled my Diet Coke—and I remember being disappointed that the Awesome Blossom was ruined. What is it with me and Diet Coke accidents?

I think I will make a wonderful wife one day. Okay, a decent wife is more like it. I think I will be affectionate and loving and mushy and affirming and appropriately attentive and jealous and all that stuff—and probably more than a little difficult to live with. But I'm not a natural when it comes to opening up my heart to just anyone. I don't have some huge heartbreak in my past that I can't let go of. It's just the way I've been—the way I am. I've had a couple regular boyfriends in the past, one in high school and one in college. Both lasted a little less than a year. I've also dated casually from time to time, but I've never been moonstruck. Ever. Does that mean something's wrong with me and I have bonding issues, like Dell claims? Doesn't feel like it to me. My lack of *smitten-ness* seems to only propel Dell forward. Like I'm the ultimate challenge.

"Hey, KC, you going to stare at the pad of paper all day or do you think we might get some work done?" Don interrupts.

I glare at him. He knows I hate that nickname. He just smiles. Don is wearing a tan summer-weight suit, a soft blue shirt with white collar, French cuffs with black onyx cuff links, and a silk tie with diagonal lines. And I do believe he has on a new pair of shoes. He's styling. No wonder he looks like he's bounced back emotionally from the trauma of his slightly scuffed Allen Edmonds. He'll give my outfit disparaging looks all day, even though in my book, there's nothing wrong with a khaki skirt and a navy polo. Even with a wrinkled collar. Last time I had this outfit on, Don said I looked like a sales girl at the Gap.

If it was anyone but Don dressing this way, I'd suspect he was on the take, because there's just no way to afford the clothes he wears on a detective's paycheck. I bet I don't spend one-third of what he does filling up my closet. And I don't have kids, unless you count the Snowflakes.

He has a little secret, though. I've been sworn not to tell anyone in the department, which makes it all the tougher to keep. Don's stay-at-home wife doesn't just stay at home. She also sells a little real estate on the side—actually a lot of real estate on the side—even in a tough economy. I've asked him how it feels to be a kept man. He just smiles and tells me it feels mighty fine. That doesn't mean he wants the guys to know that his wife is pulling down at least twice what he does. I'm happy for him. Don and Vanessa wanted their kids in private school and Vanessa's gig pays the tuition and a whole lot more.

He looks at his shoes and beams his happy smile and then immediately gets somber.

"So how'd it go this morning?"

"How'd what go?"

He rolls his eyes. "Your group therapy at the donut shop, what do you think?"

"I wouldn't know."

"C'mon, Kristen. How'd it go with IA? And by the way, if you're going to act like a horse's behind all day, we're driving separately."

I start to smart off to him but Zaworski strides around the corner.

"I got an email from Gray," my boss says.

I hold my breath.

"Sounds like your interview with Internal Affairs was a roaring success."

"Thank you, sir," I say, trying to hide the relief in my voice.

"I didn't announce you won a medal for bravery, so quit thanking me. Now listen, I've already had to go to bat with you on Czaka—"

I start to interrupt, but he immediately holds up a hand to silence me.

"And whether or not you support his decision, I don't want to hear anymore about that either. I also don't want any repeats of you grinding a kid's face in the gravel. I'm serious. You're on a short leash, Conner. On the edge of administrative leave. And if that happens, you won't land back in homicide in this precinct. No matter how good a detective you are. Understand?"

"Yeah."

"You sure? 'Cause I can't tell when someone says, 'Yeah.'"

"Yes, sir. I understand, sir. I'm sorry I—"

"Save the apology, Conner. I'm not in the mood. Glad you understand. Now how 'bout two of my finest get busy and find me the psychotic bent on terrorizing my city?"

Don and I head for the stairs in a hurry. He gives me a dirty look and keeps a safe distance in case I have political leprosy or something. I think he's looking for a promotion to the next pay grade. I'm just happy I got my gold shield. I like that Zaworski acknowledged I'm a good detective, but I'm seriously frosted that I got reprimanded by him in public. I would have told Don all about it anyway, but Zaworski doesn't know that. CPD protocol is that reprimands happen behind closed doors. Except when they don't. Don can shrug something like this off in an instant. Not me.

At the first landing he says, "We're meeting Reynolds over at FBI in the State Building. He seems to think it is a better location for our task force."

"He's probably right."

"You been over there?"

"Nope," I answer. "It's out of my league."

"I have and you're right," he answers.

"I am? About what—that it's a better spot or that it's out of my league?"

"I'll just leave it at 'you're right.'"

Payback is gonna be brutal, Don.

We're out the back door and into the parking lot. I let him open the back door for me so I can seize the inside position to grab the driver's side of our assigned Taurus. That makes me driver. Don is still looking at his new shoes and barely notices. That's disappointing.

As we pull onto Clark Street I tell him we need to stop by the CPD Armory on the way back so I can get in thirty minutes of practice shooting with my new Beretta. I switched from the standard issue Glock 22 to see if I could improve my handgun scores for my personnel files.

"I'm brave and daring when it comes to the job," he quips, "but maybe not that brave and daring."

I glare at him, which makes him laugh. I drive in silence the whole way over to the State Building on Wacker, more than a little mad. It's one thing to gig somebody for something they do well; it's not allowed when you really can't shoot worth squat. Dad always said big nose jokes were funny as long as no one in earshot had a big nose. If Don notices my pouting, he doesn't comment. He does move his feet around a lot to look at his shoes from different angles.

"Hello. My name is Walter, and I am an alcoholic."

"Hi, Walter," our circle of seventeen returns.

"By the grace of God and with all of your help, I've been sober for three months, two weeks, four days, thirteen hours, and twenty-six minutes."

He is looking at his watch as he ticks off the time. We cheer enthusiastically, but all the time I wonder how the heck someone could be that exact. Maybe he has a stopwatch feature that he clicks the second he takes a drink just in case it is his last for a while? He beams and then turns serious.

"I've lost everything this year—my wife and my boy. He's six years old now and by court order, I haven't seen him for eight months, and it doesn't look like it's going to be lifted anytime soon."

He chokes up and pauses. I take him for early thirties. He looks beat-up enough to be at least a decade older. Probably a middle-class kid who lost his way, because he definitely doesn't look tough enough for the streets. Walter, you better find your way home. You aren't going to survive out here.

I wonder if his wife will take him back. Sometimes the long-suffering ones hit a wall and when they finally boot him or her out, there's nothing left of the relationship to salvage. The toughest cases to process are when a hittee decides to stop getting hit and hits back. I had one of those when I was in uniform. The hittee was charged with murder. Everyone, including the district attorney and jury, believed her husband had a well-earned bullet coming to him, but convicted her nonetheless.

Walter talks about some job interviews he has coming up, but I'm not listening very closely. Apparently this group proceeds from person to person around the circle and everyone shares something, even if only a sentence or two. In briefing for the assignment, my understanding was that all sharing in AA groups was voluntary. I start paying attention again as the twelfth person tells about a recent setback and a recent victory. Only five more chairs and it's my turn to speak. I've read through AA's Big Book quickly and read most of their brochures. I'm now a subscriber to the AA *Grapevine* journal and worked with Don, Konkade, and Zaworski to establish a role. Don thought it was hilarious when he said my everyday wardrobe was perfect for the part. Zaworski didn't laugh and that shut him up. Take that, Don. But I thought I'd just watch and learn the meeting routine my first time out. Looks like I need to think of a quick story. I don't want to stand out by being the only one who doesn't say anything.

Eleven women from the precinct are going to attend two to three meetings a week. Seems like a long shot since our research department has established that there are over 300 AA locations across the city. That doesn't include private practices or other church and civic-sponsored meetings that don't operate under the Alcoholics Anonymous banner.

We're focusing on a five-mile circle around the crime scene. That cuts the numbers down to forty-eight known weekly or semi-weekly meetings in twenty-one locations. Again, we're assuming we don't have all of them accounted for. My assignment is to cover the Tuesday night sessions at Saint Bartholomew's United Methodist Church.

A married woman speaks next. I'm assuming she's married because she's got a big rock on her ring finger. She's wearing a tight white scoop-front shirt with a push-up bra that's generating a lot of interest from the men. The group leader, I think his name is Darren, is carefully keeping his eyes on the ground because he knows what we're all going to think if he gives her the same kind of earnest and attentive eye contact he's given everyone else. I want to laugh, but stifle it.

"Hi, I'm Bethany, and I'm not sure, but it's conceivable that I'm an alcoholic. It's probably more that I just have a . . . a sometimes drinking problem."

"Hi, Bethany," I say along with the group. This is going to get interesting.

She describes the various places she hides vodka—her poison of choice—from her unsuspecting husband's sight. She gives a pretty detailed description of the new vodkas on the market, including a revolutionary grape-based vodka, and which ones are best for the money. One of the reasons she's not sure she's an alcoholic is that she doesn't drink cheap vodka, which she heard is one of the tell-tale signs of being an *alkie*—her word, not mine. I begin to wonder if she is a liquor salesman and this is a rogue marketing scheme, but she finally gets down to business.

She tells us that she's explained her slurred speech and erratic behavior to her husband as a hormonal imbalance and that it will take awhile for her doctor to find the right level of meds to get her emotions back on track. She explains that no man wants to talk about a woman's hormone problems, so he's bought it hook, line, and sinker. Husband thinks she's with her friends playing bunko tonight. The fact that she has lied to attend an AA meeting sparks a discussion about whether it is ever right to lie to protect the innocent, which heats up and runs wild for about fifteen minutes. I look at my watch and realize—gratefully—this will save me from having to share. Thank you, Bethany.

I've never been to an AA meeting so I don't know what most of them are like, but I'm pretty sure it's uncommon for an entire group to instinctively dislike someone. This group dislikes Bethany. The consensus is that honesty is necessary to get better. Then some of the comments on the value of honesty start getting directed at Bethany. One guy leans forward and says, "Bethany, I think you are trying to mask some deep-seated problems with your lying."

Darren is all for honesty, too, but finally comes to her rescue, saying, "Bethany, thanks so much for sharing. We are honored you've decided to meet with us. I think we have time for everyone to share if we move a little more quickly. And by the way, if you don't get to say everything on your mind tonight, we'll be open for business next week—and we have a list of other meetings that meet every day."

Bethany's cheeks are flushed in anger. I don't think she was expecting to get ripped to shreds at an AA meeting. I'm no expert on drinking troubles, but I suspect she's not ready to make a go of this sobriety thing just yet anyway. Maybe I'm wrong. I wonder if her name is really Bethany. There I am being a cynical detective again.

My mind drifts back to the murderer. Wonder what happened in his childhood to start him down this path. Alcoholic mom? Abusive dad? It didn't matter—all that matters is that we catch him. It's been five days and so far we have only one clue—and that clue is based on the assumption that Virgil is on to something with this AA lead. I mull that over. Life isn't fair. About the time you make a decision to get your life together, you get hit from another direction.

"My name is Jonathan, and I am an alcoholic."

"Hi, Jonathan."

I look up and over a couple seats. Jonathan doesn't quite fit in this setting. It's not that the rest of us here have dark-rimmed and bloodshot eyes, smelly clothes, slurred speech, and a variety of involuntary tics. Bethany, for instance, is neat and trim. She's got that rock on her left hand—the day she pawns that is the day she'll know for sure she is an alcoholic. But Jonathan is immaculately dressed in a pair of gray wool slacks with pressed creases, nice polished loafers with tassels, a preppy navy jacket, and what looks to be an expensive dress shirt with sleeves showing exactly half an inch below the jacket. Jonathan actually reminds me a little of Dell, in manner. Even Don might approve of his taste in clothes.

"I've been drinking every day since my junior year in college at Northwestern. Never thought I had a problem, even though my grades slipped enough to keep me from getting accepted for my MBA at Kellogg School of Business. Now I'm thirty-eight. I've lived all over the country but always end up back here where I grew up and went to school. I've been through seventeen jobs—I always get a new one because no one will give you a bad reference for fear of a lawsuit. I don't think I can count how many relationships I've burned through. Some of you are sweet drunks. I'm an angry drunk. That said, I've come close, but I've never, ever, ever hit a woman."

He makes that sound like a real accomplishment. Am I supposed to stand up and applaud?

"I'm looking for job eighteen and it's become clear that alcohol is getting in the way of me finding and keeping the right one. Same with women. I'm jealous of the guys who have wives and kids. I'd like that, too, someday. So about a month ago I finally decided to own up to the fact that I have a problem. I want to change. It's been two days since I've had a drink and I'm dying for one right about now. I especially want to thank Walter. Just knowing you've succeeded for more than a couple months is a real inspiration to me."

Walter blushes and nods in acknowledgment. After a momentary lull, the group breaks into applause.

Jonathan continues, "I'd tell you what else I'm dying for right now, but who knows, maybe there's a cop present and frankly, not all of my substance issues are legal."

He laughs and everyone provides at least a courtesy chuckle—though a few are looking at him like they looked at Bethany. I laugh a little harder than necessary out of surprise and to cover up that I turned red when he mentioned cops. I sit back and listen to Jonathan finish up, and the four people to my left tell what's going on in their lives right now. When it's my turn I say nothing. Darren politely deflects attention from me and asks if anyone else would like to say something. He looks my direction a couple times, so I keep my head down. I'm mad at myself for wimping out, but I'm thinking about Jonathan. He fits the profile. Maybe I should have a word or two with him just to see if my internal radar sounds an alarm.

Darren looks at his watch and asks halfheartedly one more time if anyone else wants to give a testimony. Sixteen sets of eyes look my way and then give up. I guess that was my last chance tonight. Oh, darn. I missed it. Darren explains the importance of regular attendance, celebrating victories big and small, and having a sponsor you can call when the urge to drink is strong and your willpower is weak. We hold hands and recite the serenity prayer together and are dismissed.

A few attendees make a beeline for the door. Others saunter over to a side table to get another cup of wretched coffee and a store-bought cookie or two from plastic molded trays. Jonathan awkwardly shuffles my way trying to make eye contact. In my peripheral vision I see that Bethany is eyeing Jonathan and is on a path to intercept him before he gets to me. Now I'm positive she's not really here about staying sober. She succeeds in getting to Jonathan first, but only because Darren cuts me off.

"Your first time?"

"You could tell?"

He laughs. "Don't worry about not sharing tonight. We're just glad you came." So much for not standing out.

"Well, thank you, Darren. Is it always this interesting?"

"Not quite *this* interesting," he answers with a knowing smile. "But seriously, let me know if you would like the names of some female sponsors. Sometimes it's easier to share one-on-one the first time."

"Let me think about that."

"Well, don't think too hard. Really, no one is trying to trap you. These ladies are nice people who understand what you're going through. They'll drop anything to be there for you. We love to help."

"I appreciate that; that's very nice," I mumble, sincerely moved by the care and concern I feel.

"Well, I'll be honest. When we help you we help ourselves. AA has always been committed to service—it's one of our pillars of recovery."

"Makes sense." Why do I feel so awkward? I'm here as a detective, not a participant!

"I forgot to mention at the end of tonight's meeting, but we have a gift for you."

"Really?"

He hands me a white chip. It is blank on one side and the other has the serenity prayer printed in blue.

"This is a small token we like to give first-time attendees. It symbolizes your desire to quit drinking, to get better. Carry it with you as a reminder of that commitment—and to come back next week."

Jonathan keeps looking over our way for an opening, but Darren is now telling me about how long he has been sober and about how scary it is to share for the first time, but how much it really helps. Jonathan gives up on connecting with me and heads out the door. Bethany has been rebuffed and gives me a dirty look. She should have gone to bunko night with the girls.

Jonathan graduated from Northwestern, which is just up the road from Chicago in Evanston, but didn't he say something about just moving back to town about six months ago? I think so. I think of the profile Virgil spit out. Neat. Articulate. Organized. Moves around. He fits. But no way could it be this easy to find a killer.

"I gotta run," I say to Darren and I hustle for the door to see what Jonathan is driving. I step into the crisp night air. No sign of him.

Dear God, help Walter find his way home.

April 4, 2:00 a.m.

She is delightful.

Wish she had spoken up. I would love to hear what she had to say.

I have to admit that I could look at her all day. Long legs and thin, but she still has some curves. But not too many curves.

That's my kind of woman. Not a Silicon Valley type. I like soft and supple flesh. So much easier to work with when I take the stage, even if it is for an audience of one.

I'll talk to her next time for sure. I like it here in Chicago now—even with the wind and the crazy temperature changes. I think I might actually describe myself as happy, for the first time in a long while.

She should have said something even if she's new to the group. She just looked at her hands. They are lovely hands. I want to know what she's holding back, understand her, and let her know I understand her. That connection is vital for me and my girls.

I really don't mind listening to others' stories. Most spout the banal ordure of small, tedious, mind-numbing lives. But I must say, I hated hearing that guy tell about how his wife kicked him out of the house. How demeaning. Has he no pride? What real man would let a girl get the better of him?

I shared. Not my real story of course. I'm saving that for my journal. That shrink who worked for my captors was actually right about something. Journaling is therapeutic. I feel better knowing my story, my real story, is being recorded as a monument to my work—to me. If that hack Truman Capote can win the Pulitzer for writing about the killing done by others— amateur killers at that—just think what they will have to give me. A Nobel? I'm joking of course. I know they don't give prizes for my particular style of performance art. Not everyone can appreciate the mastery I possess. Their loss.

Yes, I really am happy. But I want to be even happier. And therein lies a catch-22. Happiness doesn't satisfy. It's too fleet-

ing—it leaves you wanting more. And oh, how I want more. I suspect I'm going to depart from my customary schedule. Let's call it a reward for the patience I've shown in setting up Chicago as the backdrop for my best work ever.

Cubs are on the road. Sox are in town through Sunday. All night games. I'm thinking I'll have to miss one for another form of entertainment. If good pitchers mix up speeds, then who am I to not do the same?

The call came in at 4 a.m. on Saturday. *Be at the precinct ASAP.* I whipped my Miata into the parking lot by five, as the sun rose over the lake and lit up the Chicago skyline. I was going to sleep in since today's Snowflake game—one of two left—doesn't start until noon. I need to call my assistant coach, a mother who knows nothing about soccer, but who is very good at organizing after-game snacks. Today she has to coach, too.

I pound up the steps and hear voices as I enter the office. Am I last on the phone chain or what? And if I am, is it by design? He's gruff with me, but I don't think Captain Zaworski dislikes me. He's gruff with everybody. But you can never tell with him. I hate being late. Why am I always the last one to show up for meetings? My sister, Klarissa, the perfectly coiffed news reporter, can vouch that I am not wasting time playing with my makeup. I barely put it on in the first place. A little foundation and usually a quick swipe of red on my lips, is about the extent of my cosmetic indulgences.

It wasn't the starter on my Miata that delayed me either. I got a good spot on the hill in front of my apartment, so starting it was easy. I just did my normal rolling start—shifting into first, turning the key to the "on" position, taking my foot off the brake, letting the car roll forward with the clutch pedal pressed to the floor. Once I hit fifteen miles per hour, I popped the clutch, and after only one or two jerks and heaves, was off to the races. Just slower than everyone else out of the gate. Once she starts, my Mazda's engine easily hits eighty on the crosstown highway, so yeah, I've got to be getting called last. I still need to spring for the 300 bucks to get the starter replaced. It crosses my mind to call Dell to see if he knows anyone in the supply-chain world who can get me a great deal on a starter, but it doesn't seem quite right to ask for help after the week we've had. Or more accurately, not had.

They've started without me. Don, Zaworski, Blackshear, Martinez, Konkade, and Reynolds are in their regular places, plus there are a couple new faces, most notably another woman.

I open the door carefully, but it still creaks like the entrance to a haunted house. Everyone looks up—except for Don who keeps his head down out of fear of being deemed guilty by association with his partner. Zaworski stops speaking. I feel like a ninth-grade truant and the captain looks like a displeased teacher as I bring his presentation to an abrupt halt. Everyone mumbles their greetings in my direction.

The other new face is Tony Scalia, who I've known ever since I tagged along to the precinct with my dad on Saturday mornings as a kid. Big Tony hasn't changed a bit in twenty-some years. He's got to be sixty now. Of course, he looked like he was sixty years old back then, too. He still has a full head of the darkest, shiniest black hair that a bottle of Just for Men can dye. His face is pockmarked with scars from what had to be one incredible case of adolescent acne. He's at least six foot three and has the barrel chest of a weight lifter. I'll bet he goes 260 or 270 pounds. He's actually soft spoken, but then you don't have to be loud when you exude the raw strength of Big Tony. If he wasn't a cop, he would have made a great gangster. Or better yet, he could have played gangsters in the movies.

Big Tony, ever the gentleman, is the only one to stand up. He doesn't say anything but gives me a sideways hug and a wink.

"You know Major Scalia," Zaworski says, stating the obvious. "And this is Dr. Leslie Van Guten with the Federal Bureau of Investigation."

"A pleasure," she says, giving me a firm handshake. She is wearing a matching black skirt and jacket with white blouse, which sounds rather austere, but she has a good tailor who has fitted the outfit to accentuate her nice figure without being offensive or over-the-top in the conservative "man's world" of law enforcement. Her second button is undone to show off a large diamond pendant on a simple gold necklace. No wedding ring, so I'm guessing she salvaged her engagement ring after a divorce. I'm just guessing. If I'm right, that might suggest I have the finely honed instincts of a great detective. If I'm wrong, it probably means I'm just a jealous, catty, small-spirited female who has never been married.

I don't smile because I'm embarrassed beyond belief for being late, and more importantly, the business at hand is gruesome. Pictures have been tacked to a cork strip that goes around the conference room. I'm jolted up to speed without hearing a single word. The pictures tell a familiar story. Another woman. Based on furnishings and decor, seemingly successful. Single. Living alone. Murdered. Murdered is a harsh word, but it doesn't come close to conveying or describing what someone is up to in my city. *Butchered?*

It's been fourteen days since I visited the first crime scene. In contrast to standard operating procedures, we are once again meeting off-site first. There's a downside. The clock starts ticking once a murder takes place and every minute, every second counts. Other than family members and close acquaintances—who account for half the homicides in America—if you aren't chasing a specific person with a name within twenty-four hours, there's a good chance the killer is going to get away.

The upside to huddling together before hitting the victim's home en masse is that we can each receive assignments that allow us to go into greater detail at the scene. At least that's what Zaworski thinks. And since it's automatic that all gathering, handling, and analyzing of evidence is going to be vigorously challenged in the US legal system, this gives Zaworski and Reynolds a chance to remind us to mind our *p*'s and *q*'s. No good deed goes unpunished, so if you have a question, you ask before acting—and touching. No seeking forgiveness later. Usually I chafe in this kind of environment, but I have to be honest, I am nervous as a cat on a hot tin roof. I don't have a cat so I'm not familiar with their habits, and I've never seen a tin roof, not even down by the tracks where the homeless create warrens of refrigerator box huts, but suffice it to say, the description seems apt.

"According to our experts, this second homicide proves beyond a shadow of a doubt that we have a serial killer in our city, and one who has evaded arrest and detection for close to a decade."

———

An hour later, Zaworski finishes detailing evidence protocols. Routine stuff, but a good reminder that our break in this case is probably going to come through a small detail. He looks to Reynolds and nods. Reynolds clears his throat and begins.

"If you haven't finished reading the previous factor notebooks, you need to do so within the next forty-eight hours. Come Monday morning everyone knows everything the FBI does. Nothing we say leaves our situation room. That stays the same. But before we head over to the CS, we're going to give each of you an executive summary of everything Operation Vigilance has correlated. We're then going to have you put your signature on a sworn affidavit that the materials will not leave your possession, will not be shared with anyone not on the task force—even if that someone is your superior—and will be returned within twenty-four hours. We've got to get everyone up to speed on this thing, fast. No excuses."

Reynolds nods in my direction. There're two ways to interpret it. Positively, it may be recognition that I've been doing overtime reading on six of the seven notebooks at FBI's HQ, even before it became "assigned reading." Negatively, it may be Reynolds' way of telling me to finish what I've started. I've been working fourteen-hour days since the first murder. Apparently that isn't enough. I don't care how long we are on the crime scene. I will not go to sleep without reading every page of the last notebook and the executive summaries today.

"You're going to notice a significant change in pattern with the current murder. Anyone have an idea already?"

"Time between murders," says Blackshear.

He answered way too quickly. That can't be right. I purse my lips to say something.

"Nicely done," Reynolds says to Blackshear. "He's been a once-a-month predator, but this time it's less than two weeks."

"Any chance we got a new perp at work?" Martinez asks in his heavy accent. "A copycat?"

"Great question," Reynolds answers. "But there are just too many signature acts for this not to be the same predator that Project Vigilance has identified and that Dr. Van Guten has profiled."

He nods deferentially in her direction when he says that. She must be a big shot. Good old Virgil is always on the job, but his outfits aren't as nice as Van Guten's.

"We're going to hit the scene together," Reynolds continues. "We've got transportation lined up that will accommodate all of us." Apparently, it's a Gray Line bus, which seems like a weird choice. Last time I was in a Gray Line vehicle, I was in eighth grade, and me, my parents, and my two sisters were on a trip to New York City as Kaylen's high school graduation present. But Reynolds has a plan.

"We're dropping the team off in pairs on each corner of the block. We're all walking up slowly, very slowly. We're going to look around. We're going to look people in the eyes. We're going to see who's watching, who's avoiding eye contact, who doesn't fit there. If someone wants to talk to any of us, we're going to stop and talk. Ask them what they saw and if anything has seemed out of place in their neighborhood. I know this is a different *modus operandi,* but honestly, what you're going to see at the crime scene is something you've already seen before.

"We met here at CPD because the media is stalking our FBI regional office. I don't want the circus we had at the first scene. If anyone from the media is already there, I'll assume a neighbor called or someone was paying very close attention to a very subtle message on the police band, but I'm still going to check everyone's home and cell phone logs."

I think he just looked at me. I am suddenly very self-conscious that my sister is a news reporter for one of the city's largest stations.

Reynolds gives the floor to Van Guten, referencing that she has a doctorate from Harvard, and explaining that she is a psychiatrist under contract with the FBI. She is a profiler and will now be an official and permanent member of the team until we apprehend our butcher in Chicago or he moves to another city.

"Be on the bus in five minutes," Zaworski barks. "You got anything to take care of before we leave, take care of it fast."

"Más le vale a ese tipo que no sea yo el que lo encuentre," Martinez says to Don and me as we exit the situation room. *"Va a desear nunca haber nacido."*

He strides off, his jaw jutting out, and nearly knocks the door to the men's restroom off the hinges as he disappears from sight. I look to Don for help. I took French, which was probably a mistake, but my mom pushed so hard for me to take Spanish that I suddenly developed a love for *lingua François* in eighth grade. Don isn't fluent in Spanish but is our interpreter when necessary.

"I think he wants to meet our killer in a back alley," he says with a shrug. "You never know with Antonio."

I stop to pee and take care of it fast, wash my hands—probably a mistake based on Reynolds' five-minute order, but good for public safety—and hustle down the steps and out the back door into the employee parking lot. Unbelievable. It's 7 a.m. and there are more than ten local TV and radio station vans with satellite equipment atop outside the chain-link fence, plus what looks like a fancy Winnebago from Mars with CNN printed on the side. I take back the Winnebago part. How about a country music star's home away from home? I have a fleeting thought that it would be kind of cool to look inside.

There is a horde of reporters with microphones, digital recorders, and even a few old-fashioned flip notebooks with yellow pencils. Three squad cars block the entrance to our lot and six uniforms are keeping the jackals at bay. I keep my eyes on the ground and hop up the three steps and into the bus.

I'm last one in. Everyone is looking at me. Reynolds and Van Guten have commandeered the whole front row. They are leaning into the aisle and speaking to each other in hushed tones. They have to stop and lift their heads so I can pass. The rows aren't close to being filled up, but the aisle seats sure are. I'm reminded of the scene in the school bus from *Forrest Gump*. But there's no one to play the role of Jenny and share a seat with me. I plop into a seat by myself and look at my cell phone with horror. I realize I called Klarissa on the way over to cancel our coffee date. I look forward. Reynolds is on his phone. I can only guess what order he is giving.

He's going to have our phone logs checked and think I called the story into Klarissa.

I feel sick to my stomach. But not as bad as I'll be feeling in about thirty minutes.

19

"Can I see your gun, Aunt Kristen?"

"James, you know your mommy doesn't think it's polite for me to brandish weaponry at the table."

Klarissa gives me a dirty look—she has made it known that she is not a fan of the Second Amendment and thinks we live in a gun-crazy society—which brings a smile to my face. I think it's my first smile of the week. But I guess Sunday is the first day of the week, so that doesn't quite account for the way the last seven days have gone.

"Please. Pleeeease, Aunt Kristen."

James is persistent today, so I suggest to him, "How about after we have dessert, okay, kiddo?"

He shakes his head vigorously and spoons a large dollop of mashed potatoes into his mouth. He's my kind of guy.

"Can I see it, too?" Kendra asks.

"You bet," I answer. "And if we're real careful we can take all the ammo out and I'll even let you hold it."

"Me too!" James calls through a mouth filled with mashed potatoes.

"James, don't talk with your mouth full," Jimmy instructs.

"Is it good to introduce four-year-olds to hand guns?" Klarissa asks with disdain. "Isn't that how violence gets started?"

"Guns, TV, and milk," I answer. "Seems to be a pattern or as I like to put it, a non-isolated event stream. You've got to talk to your station manager again. Have you seen some of the stuff they're showing during prime-time family hours?"

"Funny," she answers sarcastically. "But what kids watch is up to parents—and playing with handguns should be, too. We have enough violence in this world."

"Hey, us cops don't start violence, we just end it," I answer smartly. "And if Jimmy and Kaylen want to tell the kids they can't look at a Beretta 9mm, I will keep it holstered."

Nice move, I say to myself. Deflect and parry her attack. She rolls her eyes and carefully brings her fork within an inch of her lips with the smallest bite of salmon filet I have ever seen in my life, or at least since the last time I watched her eat. I watch as she opens her mouth and then thinks better of choking herself on a gram of fish. She closes her mouth and lowers her fork back to her plate. Now I roll my eyes. I've cut a decent-sized bite from what's left of the chicken breast I was able to nab—the largest on the serving platter, I would add—but bypass it and spear the bigger portion and stuff it in my mouth. No seafood for me today. I'm starved. Fighting crime builds up an appetite.

"Mmmm," I moan noisily, my eyes locked on Klarissa, who looks like she might get sick. I smile and laugh under my breath.

"So, Dell, you still enjoying our fair city? Work going okay?" Jimmy asks. I'm a little disappointed that my little melodrama with Klarissa is being ignored by everyone at the table. And that Kaylen did an end-run and invited Dell over without me knowing about it. If I'm going to get this ended completely, I am going to have to get some cooperation from my family.

"Actually, I'm loving it here," Dell answers. "Work couldn't be any better, which means the company I'm consulting for has tons of problems, and that means job security for the foreseeable future. I'd rather not move again."

"What are some of the places you've lived, Dell?" my mom asks.

"Better question may be where *haven't* I lived," he answers with a smile. "Not having family, I've enjoyed taking in different areas of the country, and honestly, I've found something I like in every place I've lived. But I've spent more time in Colorado than anywhere else, and that's where I keep a permanent address. Some day you folks need to come see it. It's beautiful." My non-boyfriend is inviting my family to his place again. What is wrong with this picture?

"So at some point you'll lay down roots in Colorado and stay there, you think?" Jimmy asks.

Where the heck is he going with that question? Maybe he aims to find out what kind of dowry the family might expect to pay out if Dell wants me for a bride.

"I think about it all the time," he answers. "I may just be a victim of circumstances. After college I worked two years in Denver with a company that ended up going Chapter 11. The economy there was miserable at the time, so I took a contract job in Albuquerque. I made more money doing contract work, so when that gig was up after a year, I took a couple months off to roam the country a little, and then signed up to do a project in Phoenix. I think Portland was next. Then it was Atlanta. I stayed there a year after my contract was finished and got my MBA at Emory. There was work waiting for me in Colorado Springs, so I printed a business card with a phone number and email address and kept moving around. I was in La Jolla before landing here in Chicago. The only thing I've done to lay down roots is to build that little home outside Durango. The problem with that is I've only been in it myself for about three months total."

I'm impressed and a little embarrassed. Am I so self-absorbed that after six months of knowing him, my family now knows as much about his history as I do? He's glanced my way a couple times. I think this is when a real girlfriend, a good girlfriend, would jump in with an encouraging comment. I'm neither so I say nothing.

"So the house just sits there?" my mom, ever the pragmatist, asks.

"I've got a real estate firm that leases it out, so it doesn't sit that much," Dell answers. "The two problems are that I always forget to reserve time for myself during ski season."

He takes a drink of iced tea.

"What's the other problem?" Klarissa asks.

"Well, with renting the place out and having strangers living there all the time, I've never figured out how I'd like to decorate it to suit my own tastes. As a result, I'm not even sure what they are. My tastes, that is. So my little cabin looks like a million other vacation homes.

When I do spend time there it feels an awful lot like a hotel. It could use a woman's touch."

He smiles and looks at me. Surprised, I frown, shake my head, and roll my eyes. Klarissa looks at me triumphantly and smiles. Thank God for Mom. She's relentless. She could work with Tom Gray in Internal Affairs.

"Well I hope that you feel at home here," she says, not about to let him swoop me off to the Wild West . . . yet. "Chicago's not such a bad place to live if you don't mind cold winters."

"You all are way too kind to me," he answers. "I've never been treated better. I always find a church as soon as I hit a new town, but I've never had so many fabulous home-cooked meals. I actually have to go to the gym an extra day every week just to keep the weight off."

Mom beams. So does Kaylen. Jimmy looks very pleased, too. James is busy shoveling the last of his mashed potatos into his mouth so he can get to apple cobbler—and my Beretta. Klarissa smirks at me. She is enjoying how uncomfortable I feel way too much. I've had enough and am suddenly ready to show young James my gun— dessert can wait.

Before I can get up and make my escape Kendra says for the table to hear, "You never asked how I did in the soccer game, Aunt Kristen."

"I'm sorry," I say with enthusiasm, relieved to have a change in the conversation. "How did my star Snowflake do?"

"Two goals."

"I had a hundred," James yells.

"James, stop interrupting," Jimmy says sternly. James gives his apple cobbler a pouty look—and then devours another bite.

"Very cool," I say. "And how did the rest of the Snowflakes do?"

"We won!"

"Way cool. Mrs. Kimberly must have been a good coach," I say, not believing my own words.

"She didn't coach," Kendra chirps. "Tiffany's dad did."

Really? No way! I'm coach!

I look up at Kaylen but she is suddenly studying one of her fingernails.

—•—

I show James and Kendra my gun. I remove the magazine and double-check that no bullets are in the chamber, of course. I give a perfunctory lecture on handgun safety and let both of them hold and aim it. I put the magazine back in, holster it, and wander from the game room where James is pretending to shoot bad guys with a candlestick. I push the door to the kitchen open and look over the counter into the living room. Jimmy and Dell are watching the Cubs contentedly and talking in low tones without feeling any need for eye contact. Dell is filling out a scorecard just like Dad used to do. I have no problem with that at a game, but it seems weird when you're watching it on TV. Of course, he has a diversified portfolio and I have a single savings bond.

Klarissa is closing her purse and getting ready to leave. She gives Kaylen and Mom long, warm hugs. I get a quick, mostly one-arm embrace and a quick peck on the cheek. I really do have to get checked for leprosy or body odor. Kaylen walks her to the door and it's just Mom and me in the kitchen.

"So when are you and Klarissa going to stop fighting and start getting along?" she asks.

"Mom, we're not fighting any more than we ever have. It's just how we communicate with each other."

"Then it's time you two start communicating better. You're like teenagers fighting over a boy."

"Well, if that's what this is all about, she wins. She can have the boy."

"What's wrong with Dell?" Mom asks with a sincerely hurt expression. "I like him."

"I know you do. I do, too," I retort. "Doesn't mean I have to marry him does it?" There's challenge in my voice.

"You're thirty, so don't you think you should start thinking about marriage? You make it sound like settling down, getting married, and having kids is something bad. You can't keep people at arm's length forever, you know."

Ouch. Not sure what hurts worse. Mom thinking I don't want to be close to anybody or the reference to thirty. I'm not thirty yet.

I say my goodbyes and head out to my car. Jimmy and Dell are engrossed in conversation about the rookie right hander that just got called up from Des Moines and barely notice my exit. Good. I need an easy escape from Dell. I've got the incident notebooks at home so I'm not going to stop by the office. I push in the clutch and turn the ignition. It grinds but doesn't start. Jimmy and Kaylen live on a flat street. Great. What now?

I end up slinking back up the sidewalk to ask for help. I get back in the driver's seat. How embarrassing. Jimmy and Dell get behind the car and push me into the street and get me rolling. I can hear them laughing. I make sure the car has enough momentum, pop the clutch, and wonder for a second if the engine is going to turn over as it pitches and sputters. It roars to life and I'm out of there. Tomorrow for sure. I've got to get the starter replaced.

But my mind's on the crime scene, not my car, all the way home.

After three solid hours of reading non-isolated event stream note-books, I jog over to the high school football stadium a mile from my house, intent on running up and down the stairs of every aisle. My surgically enhanced knee will protest, but I've got to do something to clear my mind. It's a jumble of Dell getting a family invite despite having done a revenge date two weeks earlier; Tiffany's dad coaching *my* Snowflakes and winning; Tom Gray from IA grilling me and invoking my dad's name before he left; and a bad man killing independent, successful, attractive women in my city and my desire to stop it.

It is a cool, pleasant, early spring evening that's already dropped into the upper sixties, but I sweat like it's an August boot camp in southern Georgia. My mind starts to clear and my spirit lightens just a little, but I can't help thinking about the latest victim, Candace Rucker.

Candace Rucker's apartment was as gruesome as we knew it would be. No one demurred when offered cotton swabs with a drop of ammonia at the door. The smell was still overpowering. Same MO. He—I'm not arguing that we need to be thinking it's a woman anymore—did his work and then left with the heat turned up full blast.

With a violated body nearly floating in a pond of blood, there were tons of forensic evidence. The problem is that though all of the evidence points us to a particular person, it doesn't help us find him. It simply confirms a profile and provides us with everything we need to convict him if we ever get him in our hands. I kept my focus and took copious notes like a good soldier. But the only thing we really learned was that it was the same person doing almost exactly the same thing that Virgil has already alerted us was going to happen in our city. He is careful. Precise. Sick. And good at hiding.

Candace Rucker, thirty-two years of age, a junior member of a major Chicago law firm, divorced, no kids, and no live-in, is dead.

———

"So, did you have a good weekend?" Don asks as we slide into a diner booth for some breakfast.

We spent most of Saturday at the Rucker crime scene, so it would be more accurate to ask if Sunday was good.

"So-so."

"Your girls win?"

"Yep."

"Nice. Isn't that like the first win of the season?"

"Second."

"Cool."

"We've only got one more regular-season game. Who knows, maybe we'll get win number three."

"There's the Vince Lombardi we all know and love. So how'd Sunday dinner go? Dell back in the picture?"

I cock my head and look at Don across a Formica tabletop, a cup of steaming diner coffee in my hand and almost to my lips. I want to see if he is giving me a hard time or just being a nice, normal human being who is interested in other human beings.

"Sunday dinner was nice. Yes, Dell was there."

"So you two are back together?"

"Not in my book, which made his presence awkward. He acted like nothing had happened. I guess that puts all the awkwardness on me."

"No surprise there." He laughs. "So, if you feel awkward being with him, why did you invite him over in the first place?"

"I didn't. My mom did."

"You're kidding me!" he says with a laugh. He spills a little coffee on the tabletop and nearly jumps out of his seat in fear that a couple drops will stain his monogrammed, starched white shirt. I think Reynolds' FBI "uniform" is rubbing off on him.

It's my turn to laugh. "Don't even ask why. My mom has always had a soft spot for stray cats and lost puppies. Dell is now her favorite lost puppy. Actually, my whole family adores him. Just for the record, Dell and I didn't drive over together. Kendra and James sat between us at the dining room table. He was just there and it seemed like the most normal thing in the world to everyone—except me. In fact, he was still there watching the Cubbies with Jimmy when I left."

"No way," Don says.

"Well, actually the last I saw of him, he and Jimmy were pushing my car down the street so I could start it with the clutch."

Don laughs again and shakes his head.

"Ready to order?" the waitress says. We both answer yes. We have a task force meeting in an hour, so we thought it'd be a good idea to grab a bite before the possibility of lunch or dinner disappears. Even though it's early, I order tuna salad on whole wheat. Lettuce and tomatoes, with a pickle on the side. A big glass of water and an endless cup of coffee. After living on JavaStar for the past couple years, diner coffee tastes almost watery. I can live with that if it gets the job done and wakes me up. Don orders a full bacon and egg breakfast, adds half a bottle of ketchup on the hash browns, and chases it down with blackberry pie. I notice that he's put on a few pounds since this serial killer thing started. He doesn't show it, but he must be feeling some stress, too. I promise, I will make no reference to his weight today.

"Don't you think it's a little strange," he says as we finish, "that you—the most controlling person in the world—have no say in your love life?"

"Did you just say 'love life'?" I ask him, ready to stare him down for as long as it takes. Maybe I should mention those extra pounds.

He breaks the gaze, laughs, and says, "Okay, let me rephrase that. This guy looks and acts like your boyfriend, and he's in the middle of your family life, and you don't even know what you think about him. And you're okay with that? Doesn't sound right to me."

"What I think about him is becoming increasingly clear. Now can we change the subject?" I ask.

"Hey, I'm just trying to be a good partner and I am tempted to point out that getting close to a member of the opposite sex can be a fulfilling experience. He seems like a nice guy to me."

Et tu, Brute? I look up to argue, but he holds up his hands in surrender. I hold my tongue. I'm worn out and don't have the energy for a battle of insults. Come on, coffee, do your thing.

"So, how was your Sunday?" I ask instead. He is trying to suppress a smile, which makes me think he's been waiting for me to ask.

Don's bursting to tell me his news. "Vanessa sold another house on Saturday, so it was a great weekend," Don says.

"She take you shopping?"

"Maybe she did." He holds up his silk tie. I guess I was supposed to notice that it was new. It's nice, but a tie is a tie. Don doesn't look at it that way. He then turns sideways in the booth and kicks a leg out in the aisle, high enough for me to see his foot. I'm assuming the shoes are new, too. I'm looking at a shiny black loafer with a tassel.

"Nice. New Eddie Arnolds?" I ask, teasing him.

He rolls his eyes and says, "Allen Edmonds. I've been wanting to buy some Graysons. They're not made quite as narrow as the other AE models, but they still feel great."

"That's two new pairs of shoes in two weeks."

He doesn't answer but just smiles. He and Klarissa should go shopping together. Make a Saturday of it.

"What do they cost? More than a hundred bucks?"

"Almost 400," he answers quickly, pulling his foot back under the table and crossing his arms with a frown. I've hurt his feelings. I feel a little bad for purposely gigging him. But not that bad.

We've canvassed the first crime neighborhood in Washington Park, where Sandra Reed was murdered, since six this morning. It'll be back to Rogers Park for Candace Rucker's murder later, but we wanted to catch the early-to-work crowd from the first murder as they were leaving for the office or airport or wherever they go on a Monday morning. It's been two weeks and we still haven't been able to interview everybody on the block yet; we figure that even if we catch someone for a second or third time, maybe they'll remember something they forgot to tell us earlier. It's a good idea, but not very fruitful. We talked to a total of six people, all more interested in their wristwatches than us. I wonder if anyone even remembers that a real human being—their neighbor up until a couple of weeks ago—is dead.

"Have you finished reading all the notebooks from the other cities?" I ask.

"Yeah. But to tell you the truth, I didn't find anything. How about you?"

"Me neither. This guy is a ghost."

"I love that the FBI is involved and is bringing all these resources to the table," he says, "but it seems to me that we're going to catch him with old-fashioned police work. Until he makes a big mistake, we're going to be spinning our wheels. I keep thinking that the AA meetings might lead to a breakthrough."

"Would be nice of him to leave a business card or something, preferably with his confession written out, wouldn't it?"

"We can hope and pray, but I'm not counting on that."

"Well, tell Vanessa to pray, then. You say that God answers all her prayers."

"She got me, didn't she?"

I roll my eyes. We look at our watches, finish the last bites on our plates, and get up without a word. I pull seven crumpled dollar bills from my wallet and leave them on the green check the waitress has left. Don makes a face at my offering and leaves a crisp ten-dollar bill and two more ones. I'm no math wiz, but I figure that's about a 40 percent tip.

"You need change?" she asks our backs.

Don turns and says, "Keep it." To me he says, "I bet she'll love what you left, Scrooge."

"I'm not married to a real estate mogul," I shoot back.

I hustle out the door and down the sidewalk to the driver's side. Whoever gets there first, drives. Neither of us like being second. I hold out an open palm and he drops the keys in my hand with a frown.

"You limping?" Don asks as we pull out of the parking lot. I don't answer, but my knee is barking after last night's stair run.

———

Dell called last night to see if I wanted to go out for a quick dinner. I politely declined and spent my evening again going through the remaining notebooks, created by a computer I've named Virgil. A notebook for each city. A green tab in each notebook with an overview of that area. A red tab for each victim. Yellow tabs in the back with theories and data.

It's been a tough month. Everyone I love has told me, in some form or another, that I've got an anger problem. Now everyone wants to know why I have bonding issues. I'm pretty sure everyone likes Dell better than they like me. Klarissa gives Mom and Kaylen big hugs. I get a polite sideways embrace and she misses the kiss on my cheek by a mile.

I wasn't totally honest with Don. My weekend wasn't even so-so. It was lousy.

THE CHITOWNVLOGGER
APRIL 26, 3:30 A.M.

W elcome to the jungle; we got fun 'n' games; we got everything you want," Guns N' Roses pounded out as the report title scrolled onto the screen: CUTTER SHARK ALERT: FALL ELECTIONS NOW HAVE A SHARP EDGE TO THEM.

Allen Johnson's bifocals were propped atop his thick mop of messy white hair. He sported a tan button-down shirt with a ketchup stain a couple inches above his navel that he figured most viewers wouldn't see. Nor would they catch the stubble on his face—it was a benefit of televising solely via the Net . . . a slightly grainy image that disguised such things. It saved him so much time, not having to shave every day. *Leaving me more time to investigate.* He stood in his postage stamp front yard, one foot on a step, his black Labrador Retriever obediently at his side. With puffy, dark-rimmed eyes he knew he looked like he hadn't slept since the last time he shaved. But he spoke into the camera with his best baritone that lent seriousness even in the midst of his rumpled condition.

"Welcome to my jungle, friends and foes alike—you're all welcome here. You've come to the place where you get the news that matters. The news the others don't report because they are in bed with city hall.

"Speaking of bed, I wonder how well Mayor Doyle has been sleeping lately. Is he having sweet dreams? Or nightmares? There's a killer loose in our fair city. Never a good thing for a reelection campaign, even when you are an incumbent eight times over and the city's octogenarian set thinks your daddy is still the 'Boss.'

"But the historians on his staff surely remember Harold Jefferson getting voted out of office because he couldn't shovel snow from our sidewalks fast enough, which spawned the evil Empire of Jane. Bottom line, Chitown is intensely loyal and fickle, all wrapped in one package. No, no Republican in this century or the next shall oust our mayor. But that doesn't mean a fellow Democrat will not.

"But I digress from the matter at hand. We have a new resident with a proclivity toward knives and blood. So who is this denizen of the night? A vampire? A werewolf? George Bush and Hillary Clinton's love child? Now that's a scary thought.

"We do know he loves blood. You heard that first from the Chi-TownVlogger. He's a predator with two Chicagoland hits under his belt.

But here's where the news gets worse, folks. According to my sources, I am going on record as saying it looks like he might just be warming up.

"You know my goodwill toward all men and women, and you know that I would never make light of violence. But I am officially dubbing this twisted tortured soul Chicago's very own Cutter Shark. I feel I have no choice after that moronic morning news muddler on WCI started calling our new friend the Windy City Whacker. The Windy City Whacker? Come on. I'm afraid Reporter Jenson isn't the brightest bulb on the Ferris wheel.

"It's quite clear that the Cutter Shark has a way with our lady folk. I want to give a big shout out to Nancy Reagan. She was right, girls. You can let a shark buy you a drink, but then you better just say no!

"Mayor Doyle assures us our crack police force is on the case and will turn over every stone to bring this *perpetrator of pain*, this *sultan of slice*, this *Faustian fiend of the flesh* to quick and certain justice. I will stay true to my political convictions and not buy a handgun—but I am going to break down and buy one for my daughter. I'm also going to make sure her college accounts are paid up so she doesn't come home to the Windy City, asking Dad for more cash.

"Now, if our venomous villain was piling up a pack of illegal parking citations, I have no doubt that Mayor Doyle and Commissioner Fergosi would be able to handle that. The Cutter Shark would definitely be off the streets and in custody. But give us a killer that's tough to track down? Our city's finest seem to be floundering and our mayor pretends it's not happening.

"Well, while Mayor Doyle can pretend all he wants—his only concern a reelection six months down the road—rest assured, your ChiTownVlogger will be on the case. I am going to be the first to offer a reward. I have instructed my financial planner to place $10,000 in an escrow fund, to be paid to the person who provides information that leads to the capture and conviction of the Cutter Shark.

"By the way, I asked an official at city hall why they weren't offering a reward. She told me that they were afraid of receiving a deluge of calls and messages from nut jobs. Isn't it good to know that your mayor thinks of you as nut jobs? How concerned can he be about the safety of our fair maidens?

"Check back in my jungle often, folks. It's getting wild out there. If you want the real news behind the news, you'll only get it from me, the ChiTownVlogger."

Today's meeting is not pleasant. Captain Zaworski is not happy. The press continues to be all over the case. And thanks to some nut job with a popular online video blog, who dubbed our killer the Cutter Shark, it's grown tenfold. The people of our city—specifically single women between the ages of twenty-five and forty who are at least reasonably attractive and gainfully employed—are afraid. They're staying home at night, which means the single men of Chicago are not happy either. Then there's the bar and restaurant owners. My mom's calling me and Klarissa every fifteen minutes, just to make sure we're okay. Everyone's clamoring for us to get off our tushies and make a quick arrest. Okay, then. Why didn't you guys just ask? I'll wave my magic wand and voila, the case will be solved.

There was an article in today's paper interviewing guys who feel their dating mojo has been off since the killer arrived. One guy being interviewed in the paper claimed that every time he offers to buy a girl a drink in the bar, he fears he'll be pepper-sprayed.

Mayor Doyle is not happy either, which means Police Commissioner Fergosi is not happy, so surprise, surprise, the good vibes have filtered down to Czaka and on to Zaworski. Now it's our turn to feel the heat.

"We're sitting at almost four weeks," Zaworski fumes, "and the only lead we are working came to us from the FBI. Folks, I need something. We need something. It's time to earn your retirement program."

Is that a threat?

We are back in the spacious and almost luxurious suite of the Midwest Regional office of the FBI, located on the forty-eighth floor of the State Building. I've never considered anything but local law enforcement for my career, but I could get used to the federal digs.

The meeting is scheduled to go ninety minutes, which is a relief. I might even get in a workout early this evening. Nothing too rigorous because my knee is aching. I did the high school stadium stair torture workout again. I'm not even thirty and I'm already complaining of aches and pains.

After Zaworski's chewing out, Dr. Van Guten spends fifteen minutes proving that Sandra Reed and Candace Rucker's murderer is the same killer who has struck in six other cities. This seems very important to her and Reynolds. Did any of us dispute or even question that? I guess they want us to be assured that once we find him, the information will help make sure that ten years and twenty appeals from now, someone from the state of Texas—he spent time in San Antonio and since they allow the death penalty, we're guessing that's where he gets tried—is going to stick a needle in one of his veins. But it's the *finding him* part that we need help on. That's where we need to spend our time. She doesn't know what to make of him changing the timing between kills, but she wants us to know that it is still the same man based on 137 direct connections or parallels she and Operation Vigilance have discovered. She enlightens us that, mathematically, this is a 98.7 percent certainty. I never did well in stats class—the chi tail formula just about killed me—but I'm convinced. I was convinced just by visiting the two crime scenes. This is a waste of time. She already looks tired at eleven in the morning. I think she's spending too much time with Virgil. Maybe I should invite her out for dinner.

"Has everyone finished the notebooks?"

We didn't have anything else to do the last forty-eight hours!

We all nod yes.

"Then it's time to start over because, honestly, I'm not seeing any action from local law enforcement."

No dinner invitation for her.

The detective teams report their current activities. Don speaks for us. I have no problem with that as long as I get to drive the car. And no question, he can deliver an elevator speech a lot better than I can.

I'm not quite sure what Tony Scalia's role on the team is, but apparently he's unofficially the liaison with city hall and more specifically, the mayor's office. Did I mention that he and my dad once brought down a hit man hired to kill the mayor? That was about ten years ago, but Doyle is still alive and still the mayor, so he probably wanted someone on the case reporting directly to him that he trusts. Mom still has my dad's medal—one that Big Tony undoubtedly has too—in one of those shadowbox frames in the living room.

No question, my dad's status at CPD gave me a leg up on my first job and subsequent promotions. With the run-ins I've had with

Czaka, I'm hoping his posthumous status still serves as major career protection. I met Mayor Doyle when Dad got his medal. I told him I was going to be a cop, too. He seemed to like that and made a big deal about me following in my dad's footsteps. But he's a politician, and politicians are good at saying what people want to hear. I wonder if he remembers me now. Czaka has studiously ignored me every time we're in the same room.

Cream rises to the top and in our group of detectives, that seems to be Blackshear. I'm as competitive as anyone, but I've had my gold shield for less than two years. For all my lip, I'm actually very impressed with the team we have assembled, and Blackshear has been on top of everything. Blackshear and Reynolds spend twenty minutes of our meeting going over new strategies and new assignments. Despite feeling lost and helpless, this is my favorite part of the meeting. We may not know what to do, but at least we're doing something.

Konkade goes last and reports on the number of volunteers from the force working the AA angle. No real leads so far—and no leaks to the press, thank God. He reminds us that this particular haystack is a lot smaller than the city of Chicago, so we aren't to skip our appointments and we should do more if we have the time.

I put my notes into a small briefcase, stand up to stretch the small of my back, flex my knee, and look down at my phone, which is vibrating. Klarissa. I had forgotten Reynolds' promise to check everyone's phone log in the hour leading up to our approach of the second crime scene. My heart does a quick somersault. Then I relax. I figure nothing must have come from checking the phone logs or I would have heard something by now.

I follow Don toward the door. Only Zaworski and Reynolds are still in the room, talking quietly and heatedly at the far end of the table.

"Conner."

I freeze halfway outside the conference room. That was Zaworski's you're-in-trouble-now voice. Which is the same as his "good morning" voice. I turn toward the two men with Don looking over my shoulder.

"Yes, sir?"

"Need you to stay a minute. Squires, this is going to take a little while so you may want to head back to the Second."

So is it a minute or a while?

I don't think Zaworski was making a suggestion to Don. This is an order. He moves over and pulls the blinds on the large windows that dominate one of the interior walls of our task force's meeting place. Out in the hall, Don looks at me with arched eyebrows as if to ask, what've you done this time? He heads toward the door leading to the reception area and out to the bank of elevators and I reluctantly shut the door behind me.

———

"I know you called three times, Klarissa, but I couldn't pick up. You, of all people, know that there are moments when answering isn't an option."

"So you weren't just blowing me off again?"

"No! Believe me, I would have much preferred talking to you. I was busy getting my tail chewed."

"Something to do with the Cutter Shark?"

"I don't know where you guys in the media come up with names like that, but yeah, it had to do with the Cutter Shark—and you!"

"Me?"

"Yeah. Remember the morning following the second murder?"

"I'm not sure."

"Well, we were trying to get over to the crime scene without any media interference. Someone placed a call to Mr. or Ms. So-and-So and the whole world showed up in our parking lot. So Reynolds, the FBI guy, ran a check on everybody's phone log. Guess who talked to someone at WCI-TV an hour before we rolled out the door?"

"Who?"

"Me!"

"You've got to be kidding. Who were you talking to?"

"You, you big dummy. Don't you remember?"

"Oh, the morning you decided to wake me up at four."

"It was closer to five but I didn't know when I'd have a chance to call again and I needed to cancel our coffee date. I didn't actually think you'd answer. I figured it would go into voice mail."

"I remember the call, but it still doesn't make sense. How could they know you called me? That was on my cell, not the office line."

"You think the FBI doesn't know who pays your cell phone bill?"

Klarissa pauses. "Well, that's more than a little disturbing."

"Don't go naïve on me, Little Sis. I hope you're kidding."

"I feel like my privacy has been violated."

Uh oh. What have I gotten myself into?

"Got something to hide?" I ask, hoping to move the conversation another direction.

"No," she retorts immediately. "But that doesn't mean the FBI has the right to access private communication of private citizens who are in no way suspected of a crime."

"Even with a mass murderer on the loose?"

"Your call to me would in no way hinder capturing the Cutter Shark, even if you were scooping me on some juicy crime scene tidbits—which you haven't done so far."

She leaves that hanging in the air. She may be true blonde, but she is smart.

I look at my watch and interrupt before Klarissa gets on a roll. "Hey, Sis, I don't want to be rude, but I'm getting hammered here due to no results in our investigation. What'd you call about? Because I'm going to have to hit it pretty fast."

"We were supposed to get together last Thursday night for dinner, which you cancelled. That's in addition to you cancelling coffee."

"For a little detail called a crime scene."

She ignores my protest and continues, "Despite my hurt feelings, I wanted to see if it might work out to grab a bite tonight."

I hesitate, but Klarissa and I have always had trouble connecting, so I want to keep the little momentum we've gained the last week or two going. "What time you thinking?"

"I'm not back on air until 10 p.m. Anytime between now and nine."

I look at my watch. It's six. I've got another two hours of work. I was wanting to hit my health club on the way home. I wonder if I can get everything done and then meet.

"Hey, if it's too much trouble," she starts with hurt in her voice.

"No. No," I interrupt quickly. "I'm just looking at what the boss wants done. Tell you what, I'll grab a cab and meet you somewhere in the middle. I'll come back and finish up. But brace yourself, because I may have to miss your special report tonight and I don't want to cost you ratings."

"We're only half a point from being number one, so I can manage without you for one night. Just don't make it a habit," she returns primly.

"I won't—and it's a date," I answer with a laugh. "Where do you want to meet?"

"I like that place over in Wicker Park. Not the Italian restaurant. The one with the American-fusion cuisine."

"American-fusion?"

"You'll love it. Just tell the cab to get you to Feast at the five corner intersection."

"See you in thirty minutes."

"Leaving early?"

It's Van Guten. She is wearing a mauve business suit with an ivory blouse. She usually wears her hair up, but it's after six, so she's let it down. Light brown with blonde lowlights. What do I know? I've never colored my hair. It may be blonde with brown highlights. I knew she was attractive, but wow. I wonder what it would be like to be as together and confident as she seems to be. But the slight challenge in her question agitates me.

I decide to pull a Don and let it roll. "Nah. Just going to grab dinner with my sister but I'll be back," I say over my shoulder.

"Oh, the one who works at a local TV station?"

Nothing indirect in her tone this time. This one is a straightforward challenge. I want to punch her in the nose but I'm not even looking at anyone cross-eyed because I am one outburst away from Zaworski ordering me into an anger management program. I've heard that they cure you through sheer boredom and you never get it off your employment record.

"That's the one," I say.

"You didn't happen to get a chance to talk with Reynolds and Zaworski this morning, did you?" she asks with arched eyebrows. "After our meeting?"

"Indeed I did. But I bet you already knew that."

"Anything good come out of that?" she asks with raised eyebrows, ignoring my back-at-you challenge.

"I'm not sure you'd call it good, Doctor, but we did seem to clear up a potential misunderstanding."

"Good," she says dismissively. "I trust it will stay cleared up."

I make myself turn and walk away, visualizing a certain Brazilian Jiu-Jitsu move I'd like to demonstrate on Dr. Leslie Van Guten. Don't ask me why I put so much energy into hand-to-hand training. Maybe because I shoot so poorly but score so well in fighting. Go figure. Barry Soto, one of the CPD trainers, says that pound for pound, I'm the toughest fighter on the force. I'll bet he's right.

I remember when I told Dad I wanted to be a cop, he hammered in my brain that a life-or-death moment is going to come when it's going to be just me and the other guy. *I'll be ready. I promise, Dad.* My mind flashes to a fistfight with Van Guten again. That's a scary thought. Really. Maybe I should call Zaworski and voluntarily enter the anger management program.

Dear God, help me to stop making people in charge so mad at me.

"Hi, my name is Kristen."

"Hi, Kristen."

"And I'm an alcoholic."

I almost flinch as I say it. Am I lying? I grew up in Ozzie and Harriet's household. No alcohol allowed. Mom made Dad, who grew up Catholic, quit drinking when they got married since it was against

Baptist church rules. I know for a fact he kept a six-pack of beer hidden in the garage fridge from time to time. When I was about twelve, I asked him about it and he let me have a sip of his Pabst Blue Ribbon, which promptly cured me of a craving for beer for life.

I look at the interested faces in the circle. I'm definitely lying. But is it okay with God if I lie for a greater good—like catching a serial killer? I've asked Jimmy once or twice but he hems and haws and I give up. I have to nail him down. Maybe he doesn't know. Jimmy pastors a nondenominational community church, so I'm not sure who he has to face with ethical questions. Dad grew up Catholic and they seemed to have rules to cover everything. Mom grew up Baptist and they seemed to have more.

Mom doesn't like that Jimmy is nondenominational. Kaylen met him at a Baptist college. But when he graduated from college and grad school he started pastoring a nonaffiliated church.

"Oh, so you don't mind using good Baptist education and all the money that it took to build that college," Mom would say, "but then you just get to go off and do whatever you want."

I don't know, Mom might have a point. But Jimmy's as straight-laced as they come. I somehow don't think he's going crazy with all that freedom.

Focus, Kristen.

"My problem began small," I continue, looking around the AA group.

Lots of nodding heads. They sense I'm going to need encouragement to keep this little speech from becoming a disaster.

"So it really didn't impact my work life or my social life. At first. At least I didn't think it was affecting me negatively."

More nods from some very earnest people. I'm looking for Jonathan but he's not been here the past two weeks. I'm still coming on Tuesday nights. I thought he might have a regular day of the week. Maybe it doesn't work that way if you really do have a drinking problem. Maybe you hustle your butt over to whatever meeting is available when you need it. Maybe you're not thinking about the new group member across the circle from you that much either. Unless you're a con artist with murderous intentions. Or an undercover cop.

I just wish I could remember for sure if he said that he had recently moved to town. Bethany isn't here either. She came last week. But Virgil told us our perpetrator, the Cutter Shark, almost exclusively pursues single women. In the few cases where a married woman was the victim, there was some likelihood that she wasn't broadcasting her marital status. That actually could make Bethany, who looked ready for action, vulnerable. But I'm pretty sure she did mention being married in Jonathan's presence two weeks ago. Then again, if you're a murderer, is adultery that big of a deal?

"Maybe I've had a problem longer than I think I have. I know some people at work have called me out on it. But it didn't turn into an official reprimand, even though it looked like it might. And my mom's not happy with me right now because of my, uh, problem. And my sister and I aren't getting along so hot either."

Could this be any more awkward?

"And my boyfriend—well, not really my boyfriend, I guess—but he and I, well, I guess we are in some kind of state of limbo. I'm not really sure if we're going out anymore or not. So I guess I'm here to figure out whether I have a problem or not."

I think Walter is trying to stifle a laugh. Hey, I don't laugh at him when he gives us the updated weeks, days, hours, and seconds to his sobriety every week, do I? I see amusement in some eyes and concern—or is that pity?—in others. A few people have zoned out. I'm quite the public speaker—make them laugh, make them sleep. I redden a little as I realize that what I've just said makes me sound like the world's biggest loser.

"But things probably aren't as bad as they seem," I continue quickly, in an attempt to recover. "My other sister has me help with her kids and I do pretty well at that. For the most part."

Okay, none of this is coming out right. No one is smiling now. Everyone is wide awake. I think I see some outright fear on the faces of a few women who look like they are mothers.

"I'm not saying this quite right, but what I mean is that I think things are going to go a whole lot better and you all are really helping me."

I end abruptly and plop into my seat. My ears are burning. The room is quiet. I really hadn't planned to speak but with this being my fourth visit, I figured it was time to play the part a little. I really should have written my talking points down and not tried to wing it. My sister is probably going to get reported to Children's Services for letting a drunk take care of her kids if anyone finds out my last name. Darren, the group leader, gets up and clears his throat.

"I want to thank each of you for sharing. Stick around and have a cup of coffee and a couple cookies if you can. I want to remind you that a big part of Alcoholics Anonymous is having a trusted sponsor to help you through the rough times and to help you keep your feet on the ground. Every one of us in the room is going to experience temptation and we're not supposed to go it alone. That's why God has given us each other."

I'm pretty sure he's talking to me. One clue is that he keeps looking at me pointedly. There I am being a detective again.

We stand, hold hands, and mumble the Serenity Prayer together.

"God grant me the serenity to accept the things I cannot change, courage to change the things I can, and the wisdom to know the difference."

An elderly woman comes over and gives me a hug. Oh man, I'm getting the sympathy hug. It was even worse than I thought. Darren shakes hands with me, thanks me for sharing, and asks me if I have a sponsor yet. I assure him I'll get that taken care of next week, but excuse myself and nearly run for the door.

———

I'm exhausted on my drive home. It was another twelve-hour day at the office. The long hours aren't a big deal. It's just spinning my wheels that wears me out. Two missed calls. Dell. Haven't talked to him since Sunday lunch. Klarissa. What's that all about? We've been sniping at each other for years and suddenly she wants to be my dinner partner every night. Come to think of it, Warren hasn't been around. He's never really done the Sunday thing with the family—he's the sports guy at WBC-TV, so Sunday is a big work day for him. But usually we hear something about what he and Klarissa are up to. And she didn't say anything over dinner either. No mention in how long? I really need to be a better big sister.

I zone out and find myself in a parking spot in front of my apartment. I park far enough away from the car in front of me that I can use the decline to start my car in the morning if it decides to be testy.

24

April 29, 1:19 a.m.

Call me, woman. Now.

Fine. Two can play at this game. She doesn't want to go out with me, so be it! Her loss! If she can't stand my presence, then I can't stand hers either. I'm not calling again. I swear I'm not calling. From now on, she has to call me two times for every one time I call her.

I can't believe I let that tramp get me off schedule. She's going to have to pay for how she's treated me before I forgive her. Actions have consequences. No woman rebuffs me and gets away with it.

Letting her get under my skin has messed up so much. There's a reason law enforcement has never come close to apprehending me. My system, my discipline, my point-by-point planning has kept them in the dark. It's almost been too easy. I'm playing chess and they're still learning checkers.

Until now. She's messed with my order.

Time to get back to basics. Time to reassert my self-control and my mastery of my world. I may even have to punish myself. I refused to accept the validity of any chastisement from the authorities who ran the group home like a concentration camp. But self-chastisement is acceptable. Maybe I'll go without TV or Internet for a month. Mommy always said the punishment had to fit the crime.

Maybe I should make myself wait an extra month before my next intimate encounter. Punish myself by waiting, thinking, dreaming of that moment, but not allowing it to happen yet.

Who does she think she is? She thinks she's so smart. She has that pretty girl arrogance where she actually believes she is in charge of her life. She'll learn the hard way how wrong she is. Oh, I'll be slow and gentle. I'll be so slow and gentle, she'll be begging for her ultimate release.

I lifted this morning. But I'm so angry I think I'm going to do a second circuit today.

Call, I said!

And I mean right NOW.

The car that was in front of me last night left at some point and someone else took his spot. Problem was, new guy parked about three inches from my front bumper. Thank God my trusty Miata fired right up and after maneuvering back and forth to edge out of the tight spot, I slammed it into first, gunned the engine, went airborne over the speed bump in front of the entrance to my apartment complex, and hit the road only five minutes behind schedule.

I stopped at JavaStar and got a grande Americano with a Splenda, an extra shot, and no drama. I bought a copy of the *Sun-Times*. They ran a banner on the front page directing readers to the Cutter Shark feature, a daily story featured in both major Chicago papers. We are on the hot seat. At least there was no lead story about CPD incompetence. Our lack of progress makes their job harder with nothing new to report, so they've resorted to a tabloid approach. Yesterday, the *Trib* ran a long piece on new theories about what's driving the Cutter Shark murders, which included a reference to a cult of vampires. Vampires? You've got to be kidding me. *I know vampire movies are popular, but . . .* Maybe if they'd postulated werewolves, I could have taken the story more seriously.

The *Sun's* big scoop this week was a story on a psychic from St. Petersburg, Russia, who apparently told her neighbors about this Cutter Shark fellow months ago—in detail and documented with date-stamped recording—and who is waiting for the CPD to contact her and fly her over to help solve the case. I suspect she's running a mail-order bride scam. There is already a citizen's action committee demanding that Mayor Doyle act now to bring her over if he wants to be reelected.

I haven't followed the White Sox or Cubbies much this baseball season. Both lost last night. But the Sox are in third while the Cubbies are in last. Oh well. There's always next year. If I wanted good news I'd watch insurance commercials on YouTube.

It was another day of spinning wheels. Our task force keeps getting bigger. We're covering the same territory in waves. But no one has any fresh ideas. We're all frustrated and growing more concerned and wary by the day. The killer went early with his last victim. Does that mean the four-week clock started ticking with his first murder or his second murder? Or is his clock broken?

Blackshear, Martinez, Don, and I grabbed lunch near the second crime scene in Rogers Park. That was convenient because our assignment was to ask every restaurant owner or manager if a new customer had started hanging out a couple weeks earlier. We are desperate. We ate at a strange little vegetarian place called Victory's Banner that serves great breakfasts all day—and even better coffee. If I were casing that neighborhood I'd sip their coffee a couple hours a day. We talked with a pleasant little Indian woman wearing a sari. She was not aware of anyone fitting the description—but honestly, what description could we give her? New. Suddenly here every day for two weeks. Hasn't come back since the murder. She assured us she would talk to everyone who works there and if anyone has any ideas she would have them call one of us. Same response from everyone we chatted to in a two-square-mile section of Chicago.

I was in the office at eight and left exactly twelve hours later. Klarissa, who has been incredibly sweet since our dinner a week ago, came to my office with some sandwiches from Panera around five. Sliced turkey and avocado on whole wheat. Yum. She was only with me a half hour before she got buzzed. Coldplay was in concert in Grant Park, and they wanted her ready to be on-air for a special report *pronto.*

"Don't forget to get Kendra a birthday gift," she said as she hugged me good-bye. I can't believe I got a full hug. What's up with sis? I can't believe I forgot Kendra's birthday is coming up!

———

My engine catches but turns over. I give a sigh of relief. I start driving home, mostly in autopilot mode. I remember I promised myself I would return a missed call from Dell. I look at my phone and start an internal debate. Call back or not call back. To call or not to call. I shake my head and hit his cell phone number. He answers on the second ring.

"Well, hey, stranger. I didn't think you'd ever call back. I was just thinking about you."

"Dell, I'm sorry. You know what's going on at work right now."

"I really don't . . . I just can't imagine . . . but I know this murder thing is all-consuming. That's why I've only left you one message since Sunday."

"You've got that right. Hey, Dell, we really need to talk."

"I thought that was what we were doing. Let's talk. Better yet, let me meet you over by your place and we'll grab something to drink. I've had a tough day and wouldn't mind a beer and you can have your grapefruit juice."

"I can't tonight."

"How come I knew you were going to say that?"

"I'm just off work now and it's almost nine. I've got to be in the office in less than twelve hours. I know you don't want to hear this, but I'm going to work out at Planet Fitness instead of meeting with you on the way home, because if I don't get some exercise, I'm going to explode."

"I worked out this morning, but I'd love to hit the treadmill. Why don't I come over there?"

"Dell, you're not listening. That's why we need to talk."

"Am I pushing again?" *Duh.*

"No, you're not pushing . . . I take that back. Yeah, you're pushing. Hard. I don't like it. Besides that, you're too nice a guy to put up with this."

"Nice guy, huh? Well, thank you. Is that kind of like telling an ugly girl she has a great personality?"

"No. I'm serious, Dell. You're a great guy. It just emphasizes how lousy I am to you. That girl you brought to church a couple weeks ago was smoking hot. I can't remember her name."

"Carrie," he answers quickly.

"Yeah, Carrie. Why don't you go out with her or someone who is

as nice to you as you are to them? Seriously, Dell, why are you working so hard on me?"

Big mistake. I knew I'd entered territory I'd wanted to enter with
him in person, not on the phone. In the midst of disengaging I had
just reengaged.

"You mean besides your awesome good looks . . . and your intense
and smoldering personality? Because beyond those two things—oh,
yeah, and your good morals and your incredibly nice family—I don't
know. I'm just crazy about you. I've told you that."

"I think you're just crazy about my family."

"Hey, I'm not even going to argue that point. I love your family.
The only downside of watching you all interact at the dinner table is
that it makes me realize what I grew up without."

"Well, the good news is that my family loves you. In fact, I
think—no, I know—they like you a whole lot more than they do me.
They grill me about you when you're not around."

"Shouldn't that be at least a cue that maybe you're not giving a *nice
guy* a real chance?"

I sigh and don't answer.

"Does your silence mean you are taking what I just said seriously—or that I'm hurting my chances by pushing too hard?"

I don't answer. I'm tired. I didn't want this conversation now. I
feel a little muscle spasm above my left eye. I'm tired and stressed.

"Okay, maybe I don't want to know tonight," he says quickly.
"I'm going to let you go. But real quick, let me ask how your mom is
doing."

"She's great, Dell. She's always great. You know that."

"How about Klarissa? You two getting along?"

"Things are fine with Klarissa, too. We've been hanging out a lot lately."

"I know it's tough fighting with a sibling," he says.

"You have no idea until you've lived it. But we really haven't been fighting much. I'm sure we'll make up for lost time."

"I just hope you don't have a problem with me hanging around your family," he says. I think I do, Dell. In fact, I know I don't really like you hanging out with my family. "They seem to like me a lot and who's to say you aren't going to wake up one morning and be mad, crazy in love with me?"

"Okay, you're pushing. But, Dell, I'm being serious. I'm not the girl you want to be seeing right now. I'm not thinking about dating, much less a serious relationship. I'm not at a seeing-somebody phase in my life."

"Phases change. I can wait until later."

The moment of truth is here. I just have to do it. Dad said that if you're going to cut the tail off a monkey, do it all at once, not one inch at a time since every cut hurts the same.

"Dell, I don't know how else to say it, other than to be totally direct. I don't want to see you."

He pauses and I hold my breath.

Then, "I understand. But you're going through a lot right now. Things will settle down and maybe you'll change your mind. I'm willing to wait."

I shouldn't be surprised, but I am. This is ridiculous. "You are not hearing—or simply not accepting—that I'm pretty positive that when things settle down, I'm not going to settle down with you."

"When you say 'pretty positive'—"

I cut him off before he can embarrass both of us with the "I've got a chance" line from *Dumb and Dumber*. "Dell, that won't help either of us. You hanging out, waiting for me to come around. Me knowing you're there, treating you like a . . . like you shouldn't be treated. We need to let this go."

There is another palpable silence on the line. I feel like a creep for being so blunt, but you know what? This is Dell's doing. He's relentless. I silently count to ten and then speak.

"Dell, I'm sorry. It's just not right."

He says, "Thank you."

"For what?"

"For finally being honest."

Finally? Really? "I don't think I've been dishonest with you prior to tonight."

"No, you haven't, but you've left enough wiggle room for me to keep hope alive."

"There's plenty of hope for you, Dell. Just not with me. Go call Carrie or someone else. Ask someone on a date tomorrow night. I'm being serious. Do it. Get moving."

"Okay, I hear and obey," he says with a painfully stilted laugh. "I just might make that call. But I'm not going to set up a date for tomorrow night. I'll see you tomorrow night."

Is he a stalker? Does he not know I'm a cop? "What are you talking about, Dell? What did I just get done saying?"

"Kendra's birthday party is tomorrow night. I got invited by the princess herself. You didn't forget did you?"

Klarissa told me an hour ago and I've already forgotten.

"I haven't forgotten, Dell; I just wasn't thinking about you being there."

"I wouldn't miss it for the world."

I'm stunned by this bizarre response. Maybe he really is a stalker. "Okay, Dell, here's the thing. You really need to *not* be there. It's my family, and if we weren't broke up before in your mind, I think I just made it officially, inescapably clear."

There's another awkward pause before he answers with a question. "Is me getting un-invited to a little girl's birthday party your decision to make?"

Are you kidding me? "If you want to press the issue, then yes, I'm making it my decision. If my family picks you over me, so be it. But we aren't both going to be at that party tomorrow night."

He hangs up on me. Good. And don't leave me a message in an hour pretending nothing happened.

That just got uglier than I even imagined it could. And weirder. But I don't have time to think about it now. I've got to go get Kendra a birthday present. Especially since Dell won't be bringing one.

———

"What are you doing tonight?"

It's Klarissa. Apparently, my closest friend in the whole world based on our recent food and telephone activity together.

I'm going out of my mind at a Walmart Supercenter—looking for a great present for a soon-to-be eight-year-old Snowflake—is what I'm doing.

"Just picking a few things up at the store on the way home," is what I tell her.

"I was calling to re-remind you that you need to get Kendra a present tonight. I know you've got a lot on your mind. I'm impressed you didn't forget."

I'm not going to tell her that Dell had to remind me. I pause too long while trying to think of a witty comeback, so she continues. "Just a bit of advice, but you might want to get her something that's non-sports-related. Just once."

I look at the soccer ball and new shin guards in the cart. I roll my eyes and sigh. I've let my hair down and it falls across my face. I blow it off and run my fingers through it. I'm half a mile from the checkout line and the return trip to sporting goods is pretty close to the Wisconsin state line. I put the items on a display with electric toothbrushes. I spot a two-pack of replacement heads for my Braun and put the armored plastic package in my cart.

"You there?"

"Sorry, Klarissa. I'm just having trouble narrowing down what I want to get for Kendra."

"I'll bet," she laughs. "Hey, I'm not going to keep you because I know that shopping takes every ounce of patience and concentration that you possess, but I just wanted to say thanks for going to dinner with me earlier this week and then eating with me again tonight. It was nice. I like getting along."

"It was, Baby Sis, and I like getting along, too. If I didn't tell you already, thanks for the sandwich. Just what the doctor ordered. Oh, and you promised to tell Mom that we haven't been fighting. She won't believe it coming from me."

"Already done," she says. "It made her happy."

There's a long pause.

"You okay, Klarissa?"

"Yeah, I think I am. Nothing like what you're going through with this case, but still kind of a tough time for me right now. But things are already looking up, so it's all good. Hey, I've got to review my notes one more time for my on-air segment. And you have to start over looking for a present."

She laughs when I groan.

"I love you, Kristen."

"I love you, too, Klarissa."

When was the last time we said that? There's an awkward silence. She breaks it.

"Go look for a present and I'll see you tomorrow night."

We hang up. I have the feeling there's more going on than she told me our last few times together . . . and she told me a lot more than she ever has before. Warren broke up with her. That's usually not a big deal. They've broken up a hundred times. But I guess this time it was more than one of their battles of the network stars. There's someone else in Warren's life and he admitted that she had been there for a while and that things were serious. He just hadn't found the right time to tell Klarissa. Wimp. No wonder he never got any playing time in the NFL . . . Of course, who am I to talk with how I handled things with Dell? I just hope the love of his life's name isn't Carrie. I need her for Dell.

Klarissa's a volatile mix of vulnerable and unconquerable displayed at dinner in the break room of my squad was no exception. She was tearful about the breakup, but when I asked if anything else led up to it, she locked things up tighter than the walls of Sing Sing.

Stop thinking and find Kendra a present!

I get hit by a jolt of genius. I remember that Don's daughter, Veronika, is about the same age as Kendra. He and Vanessa treat her like a princess. I'm betting Vanessa can help me find a better present for Kendra than I can on my own. Don will find that amusing and give me a hard time . . . but who cares? Desperate times call for desperate measures. I leave the shopping cart where it is, buy the toothbrush heads at the self-serve checkout line, which is thankfully empty, and head for the exit with a bounce in my step. I hit Don's home number on my cell.

empty, and head for the exit with a bounce in my step. I hit Don's home number on my cell.

Given my loitering at Walmart, I give up on Planet Fitness and head home. Three sets each of twenty push-ups—the boy kind—and a hundred crunches, followed by twenty-five double leg jumps and eagle jumps in quick succession—may have awakened my neighbor in the apartment below. But after three, three-minute planks and thirty bridges, I congratulate myself on a pretty good workout. I am breathing hard and sweating. I take a long hot shower, brush my teeth with a new electric toothbrush head that I have to wrench from plastic packaging that requires an electric chainsaw to open, and plop into bed with a copy of *People* magazine. I'm not sure I care who is together or apart or having a baby or having a mental breakdown or finding inner peace in Hollywood, but it's right there in front of me.

Klarissa had it in her tote and was reading it when she came over to my precinct for dinner. The cover story is about a nineteen-year-old actress who is in rehab for alcohol abuse. I want to read the story so maybe I can do a little better in my next AA appearances. I'm adding a second meeting tomorrow night after Kendra's birthday party. Actually, it's more like a dinner with presents. Kendra's party, not the AA meeting.

The article's actually not a whole lot of help. I'm not sure I can work the horrors of growing up as a child actress into my storyline.

I hit the lights at midnight, thinking I'll be asleep in a minute or two. Don't know what time I actually drift off. I can't get the faces of Sandra Reed, Candace Rucker, and Dell out of my mind.

Blackshear, Martinez, Scalia, Don, and I are reviewing notes with Sergeant Konkade. There are now twelve detectives and another ten techies from forensics, data, and psych on the case. That's twenty-seven full-timers from the CPD dedicated to this nightmare case alone, taking time away from the other work involved in keeping the peace in a city of almost three million people. We're trying to make sure we have covered all the bases.

We have. We've talked to every neighbor, every relative, every work associate, every club associate, and every other kind of associate of the past ten years for both victims. We've canvassed every store owner in a three-mile radius of each crime scene. We've checked every phone log. We've read every report that Virgil has spit out on previous crime cities. We've read all forty-nine case reports at least a couple times each. We've talked to lead investigators from the other cities and from similar cases. We've listened to Reynolds and Van Guten hypothesize on the motivations and habits of our killer. We're all attending AA meetings now. Zaworski feels like it was a mistake to just put women in the meetings at the outset.

Konkade heads up that part of the investigation. We've read the reams of reports this has generated. I think he has them memorized. We've run background checks on close to 300 AA attendees. None of them look good for this kind of crime, but we've gone deeper and probed into the backgrounds and current records on about forty of them anyway. Konkade has mobilized about twenty surveillance teams to pierce the anonymity of a good and innocent organization.

None of us are comfortable with it, but none of us are willing to let the only viable lead go unattended. I don't know the religious orientation of the individual team members, but I'm guessing anyone who prays is praying that the press doesn't get hold of our infiltration of a nonprofit service organization. None of us are ready to face the potential legal repercussions.

Stern and taciturn, Konkade is showing signs of stress. He keeps running a hand over the top of his head to smooth his hair back. Problem is, he doesn't have any hair.

Scalia is old-school. Just like Dad. He listens and rarely speaks. Just like Dad again. He'll occasionally interject a question about a conversation we've had with someone who might have information that can help us understand what's going on. Otherwise, he's not volunteering what's on his mind. He's a legend on the force. Could it be that he has no ideas in mind either? That's scary.

Reynolds pops his head in the room. Zaworski and Czaka are behind him.

"Sorry to interrupt. Can we steal Detective Conner from you for a few minutes?"

"We're wrapping up anyway," Blackshear answers. "She's all yours."

Blackshear is now our official spokesperson. I am predicting a promotion for him in the not-too-distant future. Maybe Martinez too. His English isn't the best but his Spanish is a very desirable trait in a multicultural city. Because of guilt by association, I may not be helping Don's cause.

I look at my watch and frown. It's 11:30. I was planning to get Kendra's present from Vanessa over lunch break. I'm hoping this goes fast.

"Is there a problem, Conner?" Czaka asks, noting my frown and hesitation.

"No, sir."

We give each other an icy stare, both willing the other to speak. Zaworski smoothly positions himself between Czaka and me and nudges me down the hall before I can hang myself. I feel like a fifth-grader being taken to the principal's office.

I look back at Czaka and Reynolds following us. We enter Zaworski's office. Van Guten is already sitting comfortably in one of the wingback chairs, legs crossed, kicking a high-heeled shoe up and down slowly, reading a report. She nods at Czaka, Zaworski, and Reynolds but doesn't look up at me. I guess what she's reading is too important to acknowledge a lowly detective.

I told Don after the first meeting that I didn't think she liked me. He scoffed and credited it to my female insecurity. Maybe we're both right. We all just stand around and get busy doing nothing. Zaworski scrapes at an invisible stain on his tie with the fingernail of his right forefinger. Reynolds races through emails on his BlackBerry or iPhone or some concept phone that only the FBI gets to test. Czaka has opened a green file folder and is looking at a two-page report of some kind. He signs the second page, shuts the folder, hands it to Zaworski, and exits without a word.

Van Guten is in no hurry to finish her reading. Power move. She looks back a couple pages, purses her lips, snaps her folder shut, and looks directly at me.

"Detective Conner, after almost four weeks of scouring for clues, it appears that you are the only law enforcement officer from local, state, or national agencies who has suggested even one possible lead for our quarry."

My mind races around trying to remember what it was that I came up with. Jonathan. I saw him in one meeting at one location. He hasn't been back. He fits the age profile that Van Guten has proposed. Even his story of multiple jobs and high intelligence fits. Could I have scared him off? Tipped him off with my inability to come up with my own story? Is that why they've hauled me in?

"As I mentioned, there are things I like about this Jonathan that you met at your first AA meeting and things I don't like. What intrigues me is that on three separate reports you expressed a question as to what he said about the timing of his return to Chicago."

"I think that says more about my memory over a quick remark than it does about him."

"I agree with you on that," Van Guten says smugly. "It suggests to me that something about this person triggered a response in you that may be LCR."

I look at her blankly.

"LCR. Latent Case Relevant," she clarifies.

Okay. Everyone in the room is looking at me intently now. What the heck is going on?

"What I'd like to do, with your full consent of course, is put you under hypnosis, which just happens to be one of my areas of expertise."

I'm not sure I'm comfortable with her knowing what's on my conscious mind, never mind my subconscious; the thought of opening that part of myself to someone else is outright scary. I'm not sure even I want to know all that goes on in my head.

27

"So are you going to do it?"

"I don't know, Don."

"I'm sure it's safe or they wouldn't ask you to do it."

"I don't know. I read a novel once where an FBI psychologist used hypnosis to murder victims."

"Did he strangle them or what?"

"It was actually a she and she didn't do it directly. She had them commit suicide."

"Huh?"

"She'd call them and speak a key word prompt she planted in their minds when they were in a hypnotic state. So there were no clues."

"Sounds like a tough conviction."

"Wasn't necessary. The good guy killed her."

"What kind of trash are you reading these days?"

"Who says I'm reading trash? It was a great book. A little far-fetched, but believable."

"Using hypnosis to murder people is plausible?"

"Well, the way it was written, sure. But getting back on topic, the thing that worries me most about Van Guten hypnotizing me is that . . . well, she doesn't like me."

"You say that about everybody."

"Well, if you had even a twinge of suspicion that somebody didn't like you, would you want them to control you when you were vulnerable?"

"No, guess I wouldn't. But I do let you drive and I even go to the shooting range with you. Both are acts of courage in conditions of extreme vulnerability."

Normally I'd punch Don in the shoulder. Hard. But my mind is racing. Don clears his throat and knocks some imaginary lint off his jacket sleeve while he ponders murder by hypnosis and my concerns about Van Guten.

"So . . . don't do it," he says.

"Right."

"I thought she said it was your choice."

"What do you think? Do I really have a choice?"

"Sure you do. You can say no—and go back to checking parking meters."

"I think I've worked every rotten job that CPD has to offer, but I actually missed the meter maid routine."

"I didn't."

I can't help but laugh. Don? Working the parking detail? How'd I miss that in my year and change as his partner? "I'll bet we've never had a better-dressed maid on the force."

"Keep laughing," he says.

"I'm going to let my meter run out just so I can see you roll around in your little meter cart."

"Like I said, laugh it up."

It's Friday morning. I have to give Reynolds, Van Guten, and Zaworski an answer by ten. We've been on this case close to a month and desperation has seemingly set in. Van Guten wants to hypnotize me based on my report of Jonathan at my first AA meeting. So what if Jonathan is the killer? He hasn't been back.

I'm all for science and any technique that might help us catch a sick killer. But you have to be realistic, too. Hypnosis feels about one step above the work of all the so-called psychics who show up when a preda-tor like the Cutter Shark emerges. My dad was actually intrigued by the psychics—or *the psychos*, as he called them. He said that if you believe in the spiritual world, including angels and demons, you never know when one of the whack jobs—his phrase not mine—was going to have an insight due to a special connection with the spiritual world.

Van Guten was actually reassuring in detailing the safety and efficacy of hypnosis with me, but there's an arrogance there that still makes me very uneasy. Zaworski handed me the green folder from Czaka, which contained a liability waiver. He gave me instructions to meet with my union rep for sure and a lawyer if I wanted. CPD would pay for an hour of legal consultation. He stressed one hour about three times. I guess our budget is already shot for the year and we're not half-way into it. I talked to my union guy, who said it was my call. I skipped the $300-an-hour legal fee for the department.

———

"So how'd Kimberly like her gift?" Don asks.

"You mean Kendra?"

"I can't keep track of all the *K*s in your family. It makes me won-der if someone in your family tree wore sheets and rode a horse by torchlight late at night."

I turn and give Don my hardest glare.

"I'm kidding."

"It isn't funny."

"You're right and I apologize," he says magnanimously.

"She loved it," I say.

Problem was the gift didn't go over very well with Mommy. No one sent me the memo that Jimmy and Kaylen were avoiding Barbie stuff for Kendra. Don said his daughter, Veronika, loves her Barbie dolls. I guess they have a black model, but according to Don, the wardrobe is still way too lily white. But no problem. Vanessa sews Veronika's Barbie's clothes . . . when she isn't selling houses and buying Don expensive shoes.

Vanessa got my text and was thrilled to help. She brought a Sporty Barbie and some accessories to the office, wrapped up in matching gift paper. She is good at this stuff. I could learn something watching her. She spent about ten bucks more than I would have, so I was feeling pretty generous when I showed up for the party.

Until I got the lowdown on the whole Barbie no-no. She and Jimmy think that Barbie sends the wrong message to girls about body image, Kaylen explained to me. Seems a little strict to me, but I don't have kids, so it's their call. I just know that Kendra squealed with delight and hugged on me the rest of the evening after opening her present. I don't think she was worried about her chest size—or lack thereof—or not having six-inch heels with her soccer outfit. Maybe it will mess her up later. I somehow doubt it.

I thought I was doing well by forgoing sports equipment for something girly but missed the boat again. No good deed goes unpunished.

Dell must have finally listened to me. He didn't show. But he did send an envelope with money in it. One for Kendra and one for James. My mom asked me if I knew why he wasn't here. I finally had to get as direct with her as I did with Dell.

"Mom, I'm not comfortable with the way Dell pursues me. You need to stop egging him on."

"But he's so nice," she started to argue.

"Mom, this is way over the top, even for you. I'm telling you it doesn't feel good to me; it isn't fair to Dell; and it needs to stop now."

Between that exchange—Mom looked like she was going to cry

—and the Barbie fiasco, I felt like a heel. Klarissa overheard the conversation and whispered some encouragement. I wouldn't have minded if she stuck up for me with Mom. Out loud.

"There now, that wasn't so bad, was it?" Van Guten asks me. "Kind of like waking up after a power nap, no?"

I resist the urge to say no back at her. First of all, I never take power naps. If I put my head down when the sun is still shining, I just pass out and slobber on the pillow. Second, what I really feel is groggy and disoriented; I don't sense even a trace of empowerment.

I am tempted to tell her that I won't be able to fully answer her question until I go for a full year without howling at the moon or running down the street naked when I hear the sound of a cell phone ringing.

I close my eyes to let my head clear a little bit more.

"Did you find out anything useful?" I ask Van Guten.

She doesn't answer. I open my eyes and realize she has left the room. I appreciate her deep concern for my well-being. I'm probably just jealous that once again she looks beautiful and completely together in yet another outfit that probably costs enough to buy three new starters for my Miata. I get up and stretch my back, then gather my purse to head to the elevator bank.

I hear a phone ring from down the hall and get very still. A minute later my clothes are still on and I'm not howling at the moon—or the sun, since it's not lunchtime yet. Maybe it's the sound of an oven timer that is the secret trigger Dr. Van Guten has imbedded in my psyche.

Good thing I don't cook much.

"Aunt Kristen, I like my new Barbie doll a lot."

"You do?"

"A lot! I really do. Her name is Kristen."

That throws me for a loop. I thought the doll's name was Barbie. Can you do that? Can you give a doll that already has a name another name? Could GI Joe become GI Jerry or Barry? Could the Incredible Hulk become the Incredible Larry? And do I want my name attached to a plastic doll that is *persona non grata* in my sister's house?

"So where'd you come up with the name Kristen?"

"It's your name, silly."

"My name isn't silly, it's Kristen."

She thinks that is very funny and squeals with delight. I'm glad one person in the universe finds me clever and amusing.

"So you really do like the doll I got you?" I ask.

"The mostest of all the presents I got for my birthday."

I'm about to ask her if she is hiding in her closet so she can play with her forbidden Kristen doll without getting in trouble with her mom, but she quickly tells me bye and says that Mommy wants to talk to me. *Uh oh.*

"I'm sorry, Little Sis," Kaylen says to me.

"What are you talking about this time?" I ask with an exaggerated sigh.

Why can't I just be gracious? Kaylen has no time for my sparring today and stays on topic.

"Honestly, Kristen, I was pretty rotten to you. And I want you to forgive me."

"No big biggie—you are forgiven."

"It's just that we had wanted to keep Kendra away from certain things, and Barbie was one of them."

She yammers on for fifteen minutes, explaining in detail again what it does to a woman's psyche when she is objectified by men. There are a few times when I think she is actually retracting her apology, and a few times when I think she is a card-carrying member of NOW, about to march on Washington to campaign for equal rights. Some of it makes sense; some of it is garbage. Most of the time I'm really not paying attention. Didn't we go over this last night?

I finally interrupt. "So were you wanting to apologize, Kaylen, or to enlighten me about the dangers of the fashion doll industry and its impact on the psychological development of the modern pre-adolescent?"

She hesitates long enough that I know my question hit the mark. *Ha.* It sounded pretty smart, too. I have to get back to my master's degree.

"To apologize. And also because I'm worried about Klarissa."

Her tone makes me fully attentive. "You too?" I ask.

"Yeah. I didn't know you were worried. Why didn't you say something?"

"I don't know if I've been out-and-out worried," I say, "but something is definitely going on with her. You know Warren broke up with her?"

"Yeah. But do you think that is really what's eating at her?"

Rats. I thought I might have the inside skinny for once.

"Hard to say," I respond. "I never figured they would actually make it to the altar. But they have been together for most of the last five years. That's got to hurt."

"Has it been that long?" Kaylen asks in disbelief. "I am getting older. Well, you too, I guess!" Go ahead and tell me I'm thirty if it makes you feel better.

We talk another five minutes about Klarissa and Warren and Kendra and how I'm personally handling the pressure of working on a high-profile murder case. That slows the conversation down considerably. I finally start to beg off because I've got to get something done today. While in a non-hypnotic state of consciousness and fully clothed.

"Hey, before you run," Kaylen interjects, "did you say that Warren broke up with Klarissa?"

"Yeah. For a hot young squeeze."

"Says who?"

"Says Klarissa."

"That's weird. Warren called Jimmy and said that he was worried about Klarissa, too, and that it wasn't just because she broke up with him."

"Well, maybe he was trying to save face for Klarissa," I say.

"Yeah, maybe," she says, "But he's always been a little more interested in his own face."

"That and his teeth," I say with a laugh. "But then again, he was the one that called Jimmy to express concern. That indicates at least a little other-centeredness on his part."

"Good point," she says.

"I love you, Sis, but got to go," I say.

"I love you, too."

I put my cell phone back in a leather sleeve I wear next to my

Beretta. I look at my landline with its message light flashing. Better start calling people back.

———

Before I hit the replay button on my phone, I stand up, stretch, roll my neck, and throw a couple imaginary punches. I step outside of my cube to see what's happening in our detective warren. Someone has put a yellow Post-it note on the carpeted wall of my office space.

DETECTIVE CONNER—YOU'VE REALLY GOT TO STOP SLEEPING ON THE JOB. NOT THAT BEING AWAKE HAS DONE YOU MUCH GOOD EITHER. YOU THINK YOU'RE SO HOT RUNNING AROUND WITH THE "BOYS" AND RUNNING THAT BIG MOUTH OF YOURS. I THINK YOU MUST LIKE MAKING A FOOL OF YOURSELF.

What the heck? Okay, Don and Martinez gave me a hard time about being hypnotized, but this is just too weird. Whenever a detective show includes a note as part of the storyline, the note is always from the bad guy to the good guys and leaves clues. But here I'm getting trash-talked by a colleague.

April 31, 3:30 p.m.

Maybe she'll be there. I'd like to talk to her. I think I'll go just in case. Even if she has been abjectly cruel. It's not her turn . . . yet. But oh, when it is her turn, the kid gloves are coming off. I picked up an anatomy book at Barnes & Noble. I already have some new ideas . . .

Not that she'll have any hint of that, before I reveal it. The next time I see her I'm going to behave with the utmost decorum. I will be pleasant, but unobtrusive. No more asking her out. I'll figure a way to get her alone later.

Asking her out again? I wouldn't go out with her if she crawled across a field of broken glass to beg me! And yet I can't deny the appealing idea of it.

How have I let this girl get to me like this? I knew I wanted to meet her, but I never dreamed she could become . . . special. And how has she repaid the honor of my attentions? I've never been treated so terribly. At least not since I escaped from the land of the walking dead.

Letting this go on, allowing her to be so disrespectful . . . I'm behaving no better than that guy who let his wife walk out on him. I will suffer her only a little while longer. My system demands I withstand her abuse for now.

I've survived a lot more attempted oppression and humiliation than she could ever generate. When you were once a pris-

oner of war—and every day of my life was war, from the time my mother went away until my great escape—you expect to be treated badly. But outside the electric fence, you expect courtesy and cooperation. In my case, I demand it. If she doesn't start being nice to me in a hurry, it really is going to be her turn sooner than I planned.

But no matter how hard I try, I just can't stay mad at her.

An elliptical machine and rack of weights and bench can only help me relieve so much pressure. I feel like my entire body is throbbing to start again . . .

I'm trying to look as casual as I possibly can, but I'm running across the church parking lot to my AA meeting in a downpour. And I'm almost ten minutes late. That started when my sporty little Miata wouldn't.

The precinct garage was full this morning so I parked in the back lot, which is completely flat, so there was no way to roll my car backward and pop the clutch to get it started. I ended up having two uniformed officers push my car while running as fast as they could. Because of the haphazard way the CPD parks—somebody needs to be handing out some tickets back there—I didn't want to maneuver half a city block in reverse, which doesn't require as much speed, so they had to push me almost 100 feet for me to get enough momentum to jerk my car to a start from first gear. How embarrassing. One of them was actually pretty cute. Where were Jimmy and Dell when I needed them most?

The problem was exacerbated because there are six plainclothes officers in three unmarked squad cars assigned to follow and watch me tonight, so my little parking lot episode will surely make the rounds in the office tomorrow. *Great.* Another yellow note is sure to follow.

I guess that under hypnosis I told Van Guten that Jonathan had indeed said that he had just returned to town. I'm still skeptical. First of all, who cares that he said it? To be running free this long he's obviously a good liar. It may just have been part of his cover story. Secondly, I'm guessing there are a hundred thousand people who are new to our happy little metropolitan area over the past six months. Not all of them, admittedly, attend AA meetings. But this still doesn't narrow down our search that much. Third, the Cutter Shark has never returned to the same city twice. Now having grown up in Chicago— if Jonathan is telling the truth—and never having killed people here, that would make returning to Chicago different than returning to San Antonio. But still . . .

Okay, I admit, Van Guten likes his age, the main points of his story, and his physical description as related by me. She let the task force know that there are eleven additional points of convergence she has identified between Jonathan and our killer. Couldn't that be a little like six degrees of separation from Kevin Bacon?

Everyone around the table was unanimous that I wouldn't be attending this particular AA meeting solo again. I didn't like it but I didn't argue. So tonight I am wearing a wire and have a cadre of bodyguards close at hand. I hope the wire is waterproof.

I walk down the half flight of steps into the now familiar basement of Saint Bart's. I've also started attending another AA meeting at Holy Family, a large Catholic church. It might even be a cathedral or basilica. There they put the chairs in rows and we all face forward and look at whoever is speaking. You have to walk up front to share. There are usually more than a hundred people there. The meeting room at Saint Bart's is a lot smaller, so we always sit in a circle and can get a good look at everyone else attending, unless they are to our immediate left or right. I don't think we've ever had more than twenty at one meeting.

There are four empty chairs, so I slide into the one closest to the door. I do a quick visual tour. No Jonathan tonight. Rats. Housewife is back. I can't remember her name. Brittany? Nope. Bethany? I think so. She is sharing and makes a dramatic pause while I get situated, not looking too happy about the interruption.

The spotlight back on her—and not too tough to pull off with that pushup thing she has going—she continues, "I don't know what I'm going to do. I don't love Jeff anymore. I know he's a great guy and is a good father and husband. He definitely doesn't deserve what I'm putting him through. He thinks I'm having an affair. And to be honest, the thought has crossed my mind. If the right opportunity had come along, I probably would have already."

She takes a deep breath and freezes. Is she a great actress or is she feeling emotion?

"But my real problem is vodka," she croaks out. "I didn't even drink until I was thirty. We went to an office party and I had my first Cosmopolitan. All the girls I drink with now love them because they're sweet and go down so easy. Funny, but I don't need the Kool-Aid or whatever they mix in there. I just like the alcohol. It's ironic, but Jeff always wanted me to loosen up and have a drink with him. Well, I've loosened up. Now I don't know how to screw the lid back on.

"I guess I lied when I started speaking tonight. I haven't been sober for two weeks. I slammed two martinis on the way over here. I don't know what I'm going to do. If I don't figure something out, I'm going to lose my husband and kids. The problem is, I'm not sure I really care."

She stops talking, folds her arms, and stares at the black-and-white checkered tile floor. A single tear rolls down her cheek. And then another. A waterfall follows. But she doesn't change expressions. Instead of looking sad, she looks angry while tears stream down her face. The kindly old woman—I have got to remember her first name—who always gives me a hug, stands up and walks over to sit beside her. She embraces her, but Bethany is not responsive. She continues to stare at the floor with tears running onto her lightweight, V-neck blouse.

I feel bad for the judgmentalism and cynicism I've felt toward her. I don't think you can fake whatever she is feeling. Our group leader, Darren, says, "Patricia, you obviously do care or you wouldn't be here."

Who is Patricia?

I'm sitting next to Walter who sees my confusion. He leans over and whispers, "Before you got here she told us she was lying about her name. It's Patricia."

Darren spends the next few minutes telling the group that acknowledgment is the first step toward recovery.

"We're proud of you, Patricia," he says. "You're on the road to recovery. Do you believe that?"

She keeps her head down and doesn't respond to him. What is Patricia feeling? Anger? Remorse? Guilt? Numbness? Has she told us the real story yet? It kind of rang true tonight, but who knows.

A few more people share, but the energy isn't there. We end our session thirty minutes early. I wonder what the six eavesdropping detectives think of Bethany . . . I mean Patricia. I'm ready to head home, but on sudden impulse, I step forward and cut her off at the door.

"Patricia?"

She looks up. Her eyes are red and puffy. She looks at me first with defiance and then softens. "Yeah?"

"You okay?"

"What do you think?"

I admit that was a dumb question.

"Sorry," I mumble. "I guess I'm just making sure you can make it home okay."

She starts crying again. I hesitantly put an arm around her and she really starts blubbering and ends up putting her head on my shoulder. Now she's just plain snotting on me. Her mouth is right next to the tiny microphone tucked into my blouse top and I'm guessing she's blowing out the eardrums of whoever is listening in. Even with a no-show from Jonathan, I don't think I'm going home early after all.

April 31, 11:58 p.m.

I liked the meeting they held at the Christian Science Reading Room. The walk to Wacker was convenient and the people were nice and friendly. The leader, Marty, was actually pretty funny.

CUTS LIKE A KNIFE

Mr. Sober But Spunky, he called himself. He always made me wish I actually had a drinking problem and belonged there.

Oh well. I won't be back. Something's off. And listening to my intuition has never steered me wrong.

I shouldn't be surprised. They must've figured out where I meet my girlfriends because I'm pretty sure they're staking me out. Some woman was paying way too much attention to everyone who walked in. I've never seen anyone at an AA meeting take notes. She looked at me a couple times. I bet she was a cop.

Well, well, well.

I considered her and what her presence might mean. Maybe if my life had started off differently, I would have taken a different path. I know I could have been a great surgeon. I find human flesh intoxicating. I find something new and fascinating every time I do my work. But the therapists confused me when I was younger. Sometimes they wanted me to accept myself. Sometimes they wanted me to know that I had serious problems and needed to control my feelings and impulses. I was in a Christian group home for a while. That was even more confusing. Every day they told me God loves me and every day they told me He punishes sinners.

Which is it? Accept or change? Heaven or hell? Just because they are confused doesn't mean I have to be confused.

I can't remember if I was eighteen or nineteen when I was set free. Not from the prison they called the Colorado Home for Troubled Youth that I was in at the time. But in my mind. I woke up one day and realized that only one person's judgment of me mattered. Mine. Not some quack psychiatrist with a lot of letters behind his name and pretty frames with fancy letters and seals on the walls of his office. I still hate the guy who always wanted me to talk about my mom. She was none of his business.

I like to watch people. Some try to rise above the strictures of society and religion, and even family. But I've not personally met anyone with my courage to be free, to stand alone. I sometimes wonder if it was becoming free that set me apart from others, made me superior . . . or if I was born superior and that's why I was able to become free.

No one can ever take away the person I've become. I don't care if the FBI, CIA, the Chicago Mafia, and the US Marine Corps all think they can find me . . . I'm untouchable. Because I know when to listen to my intuition.

So I won't go back to the Christian Science Reading Room. I'll miss Mr. Sober But Spunky. AA meetings might be off the table completely. That makes me feel a bit sad.

Doesn't mean they know everywhere I meet my girlfriends.

I wonder if she'll be there . . .

THE MONTH OF MAY

What potent blood hath modest May.
RALPH WALDO EMERSON

D̲o you realize how much overtime you cost us last night?"

Zaworski is angry. Real angry. He's not making eye contact, which is a bad sign. It's only 10 a.m. and he's already taken off his suit jacket. He's either madder than I think he is or he's forgotten to put on his deodorant. Dark semicircles of sweat have formed on his white dress shirt, which isn't tucked in quite right. It crosses my mind to compliment his tie, but I doubt that will distract him. It's an ugly tie anyway.

"Sir, I didn't anticipate that the team would stay with me once the AA meeting was over."

"And why would you *not* anticipate that, Detective Conner?"

"I, uh—"

"I'm not asking you," he interrupts. "That was called a rhetorical question. Didn't we say that we would stay with you all evening, no matter what? Are you saying that you think we don't keep our promises? That I'm not a good and honest leader? Those were rhetorical questions, too."

"Sir, that's not what I was implying. It's just that Jonathan, or the man who calls himself Jonathan, didn't show up."

"Doesn't mean he wasn't in the area. Doesn't mean he isn't using your new best friend to help him recruit a victim. Doesn't mean I'm going to leave an officer in the field uncovered."

"Sir, I'm very sorry for keeping the watch team out until midnight and away from their homes and families. I'm sorry for the expense to the department."

"Midnight? Nice try, KC. How about 2 a.m.?"

Did he just call me by the nickname I have hated and worked hard to expunge since the first time I heard it in kingergarten?

"But what was I going to do, sir? She had been drinking and was in a total meltdown. I didn't feel I had a choice. She was either going to kill people in a crash because of her hysterical crying or she was going to kill people in a crash because she was going to go out and do some more drinking."

"Or she was going to drive home and go to sleep."

Or that.

"Are you always like this? Do you save kittens from trees and push beached whales back into the ocean?"

I'm thinking about pointing out that there are no whales on the beaches of Lake Michigan, but he's out of steam and actually smiles. Then he laughs. I've never seen Captain Zaworski laugh.

"I can't believe you went home with her to help her tell her husband what is going on in her life."

"I can't either," I say, laughing a little myself now, not because I think it's funny but out of sheer relief for not being in trouble. Maybe not being in trouble. "But I figured I better help her keep things moving in the right direction."

"I've got to tell you, we were nervous. It felt like a trap."

"So I kept you up, too?"

"Unfortunately, yes. Reynolds, Squires, and I monitored the transmitter together all night. That's why I haven't decided whether to give you a good citizen award or fire you."

"I kept the FBI up until 2 a.m., too? And Don?" *Uh oh.*

"I have no clue when Reynolds and Van Guten went home. They were still here when Don and I left."

"Wow. I feel special."

He's not smiling anymore. He leans back in his leather chair and tries to stifle a yawn. As he stretches, I see dark rings staining his shirt at the underarms. I guess he didn't put on anti-perspirant today.

"Maybe we're all getting a little too desperate," he says. "Nothing else substantial has turned up and something just felt right about this lead. The others felt it, too. Martinez, Blackshear, Konkade, and I don't know how many others, were listening from their homes all night. The FBI provided a secure online site where everyone could plug in."

Oh man. How many times did I go to the bathroom? This is turning into humiliation on top of humiliation.

"I'm sorry, sir. I should have said what I was thinking. I really don't need a protective patrol."

"You don't do AA meetings at Saint Bartholomew solo, Conner. You got me?"

I nod, but my mind is on last night's conversation. I'm backtracking and trying to remember everything Patricia and Jeff, her husband, and I talked about half the night.

"If Blackshear and Martinez were up, that means the Third Precinct was dialed in, too. Anyone else listening that I should be aware of, sir?"

He frowns and then starts to smile for the second time in the eighteen-plus months that he's been my boss. He says nothing.

"DC?" I ask.

He shakes his head yes. Now I'm too numb to be any more embarrassed. I get up from the chair in front of his desk, pivot on the toes of my shoes, and head for my cubicle. I see a lot of sleepy and unhappy faces glancing up at me on my way there. Don's chair is still empty.

He's going to be a grouch. He's the only cop I know who claims to get eight hours of sleep every night.

I plop onto my seat. There's a sticky note in the middle of my computer screen. Someone—and I am going to figure out whose handwriting this is—has scribbled another note:

DETECTIVE CONNER: MY WIFE SWEARS SHE'S IN A BOOK CLUB AND THAT'S WHERE SHE GOES EVERY MONDAY NIGHT. BUT I'M SUSPICIOUS . . . I THINK SHE'S HITTING THE BOTTLE AND SPILLING HER GUTS AT AA MEETINGS. I HEAR YOU MAKE HOUSE CALLS. HOW MUCH DO YOU CHARGE FOR: (A) GETTING HER OFF THE BOOZE; (B) MAKING HER FALL IN LOVE WITH ME AGAIN; AND (C) INVITING US TO YOUR CHURCH. PLEASE ITEMIZE, AS I'M ON A COP'S SALARY!

What a jerk. Better not show how angry I feel right now or there's going to be a lot more of this coming my way. This is yellow note number three; I'm pretty sure that makes it a non-isolated event stream.

My cell phone buzzes. A name flashes up. It's my new BFF.

———

What a night I spent at Jeff and Patricia's house. Not sure which of the southwest suburbs we were actually in, but the houses were incredible, all on acre-and-a-half lots—and within a few miles of the city. The guard at the security hut opened the gate for Patricia and me to drive through, and I thought I had entered a new world. When you grow up in an 1,800-square-foot house with a half basement finished to accommodate laundry, and rec and guest rooms, then spend the next four years in a cramped college dorm with two roommates, and currently live in a two-bedroom apartment, you don't have adequate experience to estimate the size of houses like the ones in this neighborhood. Six or seven thousand square feet? Ten? Fifteen? No idea.

Jeff was confused that Patricia had brought home a friend from bunko night. He was more confused when Patricia had the three of us sit down on love seats and started chatting about her drinking. The hard thing for him to understand was how Patricia could be unhappy with all that he provided for her. I've never been in a long-term relationship, much less a marriage, but I'm guessing Jeff needs to learn something about his wife's needs. I'm not making excuses for Patricia hitting singles' bars, but he was clueless—and that's a red flag. Maybe he was so busy providing for her that he was too tired and preoccupied to notice her.

It took a couple hours, but Patricia finally croaked out that her life hadn't been right since her dad died. "We disagreed and fought over everything. I couldn't do anything right. I'm not sure I even loved him. But he was my dad. And when he died, there was no way to make anything right. When my mom looks at me, she tells me she loves me, but I get the feeling she blames me in part for his death. She said he was going to talk to me and apologize for some things. I don't know how true that was. I suspect maybe she wanted me to feel better about him and me. But it made me feel worse. I had no intention of ever talking to him again."

Heavy stuff. Jeff had stopped talking by then. He just watched and listened with a slack jaw. I can't remember much of anything I said to her. When we walked to the front door I was shocked when she hugged me and thanked me for everything I did for her. What did I do besides listen? I hugged her back and did the only thing I could think of—I did what Jimmy would do. I held hands with both of them and prayed for Jeff and Patricia. I'm not sure what Jeff thought about that, but he thanked me and there might have even been a tear in his eye. Patricia started blubbering again and held on to my neck for another five minutes.

That poor sound technician. Just thinking about it again gives me a new headache.

I'm not sure if attending AA meetings is going to help us find a killer. But it did allow me to meet someone I could help. That's a good feeling. Although Walter's wife still hasn't taken him back.

Dear God, help Walter meet somebody that can help him, too.

My hands are on my knees and I'm breathing hard after a tough workout. That's when it happens.

He comes in fast, quiet, and furious. Within a nanosecond of sensing someone behind me, he has his arms around me in a ferocious bear hug. I am going to stomp on the inside of his foot, but in a flash he lifts me just high enough to get my feet off the ground but not high enough for me to kick back and up toward his crotch. I am too slow anyway. In a single move he stutter-steps and loops a leg forward and trips me.

I am still thinking clearly on the way down and try to snap my head back and catch him on the bridge of his nose. He seems to be waiting for that move and I miss him. I'm relieved my head doesn't hit hard when we land on the ground. The fall still hurts like crazy and I can barely breathe with his arms wrapped around me in a viselike grip . . . and that's before he digs his chin in the center of my trapezium muscle. In spite of myself, I cry out when he digs into the sensitive nerve cluster. I buck and thrash, trying to create space so I can squirm forward and out of his suffocating hug. His chin in my back keeps me pinned close to the ground. His hug keeps me from using my hands. I know I have to think of something quick or I will be utterly helpless in a matter of seconds—if I'm not already.

I try the head-snap again. Not even close to the mark. Did he just laugh?

I inch my knees forward with every fiber of strength I can muster to see if I can edge out of his hold. This guy is strong. He puts more weight on me. I am seeing stars. His 200 pounds (and some change) are now doing most of the work of keeping me pinned down as he slides his right forearm up to the side of my neck. I'm pretty sure he is looking for my carotid artery to apply a sleeper hold. I am about to panic. He is planning to take me as a prisoner. I flail and try to muster a scream.

A whistle blows and my attacker immediately lets go. I roll over, gasping for air.

"Conner, you are not on top of your game," Soto says. I glance from him to my "attacker," Soto's trainee, Timmy. He's even bigger than I thought.

My breath is too ragged to say anything. Just as well. He's right. I haven't been back in my hand-to-hand combat sessions with Barry Soto, a CPD fight trainer, for at least two months. He's the best. Every chance he gets, he reminds me that what we see in the movies isn't the way fights really happen. They end up on the ground. *Always.* Fights always get your knees dirty. Either someone gets shot or knifed and goes down to stay—or two assailants engage and end up punching or kicking or wrestling each other until they are off their feet. Then the best grappler wins. Better know what you're doing if you want to survive. There's a reason high school and college wrestlers dominate in the MMA—mixed martial arts—pay-per-view fights. Violent stuff I've only watched a few times for training purposes—but they are definitely reflective of how mean real-life fights can be. I've investigated the aftermath of more than a few of them.

"Where you been?" Soto asks.

"Busy. Too busy."

"Too busy to stay in shape?"

"Hey," I snap back. "I'm in shape."

"I don't care what you look like in your bikini," he answers back with a sneer. "I want you to be in the kind of shape that keeps you alive."

"I'm not sure I believe you," I return. "Felt more like you were trying to have your goon kill me."

"May feel that way to you, but if it was the truth," Soto responds, "you'd be dead right now. Timmy's pretty good at that."

"Wow. Where's the love, Mr. Barry?"

I can't help it. If I met someone on the force when I was a kid tagging along behind my dad, they've got a title in front of one of their names. Sergeant. Lieutenant. Captain. Mr.

"Hey, princess, you said you wanted a tough, no-holds-barred workout, and that's what I gave you."

He gives me a friendly squeeze on the shoulder and laughs. Soto is probably sixty years old but he makes most of us look like softies. He's old-school. Very few weights, but tons of push-ups, lunges, and pull-ups and about a hundred isometric and plyometric floor and step exercises designed to torture and humble. I do Pilates with a workout DVD or at Planet Fitness every now and then. Whoever thinks they've discovered some new training technique never read the old Charles Atlas books and definitely hasn't been under the tutelage of Barry Soto.

He believes that all you need for a good workout is a floor and gravity. A wall can be a nice addition. A bar or punching bag is pure luxury. Bring your own towel.

He's probably not five foot six, but I've seen him put guys that are thirty years younger and fifty pounds heavier flat on their back on a mat before they know what hit them. He's probably pushing a hundred and eighty pounds. I doubt he has a thirty-inch waist. Lots of muscle and lots of hair—except on his completely bald dome.

"By the way, have you met Timmy?" he asks enthusiastically, nodding to my attacker.

"Once or twice. Three times, now."

Timmy laughs and Soto smiles. Then his face drops into a frown.

"Hey, Kristen, seriously, you need to spend more time over here. People talk to me. I know you're into the serious stuff that's out there, and I want to be able to take at least a little credit for keeping you alive. I owe that to your dad."

———

I've showered, changed back into work clothes, and am getting ready to walk out the door of the gym and grab a sub on the first floor that I'll eat at my cubicle. Soto and Timmy have put me through a grueling combat workout with a focus on handwork. Soto's given me a pair of old-fashioned spring-loaded handgrips to use at my desk three or four times a day. He thinks I'm out of fighting shape. And I have to admit, I can feel muscles in my abs and legs that I forgot I had.

"You know researchers have found that gripping exercises lower blood pressure," Soto said as I tucked them in my purse. Do I look like I have high blood pressure?

As I walk out the gym door, I about bump into Timmy.

"Sorry about that," I say as I move to my left to walk around him.

He slides to his right and blocks my path. Does Mr. Barry have more of a workout planned for me?

I move right and he slides left. *Okay.* "How about a little dinner tonight?" he asks. "I promise to be more gentle."

Timmy doesn't mess around with small talk. He'd have been a real hit in the Stone Age. Club a woman on the head and drag her back to his cave for dinner by candlelight. "Sorry, I have plans tonight," I answer. Dell has taught me to be clear.

Can't misunderstand that.

"Then how about tomorrow night?"

Okay. Maybe you can.

Were I to say yes, I'm guessing he'd pick me up by vine and we'd swing to his home in the trees and among the apes. "I really can't, Timmy."

"Are you already seeing somebody?"

This guy is not subtle.

"Well, yes, I kind of am."

" 'Kind of' doesn't sound real serious to me. Why don't you think about it and give me a call if you change your mind." He hands me his business card, like I don't know where to find him. I'm flabbergasted. I say nothing, move to my left, and finally unimpeded, head down the hall to the main atrium of our precinct. I feel his eyes on me the whole way. Yuck.

If I was faster on my feet I would have asked him if he was best friends with another deaf man I know named Dell.

———

I get the roasted turkey breast on whole wheat with tomatoes, lettuce, lots of onion—doesn't matter, I don't have a date tonight—pickles, banana peppers, cucumber, spinach, and spicy mustard. I skip the chips for a cellophane bag filled with exactly seven dried-out carrots. I pull a twenty-four-ounce bottled water out of a cooler. I've got a lot of extra change in my wallet and decide to get rid of it. I don't think the cashier or the thirty people behind me like it.

I still feel a little shaky from the workout, but eschew the elevator and jog up the five flights of stairs. On the way up I feel a pang of guilt about Dell. Not so much that I forbade him to come to Kendra's birthday party, but that I just used him to get rid of someone I don't want to go out with. I've been honest with Dell from day one, and this is the first time that I feel like I've used him.

A folder is sitting on my chair with a sticky note on it.

Need to see you ASAP! – Reynolds

There's ASAP and then there's *ASAP*. Which one is this? More to the point, do I or don't I eat my sandwich first?

I wolf down my sandwich, clean off my hands with a wet wipe that I keep in my desk drawer, and then head toward the small conference room he and Van Guten use as a temporary office when they're slumming it and work out of our precinct. Two cubicles away I stop. I can taste the onion big time. I go back and pop a tiny breath mint in my mouth. My sinuses are instantly cleared. I crunch it and it is gone

169

in a heartbeat. I shake two more from the container, vow not to chew, and walk toward Reynolds' work area. I stop again. I forgot the folder. How hard can I make this?

Finally, I'm at his door, everything in order. "You wanted to see me, Major?"

"Call me Austin."

"Yes, sir," I say with a salute. If he was up until the wee hours last night on my account, it doesn't show. He looks as together and handsome as he always does.

"Hey, sorry to just leave you a file and note on your desk but you weren't around and I wanted to make sure I got your attention."

"No big biggie. What can I do for you, sir?"

"Austin?"

"No, my name is Kristen."

"Cute. You going to call me Austin?"

"I'll have to think that one over. So what have you got for me?"

"An invite for dinner on Friday night."

"Is this an official powwow?"

"Nope. An old-fashioned date."

I'm stunned for a second. First Timmy, now the major? Did I put on some sort of male-attracting pheromone perfume this morning? It's working. "You know what, Major Reynolds? I'm going to have to get back to you on that one, too."

"If it'd make it easier for you to come up with an affirmative answer," he replies with a grin, "we could call this an official powwow."

I look at him closely, pondering. Square jaw. Brown hair parted on the side. Wide shoulders—and not just because of the cut of his suit coat. White straight teeth—but not whitened and polished to an exaggerated brilliance like Warren. I have to admit, Major Reynolds is a looker. And to my surprise, he's noticed me enough to ask me on a date. Is this a good idea?

"I'm still going to have to get back to you."

"Okay," he said with his head tilted and eyes squinted, the kind of expression on his face usually reserved for studying exotic animals at the zoo. I guess he doesn't get turned down very often.

"What about the file you left?"

"I think that's just my expense accounts from the last month. I needed a prop. My visit to your cubicle generated a lot of interest."

Oh, great. Exactly what I needed after last night's escapade.

I get asked out some. But not that much. Today it was Timmy and Austin asking me on a date within an hour of each other. Plus I had two missed calls from Dell seeing if I'd had a change of heart since we last talked. Does the guy have no shame? Or is he someone I need to run a background check on? Heck, maybe he is the Cutter Shark. That would be a sure ticket to the CPD Hall of Shame for me. Then there was a missed call from Klarissa. She left a message to set up coffee on Saturday morning before Kendra's last soccer game. Finally, Patricia called to ask me to dinner with her and Jeff. I am suddenly quite the popular girl.

No one called with any leads on my murder case.

I love Greek food. Lamb, big and fluffy saffron rice, lots of garlic yogurt, salad with some tabouli on top, feta cheese, kalamata olives, and lots of pita bread. *Ahhhhh.*

I'm sitting across the table from Jeff and Patricia and struggling to make eye contact. For one thing, I'm keeping an eye on my food. But there's also the deal that they want me to be Patricia's AA sponsor. I never thought to tell them that I'm not actually a real AA member. It's Tuesday night. They wanted to take me to dinner before the weekly AA meeting at Saint Bart's. I've been planning to skip this week so I—and my protective army—can go to bed early. I've been going to Saint Bart's on Tuesday nights and then Holy Family on Thursdays or Fridays. Throw in make-up time with Klarissa and a maybe-date with Major Reynolds, and this is getting complicated.

"So what do you say?" Jeff asks.

What was the question? *Focus, Kristen.*

"Will you be Patricia's sponsor?"

Shouldn't Patricia be asking me if I'd be her sponsor? I'm not sure if it's proper for him to speak on her behalf. Personal responsibility is a big deal in AA. But more to the point, despite reading the Big Book, as a nonalcoholic I'm not qualified to be an alcoholic's sponsor. I just read participant materials, so I'm not sure if you have go to classes or do something else to earn some special certificate to be a leader or sponsor.

"Jeff . . . Patricia, I've got to be honest with you."

"Don't say no, Kristen," Patricia pleads. She has a tear in her eye.

"The thing is I just don't know if I'm qualified." How's that for honesty?

"I feel like you saved my life the night you were at our house," Patricia says. "And we connected. When we talked I could see something in your eyes."

That my eyes were getting sleepy by midnight?

"I told you how I was lost without my dad and even though you didn't say anything I could tell you understood."

Well, I'll admit, I do know a little about missing a dad . . .

"I knew I had met someone that connected to what I was going through."

Now that's pushing it . . . "The thing is, Patricia," I break in, "I've never been a sponsor. Heck, I've only attended AA myself for a month or so. I wouldn't know what to do."

"But haven't you had a sponsor?" Jeff asks.

"Not exactly."

"What's not exactly?" he asks.

"That would be the same as no."

He pauses with a puzzled expression but then shakes his head dismissively and soldiers on. "Well, whatever you are doing sure seems to work. You look like you're doing great. I'd never guess in a million years you have a drinking problem. You are doing okay, aren't you, Kristen?"

"I'm not sure everybody would agree with that," I respond. "But I can honestly say I haven't had a drink since attending AA."

"Well, what more is there?" he says as he slaps the tabletop, making our glasses jump. "You're doing great and you and Patricia connect. What more could we want in a sponsor?"

"He's right, Kristen," Patricia says. "Just say yes."

I look at my watch. The Saint Bart's meeting starts in fifteen minutes.

"Let me try to figure this out," I say. "But you have to get moving, Patricia, or you'll be late for the meeting. I have to head home and catch some z's."

"Nope," Patricia smiles triumphantly. "You can catch up on your sleep later. You're going with me tonight. And we're driving together. Now give Jeff your car keys. He'll pay the waitress. And we can hustle on over and get there in time."

Jeff just beams.

"Unless Jeff can push and steer a car while popping the clutch at the same time, he may want to stay with his Mercedes. Though I would consider a straight-up swap if the CarFax report on his car is okay."

"Just give me the keys," he says with a wink. "I've got it all under control."

I hesitate. He may have it under control, but I don't. I can't go to Saint Bart's alone. How do I get out of this?

"Kristen, just give him the keys," Patricia says. "He's got a friend near here who is going to put a new starter in your Nissan."

"It's a Mazda," I say. "And I am definitely short on cash this month, so I can't really handle that bill right now. And I really can't go to AA. I need sleep more than the group tonight."

"I know you like your space and keep people at arm's length," she says. *Ouch.* Is it that obvious? "But this is something Jeff and I already decided we would do for you. We aren't going to take your money."

"I can't—"

"We're going to do this for you," Patricia says with a firmness I haven't heard before. "Jeff's getting a great deal and we want to do something small to say thank you for being there when we needed help the most. You know, you were a godsend. Honestly, I feel like a new person since last week. I feel like I've come out of a fog and started to get my life back. And I really need you to come with me tonight, even if you haven't agreed to be my sponsor."

I protest some more, but resistance is pretty much futile. I have no clue what I might have said a week ago, but apparently it was the right thing. Probably the prayer. She does look like she's stepped out of a fog. The way she and Jeff keep looking at each other, they are going to challenge Jimmy and Kaylen for Chicagoland Couple of the Year. This is a girl I couldn't stand the first time I set eyes on her, yet after a couple conversations over the past seven days, I do think of her as a friend. Not best friends. But a friend. I'm going to have to figure out how to tell Jeff and Patricia that I'm not who they think I am. I'll call Don tonight and ask for advice. Of course he's going to tell me we have to deal with it in group briefings, and unfortunately, he'll be right. No way can I blow my cover with civilians—they think I'm a secretary at an insurance agency—but now that a real relationship is established, I have a definite conflict of interest. No way can I keep this charade going.

We drive over in near silence, light jazz playing softly. She asks if I like Rick Braun. I've never heard of him. But I like the song that's on now. Jeff's explained that if his friend can't replace the starter in ninety minutes, I can borrow his Mercedes. Either way, Jeff will drive over to Saint Bart's to pick up Patricia and leave a car with me to get home.

We pull into a parking space with three minutes to spare. The door is on the side of the church and is at the bottom of five steps leading into the meeting room in a half-basement. We enter the hall and I make a quick left into the bathroom. I smooth my hair and pop another mint in my mouth. Between Greek food for dinner and raw onion on my sandwich at lunch, my breath could knock the flies off a trash truck. I wash my hands and splash a little water on my face.

I push open the double doors into the meeting room and spot an open seat next to Patricia. I look over and give her an encouraging smile. But then I freeze. Jonathan is on the other side of the empty seat and thinks I am smiling at him. He gives a friendly wave and pats his hand on the chair. Kristen, why didn't you call Don from the bathroom?

Two hours ago all I was planning to do was have dinner with Jeff and Patricia Williams. I wasn't planning to attend an AA meeting. I haven't told anyone from the office I would be here. As bad as last Tuesday night was with Jonathan's no-show and my marathon counseling session with Jeff and Patricia, this is going to be worse.

I'm in direct violation of Captain Zaworski's orders. I've been told in no uncertain terms I am not to attend Saint Bart's without backup. I stop in my tracks. With an embarrassed grimace, I put my phone to my ear and pretend I've taken a call. I retrace my steps and exit the double doors. I figure I've got five minutes to get hold of the team before Jonathan, if he's the Cutter Shark, gets suspicious and bolts. I walk into a stall and scroll down through my phone directory and hit Don's number. Four rings and his voice announcement instructs me to leave a message. I do. Where are you, partner?

I call Blackshear's number next. Same procedure. I stick with task force members. Konkade. No answer. Martinez. No answer but a message prompt half in Spanish and half in English:

"La próxima vez que estés sola, ya sabes a quién llamar. And baby, you know who you are."

I'm not even going to ask Don to translate that. I hang up and again leave no message. I hit Konkade's home number. He's not answering there either. I'm on a roll. Reynolds. *Nada.* He must be busy with his good buddy Virgil. Scalia. Nope. I sigh and punch in number seven on my speed dial. What the heck am I going to say to Zaworski? He doesn't pick up. I don't know if I'm more relieved or worried that everyone is offline at the moment.

Van Guten? She's not a cop but she's a task force member. I punch in the ten numbers that begin with what I assume is a DC or Virginia area code. She picks up immediately.

"Dr. Van Guten, how may I help you?"

"It's Kristen." She doesn't respond. "Detective Conner," I say.

"Yes?"

"This is going to be quick. I don't have much time. I ended up going to the Saint Bart's AA meeting tonight."

"Did you clear that with Reynolds and Zaworski?"

"No time to explain. Jonathan's here. And I'm solo."

"Detective Conner, this is highly irregular."

"Got to go."

I hang up. I flush the toilet and run water in the sink in case anyone is listening. I dry my hands, smooth my hair again, which is already perfectly smooth, and head back into the group setting.

Patricia is sharing. She is beaming. Suddenly, she and everyone in the room are looking at me.

"I've never met anyone so open and direct and honest," she says.

I realize she's talking about me and I blush.

"I can honestly say that for the first time in months, really more than a year, I feel hope in life. We talked and laughed and cried and prayed. She helped me and Jeff get some issues on the table and I feel like I'm in love again." She cried. I didn't.

She and I sit down at the same time. The old lady—is it Vivian?— who likes to hug everybody starts to clap. Then everyone is clapping. I'm sure my face is beet red. I roll my eyes and shake my head. Jonathan reaches over and gives my hand a squeeze. I stiffen and take a quick breath of air. He feels my response and lets go.

I dare to look over at him, wondering if I alarmed him. But he smiles and winks.

———

"Mom, I can't talk right now. It's not a good time."

"It's never a good time."

"I know, Mom, but this time it really isn't."

"Are you working?"

Patricia, Jonathan, and Jack, who is subbing for Darren, our regular AA leader, are looking at me with bemusement.

"I'm at a meeting."

I've been stalling. I had a ten-second conversation with Van Guten about an hour ago. Is that enough time to get backup assembled? It's after rush hour, but you never know how long it will take to navigate Chicago traffic. I may be flying solo with a serial killer in minutes.

"What meeting, honey?"

"Mom, I promise I'll call back tomorrow. I promise."

She sighs. That's the break I need.

"I love you," I blurt out quickly. "Call you tomorrow. Promise."

I click the red button. I take my empty Styrofoam cup back over to the electric coffee percolator that looks like a prop from a '50s movie. I've been chatting with Jack, Patricia, and Jonathan about Patricia's breakthrough last Tuesday night. I hate this conversation but I have to keep Jonathan here as long as possible.

Jonathan leaves Jack and Patricia to talk and follows me to the coffee station. I don't actually want another cup of coffee. It is a wretched brew with lots of grounds floating around. At least I hope those are grounds.

"Kristen," he says to my back, "I missed hearing you speak. I can't believe I wasn't there for your story."

Who told him I spoke? Did he ask or did someone volunteer that information? He's standing too close to me and I don't like it. Patricia was right. I need my space.

"And what you've done for Patricia is simply amazing," he continues. "When did you do your training?"

Crud. I don't know anything about being a sponsor. Is there a curriculum? Do you get a certificate? Why haven't I taken the time to find this out? I've just read the participant literature. I've always thought of myself as a good cop. No, a great cop. I grew up in a cop's home. And Dad was the best. He never cut corners. He got along with his colleagues. He closed more than his share of cases. I'm not sure he'd approve of the situation I'm in right now.

Jonathan takes my right hand in both of his and I glance up at him in surprise. Is he hitting on me? At least I hope it looks like surprise rather than attack mode. It's all I can do to let him speak, because what I really want to do is put a knee in his groin, push his left hand into his body and then to the outside, duck under, and wrench that thing three-quarters of the way up his back so I can start asking questions. Hard questions. Is that a sign of anger?

I'm creeped out, but let him hold my hand another second.

"I don't want to be inappropriate," he says, less than a foot from my face. The mint has worn off. Maybe I should blow on his face and ask questions when he regains consciousness. "But I'm wondering if we could go out and grab a cup of coffee. And I mean a good cup of coffee. Maybe some dessert. That's all. I'd love to talk with you some more tonight. Spend a little time getting to know you."

Seriously? I've gone months without being asked out on a date. I now have a testosterone-filled junior combat instructor, a major in the FBI, a devoted sort-of boyfriend who is fascinated with Amish culture, and a possible serial killer suspect all asking to spend time with me in less than twelve hours. Some girls have all the luck. I pull my hand away and turn to where the powdered creamer is. I like real half-and-half and never use the fake stuff. I shake some of it into the center of the black sludge, trying to look natural. I watch my hands closely to make sure they're not shaking. I'm good at action. I'm lousy at inaction. I stir the clotted mess until there are only a few clumps left.

"Jonathan . . ."

"Yeah?" he responds hopefully.

"I just don't go out with guys when I don't even know their last name. And . . ."

"Yeah?"

He looks and sounds a bit deflated, but interestingly, he doesn't offer even a Smith or Jones for a last name.

"Well, there's someone else."

Am I using Dell again? Or is it Major Reynolds? I know it's not Timmy.

"I didn't think a coffee invitation was asking you out on a date," he says. He looks miffed. Patricia and Jack walk over. They're looking at us cautiously. They sense something isn't right.

After some awkward chitchat, Patricia and I head for the exit. Jack stays back and talks to the last few stragglers. Jonathan is right behind us to make sure we get to our cars safely, he gallantly says. I figure there's no way Jeff's mechanic friend could replace a starter in less than two hours, but I'm hoping. I find myself craving the safety of my own, old, trusty Mazda.

We walk out of Saint Bart's into a glorious dusky Chicago spring evening. Jeff is leaning against his Mercedes with a proud expression on his face. It's a sparkling blue onyx Mercedes 500SE. He nods to it with a smile and tosses the keys to me. Now that's what I call a loaner. I think maybe I want to be Patricia's sponsor and chide myself for being bought so easily.

Then the world turns upside down.

I am literally picked up off my feet. I look to my left and Patricia is pulled to the side in an orchestrated takedown starring athletic men in black body suits and hoods. Jeff's smile is replaced by a look of utter shock. An agent firmly moves him around to the other side of his car with an armlock maneuver. I want to call out to Jeff that resistance is futile, if he has any impulses to fight back. The hold is designed to break your elbow if you struggle. But things are happening too fast to shout anything.

Two more men put Jonathan facedown on the ground. He is kicking and squirming and trying to yell. It ain't going to happen, Jonathan; just relax.

I hear Patricia scream my name.

I am in the back of a black Chevrolet Suburban heading downtown toward the State Building in less than thirty seconds of my exit from Saint Bart's.

Patricia, what have I done? I am so sorry. And I connected with you, too. We do have a bond.

Dear God, please, please help me sort out this mess.

It's two in the morning. We are in a conference room on the first floor of CPD's Third Precinct—this is Martinez and Blackshear's normal haunt. I am present to foster cooperation. The only problem is Patricia won't look at me at all and Jeff won't stop staring at me with anger and loathing. I am wondering if this means I don't get to drive the loaner Mercedes. The question of whether I'm a suitable AA sponsor has now been answered. Emphatically.

A bureaucrat is explaining why it is in their best interest to sign nondisclosure and nonliability forms. I didn't know Jeff was a lawyer. Patricia never mentioned it. Of course a week ago Patricia was still Bethany in my mind. Jeff's not inclined to sign nor let her sign any forms without his attorney present. I wonder why he can't just read the words and be his own attorney. Apparently, that's not how it works. His specialty is M&A, an acronym which everyone present seems to recognize, except me. Murder and Arguments? Malfeasance and Animosity? Misogyny and Apprehension?

I discreetly google M&A on my BlackBerry, hoping nothing naughty comes up. Mergers and Acquisitions. Big business and high-finance stuff. Okay, still out of my league. But I guess if I can understand some of Dell's supply-chain management business and Reynolds' non-isolated event stream mumbo jumbo, I can at least comprehend some of the basics of this.

"I'm not signing. What I am going to do is file a lawsuit against the Chicago Police Department—and a certain officer who set up me and my wife to be part of a dangerous operation."

The bureaucrat continues to speak in low tones. My guess is his response and volume are part of his training in a situation like this. Do nothing to stir emotions. Seek to be conciliatory. Appeal to the complainant's sense of duty and honor. He is laying praise for their poise and valor on a little too thick, I think. Problem is, I think Jeff has had the same training and he's not buying it. After mentioning the lawsuit, he shuts down.

I feel trapped in the conference room. I want to talk to Patricia and explain that I really do like her and that I had no idea a takedown was going to go down. I would never have endangered her and Jeff. Plus, I want to get down to the basement where the action is with Jonathan. Who's questioning him? Is he the Cutter Shark? How many awards will the mayor be giving me?

———

I'm hoofing it down a hall that is about as long as a city block. I was raised right, so I don't run inside. But I'm moving fast enough to get a tryout in Olympic speed walking. There are small signs over each door that are perpendicular to the wall with numbers on them. Jonathan is being interviewed in thirty-two, which happens to be the last door on the right. I am almost out of breath when I get there. I reach for the handle but the door opens first.

Don and Martinez step into the hallway. They look tired. I raise my eyebrows in question. Each shakes his head no and starts down the hallway from the direction I just came from. I reach for the handle again, but Don calls over his shoulder.

"I'd just let things be tonight. Come on. We'll get something to eat."

———

"I don't know who was madder, Zaworski or Reynolds," Martinez is saying, crumbs from a piece of apple pie in his goatee. Should I tell him?

"At least he was guilty of something," Don says.

"Just the wrong things," Martinez continues. "Not what we were hoping for."

Jonathan. Last name is Abernathy. First name is Andrew. Good old AA attending AA under an alias. He's married with three children. He has worked as a broker for the same company at the Chicago Board of Trade for the past eleven years. No degree from Northwestern. He does have a math education degree from the University of Illinois Chicago campus, which he parlayed into a job as junior trader.

There were nine grams of cocaine in his car. No previous convictions, but two arrests for solicitation of prostitutes. He basically admitted to liking the combination of drugs and adultery and lying about his marital status—but not murdering women in Chicago and other parts of the country.

Zaworski has already decided to cut him loose and not charge him in exchange for his signature on the nondisclosure and nonliability forms. Abernathy is more than elated to accept the tradeoff. He keeps a studio apartment downtown and is only home in a rural community south of Lincolnwood on weekends. He wants to keep his weeknight habits a secret from the missus, so all in all, he has a scrape on his right cheek, but feels none the worse for the added excitement.

"So that lawyer guy isn't going to sign?" Martinez asks me for the tenth time.

"Didn't look like it when they left," I answer. Again.

"Oh man, the captain is going to be mad, mad, mad."

"At me, me, me, me," I respond. Again.

After four chirps the voicemail comes up.

"This is Patricia. Leave me a message and as long as this isn't someone selling something, I'll get back to you as soon as I can. Ciao!"

I hang up, my unspoken apology strangling me. Heck yes, I feel bad. But I'm starting to get mad. What did I do wrong? Yes, I attended AA meetings under false pretense, but I don't think any ethicist is going to judge me for doing my job, which just happens to be in service to my community.

Okay, I shouldn't have gotten involved on the level I did with

Patricia. But I did. So sue me. I guess they are. I should be more worried, but what are they going to get? My Miata? My jazz and '80s CD collection? My savings bond?

Patricia's situation and circumstances were outside my assignment and expertise. But she was an absolute mess the night I went with her to her house to talk with her and Jeff. Do you have to be a PhD in psychology to help someone? Isn't peer-to-peer conversation sometimes the best medicine in life? Isn't that the lesson of AA? I feel embarrassed now, but I actually prayed with her and Jeff at the end of the meeting. I don't usually wear my religion on my sleeve, but God knows I've been around church and Jimmy and Kaylen enough to have a little idea on a few things to say to someone who's got troubles.

I wonder what Reynolds, Van Guten, Zaworski, Blackshear, Don—and seemingly everyone else in the universe—would say about that. Who cares.

Scalia—Big Tony—had a phrase he would say when he was partnered with my dad. It feels appropriate right now. "No good deed goes unpunished." Seems to be a thread in my thought life.

I hit the green button twice to redial. I'll leave her a message.

36

It is pouring down rain and I'm standing in a puddle up to my ankles. I can feel mud squishing inside my soccer shoes. I think the ooze has worked inside my socks and between my toes. It actually feels kind of good. April showers are supposed to give way to May's flowers. May decided to outdo April in the showers department for my Snowflakes' last game of the season.

We're trying for win number three and are playing the team with the best record for the season—coached by Attila the Hun, of course. Rematch time. Bring it on.

The rain has not dampened the spirits of the girls; in fact, they're more energetic than I've seen them all season.

They are soaked and muddy to the point that it is hard to tell the two teams apart. Before the game even started Kendra discovered that you could run at one particularly big puddle near midfield, dive forward, and slide on your belly for about fifteen feet—nature's own Slip 'n Slide. Attila didn't like it much when his girls joined in. The girls were not to be denied their fun, however. Pretty soon players from both teams were sliding past each other screeching and giggling. I winced a couple times for fear of a head-on collision—when it crossed my mind that Attila was telling his girls to aim for mine.

Sometimes you just have to admit you are a tad bit crazy—and I do.

The parents, huddled under umbrellas, were glum twenty minutes before the game, but the midfield entertainment soon had everyone laughing and the video cameras came out in force.

The referees, a father-and-son team, came three minutes before game time and asked if we wanted to cancel and call it a tie. Before Attila and I could respond, the girls jumped up and down yelling, "We wanna plaaaaaay!"

Attila and I shake our heads and laugh.

The father ref, looking stoic with mud splatters from head to toe, said, "Let's get moving, then." He suggested a shortened halftime, though. That way we could all go home and dry off. His kid, probably thirteen or so, and I'm guessing thrilled that he is still going to get his ten-dollar fee as a line judge—been there and done that at his age—looks at Attila and me and says, "It's cool when old people are still crazy."

I know he meant it as a compliment, but I'm not sure I like being lumped in with Attila—and especially not old people. I'm not thirty yet.

The first half ended up in a 3-3 tie. If we were scoring this on the basis of mud wrestling, we might actually have had a slight lead. When the ball hits the biggest puddle, sometimes it plops and just sits there. Other times it skips like a hard-rubber crazy ball. They got their second goal off a cheap bounce.

I look at my stopwatch. I can almost guarantee the old dude is going to end the game exactly on time, so we've got less than three minutes left and the score is now 6-6. Tiffany and Kendra have scored three goals each. At least I think that's who those little mudballs are. I know Attila's daughter Stacey has at least that many. He screams *Staceeeey* every time she scores. His wife is even louder.

Their goalie, Olivia, makes a save and boots it. She slips and ends up on her butt. The ball shanks out of bounds a few feet from me, so that's where we'll get to throw it in. I look behind me and see Mom, Jimmy, Kaylen, and Klarissa huddled together under Jimmy's golf umbrella. They look miserable. Weanies. They have a couple of soaked blankets wrapped around them.

Kendra runs over and picks up the ball to throw it in. In a moment of inspiration I tell her, "Score a goal and win and Coach Kristen will do a belly flop in the puddle with you after the game."

———

Coach Attila smiles and is gracious as he shakes hands after the game.

"You all really improved this year. Nice job and good win. See you in the fall if you're coaching—and no hard feelings from the first time we played."

I mumble a "nice game" back to him and try to get a quick apology out, but I'm mobbed by my team. I feel bad. I'm still holding a grudge and he ends up being a nice, normal parent. What does that make me—besides not a parent?

It's showtime, and I break away from my clump of jumping and yammering seven-year-olds and run for the middle of the field. I dive and sure enough slide at least twenty feet. My face and hair are covered with mud. I wish I had zipped my sweat suit top tighter because I think the inside of my bra is now enhanced with a couple gallons of ooze.

I hear a cheer go up from kids and parents. We didn't win the World Cup but I think we just had a successful season.

———

"More hot chocolate?"

"No thanks, Mom."

We were supposed to go to the Pizza Palace as a team, but there was no way we could take the girls anywhere, as dirty as they were. Dunkin' Donuts has four outside tables with umbrellas, so we all stopped for a quick sugar celebration. The rain was still coming down hard, but as wet as everyone already was, players and family members alike, it didn't matter. I kept thank you's and special awards to less than five minutes. No one complained. They never do when I keep it short and sweet. Everyone drove home happy.

It's just Klarissa, Mom, and me finishing off a second cup of hot chocolate each. We're all getting along and at peace. I wonder if the Cutter Shark has moved on or gone into an early hibernation. Or, with his lifestyle issues, if something violent has happened to him.

Van Guten said that the FBI estimates there are fifty active serial killers in America at any one time. But serial killers make mistakes and tend to get caught or killed.

I wonder if the turn of the calendar to May might not represent a turn in our fortunes with the Cutter Shark.

Dear God, help us not let this guy get away.

H ey, Lloyd."

"Hey, Kristen."

"Just the man I've been wanting to see."

"Yeah?"

He sees I have my serious face on and is suddenly wary. We're on the front steps of the church. Service is over.

"Yeah," I say. "I forgot to tell you something."

"Yeah?"

"Thank you."

"You are welcome. For what?"

"Your call."

"You mean about the kid robbing old people?"

"Have you called me about anything else? Of course."

"Duh. Dumb question. Glad that turned out good for you. I heard you all got him. But didn't you get cut or something?

"A scratch."

"Not what I heard. Let me see."

I roll up my sleeve and show him the three-inch cut line.

"Too bad. That's going to leave a scar."

"It is?" I ask, genuinely surprised. "The doctor told me it would disappear!"

"Look for yourself. When did this happen, a month ago?"

"Five, maybe six weeks."

"Well, it's no big deal, but it is going to leave a scar."

I didn't want another scar. I already have enough scars inside and out.

"So where you been lately, Kristen?"

"Busy with this Cutter Shark thing."

"Yeah, another dumb question. That's all people are talking about. The Cutter Shark."

"No kidding. I hate that Cutter Shark nickname. But it is obviously catchy."

"Kind of says it all. We do miss seeing you on Wednesday nights. We've been having about thirty show up for Bible study."

"Very nice. But lately I'm all meeting'd out."

"I can imagine. You got any leads?"

"If I told you I'd have to kill you."

He rolls his eyes at my cheesy cliché.

"By the way, where's that ace reporter sister of yours lately? Only time I see her is if the late news is on TV at the ER. She going to church somewhere else?"

"I'm pretty sure she is. She keeps telling us she's just visiting because I don't think she wants to hurt Jimmy's feelings, but I think she has made a change. She told me she's even going to Sunday school."

"I'm impressed. Beautiful and devout. That's the Conner girls."

"At least two of them are beautiful."

"Yeah right. I love your show of modesty, but I'm guessing you look in the mirror, too."

"Well, Lloyd, you are just Mr. Sweetness."

"That's right. And stop being a stranger so you don't forget it."

I give him a salute and answer, "Yes, sir! And how about you? You doing okay?"

"Same old same old. Doctor says I have to lose some weight. So I'm on a diet."

"No more Gas & Grub for lunch break?"

"I somehow knew that was going to come up. But nope. No more Gas & Grub. Not sure where you're going to get your hot crime fighting tips now."

"Unless you can find the Cutter Shark for me, you just need to worry about taking care of you and listen to your doctor."

"How about I return the favor and tell you the same thing? You need to make sure you're taking care of you, too. I may be a couple hundred pounds overweight but you better eat a sandwich or you're going to blow away with the wind."

"Believe me, Lloyd, I eat. Plenty."

"I know. I've seen you in action. I also know you work out like you're training for a triathlon. So I'll correct myself and say you need to eat two sandwiches."

It's my turn to roll my eyes at him.

"Kristen," Lloyd says, now serious. "You've got a lot you're working through. It's been a tough year for the Conner girls. And your mom. Even if you can't make Wednesday nights until this Cutter Shark mess is done, make sure you get yourself in a place where you can open up about the hard stuff of life with some people who care about you."

"Yes, sir," I say and salute again.

"Okay, okay. I know when you're blowing me off. But as tight as you're wound up right now, I don't want to see you snapping."

I give Lloyd a stare. He holds his hands up in surrender.

"Okay, I said too much. But I do have the special power to see when your invisible force field goes up to shut everyone out. Which is most of the time. Just remember, you can't always be the lone wolf."

Wound up too tight? I shut everyone out? Are my friends and loved ones talking amongst themselves? Is there a Fix-Kristen conspiracy going on?

I look over Lloyd's shoulder and see Dell's revenge date, Carrie, walking by, arm in arm with some guy I don't recognize. Dell obviously didn't listen to my advice and pursue her—or if he did, he scared her off with plans for an Amish expedition. She was probably too young for him anyway. I'll have to give Jimmy a hard time about running a dating service at church.

"Hey, stranger. No hello?" Dell asks, trying to look as if everything is normal, but with his face scrunched up like I've punched him in the stomach. Is the pained expression because of seeing me or because he just saw Carrie with someone else? Please let it be the latter.

I open my car door to hop in to head over to Kaylen's for lunch and Kendra plops into the passenger seat. She likes to ride with me—like it's a special treat. He bends over and waves to her.

"Hey, pretty girl."

"Hi, Mr. Dell," she answers.

"Wow," he says with a whistle, "someone has fixed up your aunt's ride."

Patricia hasn't talked to me since last Tuesday night. Jeff called the office on Thursday to set up a time to drop my car off and get the keys to the Mercedes I drove for two days—I had no choice, it was the only set of keys I had after our late-night interview with Jonathan and I had no idea where he took my car. I felt both incredibly guilty and amazed over the ride the whole time. When he called my office to make the switch—he refused to let Sheila patch the call through to me—I hoofed down with my checkbook to pay for the repairs—hope Mom has a few extra bucks to loan me because I'm not asking Klarissa even if we are getting along—but Jeff wouldn't even look at me, much less answer a single question. He handed me my keys and took the keys to the 500SE, got in, and drove off. I am going to miss that ride.

I found the work order in the glove compartment. There was no price for the work and the itemization was handwritten on a generic form, so the mechanic's name and contact information was not on it. Not only did Jeff have the starter replaced, but he had his mechanic friend do a whole laundry list of maintenance items. And then he had the car detailed inside and out. I don't know what kind of wax the guy used, but the black paint looks shiny and gorgeous again. Same with the tan leather seats and convertible top. It drives like a charm. And it starts up immediately. I'm still in the habit of parking on hills just in case I wake up and it was all a dream.

When you're a cop, you do get some freebies. Some restaurants refuse to take your money for a meal, for example. Some cops abuse the generosity of others and start expecting everything to be for free. Others won't take anything. Ever. I've read and signed the CPD ethics policy statement. This is a gray area. Jeff didn't do anything for me based on my performance in the line of duty. On the other hand, I would never have met Patricia if I hadn't been working the Saint Bart's AA meeting on behalf of the CPD.

I better get this reported to Zaworski. And even if Jeff wouldn't take my check, I'm still going to pay them back. That doesn't have anything to do with institutional policy. I just feel lousy about how things went south so fast. I'll show Jimmy the bill and have him look over my car this afternoon and ask him how much he thinks it all cost. I know I can't pay Jeff and Patricia back in one or two paychecks, but I'll start sending them something every month to settle this.

"It was time to get a few things looked at," I say to Dell. "It even starts without a long hill," I add.

"Nice."

"Are you coming for lunch, Mr. Dell?" Kendra asks.

"Not this week, sweetie," he answers. He better not be. I may not be able to keep him from attending the same church as me—which doesn't sound very Christian of me—but I do have the right to be with my family without a guy who won't let go of being there.

He looks up at me with a searching glance after he says it. Is he sniffing around for a lunch invite? Probably.

"You take care," he says.

He walks briskly to his car without looking back. I'm just not going to see him anymore. At all. Period.

Kendra and I talk and giggle the whole way over to her house. I've never seen her carry a purse to church. She shows me the reason she has it now. She used it to smuggle her Kristen doll to show all her friends. If Kendra's mommy finds out, we're both—make that all three of us if you include the Kristen doll—in big trouble. All of us might end up in time-out.

I turn off my car and park it in a turnout in front of their house. My mind flashes back to Lloyd. One more person in the long line of people claiming I have issues keeping people at arm's length.

May 14, 11:43 p.m.

I need to get back on schedule. I've never golfed before but I know about a mulligan. You get to choose one shot per round that doesn't count and you get a do-over.

I've made a decision. Candace is my mulligan. I am turning the clock back to Sandra Reed for when it is time to go again. Looking at my watch—well, what do you know?—it's time again now.

My FBI fans might argue that I'm going early for a second time in a row and that it is an indication I'm not following my pattern as carefully as before. Blah blah. First of all, it is my decision when I act. Their criticism is only meant to cover their own ineptitude. Secondly, they've probably never heard of a mulligan.

Chicago started so splendidly. Then I decided to invest in some extracurricular activity, and boy, did that blow up in my face. Her cruelty toward me has bordered on torture. I've let her be for the moment. She may think she is getting away with a blatant disregard for my kindness and my needs, but she will discover the heights and depths of pain that a human being can experience.

I have always been merciful to a fault with my subjects. It's taken a lot of trial and error, but I believe I have created the perfect mix of light paralytics and pain inhibitors to obtain an acceptable anesthetic awareness when I perform on them. I like for my girls to be awake so I can watch their eyes and imagine what is going on behind them—they kind of know and kind of don't know what I'm doing—but I do want them to be comfortable. And they are. So no one in his or her right mind can accuse me of cruelty or torture.

But I am going to treat her like she has treated me. No pain inhibitors. A large enough dose of pure Suxamethonium to completely paralyze her—but where she will feel everything. With absolutely no muscle movement, she won't even be able to blink or shed a tear. But I know she'll be crying on the inside. And I'm certain she will finally understand how bad she made me feel.

I would like to move her to the front of the line. But knowing that I am about to get back on schedule makes patience easier to bear tonight.

I was afraid that Chicago was getting too messy. Tonight should tidy things up.

I worked pecs and abs hard this morning. I am ripped.

39

"You went on a date with someone from work?" my mom nearly shouts down the table. "But you're going out with Dell."

I thought I made my feelings clear to her. She's listening about as well as Dell. And why did Klarissa have to bring up my date on Friday night?

We've only been sitting down for five minutes at Sunday dinner and I have no idea what I've done to be on the hot seat.

"Where's Dell?" James asks.

"Mr. Dell," Kendra corrects him. "He and Kristen don't like each other anymore."

"Aunt Kristen," Kaylen corrects Kendra.

"Why don't you like Mr. Dell?" James asks me.

"What's going on with you and Dell?" Mom asks again.

I give Klarissa a dirty look. She can barely conceal a smile. She pokes at the food on her plate and manages to get a single pea on a tine of her fork. She lifts it to her mouth and begins to chew slowly and thoroughly. The pea doesn't stand a chance.

"Mr. James and Ms. Kendra, listen closely," I say firmly. "I do not dislike Mr. Dell and I do not think he dislikes me."

"But can you be sure?" Klarissa asks.

She snorts out a little laugh and goes into a coughing fit. That girl has to start eating. It's pollen season and she's always had allergies, but with her weight, I'm not sure she is healthy enough to fight off a cold at any point in the year. She does look marvelous on TV, however, which everyone knows adds ten pounds. Not just marvelous. Drop-dead gorgeous. With Warren out of the picture, she'll probably make Chicago's top ten list for hot bachelorette babes.

"Aunt Klarissa makes a valid point, and it is possible that I'm wrong and Mr. Dell does not like me anymore. Nonetheless, I told him last week that we can't see each other anymore."

Everyone at the table, including little James, is staring at me, willing me with their eyes to go on. Maybe I will. This is a new experience for me. I did not always get pluses for speech skills on my high school report cards.

"Are you sure it's completely over?" Mom asks. "He's such a nice young man. And I think he likes being with us."

She is relentless today. Honestly, she's never been particularly invasive in our personal lives—as long as we go to church and come for Sunday dinner each and every week. What's the deal with Dell?

"I think he's swell, too, Mom. But I'm just not feeling the romance."

"Romance is kissing," Kendra says to James with a coy smile.

"Gross!" he nearly screams.

"James!" Jimmy yells sharply. "No yelling!" James lowers his head and quiets down immediately, but I see the trace of a smug smile on his face. He's no worse for the experience.

"So what if you don't feel romantic toward him?" Mom grills me. "It's always better to start as friends and then get romantically involved later."

"Just like you and Dad?" Kaylen asks her with a laugh.

Bless Big Sis's heart. She's come to my rescue. We all know from family mythology that Mom and Dad were instantly, magnetically attracted. They got married within a few months of meeting.

"That was different," Mom says defensively.

Now everyone has turned attention her way. I believe I'm off the hook. She gets a dreamy look in her eyes and Klarissa, Kaylen, and I make eye contact and burst out laughing.

"What? What?" Mom asks, perturbed now.

"Mom, just go on," Klarissa urges. "What made things different for you and Dad? Kaylen's got her man, but Kristen and I obviously need some serious help."

"Seriously serious help," I agree.

"You guys are just laughing at me," Mom says.

"We are not. Just tell us!" Klarissa exclaims.

Mom relents and smiles. "We just knew the first time we met that we were made for each other. I couldn't take my eyes off of him and he couldn't take his eyes off of me. My daddy was strict and I wasn't allowed to hold hands with boys on a first date, under any circumstances. And I definitely wasn't allowed to see a Catholic boy. I guess I wasn't so good that night. We met at the skating rink and held hands the whole night."

I want to laugh but the moment's just too sweet and Mom will shut down if she thinks we're still teasing her. Kaylen has scooted her seat right next to Jimmy and he is running his fingers lightly across her shoulders. I look closer and if my eyes don't deceive me, I believe I see the very beginning of a baby bump on Kaylen's belly. Kaylen is pretty but she is one of those women who get even prettier when pregnant.

Klarissa and I look at each other and sigh. Then she puts her finger and thumb in the shape of an L on her forehead. I return the compliment.

We really are getting along good these days. Even if we're both losers when it comes to romance.

—⋅—

You look down at your own peril when James has a certified weapon—a Wiffle bat—in his hands.

We headed to the back yard after lunch and I'm pitching a Wiffle ball to the kid. The kind with air holes to enhance velocity. He may be four years old, but he can already smack that ball. I'm about done throwing to him underhand. And if he keeps parting my hair every time he whacks the ball, I may have to give him some chin music to move him off the plate and then throw him the curveball away and down.

I played soccer, not softball. But I do have fabulous memories of going to Wrigley and Comiskey with my family for Cubs and White Sox games. I thought it was neat that Dad bought a scorecard and filled it out in pencil the whole game. A couple of times I caught him comparing his card with the *Tribune*'s box scores the next day. He was pretty sure he was more accurate than the official scorekeeper.

For the first couple of minutes out here, I had Kendra and even Klarissa to help shag James' prodigious swats of the bat. Both lost interest pretty quick. So now I'm pitcher and solo fielder, which means I'm running around and sweating in a jean skirt.

Jimmy's sitting on a lawn chair next to Mom on the patio, talking. She's crying about something. I'm not about to complain about having to shag James' fungoes; Jimmy's got the real work today.

I glance around. This is Chicago weather at its most beautiful. It was a deluge yesterday, but today it's breezy and in the lower seventies. The grass is a velvety green. Kaylen's flowers and her tiny vegetable plot are already bursting with color. She is showing Klarissa and Kendra something that is growing by the side of the single-car detached garage.

My phone buzzes on my hip. I pitch the ball to James and look down to see who's calling me on a Sunday afternoon. Big mistake.

James clocks me on my forehead with a scorching line drive. I put my hand to the spot where the ball hit. It feels hot and is instantly swelling. I'm going to have an angry red circle for the entire world to see; an alien crop circle in the center of my forehead. I will look like a unicorn that has had his horn surgically removed.

Konkade is calling and I ignore the pain on my forehead. My stomach does a somersault as I push the receive button and answer. "Conner."

I feel sets of eyes on me from every point in the yard. James is tugging on my skirt and asking if I'm okay. I put a finger on his lips so I can hear the details of my call.

"Got it. On my way, sir."

———

"This better be good," Don mumbles drowsily. "You've woken me from a perfectly good Sunday afternoon nap."

"Wish I could say it was good, but our friend the Shark has struck again."

Instantly alert, he says, "Already? This early?"

"Yeah. Not good."

"We meeting at the precinct again?"

"No," I answer. "We are getting back to protocol and heading directly to the crime scene. Konkade has been calling the troops to action and you didn't pick up. So he asked if I could try to reach you and give you the location while he called the others. You got something to write on?"

"Shoot," he says.

I am the first one on the scene from the task force. Miracles do happen. As I stride down a long brick sidewalk toward the front door, I see Konkade and Zaworski drive by looking for a parking spot. Looking ahead, I recognize the officer working the front door. Chuck Gibson is a tough twenty-year veteran of CPD. I nod at him.

Gibson nods back and answers my question before I can ask it: "A neighbor was out walking his dog. Hundred-pound-plus Lab basically dragged him here to the front steps. The man took the time to throw up and then called 911." He pauses, grimacing. "I took a look upstairs. We're past initial decay and into full-blown putrefaction—maybe even a little black putrefaction. You're going to need a mask."

I grimace, too. With the body in that state, the victim has been dead more than a day and a half. Maybe two days. That means it has already swollen to as big as it's going to get and the gasses are starting to leak out. I sigh. The death odors are going to be at their very worst. Even with hustling over here as quickly as we could, our team will not be on the Cutter Shark's fiftieth crime scene—known fiftieth crime scene—within a twenty-four-hour postmortem interval. Stats for apprehending criminals after the first twenty-four hours are not good. Although with the Cutter Shark the stats are never good.

My bright, beautiful Sunday afternoon has gotten dark in a hurry. With one finger I lightly touch the angry welt on my forehead from the Wiffle ball. I think I'm stalling.

I walk partway back down the sidewalk, turn, and catch the grandeur of this stately three-story townhouse just north of the University of Chicago one more time. The other two places had been very nice, even high-end by my civil servant standards, but this one must have cost a fortune.

Gibson hands me the mask as he signs me in at the checkpoint. I walk up the wide stairs of an impressive front stoop to the front door. I take four steps onto the porch and before reaching the egress, the odor is already overwhelming. I quickly pull the mask over my face. The 911 operator called the closest squad car to investigate but had a pretty strong inkling that the Cutter Shark was back in action. He called Zaworski one minute later, and he started a chain of calls to rally the troops.

I put sterile cotton slippers over my shoes. I pull the mask away from my face and hit three drops of ammonia under my nose and flinch as the chemicals make a mad charge up my sinuses and into my brain. Reynolds has ordered an extra level of care at the scenes, so I also put on a cotton version of a shower cap, similar to what the food vendors wear at Sam's Club. Nylon gloves complete my ensemble.

I step inside to view a wide front-door-to-back-door hallway with a room on each corner of the first floor, and an ornate staircase dominating the middle of the house. All the floors are open around the staircase, with a widow's perch constructed mostly of open windows on top of the third floor, so there is plenty of light in this weird mixture of classic and contemporary architecture. A second uniformed officer—I don't recognize this one—stands in front of the staircase. *He's got to be miserable getting assigned inside.*

"Third floor, bedroom in the southwest corner," he says with a nod upward.

"Anyone else up there?"

"Couple of tech guys from the ME. No detectives yet. But the tech guys will keep the scene just the way it is for you folks. The chief medical examiner is on his way in, too, so they'll be running a tight ship."

With the horde of techies from the medical examiner's office and about ten of us who are considered central to the task force, keeping the crime scene pristine for long is pretty much impossible. A perpetrator who bleeds out his victims doesn't help things.

Not only is there physical corruption at a crime scene, but there is a second kind of corruption; the spiritual state of the scene. I don't know how to explain it, but it is basically the mood, the psychology, the ambience—whatever you want to call it—that gives you clues on the emotions of a particular crime. Was it passionate and spur of the moment? Was it slow, methodical . . . premeditated? Was it violent, noisy, and angry?

Once you and twenty-five of your friends start tromping around a crime scene, it's hard to regain that initial spiritual sense of a place. It takes a weird combination of focus and imagination. Dad said that Scalia would show up to a murder scene and just stand there for as long as an hour, never saying anything, just trying to see and feel possibilities of what might have happened.

What did Big Tony do when he stood motionless in the middle of a room where someone's life has been stolen from him or her? Did he see images? Did he pray? Did he hear voices?

Dear God, help me see things I can't see myself.

I pray over and over as I tread up the steps. I don't think I've ever prayed at a crime scene.

Halfway up the last flight of stairs I can hear muffled voices from the room in the southwest corner. I look up and down the identical front-to-back hallway on the landing of the second floor. Everything is so still and muffled that the place feels like a museum—or a mausoleum—today.

Even with the ammonia and mask, the stench assaults all my senses anew as I enter the room where GiGi Baker's mutilated body is simultaneously decomposing and bloating grotesquely. Two techies look up at me. It is impossible to read their expressions behind their surgical masks.

I walk to her nightstand. There's a large ten-by-twelve picture of a happy couple. I pick it up carefully in my gloved hands and turn it over in my hands. On the back, someone—I assume GiGi—had drawn a heart and written "Alex loves GiGi" in the center of it. I hold the face of the picture out toward the lab guys.

"Is this what the victim looked like?" I ask.

"I'm guessing she's about four or five years older now," answers one who has "Bruce" stitched on his scrub top. "Pretty girl. What a shame."

"You've got that right," I respond. "Wonder where Alex is."

"Who's Alex?" Bruce asks. "The guy in the picture?"

"Yep. And if he's still alive, a certain suspect, though I doubt he's the killer."

"Do you folks have any leads?" the other tech guy asks. No name on his chest. He sees me looking and says, "My name is Jerome. We met at the first murder."

"I'm Conner," I respond. "And I can't really discuss our leads at this point."

I carefully set the picture back in place. I force myself to look at GiGi and remember that Scalia, Big Tony, didn't move for an hour or more. I've never stood still more than five minutes in my life. I am reminded of a Bible verse: "Watch and pray." Don't know where it's at and what the context is, but I make a note to myself to look it up tonight.

I hear loud thumps coming up the steps. The cavalry is about to arrive.

Martinez is first through the door. He looks paler than I do today. He is wearing one of those silk or linen button-down shirts that are popular in tropical climates—even if he's fashionably early by a month or two. He has on light khakis and a pair of sandals, which are covered by the gauze hospital booties. He has somehow worked a fedora, complete with felt band and a little feather, into his outfit. He takes off his hat, which I guess took the place of the gauze headwear, out of respect for the dead, and walks slowly to the decomposing body of GiGi, his eyes downcast. The others are close behind. *"Santa madre de Dios, apiádate de nosotros"* I hear Martinez say as he makes the sign of the cross.

I'm not sure I've translated it right, but I catch the essence of it. *God in heaven, help us catch this monster.*

———

"GiGi Baker. Thirty-six years old. Five foot ten, 145 pounds. Widowed a year ago."

Ouch. Blackshear is reading a summary of what has been learned about the victim in the past couple hours. We are back at the precinct. We switch holding task force meetings between the Second and the FBI's office over in the State Building. Once word hits the streets that there's been another Cutter Shark murder, we can't avoid the throngs of press, but keeping them guessing on location cuts the mob in half.

"Deceased husband of the . . ." Blackshear hesitates over the wording and gives it another go. "The deceased husband of the deceased wife is Alex. He died of lymphoma and complications from treatments on May 5 of last year. No children."

"Some Cinco de Mayo," Martinez says with a whistle. "Life's not fair."

My first thought is, *Thank God he wasn't alive to face this.* But then I realize that this probably wouldn't have happened if she was a happily married woman. I'm glad there are no kids, but realize there might be wonderful brothers and sisters and parents left behind who would raise their kids with love. Maybe they didn't want kids. Maybe they couldn't have kids. Maybe they thought they had all the time in the world to have kids. I hold my breath for a sec, realizing that's what I think.

Blackshear continues, "She was a certified public accountant and had her own business that she ran from the first floor of her home. But she didn't have a lot of active clients. Those she did have are big accounts. Real big. Not sure how much she has to work anyway. At first glance, her husband left her well cared for financially. No relatives from her or her deceased husband's family in the area."

Sandra Reed. Candace Rucker. GiGi Baker. A simple pattern in Chicago and a pattern consistent with the stream of related national occurrences that Virgil spit out. Single. Living alone. Successful. Attractive enough. Or too attractive?

Just another confirmation of what Virgil has told us. He doesn't force his way into these homes. There are some signs of romance and all three women have been murdered in their bedrooms. The evidence says that they haven't entered those bedrooms after a struggle. He doesn't consummate sex with the victims, which has Van Guten in psychological-profiling heaven. The possibilities for our killer's stunted development are endless.

"So he's never had sex with his victims," I say, glancing at Van Guten across the table.

"No," Van Guten answers. "Any ideas on what that might mean?"

"Impotent," I guess.

"Possible but not probable," she answers. "He's a healthy male. What else?"

Undeterred, I try again and this time pick up a little steam: "He's both fascinated by and terrified of women. He's attracted to and then repulsed by them. He goes through the motions of romance and maybe even foreplay, but his heart isn't in it. Deep down he hates women. His conquests are to show who has the real power. He is unable to love."

"Good. You read your notebooks. So how'd he get that way?" she asks, still holding me with her eyes.

I look around before answering. Konkade is smoothing his non-existent hair. Don is brushing equally imaginary lint from his shirt. This seems to be a habit.

Reynolds is staring at the ceiling, broken tiles and all, with his pointer fingers forming a tent and his lips pursed. Our date—or professional powwow as I prefer to see it—was okay. Reynolds wanted to go to the Magnificent Mile, so we did. We ate at the Signature Room on the ninety-fifth floor of the Hancock Building . . . a location that's pretty hard to write off on the FBI dime.

"Family trauma," I answer Van Guten. "The death or desertion of the father, leaving behind a mother with damaged emotions, unable to cope. Something happened and he was taken away from her—or vice versa. Really, just the kind of path that Virgil has already told us."

"Virgil?" Reynolds asks, his head snapping in my direction. "Who is Virgil?"

Don rolls his eyes. Blackshear stifles a laugh. Martinez comes to my rescue.

"Just a nickname we have for Operation Vigilance," he says.

I like Martinez better all the time. What a standup guy. He said "we" instead of "Kristen."

"So where does that leave us?" Van Guten asks.

"We'll know him when we find him," I answer. "If we can find him."

Reynolds folds the meeting and we all head home, desperately weary.

I'm at JavaStar before Klarissa on a bright Saturday morning. I catch her on the phone. "I'm here. What do you want me to order for you?"

"Grande latte, skinny."

The skinny's a surprise. *Not.* Maybe I'll order her a slice of the extra fat cinnamon swirl coffee cake.

"Go ahead and have them make mine," she says. "I'm almost there."

"You got it."

I repeat "grande latte, skinny" to the barista. I've already ordered my extra shot grande Americano with one Splenda. I need every one of those four shots.

"Just one Splenda in that?" he asks.

"In which?" I ask.

"The skinny latte."

"No, I just asked for a Splenda with my extra shot grande Americano."

"Got it. Name?"

"Kristen."

"And on the latte?"

"Kristen, too."

"That's funny," he beams. "You're meeting someone with the same name!"

There are so many things I'm tempted to say. I wonder if he can see wheels with gears spinning in my head.

"No, I'm just waiting for my sister to come. If she's not here yet, I'll be picking up her latte for her."

"Do you want me to add her name, too, in case she gets here before the drinks are done?"

I look around. Most of the seats are taken. But there's no one else in line at the moment.

"I think I can keep it straight for both of us," I answer.

"It's no problem either way."

I promise, I was in a good mood, all things considered, when I got here. I love going out for a cup of coffee in the morning. A lot of times it is very uneventful and that's what I love most about the whole experience. Because once I get the urge to jump the counter and cuff the barista, the coffee just doesn't taste as good. Oh well.

"Hey, Sis."

Klarissa saves me from charges of false imprisonment of a man with an ear stud the size of a silver dollar who's currently wearing a green apron.

"Name?" he asks her with more enthusiasm and delight than he ever showed to me.

"Klarissa," she beams.

"Two *s*'s?" he asks.

"You bet, and thanks for asking, Darrin with two *r*'s," she says with a wink.

Darrin carefully pens her name with a Sharpie, a look of rapture on his face. I think there's a little lesson in this interaction I'm supposed to learn. I don't want to acknowledge it so I give Klarissa a dirty look. She sticks her tongue out at me and laughs. She grabs the crook of my arm and pulls me toward the door.

"Let's talk outside," she says.

"I'd love to," I say, still a little sullen. "You grab a table and I'll grab the drinks."

The barista looks up as Klarissa exits the side door to stake a claim on a patio table. He looks after her wistfully. I'm guessing he wishes I had gone for the seating and Klarissa had stayed to pick up the drinks. I slowly drop a dollar in the tip box while clearing my throat. He doesn't notice. He and the entire world would have broken into a song and dance from *The Music Man* if it had been Klarissa leaving a tip.

I've got to start using people's first names so I can Win Friends and Influence People.

———

"Mom wants to talk to you, too."

Klarissa hands me the phone. A delivery truck pulls by the patio spewing diesel fumes so I don't hear what my mom says.

"Come again?" I ask her.

"I said I am so proud of the way you two girls are getting along."

"I didn't know we weren't getting along before," I say.

"Well, you weren't," Mom answers. "And stop being difficult with your mother for a day."

Klarissa is nodding her head in agreement with Mom because she apparently knows exactly what she's saying. I guess I would, too.

"I'm not going to ask you about Dell today," she says. "But that doesn't mean the subject isn't going to come up at lunch tomorrow. I want to talk to you about him. I'm worried about him. He was at church last week but turned down a lunch invite. He's lonely and he's a bit of a lost soul. Our family helps him."

"Mom," I say with the sternest voice I'll use with her. "Inviting him to lunch after I specifically said I didn't want him there was highly inappropriate. That has to stop. If he said no it's because I've told him we will not be together for any more Sunday lunches. You want to keep ignoring me on this, fine. Invite him for tomorrow. I will go somewhere else and have lunch. Your call."

Klarissa is watching with wide eyes.

"Why do you have to be so combative, Kristen?"

"No," I answer with anger. "You aren't putting this on me. I'm not the one being combative. This is me repeating for the twentieth time I am not interested in Dell—and you choosing to project what you want to happen on the situation. You and Dad raised us girls not to do 'missionary dating.' So I'm not going to date a guy—particularly a guy who is creeping me out—to somehow help him not feel lonely. You are welcome to help him find his lost soul. I'm not going to, and I'm not going to feel guilty about it."

"Okay, it's your life. But Kristen, you're a beautiful girl and I don't want you to end up alone because you don't take the time to find the right man."

"Mom, what has gotten into you? This is officially beyond ridiculous. Are you suggesting that Dell is my last hope for love?" *I don't want you to end up alone?* Gag me!

"I told you I wasn't going to talk about him today and I'm not going to."

"Well, it's a little late for that. You are going to have to trust me on this one, Mom. You are right—there's something wrong with Dell. But I'm not the one to help him."

"Okay, I'm sorry. You're right. I haven't listened to you. You have a good time with Klarissa and I'll get out of your hair."

"Don't try to lay a guilt trip on me over this."

"What'd I say that makes you think I'd try to make you feel guilty? Now finish your time with Klarissa."

I sigh and roll my eyes. Klarissa is staring at me with a look of wonder on her face. I stick out my tongue at her.

"Did Klarissa tell you she has gone out with someone new?" Mom asks.

I look up sharply at my sister. The look of wonder is gone in a flash. She knows what's up. She grabs the phone from my hand.

"You *promised* not to say anything, Mom."

My mom says something to her that I can't hear.

"Okay, I love you, too. And Kristen says she loves you, too . . . even if she is mad."

She listens to Mom another minute and signs off by saying, "No, I think she is 100 percent right. And going to church doesn't prove he's a great guy. If she gets the creeps from him, it's with reason. We're running out of time here, Mom, and I want to talk to Kristen a little more."

She hangs up.

"Thanks," I say. "Now tell me what gives. I thought we were best buds. Why are you keeping secrets from me?"

"I'm not keeping secrets from my *best bud*," she says. "First of all, I went out with somebody one time. So that doesn't even earn a mention—though there are a lot of guys out there that will give you the creeps! But the main thing is after going out with Warren—well, mostly Warren—for five years it has become a bigger deal in Mom's mind than it was mine."

"I can't imagine. Mom fixating on something?"

She laughs and adds, "And she certainly can't keep a secret."

"Nope. You don't even have to threaten to waterboard her and she blabs everything."

"By the way," she says, "I almost told you I had another date— and a slightly better one with a second guy—but you were too busy telling me about your intrepid and handsome FBI agent boyfriend. I was too jealous to interrupt. I want details on how the date went last night. You don't think I had forgotten, did you?"

"One can hope."

"By the way, I think what you said to Mom was right on. But you still have to apologize and tell her you love her."

I sigh again and look at my watch. I can't believe we've shot the breeze for an hour and a half. My Americano is long gone. Klarissa takes another sip from her half-filled cup. This is like gulping for her. Her latte has to be ice cold by now. I like my coffee like I like my clues: hot. At the moment I have neither.

Klarissa tells me about her two post-Warren dates. I just laugh. I could never keep up with Klarissa even if I wanted to. Guys flock to her like Capistrano swallows to . . . well, I guess to Capistrano.

"You really okay with breaking up with Warren and everything?" I ask her. "I feel like I've been so preoccupied with this case that I haven't been a very good listener."

"Kristen, you've never been the greatest listener even before you landed on the Cutter Shark case."

She's right and we both chuckle.

"But I'm definitely okay on the Warren breakup," she continues.

"I should have let go and moved on years ago. We weren't going anywhere. We're too much alike, I guess."

"Hey, who broke up with whom?"

"What does it matter?"

"Well, I thought you told me he broke up with you for a hot little number who does research for the news desk. Kaylen says Warren called Jimmy and he says you broke up with him."

"Warren called Jimmy? You've got to be kidding me."

"Unless he or Kaylen have suddenly become pathological liars, then indeed he did. However, I probably wasn't supposed to say anything, so forget that I told you."

"Oh, so it's okay for my sisters to talk behind my back?"

"Well, I think Mom was involved in the conversation, too, so yeah, that probably makes it okay."

"Ha ha." She pauses and furrows her brow and then says, "I can't believe that jerk called my family."

So she isn't as over him as she wants us all to think. Letting go and moving on is always easier said than done in life.

"Well, you and he did date for five years. And for the record, I don't think you two are anything alike."

"I'm going to take that as a compliment," she says with a sniffle. "So thank you."

I can see the wheels turning in her mind. She's still perturbed.

"Man, love stinks," she says, breaking the pause.

"I kind of like that song," I say. "But you're way too young to be cynical about love. Mom says it's me who's going to grow old alone."

"She might be right," she responds, "but I'll be right there with you. Kaylen seems to be the only Conner girl who knows how to land a good man."

"No doubt about it," I answer.

"Well if 'love stinks' sounds too cynical, how about it 'hurts so good.'"

"C'mon baby, make it hurt so good," I croon back to her.

She clears her throat and picks up an imaginary microphone and belts out loud enough for everyone on the patio to hear: "'Cuts like a knife, but it feels so right.'"

I hold up my hand to interrupt: "You sound great—but that song hurts too much right now with what I'm working on."

"Oh, yeah," she says. "That Cutter Shark guy."

"Yeah, it seems to always come back to the Cutter Shark guy."

"You really think so?"

"Think so, what, Klarissa?"

"You really think I sound great?"

"Yeah, you always have," I say. "If this news reporter gig doesn't work, I guarantee you could dominate *American Idol* with your voice and looks—unless you make the judges jealous and get kicked off. However, that doesn't mean the coffee shop crowd doesn't think you're a little crazy. People are staring."

"'The first cut is the deepest,'" she sings, now playing an air guitar instead of holding an imaginary microphone.

"You're almost as good as Sheryl Crow, but again, not the best song for me right now," I interrupt. "But you are definitely on a roll."

"Almost as good?" she asks with a fake pout. Then she smiles big and says, "I told you about my not-so-hot dates, but you haven't told me anything about your scorching hot secret agent."

"He's FBI, not CIA."

"So you admit he's scorching hot!"

I reach over and grab her latte and take a big swallow. "About as hot as this."

"Hey, I'm not finished with that. But no matter what you say right now, I can tell from your voice you think he's scorching hot. I can also tell by the way you keep looking at your watch that you have got to go. We can catch up tomorrow. You can tell me *everything* then."

"Hey, I've got time now."

I fight the urge to look at my watch again. I really don't have time if I'm going to get any time for myself today. I have to hit the office for a couple hours, even though it is a gorgeous late spring Saturday. I'd like to get outside and run a few miles in daylight. I don't have any plans tonight and that suits me. I look her straight in the eyes, doing my darnedest not to look even a tad impatient to move on. I'm not sure I can pull that off.

"You get to the office," she says, seeing through my lie. "Let's go to dinner one night next week and we'll swap stories later."

"C'mon, Klarissa, I can talk now."

"No. We've been sitting here getting along for almost two hours, so let's not push it. Besides, I want to make sure I have your full attention when we talk."

She stands up and says, "Get going. You know, to work? Your home away from home?"

I stand and we give each other a tight hug. Wow. I don't think we've ever been this close. As I walk out the wrought-iron fence area she points a finger at me and serenades me all the way to my car:

"'Every time you go away, you take a piece of me with you!'"

As I start up my ten-year-old Miata that looks almost brand-new, I see her stride toward her Nissan GTR sports car—I'm pretty sure it cost more than I will make in a year—with all the grace and confidence of a runway model.

She's smiling but I still can't help but think she looks somehow vulnerable.

It's been two weeks since GiGi Baker, victim number three of the Cutter Shark, was murdered. Victim number three in Chicago. Victim number forty-nine according to Virgil. We've been on the case for almost two months. It feels like a decade. We still have only one active lead and it's not one we ferreted out through our own investigative work in Chicago. It was brought to us by the FBI on the first day we met with Major Reynolds. And the clue that our serial killer might be picking up many of his victims in recovery meetings? That may not be relevant any longer. Not all the women in the notebooks went to AA—and GiGi didn't. He must have another hunting ground. Why hasn't that come up?

We keep going over the same scraps of evidence. I wonder where he is and what he's up to until it threatens to overwhelm me. I think about my family instead. Specifically, Klarissa. We were supposed to get together for a few dinners but haven't connected since singing together at the coffee shop. She hasn't been at Sunday dinner the last two weeks either. She's always come to Jimmy and Kaylen's church out of family loyalty, but it isn't close to where she lives and she has a Methodist church around the corner that she likes. Mom doesn't like it, but I'm pretty positive Jimmy and Kaylen want her to be wherever she gets the most benefit. I feel like we're losing touch already.

Our most recent task force debate has been whether to keep so much manpower focused on attending AA meetings. Ever since my Jonathan debacle, enthusiasm and volunteer attendance is definitely down.

CUTS LIKE A KNIFE

I pull up to the security gate at the CPD Armory. The guard steps out, comes to my window to look at my ID, and has me write my employment number and sign my name on a form on his clipboard. When I'm done, I pull in to find a parking spot. I'm going to spend a couple hours on the shooting range.

———

"So how'd you ever pass the test to get on the force?" Sergeant Mike Peterman asks.

He's an old friend of my dad's. He used to be lead handgun trainer but he's semiretired now. He still comes a few days a week and gives individual instruction. In my case, he spent three hours with me. I think I've worn him out.

"On the last simulator drill, I think you killed ten civilians before getting yourself shot because you didn't count bullets."

"I wasn't that bad, was I?"

"Almost. However, your accuracy marks improved throughout the day on the static range. You're almost up to mediocre."

"Man, I thought switching to the Beretta was going to help."

"Nothing wrong with that Glock you were using."

"Is there any hope?"

"Definitely," Peterman says. "But mostly for the bad guys."

I give him an affectionate punch, but I don't return his smile. I'm mad. I've never been good with handguns, but this is ridiculous. My swirling mind is clearly getting in the way. Even more so than usual.

"Hey, don't get your feelings hurt," he says. "I'm just busting on you. Just come see me more often and I'll work with you. We'll get you up to the fiftieth percentile at least."

"Is that supposed to make me feel good?"

"Kristen, making you feel good isn't my job and it's not what you want. And right now, it's not what you need. You've got some work to do. You're on a dangerous assignment."

"You must be trading notes with Barry Soto."

"Barry Soto. Haven't heard that name in a long time. What's that tough old bird up to these days?"

"Apparently the same thing as you. Trying to keep me alive."

I've been sober for eighteen years, seven months, five days, and about seventeen hours."

I'm in a crowd pushing a hundred people at Holy Family Cathedral. I like these meetings because there's not nearly as much pressure to share here. If everyone said something we'd be here all night.

I'm looking for a killer and have two significant problems. First, I have no clue what my killer looks like. I'm not beating myself up over that. You don't kill fifty people like our Cutter Shark has unless you blend in. Second, the guy speaking has me mesmerized. It's Big Tony. I didn't know he was working the AA meetings. He tells a much better story than I do. With the way he checked off his years, months, and hours, he might have been Walter's sponsor. I'm supposed to keep one eye on my surroundings to look for anything out of the ordinary. But all I can hear right now is Scalia.

"I know those times to be a fact because I looked it up this morning," he continues. "I look it up every day. That way I never take for granted the gift of sobriety. It also reminds me to say a prayer for the soul of the man who helped me get my life back, get my wife back, get my kids back, get my job back.

"I hated the son of a . . . the son of a gun. He was constantly in my face. You'd have hated him, too. But man, did I need him. I don't know why he stuck with me, but he did. Even after I took a wild swing at him one night and broke his jaw."

I freeze in my seat. That might be a true story. Dad had his jaw broken at work. I was probably only eleven or twelve when it happened. The docs wired his mouth closed for almost three months. All he could do was drink liquids and pureed food through a straw. He was never that talkative anyway, unless the Bears were on TV, but we didn't hear a word out of him the whole time. First thing he said to us when they pulled the wires out was, "I needed to lose twenty pounds anyway." That was it and then life went back to normal, the event forgotten.

Did Big Tony throw a punch at Dad?

"I hated him for making me own up to my problems. And I loved him. Like a brother. Even if he did have a little Irish in him. I grew up in a big family with eight kids. But no brothers; seven sisters if you can believe that. He was my brother and I thank him for what he did for me. I light a candle for him every Sunday morning. I miss him. I pray you have a friend like him. So, my name is Tony, and I'm an alcoholic. God bless you."

He makes the sign of the cross and takes a seat. The meeting goes another hour. I forget to look for my killer. I don't hear anything else anybody says.

I don't even know what to pray after hearing that.

44

"Dinner tonight? My treat."

I look up from the conference room table where I've been reading the Factor Four notebook again—the city of Jacksonville for us mere mortals. It's Major Reynolds. It's been three weeks since our maybe date. We had an okay time. He did a lot of the talking, which was fine with me. He's an impressive guy. Graduated from Dartmouth with a BA in Political Science and English Literature, and then he got his law degree at Princeton. Quite the Ivy Leaguer. He never said it directly, but it sounded like there's a boatload of money in the family, so I get the feeling a public servant's salary really isn't going to hamper his lifestyle. Reynolds was polite and interesting. After that long work week, I'm not sure I reciprocated on being equally interesting.

"If it's your treat, does that make it a date?"

"Based on the lead up to last time we went out, it would help me if you could give me a hint if there's a right answer," he says with arched eyebrows. "If you'd like it to be a date, it's a date. If you don't want it to be a date, then it's just two work colleagues winding down after another long week."

"I'll tell you what," I say. "Give me a couple hours to finish paperwork and we'll figure out what it is later."

"I'm very comfortable with that," Reynolds says, smiling. "Now, just tell me what a couple hours means. It's five now. If I picked you up at seven, is that a couple of hours?"

"I'm heading downstairs to do some punching. Eight o'clock is probably a couple of hours."

"I'll be at your place at eight sharp."

Van Guten walks into the makeshift office as he says that. She looks at me appraisingly with just the hint of a smirk.

"You two come up with anything like a hot new lead?" she asks.

"Well if we did," Reynolds answers quickly, "you'd already have heard about it."

I nod to Van Guten and exit in my typical graceful fashion, bumping into the corner of the table hard enough to knock over an almost full cup of coffee someone left sitting in here and spilling it on papers all over the shared conference table. *Crud.*

Van Guten takes charge and orders the junior FBI officer who just entered the room to go get something to clean up the mess. I hoof it back to my cubicle.

———

"Hit it! Hit it! Hit it! I don't feel nothing. Nothing. Give me something. Hit it!"

I'm trying to remember why I thought Barry Soto was a nice guy. Just because he was friends with Dad? He is killing me. He wanted me to break a sweat, so he put me on a steep-grade climb at seven miles an hour on the treadmill. I think he forgot about me so I kept running. I did three and a half miles straight up Pike's Peak for thirty minutes. Then it was twenty minutes of core training, fifteen minutes of grappling, and then on to punches and kicks, which is where I'm at right now.

We've done the kicks. Now we're working on cross-body punches. He's holding up two pads and screaming at me to hit. Let me say, this part of the workout is a great workout all by itself. When you're already at the point of total muscle fatigue, it's torture.

"Don't stop. Hit! Don't you quit on me, Kristen. This guy is after you. He ain't quitting. Who's got the last punch? Hit! Don't you quit on me. Hit!"

When he shouts, "Okay, finished!" I lean over. I want to vomit. I think I taste acid in the back of my throat.

"Great job, honey. Great job. Great workout. Hey, straighten up. Get your lungs open. Breathe. Great job, Kristen. You still got some fight in you."

I'm gasping for air. My heart is racing. My legs and arms feel like pudding. I contemplate fainting. I would, but then I'd have to get up again. Soto brings a towel and wipes sweat off my face. My hands are on my knees again.

"Stand up straight," he says crossly. "Get your arms over your head. Breathe."

It's working. I think I'm going to live. I look up at the wall clock. Six-thirty. I'm going to have to get moving if I'm going to be ready to go out to dinner by eight. I was going to shower here, but I'm thinking I may throw a towel on my seat so I can hustle home and get cleaned up there.

"You really are doing great, Kristen."

"Mr. Barry, I think you are trying to kill me," I say.

"No, I'm the guy who's going to keep you alive," he says with a laugh. "Hope you don't have big plans because you are going to be really tired tonight."

I consider asking him to write a note that I can hand to Reynolds to establish that there's a reason I am the absolute worst date in the universe on a Friday night. I probably should have suggested tomorrow night anyway. I'm tired most Friday nights, whether or not I've worked out with Richard Simmons' evil cousin—the one with a bald head but plenty of hair poking out his ears and nostrils.

"Just my luck," I answer him. "I've got a date."

"Then you better get out of here," he chortles. "You ain't going to be awake past eleven."

We laugh and I head for the door.

"Kristen!" he calls right before I let the door shut behind me.

I turn back to him as he hustles up to me.

"No, I'm not doing another set of lunges," I say to him.

He squeezes my upper arm and says, "You could probably use it. But I had a quick question. Did Timmy ever hassle you?"

"Timmy? No, not really," I answer a little uncertainly.

"What's 'not really' mean?" he asks.

I'm wondering why he's asking. Did Timmy push another detective for a date too? "Well, this is kind of embarrassing to say, but he did ask me out. I thought he was a little forward, but no big biggie. Why?"

"I don't know how to break this to you, kiddo, but you aren't the only one he was a little forward with. I think he asked every female in the building with two legs to her credit to go out with him."

"So I really didn't mean as much to him as I thought?" I say with a laugh.

"Like I said, kid, I didn't know how to break it to you easy. But here's the thing: I had to let him go."

"Tough break for him, but it sounds like he asked for it."

"No doubt, he did," Soto says. "But bad for me, too. He was rough around the edges but the kid could fight. He's been the best assistant I've ever had."

"He take it okay?"

"What do you think?"

"Dumb question," I say with a laugh. "But why are you telling me all this?"

"I guess I wanted to hear that he was as bad as the boss said he was. That's why I don't feel so bad about canning him. But he worries me just a little, too. Not sure he's 100 percent right upstairs."

"Are any of us?"

"Not me, that's for sure. I'm an old man still trying to mix it up with young pups. But on Timmy, I think anyone who has had a bad experience with him needs to pay a little extra attention. There's a reason he's a great fight trainer . . . he likes to fight."

I turn the ignition on my Mazda and enjoy the sound of an engine that starts right up, strong and true. I think about Timmy on the way home. That guy was a force of nature. Fast. Strong. Great anticipation. And I think I know what Mr. Barry was really getting at . . . Timmy is dangerous. Not someone you want to make your enemy.

So you've never been married, never lived with a guy, and you have no steady boyfriend in your life. How does that happen with a drop-dead gorgeous, professional, young woman? Are the men in Chicago prone to blindness or is it more a matter of low IQ?"

We're back on the Magnificent Mile. This time it's Lawry's, an old-fashioned restaurant—I really can't imagine that the waitresses' mustard-yellow uniforms looked good in the '40s either—that features prime rib. They wheel a huge silver contraption that looks like a fancy outdoor grill to your table and carve your slab of cow right there in front of you. Reynolds looked a little surprised that I ordered the captain's cut. He shouldn't have told me he graduated from Dartmouth, one of those places where blue noses go to college. Knowing he's from high society makes me suspect that (a) he can afford whatever I want to order and (b) that I'm just a curiosity to him and that he's more comfortable with sophisticated women from his social strata, ones who order the petite cut.

I'm absolutely starving. I had a cup of coffee and half a bagel for breakfast, which wasn't a bad start to the day. But Don and I met with Blackshear and Martinez from 9 a.m. to 1 p.m. to review notes and assignments. Someone put an apple on my desk—a peace offering from Shelly, I suspect, the department administrative assistant who knows I am closing in on her for writing those notes for everyone to read—and that was all I had for lunch. I had a granola bar late afternoon, but that was six hours ago and I'm pretty sure all 220 calories got burned off in that excrutiating workout.

"They're both blind and have low IQs . . . and maybe Washington, DC political-types will say anything to flatter," I respond.

He gives me an admiring smile. "Not bad, Detective Conner."

"Even if I'm not an Ivy League girl?"

"Actually, that would be young lady or woman—never a 'girl.' That would not be a politically correct form of expression at an Ivy League institution of higher learning."

"It's taken you this long to figure out that I'm not PC?" I ask with an exaggerated roll of my eyes. "What was your GPA anyway?"

"I did well enough."

"That probably means real high. So did Princeton scholarship you to law school or did your daddy pick up the bill?"

"You know it's not politically correct to talk about money at the table," he says with a laugh. "But I will confess, I didn't pay a dime for law school. I had an uncle pay my way."

"So you have a rich uncle?"

"Nah—I think my Uncle Sam's completely broke now."

I pause and raise my glass of water in salute. "So you're not from a fabulously wealthy family?" I'm starting to regret my captain's cut.

"Not quite. But I didn't take you for a gold digger. Maybe I was wrong." He leans forward, mock serious. "Does this mean you won't go out with me on another date?"

"I didn't know that we had defined this as a date."

"Oh, you're right," he says. "Since it's your call, you still need to give me the verdict. And just so you know, there's no pressure. I'm a big boy and can take any answer you give me as long as it is yes."

I cut around the fat for another bite of melt-in-your-mouth prime rib. I don't cut all the fat off, however, and after carving just the right size, I put it in my mouth and chew slowly and thoughtfully. Eating such a bite would be a month-long project for Klarissa. I look up at him several times. He's a good sport and has an amused and patient expression on his face. I finally finish chewing and pat the corners of my mouth with a napkin. I take a sip of water. Slowly, of course. He rolls his eyes.

"I can wait you out, you know," he says. "I'm very good at watching and waiting."

"Okay then, it's a date," I say.

I can't believe I just said that. I don't usually give an inch. I must like this guy. Or maybe I'm the one looking at him as a curiosity. His watching and waiting statement did get my attention. I still haven't looked up where that is in the Bible.

"Sure I can't pour you a glass of wine to celebrate?" he asks with bottle poised.

"Not even a drop," I answer with a smile. "You should probably know I attend AA meetings."

"Nicely played, Detective Conner," he says, lifting his glass in return salute. "And you don't mind that I'm having wine by myself?"

"Why would I?"

"Well, some people do."

"Not me. My mom . . . well, she would. My older sis, the preacher's wife, probably not, but she's not going to drink herself. My younger sis, the most beautiful news reporter on the planet, sips wine the same way she eats meat. She burns more calories with the effort of letting it touch her lips than what she ends up ingesting. Or imbibing as the case may be."

He laughs and asks, "What about your dad?"

Before I can answer, a shadow crosses our table.

"Well isn't this a delightful surprise?" Dr. Van Guten asks. "Austin, how nice to see you. And you, too, Detective Conner."

Reynolds stands and gives Van Guten a peck on the cheek and holds out his hand to her companion, a tall, silver-haired gentleman who obviously has a good tailor. I stand up for introductions, suddenly self-conscious that my little black dress is probably ten years old—and wasn't that expensive when I bought it. Maybe it's aged well, I think to myself with a groan. I have on some cheap imitation pearls that Mom gave me for my birthday. I want to hide them and suddenly don't know what to do with my hands, but find my bearing in the nick of time, and hold out my hand boldly for introductions.

"How are you, sir?" Reynolds says to the suit.

"I'll be much better when you introduce me to your friend and call me Bob in a social setting," he answers smoothly.

Van Guten steps in before Reynolds can speak.

"Robert, this is Detective Conner. You might recognize her name from the reports we've been sending you."

He takes my hand and holds it in both of his.

"Of course I do. I already recognized her by name."

Van Guten frowns at her miss.

"I'm Kristen and it's nice to meet you . . . Bob."

I see Reynolds tense up, his eyes wide. He might be holding his breath. Van Guten purses her lips. Bob laughs in approval and gives my hand a kiss. That's a first.

"Kristen, this is Robert Willingham, the deputy director of the FBI," Reynolds says.

"Pleasure to meet you, sir, and nice to see you, *Leslie*."

She has made no move to shake hands or give me a polite buss on the cheek, nor ask me to call her by her first name. I see a shadow cross her eyes. I don't think she is happy with the attention *Bob* has shown me.

"I'm sorry we've interrupted your dinner," Willingham says magnanimously. "I'll look forward to seeing you tomorrow morning, Austin. And, Kristen, if I may be so bold, would you mind joining us?"

"Sure," I say.

"Sure you mind or sure you'll come?" Willingham asks me with a twinkle in his eyes.

"Bob, I'd be delighted to join you all wherever and whenever."

"Fabulous," he says. "Austin will tell you, Detective Conner, that the wherever and the whenever is tomorrow morning at seven."

I smile, but groan inside. Soccer season is over. I was really looking forward to sleeping in. Willingham and Van Guten follow the maître d', the paragon of patience, to their table. Leslie has on a little black dress, too, but hers really is little, showing what I figure has to be one expensive boob job. At least I hope so—no one should be born with all that up there and so little around the waist. I think the diamonds around her throat and wrist are real, however.

"I had a nice evening," Reynolds says.

This is always awkward. I decide to be bold and get it over with. I stand on tiptoes, put my hands on his shoulders, and give him a kiss on the cheek. I might have touched the corner of his lips. But just barely. I think he turned just a little. I notice he shaved before picking me up and he has good muscle tone that he hides under a suit jacket.

"I had a nice evening, too," I say quickly. "Thanks again for a great dinner. See you in the morning."

If he's disappointed that I haven't invited him in, he doesn't show it. If he's disappointed, he'll also have to get over it. I enter my apartment, give him one more smile, close the door slowly, and then turn the dead bolt and put the chain lock in its groove.

I look at the tiny red light flashing on my phone. Three missed calls. Klarissa, Dell, and a number I don't recognize. There are three messages. I sigh. I don't want to deal with messages tonight. I'm beat. I head back to the bathroom to wash my face and hit the speaker button as I call my voicemail inbox. I'm a pretty good multitasker.

"Hi stranger," Dell says. "I would like to talk sometime. Would love to see you. I miss you. I think I'll be at church Sunday morning. See you then."

I hit three for delete. Mom will be happy. Kaylen, the most sensitive soul in the universe, will invite him to dinner without considering my feelings. I need to head that off at the pass. Hopefully that discussion won't be as rough as the one I had with Mom.

"Just got in . . . where are you?" Klarissa asks me on the next message. "Oh, I forgot, you're out with Agent Dreamboat. Coffee in the morning? You can tell me everything. Call me late if you want or just send me a text. Let me know. I want to talk. Love you, Big Sis."

I hit delete.

"Thanks a lot for getting me fired," the third voice says with a seething anger. "I was hitting on you in your dreams." I hear the phone slam hard enough that I jump. I hit delete quickly—not smart, should have saved it. I couldn't testify in a court of law that it's Timmy—but it's Timmy. The Cutter Shark isn't enough. I have another dangerous enemy.

I shake my head, go find my cell phone, and send a quick text to Klarissa:

Yes, had nice date 2night. Got called into office 4 early meeting @7. Will call u after. Maybe coffee then. Luvs and hugs. K

Face lotion on, I gargle and floss. I let my electric toothbrush do all the work while I check the corners of my eyes for lines. I do have decent skin.

I really ought to do something about my wardrobe, though. I put my toothbrush on the charger, turn off the light, and go straight for my closet. I pull out the little black dress and throw it in the wastebasket to force myself to buy something new. Then I give myself two-to-one odds that I'll pull it out and hang it back up in the morning.

As I fall into bed, I muse over the fact that I met a legend in law enforcement tonight. Robert Willingham—Bob to me—was involved in the TWA Flight 847 hijacking in 1985. I read about him in a case study in a class at NIU. He was also the behind-the-scenes hero who did the legwork that led to the secret indictment of Hezbollah's Imad Mughiniyah. He was the lone dissenter when Janet Reno sent the tanks in against the Branch Davidians in 1993. He got demoted and was exiled from the Bureau for a couple years. That was a case study I wrote about on "group think."

I wonder if Chicago PD or FBI will get credit if we apprehend the Cutter Shark. When we apprehend him. Then I must have fallen asleep with no reading, no crossword, no prayer.

Because next thing I know, my alarm is crowing like a rooster.

THE CHITOWNVLOGGER
MAY 16, 2:00 A.M.

W elcome to the jungle; watch it bring you to your knees...," Axl wails. The words "HOT FLASH IN CUTTER CASE" flashed on-screen ten times. Johnson liked that. He was back in his desk chair, crumpled sweater—a new ketchup stain—running his fingers through a mop of silvery white hair one more time as he started.

"I hope you are sitting down, my friends and loved ones in Chicagoland. A little birdie has told me, your ChiTownVlogger, that the Cutter Shark has been very bad and very busy. I wonder why our esteemed city government and crack police force aren't telling us everything they know about our most famous resident? Sorry, Oprah. You are now so yesterday.

"Mayor Doyle and Commissioner Fergosi have a secret they're not telling us. Only your ChiTownVlogger has the sources—and digs deep enough—to give you the real scoop. Here it is, folks. This isn't the Cutter Shark's first rodeo. That's right. You heard it here first. Chicago is not his first city. Serial killers can be such pigs. Our Sultan of Slice has led us on with promises that we really were different than all the others. Only we now find we're the latest in a long line of love-sick and jilted lovers at his various ports of call. I just find it curious that no public official—*not* the mayor, *not* the chief of police, *not* even the head of sanitation and sewage, has seen fit to tell us that we're his fourth or fifth city!

"Who's the birdie whispering in my ear? Wouldn't you like to know, Mayor Doyle? In this day when Big Brother Government feels enabled—or is it ennobled?—to trample on our fundamental freedoms as private citizens, I'm sure the mayor will simply ask one of his cronies in the police department or at the FBI to find a name. I'll bet they put together a task force to plug that leak in city hall—or is it from the Second Precinct?

"I just wish they'd work as hard finding the killer.

"Check back often. The jungle is getting even wilder than we thought. Anything you need to know you'll hear here, from the ChiTownVlogger."

Johnson smiled as the report ended. *I'll get three million hits on this. CNN will be calling for an interview in fifteen minutes.*

He was dead wrong.

A producer for CNN called five minutes after the story was posted.

CUTS LIKE A KNIFE

47

Honestly, I'm not interested in all the reasons we can't find this guy," Willingham says. "And I don't care to hear again all you've done so far. It's not working. I want to know what you're going to do differently today. And tomorrow. This guy is going to hit again—and we don't know how soon because his timing has changed—so we've got a near crisis on our hands. The local media is out of control, and they've yet to find out we're dealing with a multi-theater phenomenon. We can thank God for small blessings. You think the rabble out in the parking lot trying to sneak into off-limit areas of your building right now is a hassle? Wait until every journalist from Tokyo to Tel Aviv shows up. From personal experience, you don't want that happening."

The deputy director of the FBI takes off his rimless glasses, pauses dramatically, and looks at each person in the room, right in the eyes. I feel like he's trying to peer into my soul. I don't dare think of a sarcastic response to his comments. I'm afraid he would read my mind. Van Guten breaks the silence.

"This is a fascinating case, Deputy Willingham," she says. "Honestly, with the break in pattern, I suspect our friend might be going into an acceleration cycle. I hate to sound crass, but that's not always a bad thing. That's when organized killers get careless, make mistakes, and start leaving clues. None of which he has done to date."

Despite her best efforts, Leslie did sound crass.

"Another death is never acceptable," she continues. "But if it leads to our capturing him, it clearly beats the alternative of him just disappearing."

"Disappearing? What are you saying, Dr. Van Guten?" Willing-ham asks.

"I know this isn't what you want to hear after all you've been through," she continues with a pointed glance at Reynolds, "but there is evidence that some serial killers burn themselves out at the accelera-tion stage and return to a normal life."

"Really?"

Did I say that out loud? *I did.* I have never heard that before and here I am a college graduate with a degree in criminal justice. And I'm about halfway done with a master's degree.

"Let's put it this way," she says directly to me. "Many serial kill-ings have gone unsolved with no record of similar patterns in the future. Did all these killers die? I doubt it. A few have quietly sur-rendered to the police; we suspect others have been killed due to their dangerous lifestyle or committed suicide; and yes, we believe some have gone underground, never to be heard from again. I correlate the organized killers who go underground with the general psychopathic population."

"How so?" Willingham asks.

"A lot of people have never heard—and probably wouldn't believe it if they did—that psychopaths cure themselves as they age. Starting at age twenty-one, approximately 2 percent of all psychopaths go into remission every year. In other words, the older a psychopath lives to be, the more likely he—or she—is to become a functional member of society." She drones on, but I stop listening.

I don't quite believe the "cure themselves" angle. How could I? I attend AA and am pretty well versed in the principle that you have to acknowledge a Higher Power. That, and the fact that I've gone to church all my life, means I believe we need the help of God and other people in order to get better. Not sure I practice my beliefs like I should, but I do believe it.

AA meetings never cease to amaze me. I'm not an alcoholic, but it does seem kind of natural to be there. *Hi, I'm Kristen and I have an anger problem.* No, that's distancing the problem from myself. *Hi, I'm Kristen and I'm an angerholic. Started small, but man I am all in, these last few months in particular.* When I talk about my anger, not by name of course, everyone in the groups I've attended perk up and think I'm talking about vodka or cocaine. I wonder if my anger will be cured with age. Gray, the guy from Internal Affairs, suggested I'm heading for a burnout stage. That's a scary thought.

We're at the State Building on Wacker, just south of the Chicago River and on the north edge of the Loop. I like meeting at the FBI's place better than at our precinct. They have carpet on the floors; we have linoleum. Their conference room table is made of mahogany; ours is made from Formica. Their chairs are covered in soft leather; ours might have had cloth completely covering foam at one time. They have art on the wall; we have rust-colored water stains. Their ceilings have geometric flourishes and trims. Half our ceiling tiles have at least one major chunk missing or some discoloring we'd rather not investigate.

But what makes meetings at their place infinitely better than ours is that they have a cool space-age machine that grinds coffee beans and brews an individual cup of the freshest joe in the world. Oh, and they have real half-and-half. As in liquid. The fresh bagels and lite cream cheese are a nice extra.

An attractive young lady, young now being anyone that doesn't have three or higher as the first number of their age, walks in and stands at the FBI deputy director's left shoulder, waiting for him to acknowledge her. I wouldn't interrupt him either. I didn't refer to her in my mind as a girl, so maybe I am becoming more politically correct. I'm not sure that's a good thing.

"Thanks for the insights, Dr. Van Guten," Willingham says. "I think you might have thrown us all for a loop on that one. Bottom line, we've got to catch this guy. I hope it doesn't take our killer entering a period of frenzy to do so. But I sure as heck hope this guy doesn't go underground. As much pain and suffering as he has wrought on this world, I want us to be able to tell some families that we have apprehended the man who killed their son or daughter."

"He's killed men?" I ask.

That was for sure out loud. I blurt it out quickly, interrupting again. Is my name Chatty Cathy?

There's a pause in the room among the FBI personnel. Zaworski looks up at Willingham and then Reynolds sharply. Willingham makes a church steeple with his forefingers. He looks at me and I can't tell if he's mad or amused.

"What gives, Bob?" Zaworski asks.

"At least three instances," Willingham answers.

"That's not in any of the reports Virgil has generated," I say, my voice cracking.

How come everyone else can speak with poise and modulation and I sound like a blathering fool? Willingham looks at me, puzzled.

"That's Detective Conner's nickname for PV, Project Vigilance," Reynolds answers for me.

Willingham narrows his eyes. Now I'm sure he's mad. Then he smiles at everyone in the room. "Virgil. I love it." He lets out a loud laugh and everyone joins him except Van Guten. She has the start of a smile on her lips. Might be a sneer.

"What gives, Bob?" Zaworski repeats. "Are you holding out on us?"

"Believe me, Captain Zaworski, I want you to have anything and everything you need to catch this guy. But you and your team do know that if we gave you every bit of data PV . . . uh, Virgil . . . has generated, you would have ten times the material to sift through than the 1,400 pages we've already handed you. In addition to that, we have another thousand pages on three unsolved murders that he might have committed but that we can't definitively correlate. We believe he has killed three men, all of them homosexual. But all three murders predate Denver when the pattern we see emerging in Chicago began."

"Deputy Willingham, I think I'm to blame on this," says Van Guten. "I think it was an oversight on my part to stress that the non-isolated event stream notebooks are thorough, but in no way complete. I hadn't even thought of the male angle in years. We believe it was an experimental stage in his life that he did not pursue."

"I don't care what you forgot and who is to blame," Zaworski storms. Van Guten turns a deep shade of red. "But I do care that the FBI has been busting our chops over lack of progress and not indicated that there are more options we should be considering. This sicko has been in your jurisdiction a lot longer than ours. Make sure we know what you know."

The tension at the table is palpable.

I break it by saying loudly, "I think I know one of the option areas we need to be considering."

Everyone is suddenly staring at me. I always have great things to say in meetings—but never seem to think of them until after the meeting is over. I think I'm in shock that I now hold the floor.

"Well, you gonna tell us or do we have to play twenty questions?" Zaworski growls.

"It's his pickup grounds," I say. "We've focused everything on AA meetings. But only twenty-nine of the forty-seven victims prior to Chicago attended AA. One out of three here have. He's finding his victims in other places."

"Any ideas?" Reynolds asks.

"Not yet," I answer. "But can you ask Virgil to go back and see if there are any other settings that show up more than once?"

"Consider it asked," Van Guten answers for him. "Off the top of my head I know that bars will show up. I know he bought opera tickets somewhere and met a victim there. Not sure that happened again. But nothing else has seemed statistically valid. Oh, he has found several victims in health clubs. Beyond that I can't think of anything. But I think Detective Conner's idea warrants some further study."

"Some immediate further study," Willingham interjects.

"My apologies, Tom," Willingham says to Zaworski. "If it seems like I'm pointing a finger at the CPD for lack of progress, let me assure you, I'm even more disappointed with my team's failure to generate anything here."

If my eyes don't deceive me, both Van Guten and Reynolds have a slightly red coloring on their faces.

"We're on Conner's train of thought. And we at the FBI are going to get better and sharper in the days ahead or make some wholesale changes of our own. That brings up something else I need to mention."

Zaworski's eyes narrow.

"I'm bringing in another eight street soldiers from Fairfax. But we need more local investigators in the field as well. Reading the reports I see you've only got eight detectives, another sixteen officers, and maybe seven or eight tech and forensic specialists full-time on this. I question whether your team is big enough."

"We've got our best on the case," Zaworski responds, unruffled.

He barely glances in my direction. Other than Zaworski, I'm the only CPD present at this cozy little meeting. He's probably wondering how I ended up invited to this high-level power breakfast. I also get the feeling he's wondering if I'm really one of his finest.

"And you're not factoring in that we have another hundred and fifty officers and staffers working the case part-time. All told, we're working the equivalent of sixty-one full-timers every day since the first murder. I know that for a fact because I just came out of budget meetings."

"When the Green River killer moved from Washington to Missouri, the Kansas City Police Department had the equivalent of fifty-nine full-timers per week," Willingham quickly rattles off. "New York City had thirty-four officers, not counting background support, on Son of Sam for an entire year. Los Angeles created a whole unit that ran for a decade for the Zodiac Killer. Your Cutter Shark makes those guys look like amateurs."

"Help us out with some leads and I'll put the whole Second Precinct on this," Zaworski answers, his face red, his eyes flashing. "We have three murders and a very limited number of clues. We're sifting the same bag of dirt over and over and over—and there isn't any gold in it. I'd put more detectives on this if I had any real work to give them."

"Captain, I admire you and your track record," Willingham responds. "But I'll also echo what I've been suggesting for the past hour. Whatever it is we're doing, isn't working. Let's do something different. Anything. Start there. There's something you could be doing that you haven't thought of yet."

Willingham pauses and looks at his aide who has been waiting patiently at his side for ten minutes.

"Yes, Megan?"

"Thought you should see this, sir."

He takes off his glasses and reads a printout she hands to him. It takes him about thirty seconds. He hands the sheet of paper back to Megan. He pinches the bridge of his nose as he looks at each of us around the table.

"Anyone here ever heard of the ChiTownVlogger?" he asks.

"A hack journalist," Zaworski answers. "Sees himself as a friend and defender of the people. Used to be mainstream but now does some Internet report. He peddles every rumor and conspiracy theory associated with city government and he hates Mayor Doyle. He thinks Doyle got him fired from WCI. He's got enough of a following that everyone in the city knows who he is. What's he done this time?"

"Let's just put it this way," Willingham says. "Brace yourself for a media invasion like you've never experienced before. I'm guessing that while we've been talking, 90 percent of Chicago now knows that this guy he named the Cutter Shark is a multitheater phenomenon. He posted a report that specifically listed Chicago as the latest of many cities. Oh . . . and he went live on a CNN Headline News interview an hour ago—they'll be airing that once every thirty minutes all day."

"Doing anything fun today?" Zaworski asks me.

We're in the elevator going down to the parking garage, which starts two levels below the street entrance to the State Building.

"Not really," I answer.

"I was going out on Lake Michigan with my wife, daughter, son-in-law, and three grandkids."

"Sounds nice," I say. "What kind of boat you got?"

"I've got the Bayliner Buccaneer. It's a thirty-five-footer that can sleep all of us. My one indulgence through the years. Know anything about boating?"

"Not a thing."

"I won't bore you then."

"I wasn't bored a bit, sir. And I'm glad you get to go out with the family."

"Not going to happen for me," he says. "I'll call my wife on my way over to the mayor's office."

"Uh-oh. Will that get you in hot water?"

"She isn't going to like it, but she'll understand. We've been married forty years and a good part of the reason we're still married is she understands a cop's life well enough not to complain or waste her time getting bitter and trying to lay guilt trips on me when plans get messed up."

"Bummer."

Bummer? I've got to get better at this professional interaction thing. I'm not looking for a promotion for a long time, if ever. My goal was always to be a detective. It's what I am and it's what I love doing. Some teachers teach their whole career. Others want to be principals. I think I'm the be-a-teacher kind of detective.

"The mayor and chief aren't going to like what I've got to tell them either," he says, now with a preoccupied tone. "And they aren't going to be nearly as understanding as my wife," he says with a forced laugh. "The city is nearly broke and they want us to do more with less—'work smarter not harder' is the phrase they used. Willingham wants us to work with more. In this case, as mad as I am at him, he is probably right."

The car stops, a bell rings, the doors open, and we exit the elevator and give each other a nod as we go opposite directions for our cars.

"Conner," he says.

I stop and look back at him.

"Yes, sir?"

"Do something fun with your family today. Life is about to get miserable."

I nod awkwardly.

"In case you were wondering," he says, "that's not a suggestion. It's an order."

I'll pick the kids up at six," I say to Kaylen for the sixth time.

I'm ready to hang up. I've got a few more calls to make and I need to think. I'm driving from the State Building to the Second Precinct. A whole lot of dynamics were going on this morning at FBI headquarters that I didn't understand.

"Are you sure, Kristen? Jimmy and I were just talking about all you're going through right now. Life's been so crazy this past year for all of us, we haven't been there for you. This Cutter Shark thing is so scary. What happens to people that they become monsters?"

"Hey, Kaylen, I'm actually doing okay today and I want to take the kids out and have them spend the night. I miss them! You and Jimmy do something fun, you know, get out the old Scrabble board or maybe play some Parcheesi. Jimmy can pop popcorn over an open fire in the back yard and lead Mitch Miller choruses."

"Ha ha," she says with not even a scintilla of humor in her voice.

"Hey," I add, "if you've got other ideas, maybe even romantic ideas, you're adults and you're even married, so have at it."

"You are so dead when you get here, Kristen," she says. She pauses and continues, "You know, that's probably not the best choice of words right now."

Then she starts crying. I immediately swear to myself I'm not going to join her in crying. Kaylen cries easily. I don't. This Cutter Shark guy is a shadow over the whole city. He's getting inside people's minds. Either that or big sis is about to finally own up that she's preggo.

"Kaylen," I say as I bump into the parking lot, "I'm sorry I have to sign off but I'm at the office. We will talk more later. I promise. But I have to run now."

I sit in my car for five minutes, trying to get my thoughts focused on what I can get done in the next hour or two so I can obey Captain's orders and do something fun with family. I crank up a classic rock station and listen to Chicago belt out "25 or 6 to 4." I once heard a deejay earnestly explain that the "25 or 6 to 4" phrase was just something nonsensical someone in the group came up with at the end of a studio session so they could go home. Nonsensical? Gee, do you think so?

Whether it was the peppy beat or a flare-up of my sarcasm gene, I now have my game face on and head into the building. I nod at the officers working the front desk and sign in. I eschew the elevator and jog up four flights of loud, metal stairs. The floor is reasonably quiet this Saturday morning but I can hear voices here and there. I get to my cubicle. There is another yellow sticky note in the middle of my computer screen:

ROSES ARE RED
VIOLETS ARE BLUE
DOES THE FBI STUD
REALLY LOVE YOU?

Someone is going to pay for this. Shelly, if it's you, leaving an apple on my desk is not going to get you out of this.

It takes me almost an hour to stop fuming about the Post-it note and get my mind fully on task. In terms of progress on the case, no one would be able to tell the difference.

Dear God, something has to give. Please give us a breakthrough.

A lot of people have all sorts of questions about God. I guess I took to heart early on that faith should be childlike—or it isn't faith. So I don't try to figure everything out even if I have a few specific questions, like the "once saved, always saved" debate I ponder every now and then. I'm simple-minded. I believe in God with all my heart. But right now my real question is why he doesn't seem to hear my prayers.

49

May 16, 2:00 a.m.

Can you say breakthrough? Everybody is talking about me now. Not just local media and an occasional mention on national outlets. The world is talking about me. And the reporters are finally getting some of the details right. I like that. I want my legacy preserved. I'm tired of writing in my journal. It doesn't look right in pencil, and when I write in pen there are smudges. The whole thing looks like a mess. I wanted it to look neater. So I'm not going to do it anymore. I can't let anyone read it now anyway. It's better the way it's unfolding, slowly. Give the media some juicy details to get everybody hot and bothered—but not enough details that they would ever be able to apprehend me. There are gaps they will never fill in.

I hate that ChiTownVlogger guy—contacting him might have been a mistake. He wants too much glory for himself. He's a typical media hack. He thinks the story is about him. But this story is about me. He'll get his fifteen minutes of fame and then they'll forget him—but they'll always remember me. I hated when he gave me the Cutter Shark name. Even if it is catchy. I have to admit, he does get results. He's already been on Fox, CNN, and the BBC.

But I will not tolerate it if he continues to speak caustically of me. I will show him the true meaning of cutting. So if he wants any more exclusive news tidbits—and if he wants to continue breathing—he will show me the respect I deserve.

This vlogger—Allen Johnson—is one messed up individual. He has an acute sense of paranoia. He thinks the mayor got him fired and monitors all his electronic communications. But it won't be the mayor monitoring his emails and Internet activity now. No, the FBI has to have taken on that particular task. That's why I've already sent him another message via the old-fashioned route: the post office.

I'm always one step ahead.

The most important thing is I'm building my legacy and receiving some long overdue fame. I have been punished with obscurity because of my own brilliance. The only thing that will knock me from the lead spot of all news programming is if some some teenage actress gets drunk and runs over a paparazzi again.

Two weeks ago, GiGi was a perfect one-month schedule behind Sandra. But what if I decided Candace wasn't a mulligan? That would mean I could go back to work this weekend and be perfectly on schedule.

I like the way I'm thinking! I make the rules, so I can bend them or break them. At will. Track that, FBI psychologist!

It would be good to wait for a full moon, but the pressure is building. I know myself too well. I can't wait. And I have a date tonight . . . even if she doesn't know it yet.

This city is going to explode when they find out who she is.

She's going to explode when she finds out who I am!

Freedom. It is hard for average, normal, pedestrian individuals to cherish that like I do. I once was a prisoner. Now I'm free. Free to live life to the fullest. Free to soar.

I told you why I can't go out tonight. I've already got a date with my adorable niece and fabulous nephew. Even if I hadn't made plans, I'm not ready to go out two nights in a row."

"And why would that be?"

I shift into fifth gear and drop the phone off my shoulder. I've got to get a hands-free earpiece. I fumble around with my right hand while keeping both eyes on the road. I'm doing seventy-five in a sixty-five zone and Saturday afternoon traffic is surprisingly heavy.

"Are you still there?" Reynolds is asking as I get the phone back up to my ear.

"I am."

"You haven't answered my question."

"Sorry, I dropped my phone. But you know what, Austin? I don't think I'm going to answer anyway."

"That hurts. However, you did use my first name, I believe for the first time, so I'm not going to complain."

"I'm honored, Major."

"Listen, I think it's great that you've got your sister's kids tonight. But you've got three hours before you pick them up and knowing you when you get working, you haven't had anything to eat since you poked that bagel around your plate this morning. Meet me for a late lunch on your way home."

"I've got to get cleaned up and do some housework."

"You've got to eat lunch sometime. We'll just sit down for an hour."

"I'm thinking."

"Keep thinking and see if this helps. There's a great little Philly cheesesteak place near the corner of Clark and Belmont."

"After eating a pound of cow last night, for some reason the thought of a sandwich piled with meat is not making me lean in your direction."

"There's a vegetarian place a couple blocks away. The Chicago Diner. Are you still thinking? Does that help?"

"Okay, I'll meet you there, but two things."

"Name them."

"First, I buy my own meal. Strike that. I buy both meals. Just make sure it doesn't go over twenty bucks between us because they don't take credit cards and that's all the cash I've got."

"Sounds good. I like a strong, independent woman and I can eat on a budget. Been there, done that. What's number two?"

"Forty-five minutes, tops, is all I've got. I have to have some down time at my place before I pick up the kids."

"Doesn't sound as good as number one, but you got it."

———

Lunch was great. Austin is a good conversationalist and the more I relax with him, the more fun we have.

The Chicago Diner is vegetarian and organic, but that's not the same thing as low calorie and small portions. I was in the mood for an omelet so I ordered up one with tofu bacon, caramelized onions, asparagus, olives, fresh basil, and feta "cheese." I get after Klarissa for never finishing her food, but I left half the omelet uneaten and didn't touch the potatoes or whole-wheat toast. I did drink one of their juice mixes with carrots and apples and wheat germ. I may wear my love beads and Birkenstocks tonight.

Agreement number two was that I had to be out of there in forty-five minutes. I should have stuck to the plan. We went twenty-five minutes over. That's when things went downhill in a hurry. I went to pay the bill at the cash register and was a couple bucks short. Austin dropped my twenty back in my purse and pealed off a ten and a twenty from a pretty fat wallet. He told the cashier to give the change to our waitress.

As we turned toward the door, Austin put his hand lightly on the back of my shoulder, which shouldn't have taken me by surprise, but it did. I know I stiffened and reddened a little. But I went beet red when I looked up to see Dell standing ten feet from us. His mouth was slightly open in surprise and he was still as a statue. I froze, too. I hadn't talked to him in . . . what? Two or three weeks? He had called and left messages at least twice. I never returned either call. I finally snapped out of my shock and walked forward. Dell seemed to recover, too.

"Well, Kristen Conner, it's good to see you again," he said.

"Hi, Dell. How you doing?"

"Not bad? You?"

"Dell, I'm Austin," Austin said, interrupting to introduce himself, for which I was grateful. They shook hands.

"A pleasure to meet you."

"Yeah, you too, Dell."

Reynolds does the same thing as Klarissa with people's names. Repeating them, so he remembers them. That's why he's a major.

As we exited the restaurant, I looked back in and Dell was sitting down at the counter. Austin wanted to know who Dell was. I told him I didn't have time to get into that now and almost sprinted to my car. I was embarrassed. I felt like some of the muck in my life splattered on my relationship with Austin.

I didn't feel good about myself the whole drive home. No one can make me reciprocate romantic interest—not even with my mom's assistance—and I have no qualms with that. But I was pretty abrupt when I told Dell it was over. Maybe I could've done something to soften the blow. Nah. Dell made that impossible. Stop beating yourself up.

I used to think of myself as a very nice person. Christian. Caring. Interested. Ready to get involved and help. Conflict—even when it's not your fault—has a way of making you pull back and retreat within yourself. It does for me. Plus there's all the conflict in my life that is my fault. A lot of it is little and petty, no big biggie. But I still don't feel good about myself.

I think you are supposed to vacuum before you dust. Vacuuming stirs up dust, so it undoes—at least in part—what you've just got done doing. That's what Mom always told me, anyway. I always remember her words of wisdom after I've dusted first. Resigned, I wind up the cord on my vacuum cleaner and push it in the back corner of the small coat closet in my front hallway. The thought robs me of some of the satisfaction I feel for having a top-to-bottom clean apartment—even if I never get to the cobwebs in the corners of the crown molding.

I still feel much better than I did after seeing Dell at the Chicago Diner. Clean bathroom; clean kitchen; clean everything. I got two loads of laundry done, which is all my laundry. I've got a pile of warm whites on my bed. Won't take me more than fifteen minutes to fold them and put them away. Even my desk is cleared in my second bedroom. Okay, the top right drawer will barely shut with all the junk mail and unpaid bills I've still got to sort through, but the clutter is out of sight. Fresh sheets are on the spare beds for the kids.

Kendra's eight now and doesn't want to sleep in the same room with James. James has trouble going to sleep by himself unless he's in his own room at his own house. I'll whisper in Kendra's ear to lie down in the bed next to him for twenty minutes until he falls asleep. Sometimes that even works and then she runs over to my room and jumps in bed with me. Once she fell asleep before James, and I left her to sleep in the guest room with him all night. She was so hurt and distraught, she wouldn't talk to me the whole drive back over to her house. So if she does fall asleep with James tonight, I'll pick her up and carry her over to my bed before I drift off.

But sometimes neither kid can fall asleep. Then I let both of them come over to my bed. One of my few extravagances in life is having a king-size bed, which means there should be plenty of room for the three of us. It doesn't quite work out in real life, however. James never stops moving. He wiggles. He tosses and turns. He gets sideways and starts using his feet to claim new territory. He is fundamentally a sprawler. I end up on the very edge of my bed, one arm draped over the side. Kendra ends up snuggled tight against my back, her breath on my neck. Sir James ends up with two-thirds of the bed.

Clothes put away, I lace up my Nikes and head out the door.

———

I do a fairly hard 5K run in just a little under thirty minutes. Back in my college days I could run a 10K in thirty minutes. That's five-minute miles. Back in my college days, I barely noticed my oft-repaired right knee either. The knee is barking at me again. Is that what happens when you turn thirty?

I strip down and take a glorious fifteen-minute shower. I'm not going to have time to dry my hair if I'm going to pick the kids up at six. Doesn't matter. It's in the upper seventies and I'll just pull it back in a ponytail and let the wind do whatever it wants to with it. My niece and nephew love me, regardless of what my hair looks like. I put on a jean skirt, just a little shorter than Mom and Kaylen approve of, but a couple inches longer than Klarissa, the beauty queen, wears. I pull a black cotton, sleeveless shirt over my head and look in the mirror. It used to be half a size tighter than Mom's standards of modesty—which are pretty strict, I might add—but I notice that I really have lost weight. Maybe Lloyd had a point. I was already small up top—I think I've disappeared now. Looking for a serial killer for a couple months has been tougher than I thought. No wonder Major Reynolds is doing his part to try and put some meat back on my bones. He's asking me out for mercy dates.

I grab my purse and phone and head down the stairs to my car. Two missed calls. One is from Don. That's unusual for a Saturday. He's a hard worker, but he is also able to separate the job from family time with Vanessa and his kids. The other is from a number that I don't recognize. It's not a Chicago area code.

I key in my password and listen to the first message. "Kristen, this is Don. Wanted to catch up with you before Monday. I hear you've figured out a way to get invited to the executive task force meetings. I'm impressed—and a little surprised—by your strategy of dating one of the big dogs. Don't forget us little people on your way to the top. Hey, I'm kidding, so don't get your nose bent out of shape. I do want to hear what was said, though."

What a jerk. I know he's joking. But sometimes when people tease, there's some real feeling packed into it. I get accused of being paranoid, but anyone would hear a barb in his message. But it doesn't make me as mad as the next.

"Kristen, this is Dr. Van Guten. I stopped by your cube over at CPD. You were already gone." She paused, as if to emphasize that I should have still been at work on a beautiful Saturday afternoon if she was. "I was talking to Director Willingham and at the risk of being rude, we wanted to make sure you know that we take this business with the ChiTownVlogger very seriously. We don't want anything that was said in today's meeting being repeated over at CPD outside of direct task force members—or with anyone in the media. That includes WCI-TV and family members. Just in case you are wondering, this isn't Reynolds' call. This is straight from the deputy director. Call me on my cell if this isn't clear or you have any questions."

At the risk of being rude. If this isn't clear? She's accusing me of sharing secrets from our investigation with Klarissa?

God, I know that vengeance is yours, but I want to pop her in the mouth so bad.

———

I thought the kids were spending the night. Maybe they're moving in with me for good. Both have suitcases on wheels.

"I'll have them to church on time," I say in response to Kaylen's admonition that I do so for the third or fourth time. I suck it up, since to be fair, I have been late more than once.

Jimmy slams the trunk shut. The kids share a seat belt on the passenger side. Kaylen looks worried. She always looks worried when the kids get in my car.

"I'll drive safe and slow," I say to Kaylen with a stern voice.

She laughs and bends over and hugs my neck.

"Are you eating?" she says. "You're getting as thin as Klarissa."

"Same as always . . . everything in sight," I answer.

"We're either going to have to feed you more or you're going to have to cut back on your crazy workouts."

I've never noticed Mom's tone of voice in her before. I hear it this time. I roll my eyes at her, blow her a kiss, and we're off to Chuck E. Cheese's for lukewarm pizza and a scary mechanical gorilla singing oldies.

I'm glad the top is still down. It's too noisy to talk to the kids and I still need to cool down after hearing Van Guten's message. I'm hoping Jimmy and Kaylen didn't see how angry I was. I shouldn't have listened to my voice messages before picking up my angels.

52

May 16, 7:30 p.m.

I need to change plans. I don't like that. If I had wanted something different to happen I would have planned it that way in the first place. The Cutter Shark is not happy. And I'm not happy that I'm using that stupid name the ChiTownVlogger gave me. Bad name begets bad name. This is my story, not his.

My tool kit is carefully packed. Hypodermics—check. Axe— check. Carving knife—check. Butcher knife—check. Scalpel— check. Bolt cutter—check. Whetstone for sharpening—check. Rubber suit, nylon gloves, and boots—check. Plastic bag to discard items—check. Wet wipes—check.

Where is she? This was my special night. Mine. What about me and my feelings? She has never shown an ounce of consideration. She is all about herself. She is selfish. I hate country music, but I like the song that big-buck Okie sings, "I wanna talk about me." Me too. I want to talk about me. And I want everyone else to talk about me too! For once.

Okay. Time for Plan B. What to do, what to do, what to do? Abort? Wait and see if she returns? Settle for someone else? I hate to settle. It's never as satisfying.

I'm going to use Occam's razor; when in doubt over two possible explanations, go with the simplest one. I'm in doubt as to whether I should press forward or fall back. What's simplest? Press on. Because despite a setback that would crush the spirit of lesser individuals, I am resourceful. I am resilient—as resilient as soft supple skin. I am charming—though apparently she is immune to my charms, a deficiency for which she will be punished. But I'm out and dressed for success and I intend to have my success.

I've always like Occam. He was smart—and he always had a razor. My fellow man.

I have been cheated of total satisfaction. By a woman. That's just insulting.

But I will set it right. I always do. Even if she has eluded me tonight, she has merely postponed the inevitable.

I will be coming for you, Sweetheart . . . soon.

I wake up with a start, light streaming on my face. It's 8:45. The kids' Sunday school starts at 9:25. I have no idea why it doesn't start at 9:30 or, even better on this particular morning, at ten or some other round number. I just know that it takes thirty minutes to get there and the kids are gone to the world. Kendra is one foot from the edge of the bed. She'd be all the way on the edge, but that was the space afforded to me. James is at a forty-five-degree angle, his head in the direction of the foot of the bed. He looks very comfortable. He ought to; he worked hard to get the whole bed to himself.

I throw the bedroom curtains all the way back and start barking for the kids to get up and get ready in a hurry. Neither looks so inclined. Kaylen is going to be mad.

We had a great time at Chuck's. Klarissa ended up joining us and that was a blast. After winning close to a million tickets, most of them based on my mad skills at skee ball, we were able to cash in and get both kids a prize worth at least one buck each.

We invited Klarissa to make it a slumber party, but I think the mechanical gorilla was all the youthful frivolity she could handle, so she booked it back to her place, winding her GTR's engine into a loud whine before she exited the parking lot. Kendra, James, and I pulled up to Chez Kristen at ten with yet another voice message waiting for me. I keep saying I am going to get rid of my landline since I never talk to anyone on it. It is, however, my defacto message machine—and who would I hang up on if salespeople didn't have it to pass around?

I hit the flashing red button and put it on speakerphone. It was Dell with a tone of voice the kids had never heard. Me either.

"Well, well, well . . . I guess you're really not at a seeing-somebody phase in your life," he said, his voice dripping with sarcasm, loud enough for me, the kids, and my neighbors on either side to hear before I could snatch up the receiver and click off the speakerphone.

"Nice way to repay someone who treated you like a queen. That's right, a queen. Thanks for kicking me in the teeth. I deserved better and you sure as heck didn't deserve to be treated as good as I was to you. I have assumed you have had a rough year because of your dad—but now I'm not so sure. I'm not sure you have feelings. No one has ever treated me as poorly as you. Lucky you have a nice family or you wouldn't have a friend in the world. You asked for space and I gave you all the space in the world and boy did you run with it. Your day will come. You'll know how it feels to get hurt and abused by someone you care about. Payback is a killer. And, princess? I know the world revolves around you and your whims, so good news, you won't be hearing from me again."

I put the phone down gently. The kids were looking at me with curious eyes. I forced a smile.

"Is Mr. Dell mad at you?" James asked. "Is he going to beat you up?"

"Don't be stupid," Kendra said to him. "Boys aren't allowed to beat girls up."

"They are too!" he yelled. "And you're not allowed to say 'stupid,' stupid!"

"And neither are you," I said, tickling him. "Now get your pajamas on and let's watch a movie, you two!"

I wish Kendra was right. But sometimes boys do beat up girls. I will be running a background check on Mr. Dell first thing Monday morning.

I didn't even bother putting the kids in the spare bedroom. We all climbed in my bed and watched half a Disney movie before the kids—actually all of us—finally succumbed to the call of sleep. I woke up an hour later to check all the locks on my door and was wide awake. So I watched the rest of *Beauty and the Beast* by myself. When I was a little girl I liked to think of myself as Belle—the hair color was even right. But I wonder if I became the beast when I grew up.

Klarissa always claimed to be Ariel from *Little Mermaid*. Kaylen clung to *Snow White*. Even as a kid, she was old-school.

I think I dreamed that Lumiere, the candlestick with the heavy French accent, was scolding me for turning my back on true love. I don't think that little clock guy was very happy with me either. His face looked like Dell.

Kaylen is waiting for us as I run in the door to the children's area of our church. We got out of my apartment in fifteen minutes flat. But the kids were starving and we stopped at Dunkin' Donuts. I'm obviously not a mom or I would have known not to let James get a powdered sugar donut. His mouth and the front of his shirt are coated in white. I brushed Kendra's hair out and put it in pigtails. I now notice that the part is a jagged line and that the left pig tail is twice as big as the right. So does Kaylen.

I give a sheepish smile. She just shakes her head. I want to say something smart, but just walk up to her and hug her tight.

"I love you, Sis," I whisper. "Sorry."

I then do the only thing I can think of under the circumstances because frankly, between Dell and Van Guten, I've been scolded enough for one twenty-four-hour period.

I turn around and walk out the door.

I drove south after my dramatic exit from Kaylen and went to Don and Vanessa's church. I read a sociology textbook back in college that had a highlighted sidebar noting that Sunday morning is the most segregated window of time in America. I'm not sure how much that bothers me, but nonetheless, even if I don't bow at the throne of diversity—something you don't say out loud when you work for the city of Chicago—I know it would be a good thing if people from all walks of life got together for worship. I remind myself of that when I discover that I am a minority—of one—at Don's church.

The sign out front indicated that it was a temple. It was a one-story converted strip mall and wasn't very ornate, so in my mind, it's a church. I got there at 10:15 and no one seemed to care that I was late. *Ha!* I say to Kaylen in my mind. A lot of people came in after me. No one seems to feel guilty about timelines here.

The service didn't end until after one. I think we stood for more than an hour of singing. And dancing. And shouting. Don has invited me to attend church with him and Vanessa a bunch of times. I'm not sure he thought I'd actually take him up on the offer. I think I'm putting a damper on his freedom of expression. Vanessa feels no such inhibition. Not only can that girl sell real estate, but she's got moves.

I liked the people, the music, and the preaching. Even the announcements were pretty good. I might have some helpful suggestions for Jimmy on livening things up at our church. I do have one problem with Don's church—and I know it shows a lack of character and spirituality for me to admit this—but I can't handle three hours of church. Sometime after noon, I committed myself to working things out with Kaylen. I could go to church with Klarissa one Sunday as a power play—but I suspect this will be my sole excursion into discovering the diversity of worship experiences in my community.

Afterward, Vanessa invited me to dinner at their place. The place was nicer than I had even imagined—and I assumed the Squires' lived in a nice place. Don and the kids showed me around while Vanessa finished pulling everything together in the kitchen.

It wasn't a new house, but it was big, at least 4,000 square feet—probably more—with a whole lot of remodeling and upgrades like a marble foyer and everything granite and copper in the kitchen. The hardwood floors look fairly new. Jimmy and Kaylen keep talking about some things they want to do with their place and Kaylen's lament is that it costs more per square foot to build out and remodel than what you pay per square foot if you just buy what you want new. I live in a two-bedroom apartment and don't have to deal with things like that.

Vanessa may make the money but Don's the king. Both he and Vanessa have their own offices, but his looks more like the lounge of a British private men's club, with brass-studded maroon leather chairs and a lot of pheasant and fox hunting scenes on the wall. I'll have to ask Don at work if he's ever been pheasant hunting. Having never been to a private men's club in the British Isles—or to the British Isles at all, for that matter—I'm using my imagination here. Vanessa's office is nice, but Spartan in comparison. I'm guessing a lot more real work takes place in her space than his.

The kids' rooms are way cooler than anything me or my sisters grew up with. Devon's nine. He has bunk beds, his own space-age desk, a nicer media center than I have at age twenty-nine, a basketball goal over his laundry hamper, and a bunch of those oversized Fathead posters of sports stars on the walls. He likes Brian Urlacher. Everyone in Chicago likes Urlacher. There's also a whole collage of posters dedicated to Walter Payton. That was Don's influence. He has an informal shrine to the immortal number 34 of the Bears on his desk.

Veronika is eight, same age as Kendra. Vanessa has had one of her walls painted by a local artist with a scene out of a fairy tale. It actually has a *Beauty and the Beast* look to it, though I don't remember Belle being quite that dark skinned, which makes me remember the lousy feeling I had all last night.

We spend ten minutes looking over things in the half-basement game room—pool table, foosball table, Ping Pong table, Xbox set up

with a huge flat-screen TV, a couple of old arcade games—I had forgotten about Space Invaders—a table that might be for Monopoly
with the kids and poker night for Don and his heathen friends if Vanessa lets them in the house, and a wet bar. Then we walk up another
flight of stairs and down a back hall into the formal dining room. The
paintings look real. The china is something out of a Martha Stewart
decorating special—and I'm not talking her prison phase.

I'm not sure Vanessa was expecting me to accept her lunch invite,
because she told me numerous times that the meal wouldn't be much.
And she's absolutely right, if salmon with dill sauce, creamed spinach,
new potatoes baked with a fresh rosemary and garlic seasoning, fruit
compote with the fattest blackberries I've ever seen in my life, steaming mini-loafs of sourdough bread, and some kind of sweet potato
casserole that ends up tasting an awful lot like Mom's pumpkin pie,
isn't much. The iced tea flavored with peach nectar was a particularly
nice touch that I want to remember when hostessing. *Ha.*

We were almost through with dinner, the unbelievable aroma
of an almost-baked apple pie now wafting through the room, when
my phone buzzed four times. I figured it was probably Kaylen so I
decided to ignore it. Good, she misses me. When it started a second
round of buzzing, I looked at the tiny screen.

Zaworski.

"I wish you didn't have to run."

"I know, Vanessa. This was wonderful. I feel so bad running off
before dinner is even over. I would have helped with the dishes."

"We're just glad you could come, girlfriend!"

Cool. I'm a girlfriend. Vanessa and I are in the doorway with Don
and the kids dutifully in the background. He doesn't look happy. I

went into the living room to talk with Zaworski, but I know he probably figured out who I was talking to. His phone hasn't made a peep. He keeps glancing down at it.

After what he said about me seeing Reynolds to move up the food chain on this case, I refuse to explain. He'll find out soon enough where I had to dash off to, and he will feel bad. Maybe even get a grip so he doesn't leave me any more "poor me, left out of the big boys' club" messages.

"You know, Kristen," Vanessa says as I'm halfway through the door, "I bet we've said 'let's do lunch' a hundred times and we've never done it. We need to do it. Really."

"I'd love that," I say.

We hug, everyone calls good-bye at my back, and I'm on my way to Saint Elizabeth's hospital.

Jeff made a couple of calls and finally reached Zaworski. He has asked for me to get there as fast as I can. Patricia's in intensive care.

I don't know what I'm going to do. I love her so much."

Jeff is sobbing, his face in his hands. We're sitting at a forty-five-degree angle in the family waiting room of the ICU at Saint Elizabeth's. A 911 call came in at five in the morning. Patricia was found in an alley, just outside the back door of a biker bar. Raped—presumably—and beaten to a bloody pulp. I barely recognized her pretty features when I went to her bedside. Nose broken in three places. Broken jaw. The emergency room doctor wasn't sure, but he thought she might have a detached retina. Blood alcohol levels high enough to have drunk herself into a coma or even to death. She would've been in the hospital even if some Neanderthal hadn't decided to make her his punching bag.

"I'm so sorry, Jeff."

He looks up at me, eyes red and puffy. He doesn't look like a high-powered mergers and acquisitions lawyer at the moment.

"What do I do?"

"I don't honestly know, but you're here right now and that's the best thing in the world a man can do for his wife in a moment like this."

"Do I stay with her? For good?"

"You're here now, so I'm guessing the answer is yes. You're going to do all you can to hang in there with her."

"I screwed up driving you out of her life. You were good for her."

"Jeff, I barely knew Patricia. For all intents and purposes, we had one major conversation in our entire lives—and you were there for most of it."

"Something about you rang true with her."

"Despite the fact that I was lying to her about why I was at AA?"

He actually laughed and snorted at that.

"Yeah, despite the fact that you helped her under false pretenses. I'll drop the lawsuit tomorrow," he says with a shake of his head. "But I need your help tonight."

"Jeff, drop the suit if it's the right thing to do. But you can't attach strings to it. I don't know if I can be there for Patricia."

"I'll drop the suit against the church, the city, the police department, and you—because it's the right thing to do. I'll also keep tearing up the checks you send me for that bucket of bolts you drive because that's the right thing, too. All I ask is that you consider being a friend and sponsor to Patricia."

"Jeff, you do realize that I'm not really an alcoholic?"

"Yeah, but somehow, someway, you're a wonderful mess, too."

We both laugh. Then he starts to cry again. When he halfway pulls himself together, I ask, "How'd you guys get together in the first place?"

"I met Patricia when we were undergrads at Northwestern. I was a senior, she was a freshman. We dated the whole time I was in law school. She got her English degree and a teaching minor. She never went into the classroom. Might have been good for her. Believe it or not, she was the prude and I was the party animal. I don't know how things got so out of control for her."

"Nothing out of the ordinary happened?"

"I guess just what she told you that night at our house. Things went south in a big way when her dad died. They never got along. When he passed on, I think she got hit with a wave of guilt and remorse for never getting things worked out."

I don't say anything. I just wait him out, just like they taught me in cop school. Most people can't handle silence, so they talk. As Don says, I'm the master of the awkward silence. But with Jeff right now, silence feels just fine. Comfortable.

"It's a tough thing losing a dad, but to be honest, I never liked the guy, so I probably didn't pay attention like I should have. I've always worked too much. I didn't spend enough time with Patricia."

"You don't have to apologize for working hard," I say. "I've seen a lot worse habits from husbands in my time on the force. And that's just the cops. You should see the bad guys."

He gives a half-hearted laugh.

We talk some more. We motion for an investigating officer to come over and the three of us cover some incredibly uncomfortable questions that may or may not help with finding who messed Patricia up. My guess is Jeff won't be much help. Any answers will come from finding and talking to everyone who was in the Sexy Hog last night. No easy task. I can't even imagine entering an establishment called the Sexy Hog, let alone questioning all her patrons.

I walk back into Patricia's room with Jeff. She woke up for just a minute or two when I first got there. Her eyes were filled with tears when I hugged her. I hug her again now, kiss her forehead. I whisper the serenity prayer in her ear. She opens her eyes as I finish. I tell her I love her. I tell her that Jeff is here for her and to let him love her. I don't know if she hears me or not.

Jeff walks me outside the door and down to the lobby.

"So what do I do?" he asks, dried tears streaking his face.

"Just do what you're doing now. Be here for her."

"Can she get better?"

"Yeah, I think so," I answer. "She's got a good man who loves her. And she loves you. That's a heck of a start."

It must be nice, I think as I push out the door into the bright sunlight and wonder how obvious it is to the rest of the world what a wonderful mess I am.

I'm sorry, Klarissa, but I just can't break free tonight. You know how bad it is right now."

"You're there for the drunk."

"Klarissa, be nice and please don't call her that. She needs me right now."

"Who says I don't need you?"

"Do you?"

"Does it matter? Hey, I don't have to beg to get a dinner date. So please, don't go out of your way for your sister. I guess booze is thicker than blood."

"Is this still about Warren?"

I shouldn't have asked that, but her calling Patricia "the drunk" made me mad. There is a pregnant pause on the line.

"I cannot believe you just said that," she says, barely controlling her anger. "When have I once mentioned that my breakup with Warren is a problem? Give me one example. Now you and Kaylen and Mom talking about it is another issue. Behind my back I would add!"

"Don't bark at me, Klarissa. The fact that you haven't mentioned him makes me figure you're having a tougher time with the breakup than you admit. I wasn't trying to make this into a big deal."

"I am not barking," she yells. "You just don't listen. No wonder you're having a tough time being a detective these days."

"I'm not listening to this," I storm back.

"You don't listen to anything anyway."

I was going to let her have it with both barrels, but she hung up on me. I can't believe she just said that. What the heck is this all about? She never yells. That's my domain.

What a week. It's Friday afternoon. I was in a hospital room last Sunday with Patricia. I made it home for fifteen minutes. I was at the scene of a murder half an hour later. Victim number four. Stefani Allen. Forty. Single. An attorney, specializing in intellectual property rights, specifically scientific patents. A very posh condo with a lake view.

Over the next several days our team interviewed all 634 people who live in the 412 condos in Stefani's building. Plus another 250 maids, security guards, salespersons, maintenance workers, delivery truck drivers, and anyone else who had consistent contact with her building. The city would shut down without our large illegal immigrant population, so getting to everyone who has access to the Marina Palace is impossible.

No one can remember seeing anything out of the ordinary. Stefani did use her ATM card the night the coroner says she was killed, and from that we have been able to trace her steps on at least a three-stop bar crawl. Problem is that no one remembers her leaving the third bar. So she might have hit one more spot where she met the Cutter Shark or maybe she left from there with him. We've checked security cameras in the Lakeside Room, bar number three, but they're limited to the back hall leading to the public restrooms. We've been working with the bar management to identify and visit everyone that showed up on the camera who can be identified, as well as everyone who used a credit card. We've also canvassed every bar in a three-mile radius with her picture in hand. No luck so far.

The press is having a field day, of course. The ChiTownVlogger is now officially a rock star. In our task force meetings we continue to review previous cases looking for additional hunting grounds for our predator. Bars are in a solid second place behind AA meetings. Health clubs are running third. Everywhere else the Cutter picked up his victims is clustered together, giving too many options to realistically narrow the search down.

I went to lunch with Vanessa earlier today. We had a nice time. But there's a reason we've promised to get together and have never done so until now. Both of us are swamped in our personal and professional lives—and we really don't have that girlfriend chemistry thing going on, no matter how many times she calls me girlfriend. We talked the whole ninety minutes, but it was hard work.

She made reservations at Oceanique—very chic and expensive. I felt out of place in my off-the-rack ensemble and comfortable Eccos. She insisted on picking up the bill because it was almost a hundred bucks for lunch. Good thing. Out of my price range. I'm not a big fish lover, but the sea bass with some kind of chutney relish was out of this world. I could get used to fine dining.

I've experienced it more in the past month than in the previous year. I wasn't going to, but I did end up going out with Reynolds again. Twice. Once for an early power breakfast in the lobby restaurant of the Hotel Intercontinental on Michigan, which is pretty close to the State Building where we had a meeting. The second was for dinner at Sushi Para II in Lincoln Park. Very nice. Very expensive. Again. I need a raise if I'm going to continue hanging out with these kind of people.

But curious for me, I look forward to going out with Austin again. What's happening to me?

"I've got to cancel dinner tonight."

It's 4:30 and my eyes are bleary from looking through notebooks yet again. I'm working the back tabs. I have an idea. Strike that. I had an idea. My mind was roiling and I'm not even sure what I was looking for in the first place.

"Hunkering down with Willingham and the Ice Queen?" I ask Austin.

"Funny how I know just who you're talking about," he says with a laugh. "Actually I've been hunkered down with those two for a couple hours over here. Willingham doesn't trust the office setup at the State Building. But something's come up from one of the other cases. I'm catching the 7:00 United flight to Denver and a car is picking me up for O'Hare in twenty minutes."

"Good luck with rush hour."

"I think Willingham put in a call. If I'm late, the plane will still be waiting for me with a quick 'maintenance issue.'"

"He can do that?"

"If you ran an airline in the US, would you do a favor for the second in command at the FBI?"

"Good point. Do you keep a toothbrush packed?"

"Yes, I do. Plus clean underwear and fresh dress shirts and ties. I'll wear the same suit for as many days as I'm gone."

"Let me guess on the shirts. White button-down Oxford with your initials. Both of them."

"Lucky guess—or you're a mind reader."

"So what's up in Denver?"

"I sense you're detecting right now and you need to know that I've been trained to withstand torture, including time on the Chinese waterboard, so you're not getting any information out of me."

"Really? The FBI teaches you to withstand torture?"

"Not the FBI. I may have forgotten to mention that I was in Army Special Ops before I joined the Firm."

"I'm used to you and your colleagues leaving vital information out, so this little bit of personal data shouldn't come as a surprise."

"Sorry," he says with a laugh that indicates he's really not sorry. "I've lived on a 'need to know' basis too long and it's permeated my entire life. If it makes you any happier, my mom isn't very happy with me either."

"So you have a mom? I thought to be in the FBI you had to be hatched."

"Believe me, if they get any better at this test tube cloning thing, all future agents will be."

"So you really can't tell me what's going on in Denver?"

"Actually, I'm going to brief the whole task force when I get back. I'm not stopping in Denver. There's a private jet waiting for me at a small private airport on the other side of the city and I'm going to connect to Durango."

"Isn't that where all the UFO sightings take place?"

"Yep. And there are a few things that suggest it might be the home base of our killer."

We hang up. And it hits me. *Durango.*

My mind—and stomach—immediately start churning.

Single. Professional. Smart. Unconnected.

No, that's just too bizarre. That could not be. I would never live it down. If it were to be him, he singled me out. No way.

———

Klarissa is either still mad or on-air with one of her special reports that she does most nights, because she won't pick up. It's Friday so she might even be working as guest anchor. I don't want to make up, but I've liked being friends. So I'm going to eat humble pie and apologize for my temper. She better apologize, too. I should go over and see Mom, make a preemptive strike before Klarissa can get to her first. But I'm thinking I really need to make another quick stop on the way over to see her.

Much as I hate it, I have to find out if the only person I know from Durango has an alibi for the night Stefani Allen was murdered.

If he'll talk to me.

God, I want to find this killer so bad. Please don't let it be Dell.

57

Absolutely not," Zaworski says to me.

"Boss, I was just giving you a heads-up. It's probably nothing. If it's something, I can handle it myself or call the team then. I don't want to mess up everybody's Friday night plans on a hunch."

"Let's be clear," he says. "This is a direct order. Stand down. Pick a location within a mile of the destination. Support personnel will be thirty minutes behind you. You can then make contact with appropriate backup."

"Can I at least drive by and see if his car is in his parking spot?"

"Negative."

Oh boy. I called Don first to get his thoughts. He said what I was afraid he was going to say: "You have to call the boss on this one."

So I called Zaworski—hoping he wasn't out somewhere with his long-suffering wife. He picked up on the second ring.

"What you got?"

Reynolds said I couldn't get any information from him but I know he's on his way to Durango—so I let the boss know that, and the connection to my one-time sorta boyfriend.

He whistles and says, "If he's our guy, you were probably singled out shortly after he arrived. Where did you meet him?"

"Church."

"Oh man, oh man, oh man. And he fits the profile?"

"Captain, I'm praying he is not the killer, but yes, Dell is a high-end drifter who moves about every year. He has no family or social bonds that I'm aware of. He's intelligent. He's neat. He's organized.

He blends in. He is no one you would ever suspect of any kind of crime. Reynolds is on his way to Durango, and that's where Dell keeps a home. But I'm not saying he's the Cutter."

In this next hour, I can foresee two embarrassing scenarios playing out. One is that Dell is the Cutter Shark. How bad would that be for me? Ace detective dates the man she was supposed to be hunting. I can see the headlines: She Never Suspected a Thing. I just can't believe Dell is connected to this, but it is eerie how well he fits the profile of a serial killer—all the way to the fact that he is someone you would never suspect. And what about that harsh phone message he left? He sounded threatening and ominous that day.

But there's yet another possible embarrassing scenario. Just like the takedown of Jonathan at the Saint Bart's AA meeting, what if Dell is innocent? I'm going to look like the boy who cried wolf all over again. I was going to just drop by and say hi and get a feel for things. Maybe find out where he was the night Stefani died. Then I realized I better not go without anyone else knowing, so I called Don and then Zaworski.

I might as well have walked into a crowded theater and shouted, "Fire!"

———

Dell's Lexus is parked in the diagonal space reserved for him in the alley behind his brownstone on North Dearborn, about a ten-minute walk from the Magnificent Mile. I don't know if the Porsche is in the small one-car garage that is a small basement at the bottom of a steep slope in the alley. No windows to peek in. He might be out for dinner. An officer then drives me around to his street and drops me off at the corner. I walk up the five stairs to his impressive front door, side-by-side oak doors with an ornate wrought-iron grill for security. A very nice place in a very nice neighborhood. The only furniture Dell owns is in Durango—at least that's what he's told me—so he rents stuff from a decorator every time he moves to a new city. I shudder again at the thought that he could be our killer.

I've got a wire on; Zaworski sent a techie over to outfit me. I politely demurred, but rank has its privileges, and apparently his rank is bent on telling me what to do.

I pause on the landing before ringing Dell's doorbell. I get a wave of nausea. He wouldn't have done something to himself over my breaking up with him, would he? Surely my imagination is just running a little wild. Isn't it?

Don, the techie, Blackshear, and Martinez have parked a sedan a couple houses away. If Dell so much as sneezes wrong, there are going to be three serious men breaking his door down, and a techie is going to be calling the Navy, Air Force, and Marines for support.

I can take care of myself, though. I have the Beretta in a holster on the small of my back and also have a knife sheathed on the side of my ankle. I know Dell is probably not the Cutter Shark, but a rough paraphrase crosses my mind: live by the knife; die by the knife.

Zaworski, I think sensing my unease that Dell probably isn't a real suspect, has decided not to call the FBI. He hasn't said anything out loud, but I think everyone in this little fishing expedition knows what the rules are. None of us are eager for an AA false call re-do. So if we take down a bad guy, the techie will send out an all-points alert, and we'll just say we didn't have time to include anyone else before we got there. But if Dell is the nice, God-fearing, churchgoing, Amish-loving—though isolated—man that I think he is, no one says anything to anybody at any time. This will never have happened.

I ring the doorbell. I don't hear footsteps. My heart starts to race a little. I try to breathe deeply to get everything under control. If he's here, whether he's guilty or innocent, I need to look natural. I wait fifteen seconds—I know because I count them off with Mississippi's in the middle—and ring it again. There are about ten newspapers on the stoop, some of them already turning yellow. Some sales flyers are crammed inside the wrought-iron door. Nothing. Ten seconds go by this time, and I creak open the surprisingly unlocked iron outer door and knock hard. The wooden doors haven't been shut all the way and groan open. My heart is pounding.

"What's happening?" Don asks into my ear piece.

"Door was open. I'm going in."

"Don't do it," Don hisses. "Anything you find in there would be tainted evidence for a jury trial."

I ring the doorbell a couple more times, staring at the clearly abandoned room, and then retreat to the car. Martinez is on the phone with Zaworski.

"Yeah, at least one car's here, but we don't think it's been moved for a while," he's saying. "He has a second, but we don't know if it's in the garage or not. Newspapers are piling up on the front porch. Conner just looked through the crack in the door and the front hallway is filled with letters and junk mail."

He listens.

"No. She didn't do anything to open the door. She just knocked and it opened a little bit. No one's gone inside, Boss."

Another pause while Zaworski gives him orders.

"We'll sit tight, Captain."

He tells us Zaworski is getting a search warrant from a judge—and is going to call the FBI. If Dell is the Cutter Shark—or is guilty of any other crimes—we aren't going to do anything to jeopardize a righteous conviction.

—•—

"I'm sorry, Mom. Honest, I was looking forward to coming over and being together, just you and me. It's this da—this darn case."

"Are you okay?"

"I am. I'm even getting along with Klarissa these days."

"That's not what she told me an hour ago." She got there first.

I groan inwardly, wishing I'd been able to get to her first, as planned. "We had one little fight. It was nothing. I tried calling her back to apologize."

"Have you talked to Dell lately? I still worry about him."

"Believe it or not, Mom, I tried getting a hold of him tonight. He wasn't there. Look, I'm pulling into my parking lot. I've got to get some things out of the car, so I'm going to sign off. But I'm coming by tomorrow for lunch. Just the two of us. We'll talk. I swear."

"Well, if you're not here by noon, I'm going to come find you wherever you are. I still have contacts on the force, you know."

We laugh.

"Love you, Mom."

"I love you, baby girl. And Kristen . . . be careful."

"You got it."

"Listen to me. I mean it. Be careful. I couldn't stand the thought of something happening to you."

I hang up before she can start crying and pull into a good spot near the stairs to my walk-up. I turn off the engine. I just sit and look at a brilliant full moon. I sigh and shake my head. I rub my temples. I can't believe it. Dell is gone. The warrant signed by a judge, we invaded his rental house. The rental furniture's still in his apartment along with the two cars. They were both rented as well. Officers started making calls and it looks like everything, including the house, is paid for through the end of August. Otherwise, every stitch of clothing, every book, every knickknack, his toiletries, cleaning supplies, linens, plates—anything that was a personal item—has been cleared out. The place is dusty now, but when he left, probably close to the time he left me the angry message last Saturday, he or someone cleaned the place thoroughly. Top to bottom. Everything. When the full tech crew got there, they weren't sure they were going to find any evidence of a human presence.

"This guy even vacuumed the traps in all the sinks," Jerome tells me. "That's a sure sign of someone with an obsessive-compulsive disorder—or more likely, something to hide. I'm not a detective but I suspect the latter."

"Thanks for the tip, Jerome."

He and Bruce, who I've now been with at four murder scenes, were called in to maintain consistency on examining any evidence that might be tied to the Cutter Shark case. They are apparently on the same bowling team because they had matching shirts with their respective names stitched on the chest and both were still wearing bowling shoes. They must be good bowlers, I decide, because those weren't rentals.

We knocked on every door up and down the street. We've discovered two things. First, Dell didn't know his neighbors. Second, his neighbors didn't know him. No one can definitively say whether they even saw him in the previous month, but some are quite certain they have never seen him. One guy distinctly remembers the Porsche—but not the driver. Now that's a commentary on society.

I supplied his work number and through some calls back at the office, we got the number of the person who issued a freelance contract to Dell and who is his project liaison at Goff & Duncan, the manufacturing company he is consulting for. Blackshear finally located the guy at an engagement party for his niece; he wasn't happy that two uniformed officers showed up and insisted that our investigation was a higher priority than a family celebration. They impressed on him the importance of being a good citizen and he got busy helping Blackshear understand Dell's business arrangement.

Blackshear gave us a synopsis later. On Monday or Tuesday—the guy has to double-check when he's back at the office tomorrow morning—Dell exercised the "out" clause in his contract. He handed the liaison a final invoice with instructions to send his last expense and fee payments to a drop box with a bank in Durango. He cleared out his temporary office and was off the premises almost immediately. The guy thinks he was in a hurry. Dell's work was exceptional from start to finish and the guy hated to see him go. He said the company CEO had recently let Dell know that they were prepared to offer him a full-time position. He thought Dell was interested. So he remembered thinking Dell's sudden departure caught him by surprise.

I unbuckle my seatbelt, push open my door, slide my legs outside the car, and stand up and feel a gentle summer breeze. Actually, summer doesn't officially start until June 21, but growing up, summer always began on the last day of school—at least in the mind of a school-aged kid. It's now the end of May. Have we been on this case for two months? It's been in the eighties during the day, but it's probably seventy-five degrees right now and it feels great. I push my car door shut and take another deep breath, stretching my tight back.

I feel an explosion on the left side of my body as someone slams a fist into my kidney. I throw up in my mouth as I go down like a rag doll.

Someone whispers, "Don't even think you can get away with messing with my life," in my ear before I pass out in a swirl of dark, all-encompassing pain.

I lift my head slowly. I am laying in a small bed, but have no clue where I am at or what my situation is. A light shines through a crack under the door. My instinct is to call out and find out what I am up against. Stupid idea. A brass band is playing Pavarotti meets the Rolling Stones. I breathe slowly. In and out. My head begins to clear. I lay still—I don't want to alert my captor or captors that I am awake. I keep my breathing as slow and quiet as possible.

I take stock. I wiggle my fingers and toes. Check. All present and accounted for, even if they feel slow and unresponsive. Drugged. Not good. I roll my neck back and forth. Everything in working order there, too, but there is now a group of renegade dwarfs that have booted Pavarotti and the Stones and who are swinging pick axes on the inside of my cranium.

I lift one arm and then the other, glad to find I'm not restrained. That is a big mistake on someone's part. Just because some gorilla can punch like a heavyweight boxer when I'm not looking doesn't mean he is going to withstand a quick shot to the trachea if I get even half a chance at him. I clench and unclench my fists to get the blood circulating. I begin practicing a couple of attack moves in my head. You are going to have to seize the element of surprise.

I hear footsteps outside my door. I barely breathe. I am pretty sure there are at least two sets of shoes on hard flooring. Maybe three. Might be one person wearing some kind of soft sole. Not what I wanted to hear. More than one captor is going to make escape more challenging than I was hoping for. Does the Cutter Shark have a partner? Multiple partners? My mind quickly runs through a list of drills and strategies for neutralizing two opponents.

The door swings open. One of my assailants creeps slowly toward me. Have I alerted them I'm awake? Then the other turns on glaring lights to blind me. I am as ready as I am ever going to be. I was already moving before he reached the bed, and now I drive the heel of my hand in the direction of his face with the simplest karate punch in the book. He twists his head sideways and gets a forearm up to partially block my punch in a trained move. I know I landed a decent blow that did more than graze his cheek. I was hoping to catch him on the bridge of his nose, which would have temporarily blinded and immobilized him.

I spin up and off the bed to kick and throw another punch. I aim at his groin and throat in a split-second combination—but I don't think either landed enough to do any damage. Not good. I am lightheaded from the sudden change of positions—the drugs haven't worn off as much as I'd hoped. My movements are too slow. Before I can continue my attack, a pair of muscled arms from my second captor wraps me up tightly from behind. I'm not done fighting. I kick up and backward and hear a heavy oomph. I got him in the groin but not as good as I want because instead of falling down in a fetal position he holds on, cursing in English and Spanish. He pushes me face down on the bed and brings his weight to bear on me. I snap my head back and catch him on the eye's orbital socket. But I still can't get free.

Now a second set of hands is holding me down and yelling something. I feel the pinprick of a hyperdermic needle enter my upper arm. There was a third person.

I am sorry I wasn't better prepared, Mr. Barry. I'm sorry I wasn't careful enough, Mom.

———

I'm sitting up in bed drinking a glass of water. A tray with a bowl of untouched chicken noodle soup is beside me.

Don is sitting across from me, an ice pack on his left cheekbone. Zaworski is standing by the door shaking his head and trying not to smile. Martinez is sitting on the other side of the bed. He has an ice pack on his lap. Enough said.

"*No nos pagan lo suficiente para este tipo de trabajo,*" Antonio says to me with a weak smile.

"What's that mean?" I ask him.

"I can answer that," Don interrupts. "'We don't get paid enough to do this job,' and for the record, I think I agree with Martinez on this one."

Zaworski walks back over to my bedside. "Kristen, now that your head is clearing a little, you're sure you can't tell us anything more about who attacked you?" he asks again. "I'm talking about the parking lot where you live, not here in the hospital," he says, looking at Don and Martinez with a barely concealed smile.

"I can't say with any degree of confidence, sir," I answer.

"You didn't get a look at his face? Not even a glimpse?" Martinez asks.

"I never saw him coming."

"You didn't recognize his voice?" Don asks.

"I didn't."

"Was he disguising it?" Zaworski asks.

"Possibly, but I'm not sure it mattered. I was fading fast when he spoke. He did whisper."

"What did he say again?" Don asks.

"Something about me not getting away with messing up his life."

"So it's possible it's this Dell guy?" Zaworski asks.

"I know he was angry with me. We dated off and on for almost six months. He was having a real hard time accepting that I didn't have feelings for him and was cutting him off completely. Then he saw me having lunch with Reynolds last Saturday afternoon and left me an angry message."

The three men say nothing. Zaworski tries not to look surprised. Sometimes the boss is last to know.

"He's got to be the guy," Martinez says with enthusiasm and then immediately winces from the movement.

"I don't know," I say. "First of all, I have never seen any evidence of violence in Dell. Really, he's a gentle soul."

"But you said yourself you never really got to know him," Don says. "Heck, I'm your partner and I don't remember you saying anything of substance about him; just that he had wormed his way into your family."

"Yeah," I agree, "I really didn't get to know him. That voice message took me by suprise."

"So why don't you like him for being your attacker?" Zaworski asks, puzzled. "He seems perfect. He was obsessed with you, it sounds like, so he definitely has the motive."

"Well, for one thing," I answer, "I'm just not sure Dell could hit as hard as this guy did. I've never been punched like that. I'm not saying Dell didn't work out and was weak or anything. I'm saying this guy knew how to *punch*."

"But you don't got no meat on you, girl," Martinez says. "And who stands up to a well-placed kidney shot?"

"I could have had a thirty-pound spare tire and the result would have been the same. Martinez, you would have gone down same as me."

"That's not saying much," Don says with a wicked smile.

"You want to see how easy it is to take me down, *amigo*?" Martinez challenges back.

"Ladies, not now," Zaworski says, cutting them off. "Kristen, can you think of anyone else? No other enemies or scorned lovers?"

"He wasn't a lover," I say with a sternness that makes even the captain back off. "If you don't count my family or Internal Affairs and someone in the office who writes me nasty Post-it notes, I really can't think of anyone else that mad at me right now. Everything's good with Jeff and Patricia as of last Sunday, and you met Jeff yourself, Captain, so you know if he wanted to hurt someone, it would be in the wallet and happen in a court of law. Honestly, I'm flying below the radar these days."

"What is this Post-It notes thing you are talking about?" he asks, frowning.

"It's nothing," I answer. "Someone is having some fun at my expense. Just a harmless prank."

"We don't prank in my office," Zaworski answers. "I want those notes."

"I'm not sure I kept them."

"And you deleted a threatening phone message from this Dell Woods. Use your head, Kristen. If there are any more notes or messages, you keep them. And you give them to Shelly to give to me."

Shelly is still my chief suspect. I wonder if he will get them . . .

"Now think, Kristen," Zaworski says. "Because if you can't come up with somebody else, I'm going to assume it's this Woods guy."

"What about the punk we collared a couple months back?" I ask, looking at Don. "Hard last name, Polish or Russian I think. Started with an *I*."

"Couldn't be him," Zaworski breaks in. "He'd still be locked up." He squints at me, like I should remember that. Maybe the drugs they've given me are stronger than I thought.

Don's frown deepens. He slaps his leg and mutters something.

"What?" I ask.

"Incaviglia. The punk. He got cut loose. I stayed late at the office so I could do something with the family tomorrow morning. As arresting officers, you and me got an email after hours tonight. There was a big bureaucratic snafu. The punk got in line and gave somebody else's name and walked out of Cook County Jail."

"You have got to be kidding me," Zaworski says.

"Not the first time something like this has happened recently," Martinez adds. "With all the budget cuts they can't keep up down there. My *el primo* works there and says it's getting sloppy."

"You're telling me the punk who about beat an old man to death and who gave me a brand-new scar just walked out the front gates of our judicial system?" I ask. I'm stunned. I feel sick to my stomach. I want to let someone have it. I count to ten and take a couple deep breaths. Weariness overwhelms me. I'm too tired to stay focused.

"Guys, I can barely keep my eyes open," I say. "But I don't think it was Incaviglia. Now that kid was tough, I'll admit. But I don't think he weighed 170 pounds. I don't think he could generate the power the guy who punched me had."

"Well, we're going to let you catch some sleep and get rested up," Zaworski says. "You think of anything or anybody, you call me directly. Not even Squires gets the first call."

Before they have a chance to exit, Big Tony Scalia comes through the door and beelines over to my side.

"I promised your daddy I'd look after you and I'm doing a crummy job of it," he says, giving me a kiss on the cheek and smoothing my hair down.

He turns to look at Don and then at Martinez and starts laughing. Zaworski, who I've seen smile maybe two or three times in the not quite two years I've been in his department, finally lets loose and joins Tony. Don rolls his eyes. Martinez still looks a little glazed.

"I guess you can take pretty good care of yourself," Scalia says.

Don and Martinez are not amused.

"You all got anything on the attacker?" he says to the three men present.

"We're not sure. It might be this Woods guy or maybe an escaped prisoner that Kristen collared," Zaworski says. "But she doesn't think either could punch like the guy who hit her."

"I got a call from Soto," Tony says to me. "He heard you got sucker punched and wondered about that guy he had working for him in the training room. Says he hit on you."

"Timmy," I respond with my eyes half open. "He's a lot more likely than Dell or the punk."

"We got a name?" Zaworski asks Scalia. "If so, let's get an APB out and bring him in for questioning."

"Consider it done. We'll get some officers on it." He turns toward me and continues. "By the way, Soto is on his way down here. He swears he's going to kill Timmy or whoever it is that did this. With his bare hands. He's also not happy with someone in this room. He thinks she's not taking the personal threat of the Cutter Shark case seriously enough and is being way too careless."

"Any truth to that?" Zaworski asks.

Before I can answer, more visitors arrive. Konkade and Blackshear enter the room first. Is anyone going to let me sleep off the rest of the knockout shot they gave me? Both come over and give me a pat on the shoulder. Both look at Don and Martinez with incredulity. Konkade whispers something in the captain's ear. Zaworski quickly glances up toward the door. On cue, Willingham and Van Guten enter. This is getting interesting. I think we're having a party. I'm starting to wake back up now.

Willingham ignores Zaworski and walks over to the side of my bed. He takes my hand and looks at me kindly. If Willingham hadn't decided to be an FBI bigwig, he would have made a great doctor. His bedside manner is impeccable.

"How are you doing, Detective Conner?"

"Fine, sir, thank you for asking. As soon as the pain medicine wears off, I'll be out of here and back to normal."

"I hear you don't have the doctor's clearance."

Despite the ice packs—sure hope their ice machine is industrial strength—my side still aches dully. I was also passing a little blood as of an hour ago. Until there's no blood in the urine, Dr. Singh is not letting me go home.

"They're just being cautious," I say.

"That's good," he says. "Wouldn't be a bad idea for you to do the same. Don't get in a hurry to get out of here. You'll slow down recovery."

"Yes, sir," I answer as he gives my hand a reassuring squeeze.

"When did I become 'sir' to you?"

"Sorry, Bob. I promise to be cautious."

He likes that and chuckles. Then he turns toward Zaworski and the smile is immediately gone. The two men lock eyes. I don't think either is willing to blink first.

Van Guten breaks the impasse. "Why don't you gentlemen clear the room and let our intrepid detective have some privacy. You can run your task force meeting out in the hall."

"Good counsel, Leslie," Willingham says. "However, I think Captain Zaworski and I might have a private conversation in my car. Can you get a ride back?"

"No problem. I'll catch a cab," she says.

"I can give you a lift," Martinez says, straightening his collar. Leslie doesn't look very excited about that suggestion.

She gives Don, who is now standing, a playful but firm nudge toward the door. Everyone but Leslie begins to shuffle out. I notice that Don has ditched his ice pack, probably in the foolish hope that everyone will forget I got a pretty clean punch off before I was subdued. His dark skin might hide discoloration—but he's already got a golf ball swelling on the side of his face.

Martinez isn't letting go of his ice pack. But he seems to be taking my counterattack more in stride than Don. He moves gingerly as he follows the others out of the room. With the men gone, Dr. Leslie Van Guten closes the door and walks over to me. She looks at me without saying anything for a moment. I feel like a bug under a microscope.

"So what was my ex-husband working on tonight?"

"Come again?" I answer, confused.

"In Durango."

"I have no idea what you're . . ."

My head is spinning. I'm sure it's the reaction she was hoping for. She is now looking at me with detached amusement.

"I guess he didn't mention that to you. Typical Austin. What I want to know is why he's in Colorado."

"You're the Mensa member; why are you asking me?"

"Clever and correct," she deadpans. "Let's just say the deputy director and I are not absolutely sold on the way Major Reynolds is conducting this entire investigation, and he's not keeping the chain of command as apprised as he should."

"Well, Leslie, at least he's doing something."

And I'm sticking up for the guy who didn't bother to let me know that I am working a case with his ex-wife? Why?

"We have processes for a reason. But no matter. Reynolds is good. *Very* good. And after tonight, I think the threads are all coming together anyway. We have you to thank for that."

"How is that?"

"What sedative did they give you—or are you just that slow? I think you're the only one on the team who hasn't figured this out yet."

I say nothing. I am too doped up to work out anything hard and I'm fading fast. I can't for the life of me figure what she's talking about so I say nothing, but it must center around Reynolds and this Durango lead. Thanks for making me look like a fool, you jerk. She just looks at me, I guess to see if the uncomfortable pause will coax me into blabbing.

Not going to happen, girlfriend. I'm basically shutting down and she realizes it. She turns and leaves without another word.

She could learn something from Willingham's bedside manner.

Dell can't be the Cutter Shark . . .

59

You're staying at our house," Kaylen says. "There is no way you're staying here by yourself."

Kaylen, Klarissa, my mom, and I are at my kitchen table. It's eleven on Saturday morning. I left the hospital twelve hours ago, but suddenly I wish I was still there, safe from my overly protective friends and family. Don and Martinez, fortunately not holding grudges, drove me home. Vanessa was already at my place when we arrived and had brought flowers, stocked my fridge, and done some cleanup, including a couple loads of laundry. I was thankful beyond belief that the place was fairly clean before she got there, though I don't think I've ever vacuumed the traps of my sinks.

Vanessa also whipped up the most unbelievable coffee cake that my mom popped into the oven before I woke up. I am currently on my second piece. Even Klarissa, who eats less than anybody not living in a famine-stricken country, has cleaned her plate. Granted, it was a small piece to begin with, but this still represents a breakthrough in my mind. I may have even caught her looking at the half-eaten second piece on my plate with something other than disdain. *Interest?*

"She can come home with me and stay in her old room," Mom says.

"We have room for her and you," Kaylen says.

"She can come to my place," Klarissa says.

"She's in the room, guys," I say. "So you can talk *to* her, not *about* her. And we've already settled it. Kaylen can spend the night. Just one night."

I've been up an hour and still have a summer-weight nightgown on. My hair is pulled back in the default ponytail I wear when I'm out of time or too lazy to fix it otherwise. That would be almost all the time.

"I have two of Chicago's finest as my bodyguards. They're sitting in the parking lot right now. I'll be fine."

"Bodyguards? I'm impressed," Klarissa says. "Are they cute?"

"Think they want something to eat?" Mom asks. "We could take them a piece of Vanessa's coffee cake and a cup of coffee."

"We're not supposed to do that, Mom," I say, trying not to roll my eyes. "Remember Dad's undercover days? And Klarissa, we can't go on a double date with them until this case is solved."

"And you're sure it wasn't the Cutter Shark who attacked you?" Kaylen interrupts with a shudder.

"If it was the Cutter Shark, I wouldn't be here," I answer. "We have no way of knowing who attacked me, but I doubt it's connected to the case I'm on. I think my attacker might be a guy named Timmy. He was one of the fight trainers at CPD for a month or two. He was working for Barry Soto."

"And Barry didn't know this guy was trouble?" Mom asks. "I always thought Barry was sharp. He must be slipping if he let a murderer work for him."

"Mom, I didn't say Timmy is the Cutter Shark," I say again. "This could be a random attack, which is doubtful, but there are at least a couple options we're exploring."

"If you've got colleagues attacking you," Klarissa says, "you must be a real bear to work with."

"Thanks, Baby Sis," I say. "You really know how to brighten my day."

She laughs and gives me a punch on the shoulder. I wince. Every movement still hurts. I guess everything is fine and she forgot about how our last conversation ended with her hanging up on me. I haven't forgotten.

"Sorry," Klarissa says, giving me a rueful look. "Who else is an option?"

"I just can't say," I tell her. "Honestly, I'm not even going to speculate. I got no look at his face and he whispered when he spoke to me. After working this case for a couple months, honestly, I am just grateful that whoever attacked me left me laying where I was."

"That gives me the creeps," Klarissa says with a shudder.

I haven't been up long, but I'm considering a nap. My family is wearing me out and it's obvious they are not going to leave me alone any time soon. Sweet, I think, but irritating. It's been tough this spring and early summer—really, the whole past year—so it's nice to have everyone close.

We finish the coffee and Mom goes to the kitchen and puts on another pot. Kaylen pulls Scrabble out of her overnight bag. Scrabble? That's only for Christmas holiday. She sets up the board deliberately and wordlessly—I think to make sure I know that this is what we're going to do and there's not going to be any debates or jokes about it. I get up and take one of my many bathroom breaks—the doc has me drinking a six-ounce glass of water every hour. I look down; no pink in the fluid. As I return, Mom is pouring coffee refills. *I'll be back in the bathroom in thirty minutes*, I think. I take the fourth chair at my kitchen table, giving up my ideas of an escape. Kaylen draws the *A* tile and gets to go first, which means an automatic double-word score. She gets a cute little smile on her face and plays all seven tiles first move. Not only does she get a double score on a word with a *Q* in it, but she gets fifty points for playing all seven letters in one turn. Basically, none of us have a snowball's chance in Death Valley to win after she adds up 140 points. I think about suggesting that this is a sign that maybe we should watch a video or that everyone should go home and I should go to bed.

"Oh dear," Mom says. I think she's figured out that resistance is futile.

I open the little drawstring game bag and make everyone put their tiles back in. This time I shake it up extra good and we start over. I pull out a Y. Guess who starts last? Talk about a blast from the past. Scrabble with Mom and my sisters. Beats getting grilled about who my attacker might be.

———

I look at my wall clock. It's four in the afternoon. I couldn't take any more excitement from Scrabble—and yes, Kaylen won again and again—so I fell asleep on my couch at about 1:00. I feel groggy now. But the vibration of my cell phone has wakened me.

"Feeling better, honey?" Mom asks. "What can I get you?"

I look around. Kaylen and Klarissa are gone at the moment. It's just the two of us now.

"I could use a glass of water and another pain pill," I say.

Percocet—a witch's brew of oxycodone and acetaminophen— definitely makes pain management easy. When I was a uniformed officer, painkillers were becoming a real problem on local college campuses. I guess all you have to do is take one of these bad boys and chase it with Jack and you've got a major buzz for the evening. Kids were paying thirty or forty bucks per tablet.

"Is it time for your antibiotic, too?" she asks as she puts down a crossword puzzle book and gets up from the recliner to head for the kitchen.

I'm no longer thinking about pain pills. The vibration isn't from a call. Two text messages have popped up. The first is from Reynolds:

On my way back. Lots happening in Durango. Late dinner tonight? Carmine's on Rush? I'm starved! I want to see you!

I want to text back that he is on a "need to know" basis with my dinner plans and that he probably needs to touch base with his ex-wife when he lands. I go to the next message instead. It's from Don. I'm surprised. I didn't think he could text with his fat thumbs. I read it and my heart sinks:

Our friend strikes again. Another body found. Sit tight and get better. I'll call u later w the details.

In your dreams, Don.

"Mom, can you make me a sandwich?"

"Sure, honey. Go sit down and I'll bring it over to you."

"Better wrap it. I've got to take a shower and get rolling."

"What? Tell me you're not serious. Kristen, no."

I look her in the eyes. "Our guy has struck again."

She shakes her head and sits down on one of the kitchen chairs, tears in her eyes.

"Why do people have to be so hurtful? So evil?"

I walk over and give her a careful hug. Not for her benefit—she's fine—but I'm still aching. I gently touch a scrape on my forehead that has started to scab over but is still oozing yellow a little. It's in the same spot where James whapped me in the head with an oversized Wiffle ball last week. Am I going to have a permanent red mark in the middle of my forehead? Would that mean I have to change religions?

"I don't know, Mom. But I'm going to put this guy in a place where he can't do any more harm. I promise."

I give her another quick hug and a kiss on the top of her head. Then I break away and head for the shower. I call Dispatch first, identify myself, and tell them I need the address of the latest murder repeated.

———

I wipe mayonnaise off the corner of my mouth with my sleeve. Glad Mom didn't see that. She's already very unhappy with me. I walk straight to the unmarked police car where the two officers assigned to guard detail are sitting. They're out of the car before I get there.

"Yes, ma'am?" a kid with a buzz cut and acne says.

Ma'am? That hurts worse than a kidney punch. I'm still not thirty.

"I'm heading over to the crime scene. You all going to stay here and watch my apartment or come along and keep an eye on me?"

The two officers look at each other, both hoping the other knows the right answer. Their instructions are that no one enters or even gets near my place without clearance. They're not sure if that includes me since the assumption was I wouldn't be going anywhere anytime soon.

"I think we need to call it in, ma'am," Buzz Cut says.

"Well, while you do, I'm going to be driving over there. Stay or come. Your call. But if you do stay, my mom will be leaving in a few minutes and she is authorized to move freely."

The young men look at each other and shrug. The second one speaks for both of them and says, "We'll follow you."

I nearly go airborne over the speed bump halfway around the circle drive in front of my apartment and bite back a scream. Bad move. That hurt. My guards follow close and bounce out of the parking lot right behind me. I pound through the gears and drive fast through city traffic on my way to the toll road. I run at least four yellow lights, so I don't know how the heck they keep up with me.

I've got an EZ-Pass on my windshield for the toll booths, but as I enter the highway, already doing sixty-five, I think I pass through the automated lane too fast for the camera to scan the barcode on it. I hear a loud buzzer behind me as I immediately cut across three open lanes on my left, downshift into third, and push the pedal hard to zip around two cars that are poking along, and then zip back across two of the lanes to the right while shifting into fourth and fifth in rapid succession. I am not going to let slow drivers get in my way as I head for the crime scene. I look in the rearview mirror. Buzz Cut is doing a nice job of not losing me. He's kind of got that NASCAR look about him.

There's a rumble in my brain that's about as loud as the buzzer at the toll booth. Every part of my body hurts, particularly at my temples and on the lower left side of my back. I should have taken two Percocets. But then I couldn't be driving. I look down at my phone and see the red light is still flashing. I got to my text messages before hopping in the shower, but didn't check to see if anyone had called. I scroll down and see that I have a missed call from a private number and that I have a voice message. I press down on the one key and listen.

It's Dell.

I almost swerve off the road.

"Kristen. I need to talk to you. You can't reach me, so I'll call back later. I know I got out of town in a hurry and I'm sure my last message on your home phone freaked you out. I apologize. Sincerely. There are a few things about my life I never mentioned to you that have come up and that I have to deal with. I'm in a little bit of trouble right now. I know you probably hate me, but you're still the only one I can talk to. Keep your phone close, would you?"

THE MONTH OF JUNE

It is dry, hazy June weather.
We are more of the earth,
farther from heaven these days.
HENRY DAVID THOREAU

June 1, 4:30 p.m.

Let's be honest. Not all people are created equal. Equal rights, equal value, equal needs—all nice thoughts. But some people matter more than others. I didn't have any say in the matter. God just made me one who rises above the masses, who matters more.

When I spent that year in a group home run by some church, a group leader asked us to share as honestly as possible what we really thought about ourselves. He was earnest and persuasive.

So I shared. "I matter more than others," is what I said. So much for being honest. Next thing I knew he wanted to cast demons out of me. I don't have demons; I have angels. They go before me and see that my plans always work.

But I'm going to have to fire the current host of angels working on my behalf. They aren't doing their job very well. I don't like my recent work. Oh, I like the work part, just not the results. They aren't neat. They are messy. Just like that stupid journal.

It all started with her. Nothing has gone quite right since I let her get under my skin.

I've always made sure I'm the only that gets under other people's skin.

I taught her a little lesson she won't forget soon last night. But even that feels hollow. It's not commenserate with the pain she has caused me.

I went with Plan B two nights ago. I had to hurry and find someone new. I don't like hurrying. The moment just didn't feel as good as it should have and that's not fair to me. Now I'm probably going to want to start early to get things right. Again. When will people stop messing with my perfect plans?

It's interesting to watch the FBI team grow. When I leave Chicago, they're going to love disbanding and starting all over again. The psychologist from the FBI is going to get a lot of undue acclaim when she writes about me some day—and she's the type that will. I've watched her. She's cold and arrogant. Full of herself. Just like so many others who came to see me and analyze me. Her exalted sense of self-esteem will lead her to underestimate me. She will write about this period of my career with pejorative adjectives—hurried, desperate, frantic, and the like. I read too. I know how these shrinks think. But despite the pseudo-sophisticated veneer of her beloved academia, she will never fully understand me, my greatness. I am too complex, too nuanced to be put under her flawed microscope of psychobabble.

It's interesting that even as the Cutter Shark Team grows, they still haven't shown up at my latest venue. It may not be up to my personal standards, but in a sloppy way, it is still a work of art. More Jackson Pollock than Mark Rothko.

I like my use of the word, pejorative. Clothes and vocabulary make the man.

A ripped physique doesn't hurt either. Helps to grab the ladies' eyes . . .

61

Zaworski is waiting for me as I drive up. My babysitters called ahead, as I knew they would.

"Who told you?"

"I am a detective, Captain," I answer. "I detect for a living."

"Don't get smart with me, Conner. I know it was Squires and I'm going to kick his tail back to parking meters over this. Everyone had strict orders to leave you out of this one. I want you to get back in your car and drive home right now. You don't need to be here."

"Sorry, Captain, I'm not going to do it . . . And before you say it, I'm not leaving, even if you give me a direct order."

Please don't give me a direct order.

We stare each other down, hands on hips, jaws set. Out of the corner of my eye, I see a mob of journalists, photographers, and video cameramen hustling to get as close to us as the perimeter tape will allow. Digital cameras are taking in everything. Zaworski takes me by the arm and walks me toward the front door of the crime scene to get us out of that particular line of fire.

"I knew you were going to be even more difficult than usual when they let you out of the hospital against everyone's better judgment but yours," he says with a dull tone. "Keep moving and don't smile."

He looks back at my two bodyguards who have caught up with us and says, "You have a new job. Help out the border patrol. The mob is getting unruly. No one gets past the tape. And you don't leave until we do."

He nods for me to follow him. I'm an hour behind Don, Blackshear, Martinez, Konkade, Big Tony, a couple of other detectives from the Third, and a host of new FBI faces. Everyone on the perimeter—reporters, uniformed cops, spectators—follow Zaworski and me with their eyes and cameras and shout questions as we walk up to the front door of a small ranch house with beat-up aluminum siding. There are brown patches all over the yard. The shrubbery, which looks like it hasn't been trimmed in years, is growing in wild and grotesque shapes, half covering the front picture window. The sidewalk is uneven and cracked and missing whole chunks of concrete. One of the downspouts has broken free of its moorings and is hanging away from the eaves of the house, ready to fall in a twist of metal. A pane is missing an entire corner in one of the front windows. Tar paper shows through some areas of the roof with missing shingles. I take it all in. This is different. Whoever victim number fifty-one is, she is no Sandra, Candace, GiGi, or Stefani.

Without turning my head, I say to Zaworski, "Dell Woods called and left me a message while I was sleeping."

He stops in his tracks in the doorway and looks at me.

"He says he's calling back. I figure you'll want to huddle the team and let them listen to his message."

"You got that right."

"And I'm guessing the FBI is going to patch into my cell line so they can triangulate his location when he calls back."

"How do you know he'll call back?"

"He said so in the message."

I hold up my hand before he can say anything else, pull out my phone and get into my voicemail, then let him listen.

When he's done, he hands it back to me, and I save the message, then hand it back to him again. "You gather the team to listen in and discuss and that will give me fifteen minutes to catch up on the crime scene. You all will know as much about Dell's most recent contact with me as I do at this point."

"Anything else, Conner?"

"No, sir, that will be it."

When did I get so sassy with my boss? He's giving me a lot of rope these days—I better cool it before I hang myself.

I know everyone is enthralled with crime scene investigation dramas. That's because they've never been to a crime scene. A quick camera shot of a dead body is one thing, but when you're actually there and have to take in real flesh and blood that has been traumatized with a knife or blunt force, the sights and smells of decomposition, then it's not so glamorous. I've watched the show set in Miami a couple times. Sure they put plenty of white and blue makeup on the corpses, but the victims still tend to be beautiful. That's not the stuff of a real crime scene.

I don't know how Jerome and Bruce do it. Our two techies are working murder number five for us. The Cutter is definitely in the acceleration mode that Van Guten anticipated. They are putting items into clear bags and then writing notes on the bags with Sharpies. The medical examiner is leaving as I arrive. Once we give the green light, the body will go into a big black bag, which will be zipped up and taken to the morgue so the body can be seriously studied.

Grace Mills. *Grace.* Pretty name. Her background is a little different than the others. She doesn't have a professional job—she was a waitress at a cocktail lounge about ten minutes from her 900-square-foot house—and obviously, her place isn't nearly as nice inside or out as what the others lived in. Not the same zip code—literally.

I cover all the rooms in a slow and methodical walk-through. When I get to her bedroom, I just stand at the door and watch the workers preparing to move her from the blood-soaked bed, trying to imagine the place with just her and him. I breathe slowly. I say a prayer. I have an impression. Of what? I think I can feel some of his emotions. Elation. Frustration. Disappointment. Fear?

I try to hold on to a soft blurred image in my mind, but then it's gone.

———

Don rides with me from the crime scene.

"I know you all are convinced that Cutter Shark attacked me," I say, "but you're ignoring one simple fact. If he attacked me I wouldn't be here. According to Virgil, our killer hasn't let anyone go free yet. Once you swim in his ocean, you don't make it to shore."

"You might be right," Don says, "no matter how contrived your word picture. But Van Guten likes Woods for your attack and for being the Shark."

I shake my head. Dell just didn't feel right for either role.

"This is not the MO of the Cutter Shark. He hasn't snuck up on people in parking lots. He has charmed his way into their bedrooms. He hasn't attacked them and drug them in there by the hair."

"Maybe Dell thought he was going to charm you and when it didn't work out, he attacked you."

I give that serious thought. "Even if you're right, I'll ask again: why am I still alive then?"

"That's a great question, KC. Maybe he has real feelings for you in his twisted, perverted mind. He is crazy, you know."

"Did you just call me KC?"

"I did. My bad. But bottom line, the shrink thinks your ex is our man."

"Bottom line, she's wrong. It's not Dell. And Dell is not my ex."

There is no way he could punch like that.

We met back at the State Building at 7 p.m. Fifteen of us sat around a long conference table, like a big family settling down for a dinner of information. Willingham was at the head of the table, with Zaworski right next to him. Reynolds entered a few minutes late, arriving by helicopter like some serious hotshot. He sat at Willingham's left hand. I look at them. The holy trinity of the Cutter Shark murder investigation.

Van Guten had been sitting in the seat next to Willingham when the meeting started, but left the room to answer a phone call. When she got back in, Reynolds had taken her chair. She gave him a decidedly dirty look and appeared less than thrilled to get stuck down at the other end of the table next to me. I glance at her several times out of the corner of my eye. How can anyone have such perfect fingernails? I can't stop stealing looks at them—honestly, I don't think they're fake. Her hair is perfect—she could walk away from this place and into any restaurant in the city fifteen minutes later—without stopping in the powder room—and fit right in. I've never wanted to win a beauty contest but I feel just a little self-conscious looking at my short, clipped nails. No polish. Maybe I'll get a manicure tomorrow. And maybe I'll join the circus. Just as likely.

We'd been going at it hard for ninety minutes. We spent the first thirty minutes on Dell. I got my phone back and was given explicit instructions to pick the thing up the second a private number vibrated, no matter what time of day or night.

Reynolds confirmed that Dell's home has been linked to Cutter Shark activity. There's no sign of him being there recently and even though they've been tossing the place for almost twenty-four hours, they've found no physical evidence explicitly tying him to any of the crimes. No way is Dell a serial killer. I did not date a serial killer. But the thought crosses my mind that it would delight a sicko like the Cutter Shark to play with a detective. But it's not Dell. No way.

I feel incredibly sad for him. And I'm very bothered by the fact that I could hang around with someone off and on for most of six months and never have a clue that there was something terribly wrong with him. He's not the killer. But he did tell me he was in some kind of trouble. Did I sense something? Anything? Besides a die-hard pursuit? A lot of guys are weird when it comes to dating. And he's not the killer. Or am I just a lousy, blind, deaf detective?

Right before we transitioned to the postmortem of the Grace Mills crime scene, my cell buzzed and sure enough, it was a private number. Everyone in the room froze and my heart was racing as I hit the green answer button on my Nokia. It was my credit card company wanting to know if I wanted to try their identity theft protection plan free for a month with no obligation to buy. I thought it might be funny to ask a few questions about costs and benefits with everyone listening in, but Don's audible sighs and angst-ridden expression were helpful deterrents. *Don, I wasn't going to fool around. I'm not that stupid.*

Willingham looked irritated. Not my fault, I wanted to say to him. Any thought of actually voicing such sentiment and defending myself was cut off by Zaworski's stern gaze. Has he been talking to Don? Reynolds was trying to make eye contact with me the whole time. Not going to happen, Major.

I've kept my mouth shut since explaining for the seventh time everything I know about Dell's call. How many times can you say you were asleep, he called, you didn't pick up, he left a message, and you listened to the message while driving over to a murder site? The same message they heard from a guy they think is the killer, but who isn't the killer.

A number of theories were espoused as to why the Cutter Shark picked Grace Mills. She wasn't really that less attractive than the other women and yes, she met the qualification of being single, but she definitely stood apart from the rest in her occupation and residence. She didn't show signs of illegal drug abuse but she definitely liked her alcohol. Another AA target? We don't know yet. There were empty beer and whiskey bottles everywhere. Pabst Blue Ribbon and Jim Beam were her poisons of choice. There were enough cases of PBR stacked on one side of her garage that she could weather a couple years of famine, pestilence, and nuclear fallout without having to drive to the corner convenience store for a six-pack. My guess was that the guy who owns the bar she works at, downstairs for questioning even as we spoke, was going to have a lot less beer missing from his inventory in the years ahead.

Don started things off by asking if Grace's murderer was even the Cutter Shark—or maybe a copycat killer instead. One of the FBI forensics experts got Bruce on the speakerphone and after about ten minutes of question and answer, the group was reasonably certain that this was the work of the one and only Cutter Shark.

Konkade chalked up the perpetrator going for "a drunk slob"— his phrase, not mine—rather than a sophisticated lady, to the law of averages. If you go out with enough people, some of them are going to look better, have better habits, and generally be better off than others. Grace just happened to be on the very right edge of the murderer's bell curve as applied to victim selection.

That didn't really fuel a lot of discussion. Reynolds was flipping through notebooks the whole time to see if there was precedence. He was sure he remembered another woman who might be a little like Grace. He found the page he was looking for, and it ended up that one of the Cutter Shark victims in Charleston, South Carolina, was almost as messy as Grace. But then the comparison broke down. She was actually a very successful artist who kept her studio in her home, which was on the National Register of Historic Places and worth a couple million dollars. She was also beautiful and from the pictures had good personal hygiene. She just kept a messy house.

Konkade argued that this just might prove his point; over time not only would the killer find women who were more or less messy, but he would also find some women who were richer and some women who were poorer. He still didn't have anyone convinced. He looked deflated as he smoothed the hair on his bald dome.

Van Guten took over the conversation and discussed the Cutter Shark as a man in and out of a killing frenzy, not quite on top of his game, showing cracks in his veneer, and making mistakes. The only problem, Willingham pointed out, was that the guy really hadn't made any mistakes; at least none were immediately identifiable at his latest killing ground. He still hadn't left the proverbial calling card with his current address. Van Guten didn't like this response. I watched her swinging the toe of her right foot, higher and higher over her left-crossed leg.

The conversation ground to a halt and it looked like things were done for a Saturday night. I started organizing my papers into a neat pile.

"Conner, you haven't said much. Why do you think he went after Grace?"

Willingham was looking at me intently. I snapped out of my reverie.

"Why Grace?" I asked rhetorically. "Why not another accountant or attorney or human resources director or media personality or studio artist? Why someone in a filthy little hovel when every other person had a ritzy place that was clean as a whistle?"

I wondered where that phrase came from.

"I think his plans got messed up at the last minute," I said. "And he had to improvise. I think Grace was Plan B. Maybe even Plan C."

There was a silence in the room. Every eye was focused on me. I like creating awkward pauses for others, but hate them for myself. I wanted to explain my thought further or apologize for wasting everyone's time with such a stupid idea or let the group know that I had to get home and go to bed because I didn't feel well. Using all my willpower, I held my tongue and said nothing.

"Ding, ding, ding, ding, ding . . . I think we've got a winner," Willingham said, breaking the silence.

A winner? Right. They think I dated a serial killer.

He dismissed us and set another meeting for ten the next morning. I looked at my watch. If I could climb in bed in an hour, I thought, I could cop a whole twelve hours of recovery sleep. I needed every second of it. I walked out of the conference room. My bodyguards were drinking coffee and looking at magazines in the reception area. I suddenly loved my bodyguards because they meant I could leave my car in the parking garage and get a ride home from them and then a ride back over here in the morning. I headed their way.

"Nice job, hot shot," Martinez said as he held the door for me. "I like that Plan C theory you came up with. How'd you come up with it that fast?"

"I've learned from the best," I answered him.

"And that would be me?" Don said, walking into the conversation.

Konkade, Blackshear, Big Tony, Zaworski, and Van Guten overheard and joined the circle to see how this would turn out. Reynolds was still back with Director Willingham.

"Tell them," I said to Tony.

"That's easy," he said to an interested audience. "Her daddy."

Good answer. But my daddy would have known he was dealing with a serial killer—though Dell is not the serial killer. We headed our separate ways. One of these days I have to ask Scalia about his AA story and whether he really broke my dad's jaw.

I call my mom from the back of the squad car on my way home. I like being chauffeured; it feels different than when Don drives and I get shotgun. Mom lets me know she went back to her house for a couple hours to pack some things and feed the cat and is already back at my place. I tell her again that she doesn't have to spend the night, reminding her Kaylen said she'd stay, which makes her indignant and hurt. I give in.

Kaylen is already back at the apartment, too. Mom tells me they've made my favorite chicken salad for me. Mom made me a quick ham and cheese sandwich earlier, but I suddenly realize I am starving and chicken salad with golden raisins, fresh dill, walnuts, grapes, celery, and a little mayonnaise sounds wonderful. I ask about Jimmy and the kids and Kaylen gets on the phone to tell me that it's good for him to be on his own. All he has to do is finish a sermon and get James and Kendra to bed. I wonder how long it takes to write a sermon and practice it. I know how long it takes to get those two kids into bed. Kaylen tells me she isn't planning to go to church in the morning, but is going to stay at my place and make sure I don't go anywhere for the rest of the weekend, even if she and Mom have to form a human barricade in front of my door. I decide not to tell her just yet that I'll be back in the office at ten. I wish I had one of those rope ladders so I could make an easy escape in the morning.

As far as Kaylen asserting that she is going to miss church, I think I'm going to pass out from shock. I'm not sure she's ever missed church. When we were little kids, our church had a perfect attendance award system. You got a medallion for your first year with no Sunday misses, and then you got a gold bar that hung on tiny hooks from the medallion for subsequent years. She looked like a five-star general when she wore hers. I never made buck private. I didn't dislike going to church; I just came up with excuses for missing from time to time. I know when we were teens my sisters—and my mom—resented that Dad took me to my weekend soccer tournaments in St. Louis or Champaigne-Urbana or Indianapolis or Springfield—and Mom took them to Sunday school. Nobody said they couldn't try out for a travel soccer team.

My cell beeps twice while we talk. I pull the phone from my ear and look each time to see if it is a private number that will end up going live with me and about a hundred FBI agents at the same time. It is Reynolds, both times. I'm not taking his calls. But if I do, it will be to let him make a fool of himself within earshot of his colleagues.

My cell starts beeping again. It's Don. I tell Kaylen I have to take it and that I'll see her in a few minutes.

"What's up, Don?"

"Just talked to Vanessa. Need a roommate tonight? She's already packed if you need her. She says I can get the kids ready for church all by myself tomorrow."

"I would say no, but the thought of you being a mommy and getting those angels of yours ready by yourself makes me want to reconsider my first response."

"Ha ha. KC, consider it done. She'll be there in less than an hour."

"Don, tell her to sit tight. My mom and Kaylen already have dibs on the beds in my guest room. I'm calling Klarissa next and if she comes over, she'll get half my bed. That would leave the couch for Vanessa. I wouldn't wish my couch on an enemy."

"She's made dinner to bring over," he says. "Wouldn't have to spend the night."

"Tell her to get moving now," I say without hesitation, laughing. "And tell her to bring her pajamas and a sleeping bag, just in case."

"Done."

"And Don?"

"Yeah?"

"Stop calling me KC."

"Got it."

I love Kaylen's chicken salad. But Vanessa is a gourmet and as I've noted, I've taken a liking to fine dining. I hold down the number four and Klarissa's cell starts chirping Beethoven's "Ode to Joy." Her voice message comes up: "You've reached Klarissa Conner, reporter at WCI-TV, Chicago's number one source for news. I can't come to the phone right now, but your call is important to me. Please leave your name, a detailed message, and the time you called. I will get back to you as soon as I can."

"Hey, Klarissa, this is Kristen. Call when you get this. Better yet, just come over. It's slumber party night."

She wasn't very talkative at my apartment earlier today, which now feels like a couple of weeks ago. She's probably jealous of the attention I'm getting from Mom and Kaylen. She probably feels left out and she for sure feels I'm not listening to her. *Okay, cool it,* I tell myself. *You two have been getting along fine until that last blowup. Better than fine. Better than ever. Even if you are a little mad at her, let things go.*

Dear God, help me get along with my sister.

63

THE CHITOWNVLOGGER
JUNE 6, 8:40PM

Axl wailed, "We take it day by day; if you want it you're gonna bleed, but it's the price you pay . . ."

GUESS WHO HAS BEEN OUT ON THE TOWN? scrolled across the screen. Then, THE CUTTER SHARK HAS BEEN A BAD BOY . . . AGAIN flashed over and over during the Guns N' Roses intro.

"Your ChiTownVlogger hears that we are America's number one city in the heart of the FBI. In fact, the national headquarters has set up shop and has just sent another ten agents to their posh new digs on the forty-eighth floor of the State Building. They are being led by Deputy Director Robert Willingham. And wherever he shows up, the bad guys tremble. He's not only smart but he also brings his impeccable style and taste—at a significant cost to taxpayers. I hear he brought in a corporate designer to decorate and furnish temporary offices and is paying twice the going rate for downtown office space. The perks of being a legend are excellent, all the way down to the Blue Mountain coffee he has flown in at the beginning of every week.

"I happen to know the designer's total bill. Get this: 150,000 bucks. For a temporary office space. That didn't include the actual furniture. I don't even want to guess what Willingham's expense report is costing us. I don't think he does the dollar menu at McDonald's. I hope they catch the Cutter Shark before our government goes bankrupt. Too late. I think Bush and Obama already tag-teamed to make that happen.

"Sadly, it appears that Citizen Willingham is much like Citizen Doyle. Both like to sit on their tail ends all day. I guess that's one reason they both feel free to spend so much of our hard-earned dollars making themselves feel very comfortable. Even with all that to-do, there are no new leads on the Cutter Shark case. Where is J. Edgar Hoover when you need him?

"The big guns have indeed rolled into town. You didn't hear that from the mayor. You won't read it in the *Tribune*—until after they learn it from the ChiTownVlogger. But it makes me wonder, what else aren't they telling us? Methinks our deputy director has spent too much time cloaked in the veil of 'national security' while fighting the fight on terrorism. Maybe he's forgotten we live in a free society, with a free press. Well, the mainstream media doesn't seem to care—too much work—but I'm old-school and I do. That's why you tune them out and tune me in.

"If you want to know what's really going on with the Cutter Shark investigation, check back in my jungle, early and often. Because if you want to be in the know, you have to get it from your ChiTownVlogger."

Satisfied, Johnson hit the upload button. He stood up with a grunt to stretch his legs and looked down at the front of the polo shirt stretched across his belly. He brushed crumbs from the tacos he had for dinner.

More company," Randy says. "They say they know you. Jeff and Patricia Williams. Want to come to the front door and verify?"

"On my way."

I hit the red button and put down my cell phone on the coffee table. I've got two new babysitters guarding me outside, and Randy is one of them. Mom, Kaylen, Klarissa, and Vanessa are in my living room, all staring at me to make sure I'm okay. I think they're all spending the night now, couch threat and all. Mom's in my recliner, I'm laying on the couch, and my sisters and Vanessa are leaning against big cushions on the floor. It's like I'm back in sixth grade. And my mom has insisted she be a part of the party. I get up with a groan.

"I can go to the door for you, honey," Mom says.

"That'd be great, but Randy needs me to identify who is there," I say.

"You just want to do it yourself because you think Randy is cute," Klarissa says.

Yep. I'm back in sixth grade, I think as I grimace a smile at Klarissa.

I walk slowly to the front door and look out past a kid with a shaved head, not Randy—I think this one's name is Carter—in a neatly pressed dark blue uniform and shiny black shoes. He's got to be ex-military. You can usually tell. He can't be twenty years old, can he? Did he do a turn in Afghanistan and still have time to go through the academy? I'm still almost a month from turning thirty, but I suddenly feel old. I look past him.

It's Patricia and Jeff. She has a splint on her nose and her face is bandaged. She looks worse than me by a long shot. I talked to her earlier and told her what happened and she said she wanted to come over. But I didn't think she would. I don't quite know what to do, but she just gives me a hug and strides in like she owns the place. Jeff hands me her small overnight bag with a shrug, a smile—sincere but slightly strained—and does a quick about-face.

"Have fun, ladies," he calls over his shoulder.

—

I can't keep my eyes open, but for once, the party is at my house and I don't want to be left out. So I'm sort of in and out of sleep on my couch. Every time I lift my head, I see Mom and Kaylen talking with Patricia at my kitchen table. They're laughing, crying, hugging, praying, and heaven knows what else. I wish I would have thought of them earlier to help with Patricia. I couldn't be her sponsor or provide the support she needed after what happened, but the combined forces of the Conner family led by my relentless mother, might have kept her out of the hospital.

Klarissa and Vanessa are sipping chardonnay and sitting on the floor talking about the contemporary furniture exhibit coming up at McCormick Place. Mom gave Klarissa's glass of wine one disapproving look and hasn't glanced that way since. I can't quite follow the conversation but I think matte pastels are back in. And it doesn't sound like pink and brown are going anywhere soon. I'm not sure if they said chrome and painted concrete are making a serious comeback or not. Might have been the other way. But I'm pretty certain they said that the rich-grained mahoganies and other dark woods have got to be on the cusp of a breakthrough. That's good to know. I drift back to sleep. Again.

Vanessa brought a chicken casserole that was to die for. Even better than my favorite chicken salad. Rosemary and thyme, straight from her garden, she explained. I tried to make a joke about a song from the '60s but couldn't quite get it out. Wouldn't have been very funny anyway.

I wake up with a start. I look at the clock on my nightstand. It's 2:55. I don't know how I got into my bed and under the covers. I just know I was dreaming. I was being chased. I was sure it was Timmy, but when I looked back it was Dell. But then when he caught me and knocked me to the ground, it was the punk. He was leering and slowly moving a blade side to side, inches from my face.

My head clears a little. I had forgotten about him until I mentioned him in the hospital as a suspect and Don told us he had been cut loose. I wonder where the punk is now.

So who attacked me? Dell? Timmy? Incaviglia? The Cutter Shark? *Who is not Dell.* I try to sort it out but can't. Then a crystal-clear thought jumps into my mind: *If Grace Mills was Plan B, who was Plan A?*

I'll bring that up when we meet. I fall back into a restless sleep.

I swing my legs over the side of the bed at a quarter past four. I really have to go to the bathroom. I finish and look down before flushing, relieved to find no blood in my urine. I pad out to my kitchen, pour a glass of water from the dispenser on the door of my Frigidaire, and

pop a pain pill in my mouth. *Last one,* I think. If things still hurt, I'll just take an over-the-counter ibuprofen. I creep around my apartment; look in the door of the guest room. Mom and Kaylen are asleep. Usually it's James and Kendra in there. I miss them.

I walk into my living area. Klarissa is asleep on the floor. She has made a nice pallet with blankets I inherited from Grandma. I offered her half my bed but staying up and talking must have been a better offer. I look at her face. She is so beautiful, my breath catches. She is an angel. She can be so hard and tough, but right now she looks childlike and elfin.

Patricia has made a little bed on the floor, too, and is at a ninety-degree angle from Klarissa. Her face is about an inch from Klarissa's feet. She's going to end up with a toe in her ear. I want to laugh, but my side and back still hurt too bad. She called Jeff earlier in the evening, and he spent an hour on the phone with my mom. He is going to go with the kids to Jimmy's church in the morning. We're all meeting at Jimmy and Kaylen's for lunch. They think I'll be there, too, and I'm not lying; I'm just not telling them that I have to be at the office at ten.

Patricia continues to be a mess, but I somehow think things are going to work out for her and Jeff, now that they have a real support system. I think I'm good for a shot of adrenaline to kick your butt in the right direction—Red Bull for the soul—but it's the saints of the world like Kaylen who can help you make it over the long haul.

Vanessa is asleep on the couch. She is on her back with one arm hanging over the side at a weird angle. She's going to be sore in the morning. Probably not as sore as Don when he actually has to get the kids ready for church by himself. I bet they get there late. But then I remember at their church, it doesn't matter. I walk back through my little home and look out my front kitchen window. An unmarked Chevy Malibu is in the parking lot with an interior light on. No Carter tonight. One guy is obviously asleep and the other is reading. Some bodyguards. But I'm not worried. I feel very safe surrounded by my friends and family.

I go back to my room and climb into my huge bed. I feel guilty for having all this space to myself, but only for an instant. I feel myself falling back asleep while rubbing my feet together. A professor in one of my psych courses said that we rub our feet together to comfort ourselves. A punch to the kidneys always demands a little comforting.

My phone chirps on the nightstand. I fumble for it so I can turn off the alarm. Then I realize it is not the wake-up signal but a phone call. I look at the small display. It's only 4:58. It is a call from a private number. I pick up at the very end of the fourth ring, hoping that whoever is calling hasn't already been transferred over to voicemail.

"Dell?"

"Yeah, it's me. How are you, Kristen?"

"Uhh, just so-so."

"What's the matter?"

"Other than getting attacked in the parking lot two nights ago, I'm still in the middle of the city's biggest homicide case in decades."

"Are you serious? Someone attacked you?"

"Very serious. Imagine that. Someone not liking me enough to get violent."

He laughs. And then he starts to cry. I consider how I'm going to play this. What I can—and can't—say. One way or another, I am going to find out, right now, what I know to be true—that Dell isn't our man. But his crying? Well, yeah, that's troubling me . . . "Dell?"

"Yeah?"

"What's wrong? What's going on?"

"I can't tell you."

"Yes, you can. That's why you called."

"I can't. You wouldn't understand."

"Probably not. But I think you're in a lot of trouble and you're going to have to start talking to someone, sometime. Why not now? To me?"

"This call is probably being recorded, isn't it?"

No use lying. Dell knows technology. It could be his tagline. Dell Knows Technology. I shake my head and force myself to focus. "It is," I answer.

"So I wouldn't really be talking just to you, would I?"

"No."

"You've probably been told to keep me on the phone as long as possible, haven't you?"

"Yes."

"They probably already know what city I'm in right now, don't they?"

"I'm not sure about that," I answer truthfully, though I suspect they do.

"It's funny, but you were always afraid of hurting me . . . that's why you didn't just break things off completely even though I knew almost from day one that's what you wanted to do. But you went ahead and kicked me in the stomach anyway. You know something that might surprise you?"

"What?"

"I was always afraid of hurting you, too. I have a secret, you know."

"That's what you said."

"Know what it is?"

"I think so," I answer, my heart hammering in my chest, afraid of what he's going to say next.

"I'm not sure you do."

"Come meet me, Dell, and let's talk this through."

"Alone?"

"Absolutely."

He laughs under his breath. "Kristen, even if I accused you otherwise, I always respected that you were honest with me—even when you were a little *too* honest for my state of being. But I somehow suspect you aren't telling the truth right now."

"Dell, I promise, if it is within my power to make it so, we can meet alone."

"Empty words. You know it's not within your power. And it's too late for that. I need to hang up now. But I'll call you again in the next couple days."

"Dell? Dell, don't hang up."

He's already gone.

He's either the world's greatest actor or he's broken up over things. The guy can't be the killer. No way. Surely they can hear that when they listen to this call. But what's this secret?

———

It's seven. I'm showered and dressed. I actually feel pretty decent, despite having had my sleep interrupted a couple times. I have three hours before the task force meets in the dingy, gray conference room at our CPD precinct. My plan is to sneak out without anyone hearing me. I never told Mom or Kaylen that I was heading back to work today. I am about to pull the door open, when I hear footsteps behind me.

"You could have told me," Patricia whispers.

"Told you what?"

"That your dad was shot in the line of duty. That he's dead."

I say nothing. I just look in her tear-filled eyes that peer out from the bandages.

"You never said anything."

"I know."

"Why?"

"I don't know why. I just know it's something I don't talk about."

"I *knew* you were hurting inside, just like me. I could tell. And as we've learned in AA, alcohol is not the problem, but a symptom of the problem. We just have different ways of coping. I turned to vodka and you keep people at a distance."

"I can't argue with that, Patricia, because everybody else is saying the same thing. But I will defend myself and say that some things, like how many open relationships we have, is a matter of personality, too. Even when nothing is eating at me, I've always preferred to do things with people rather than sit around and talk with them."

"*Really?* I couldn't tell," she says sarcastically. "I'm sorry," she continues, seriously. "This isn't a joking around time. So I'll just say, you're going to have to talk about what happened the past year sometime. A year is a long time to hold things in. So when are you going to open up to someone?"

"You've met my family. My life is an open book."

"Really? How come your mom and sisters told me you won't open up with them either?"

"Because they obviously can't help sharing with others," I say with a laugh.

"You really aren't ready to talk . . ."

"Even if I think talking about things is overrated, I agree it is a very good thing to connect with others when we have problems. I at least learned that from AA. But even if now was the perfect time to talk, you wouldn't understand everything that goes into my situation, Patricia. Not all of it."

"Try me. Trust me. I trusted you."

I start to speak and then pause. The words won't come out. I try again, still no words.

"Just say it," Patricia says.

"Your dad died of a sudden stroke, Patricia. That's awful. You didn't have time to work out the things that came between the two of you and that makes it even more awful. My dad didn't die the same way."

"He died a hero in the line of duty. Doesn't that help a little? You had a great relationship with him. I didn't."

"He didn't die in the line of duty," I answer dully. I can feel the familiar, deep-seated wave of emotions rising in me—grief and then anger—ready to spill over and cover everything in my path. She just looks at me, confusion on her face. She doesn't get it. "I'm angry because someone shot my dad in the line of duty—but it took him a year to die. We still don't know who shot him and there's nothing I can do about it. They closed the case in February of this year. Now I can't poke around the files—even if it's on my own time—without permission from the commander's office. And he's not giving it. He doesn't think it's healthy for me. I can't do anything without getting fired and that's driving me crazy. Like I said, I prefer doing over talking."

Her eyes are a little wide from my vehemence. We look at each other in my little hallway, neither knowing what to say.

"I'm so sorry, Kristen," she finally says. "I don't think anyone would know how to handle what you're going through."

She steps forward and gives me a hug. I nearly flinch because the last thing I want is sympathy right now. I don't want a hug. I don't want comfort. I want to set this right—and that requires some anger. I pull away and start talking fast.

"My family is worried about me and my anger. They seem to be coping okay, but they're all struggling, too. Klarissa's always been a twig but I don't think she's eating enough to feed a cat. Kaylen has Jimmy and she's a rock, but that's because he's a rock. But I don't hear her talking about the dad thing either. No one's busting her chops— she can hide behind two kids and another on the way. Mom is from another planet these days. So bottom line, we all feel betrayed but it shows up in different ways. With me working the case, even when it wasn't mine, it did help. All of us. But since CPD closed the case and moved it to the cold files . . . I'm . . . I'm angry. I've grown up with the CPD. The CPD helped raise me. My dad even worked for the guy who put his file on the back burner and took away my access. Czaka has had dinner at our house. He's known us girls since we were babies. The CPD I know and love would never put a cop-shooter case in the cold files. But they have. And it makes me furious."

"Listen to someone who has screwed up her life so much that she's holding on to her world by a thread. Deal with your pain somehow, some way. Right now. I know you don't want to hear this and I have no right to say it, but it's possible to end up in a hospital—or some other equally bad place—even if you're not a drunk."

I close my eyes at the memory of Patricia in ICU. Was it just a week ago? Her beautiful face will come back—but it's gonna be a while.

"Patricia, I am dealing with things right now. At least a little. The funny thing is, AA actually helped me. A lot. That was the farthest thing from my mind, getting help, when I showed up at that first meeting. Same as you. Over time I kept trying to make up a drinking story, and I finally just started substituting the word *alcohol* for *anger* and you all ate it up."

She has a hurt look on her face.

"I'm sorry. I didn't mean it to sound that way. Diplomacy has never been my strong suit. What I mean to say is that I was finally one of you—one of the group and I fit in. And it wasn't that I had a better cover story—I could relate and get help. And maybe even help others."

"You did help," she says. "A lot. I still mean what I said to the group: you saved my life. And one of these days you might let me help you back by talking to you about your dad—not just your anger?"

"Maybe." Was she not listening? That's what I just did. I just told her everything inside me that can come out.

"I know, I know . . . you're already out the door and you'd agree with anything I say to be on your way. But it would mean an awful lot to me if you'd let me be there for you. When you're ready."

"Maybe."

"Well, you are being honest, and that's good enough," she says. She pauses and continues, "I'll tell you something else funny before you run. I definitely did not like you the first time I laid eyes on you . . . and before you pretend it was otherwise, I know you absolutely despised me, too."

"Was it that obvious, *Bethany?*"

"Oh yeah," she says with a laugh.

"Patricia," I say hesitantly, "I know there's a lot more we could say to each other, but I've got to get out of here."

She smiles and retorts, "And you don't want the others to know you're sneaking out?"

"Maybe."

"So get out of here and go save the city from the Cutter Shark before I wake everybody up." Patricia gives me another hug and I accept it this time. Okay—a little comfort is okay. But only for a second before I'm on my way. I think I'll be fine from the attack in no time. But all this sharing wears me out. I just breathe in and out with my game face on as I stride purposely into the parking lot.

Everything I said to Patricia was true. I just didn't tell her everything. And of course, Mom and Kaylen didn't tell her everything because they don't know everything I do. Lying by omission. I still have to ask Jimmy about that. What does God think about such things? I keep the last letter Dad wrote me locked in my safebox.

Not everything can come out . . . Some things are better left locked up.

I drop my change from four crumpled dollar bills into the tip box at the drive-through window. I greedily snatch my steaming grande Americano with an extra espresso shot and one Splenda that Randy hands back to me. I am sitting in the back of a police cruiser. My two babysitters have been sipping coffee all night and aren't interested in any more caffeine. I have enough aches and pains that I'm content to skip my ritual of going inside because I don't want to have to get in and out of the cruiser an extra time. Their shift ends in an hour and I'm guessing they'll be asleep within five minutes of getting home and putting head to pillow.

Randy is driving and Carter is riding shotgun. I'm separated from them by a metal mesh protective screen with a window that is opened. It's no fancy limo, but it's a ride. Randy wheels out of the drive-through lane as I take my first sip. My friend with the tongue stud and green apron has forgotten to put a Splenda in my drink. I need a little sweetener in my coffee.

"Hit the brakes," I order. "Pull into that parking spot by the front door and let me out."

"Everything okay?" Carter asks.

"Definitely not."

They look very concerned. I fumble to open the door, but realize there are no handles in the back of a cruiser.

"Can someone get the door open?" I demand.

"Sure," Randy says glancing nervously at Carter.

He kills the engine, gets out, and opens my car door for me, quickly stepping aside. I head through the entrance with two very worried bodyguards on my tail. Their heads are on swivels as they look left and right for possible threats against my person. It's not me they need to be worried about.

Can I not speak clearly? Do I stutter? Mumble? Why is ordering a simple coffee drink such an ordeal for me? And since no one else has mentioned they have problems, I guess it is me. I step to the front of the line right in front of a guy who is about to order. He turns to let me have it for cutting. He sees my expression, and then my bodyguards, and immediately backs down. Smart man. I explain to a cheerful young blonde that I didn't get the drink I ordered. The girl at the counter assures me that it is no problem if I changed my mind. They want me to be happy. That's not what I want to hear. I tell her that I will only be happy if she or someone else from the establishment admits that they are the ones that made the mistake.

"Uh, sure," she says. "My mistake."

Since she's not the one who took my order, her mea culpa doesn't feel very satisfying. I look over at Carter and Randy while tapping my fingers on the high, amoeba-shaped counter where my replacement drink will be delivered.

They think I'm crazy. They might be right.

On the freeway I hear the sound of a submarine's sonar system. I look at my cell and see that a text from Reynolds just came in.

I was going to tell you. You have every right to be mad. Let me explain. Let's talk. Please?

I hit delete and lay my head back against the seat. I close my eyes and take inventory. I'm feeling better physically, all things considered, but am wondering if going to this meeting really is a very bad idea.

Randy and Carter weren't quite sure what to do when I came out into the parking lot earlier this morning. They had explicit orders to watch over me and anyone else at my apartment. No one added a note that they were to drive me down to precinct on their assignment report. And after yesterday, they weren't as apt to just jump when I barked. I would've just hopped in my own car, but it was parked in the garage at the State Building. Thankfully, they called Dispatch and another car was sent over to take their place on guard duty so they were freed to drive me to CPD.

I'm in my cubicle before eight. I attack everything relating to the Cutter Shark case on my desk with a passion. I bury my head in the mountain of paperwork—notebooks, documents, photographs, profiles, and more. I worry about the trees in the rain forests for just a second.

A half hour before our meeting is to start, I find something in a back tab of one of the notebooks. San Antonio. I tab the spot with a bright pink adhesive strip and jot a note on a blank sheet of paper and start skimming through Jacksonville, Denver, San Diego, and the others as fast as my fingers and eyes will work. I furiously scribble more notes for the next hour and when I look up I realize I am already thirty minutes late. I've pieced together some random observations and have discovered a non-isolated event stream. I grab my notepad and hustle to the conference room.

I open the door and it hits the doorstop with a bang. Always the graceful entrance. Everyone looks up at me.

"You didn't have to come in," Director Willingham says. "We would have understood. I don't think you're being as cautious as your doctor would like."

"No problem, sir," I answer. "I wouldn't miss this for the world."

As I make my way around to the only open seat, between Blackshear and Don, I remember that Vanessa is snoring at my house and wonder who is watching Devon and Veronika and getting them ready for church.

Don reads my mind and whispers, "They're with the neighbors."

Van Guten looks at me with disdain and gives Don a dirty look. I guess students are not supposed to speak without the teacher's permission.

"Any more ideas on finding Dell Woods?" Reynolds asks. "Besides keeping our eyes on Kristen."

Keep your eyes to yourself.

He had already reported at length on his trip to Durango. About the time Zaworski was getting a search warrant for us to crash into Dell's rented brownstone here, an FBI analyst created a graphic model and plotted southwest Colorado as the likely geographic home base for our murderer. The FBI then rented one of the US Army's supercomputers for a day—at a cost of more than $875,000 per hour, we were informed—and cross-tabulated calls and financial transactions between that area of the country and the target cities during corresponding dates.

To the FBI analyst's amazement, the computer was able to narrow the search down to a list of fewer than seven potential residents. They gathered a small army of financial and logistical analysts in Washington, DC, to work a graveyard shift in order to understand everything about the movements and patterns of members of those households. Dell's home and travels and a few select accounts came out as the winner. We don't know where Dell is—couldn't keep him on the phone long enough—but that's just a matter of time. The plan is to put his face on every news outlet in America starting at 5:00 EDT. Government lawyers are getting federal warrants and vetting the entire process to make sure nothing is done that will let a bad guy off the hook based on inadmissible evidence and that no lawsuits come our way.

It's been well over a decade, but the memory of the FBI announcing Richard Jewell as the prime suspect in the '96 bombing outside the Atlanta Olympics venue, and how the press subsequently crucified him, is still a textbook case of what not to do. Putting an innocent man's face on a couple hundred million TV screens is no small decision. In Jewell's case, it probably killed him.

What will it do to Dell?

I look around at the feds and see a lot of competence. I don't see anyone in this group as mistake-prone. But it wouldn't be the first time. I still can't believe the Cutter Shark is Dell, no matter how many thousands of dollars have been spent to prove it. But I'm seriously conflicted. Willingham went through a purgatory of sorts, due to others' mistakes. There's no way he could get something like this wrong, is there?

Willingham looks around the room one more time. He's very relaxed. He even laughed when he told the group he watched the ChiTownVlogger's latest report that included the cost of designing the FBI's ad hoc headquarters. He didn't say if the number was right. Everybody's ready to leave. I start to lift my hand, put it down, and then just blurt out a strangled "Sir."

"Yes, Conner?"

There is a nearly audible sigh in the room. Task force members who were halfway out of their chairs settle back in.

"I'm still not convinced Dell Woods is the killer." I raise my hand before Van Guten or anyone else can explain to me the error of my thinking. "But whether or not he is—and especially if he isn't—I believe I found another hunting ground for the killer."

"Oh? Let's hear it."

"We already reran all data points through Operation Vigilence," Van Guten interrupts. "Nothing was found."

"That's because of how you coded the data," I say. "But I've found eighteen victims—almost as many as he found at AA meetings—in one place. Virgil could have told you this, but you never asked him."

Okay. Everyone is looking at me and holding their breath. I can't believe it. I'm doing the pregnant pause. Van Guten is going to chew her lip off.

"Let's hear it," Zaworski demands, breaking my pleasant reverie.

"Church," I say. "He goes to church to find victims. Eighteen of our victims, including Sandra and GiGi in Chicago, have been regular church attendees."

"Is it possible, Dr. Van Guten?" Willingham asks.

"I'll have to look at the report protocols before I answer that," she says.

"Then get looking. I personally think we have our man, but if we don't, we need to make up for lost time on the church angle. How in the heck does something like this happen?" Willingham demands, looking at a blushing Van Guten.

"Church affiliation was given to Virgil as background data," I answer. "But somehow no one thought to add that line to any of the crosstabulations."

"I think Detective Conner has stumbled onto something," says Van Guten. "After all, that's where Woods located her."

Stumbled onto? Give me a little credit, Ice Queen. But oh man, I wasn't wanting to put more focus on Dell as the bad guy, and I just did exactly that. I'm still not sold . . .

"Great work, Conner," Zaworski says, slapping the table. "We're getting close, people. Now let's finish the job."

66

"Conner, you are the man," Martinez says again, his mouth stuffed with a jumbo hot dog with more trimmings than the bun can hold. He has mustard dripping down his chin, along with half a cucumber slice that just won't fit in the door.

I'm glad someone thinks I'm "the man."

He, Blackshear, Konkade, Don, Big Tony, and I are at a hole-in-the-wall a mile from HQ called the Devil Dog. Reynolds asked me to go to lunch with him. I politely declined. He kept trying to make eye contact while asking. I finally did. That helped him understand I wasn't going out with him. At least he's more perceptive than Dell.

What do I think of Reynolds? I'm not too hung up on looks, but he is attractive and he caught my eye the first time I saw him. I do like a confident and fun personality, and he has that in spades. He can be appropriately self-deprecating with his humor but you can easily tell that underneath he's comfortable with himself. He's very confident. I like guys who like their work—I am my daddy's girl after all—and that was another checkmark in his favor. I don't like needy. And Reynolds, despite trying to give me a hangdog look for sympathy the last two times I've seen him, really isn't. I know some women want tears and sensitivity from a man. Not me. Doesn't mean I want a Neanderthal. I do want caring and considerate. At least someday I do. I just don't want wimpy. I'm sorry if that means I lose my official Gen-X membership card.

"Nice job, Kristen," Big Tony adds. "Your dad would have been proud."

"It's hard to admit," Don says, "but even her partner is proud."

Okay, this is getting as thick as the mustard on Martinez's hot dog.

"Buen trabajo!" Martinez adds. *"Muy bien."*

"No applause, just throw money," I say, embarrassed at the attention.

"You got it," Blackshear says. "Your lunch is on me."

"Mine too?" Konkade asks quickly.

"Yep." Blackshear answers. "Just as soon as you figure out something before Virgil does."

Everyone laughs.

"We haven't caught anyone yet," I say. "And sorry, I still don't think it's Dell."

The table falls quiet.

"Esto tipo es un loco diablo—and whoever he is, we're gonna catch him," Martinez says with his flair for words—even when we don't understand all of them.

"I'm taking a long vacation after this is done," Don says. "I don't think my kids know who I am anymore."

"Good point," Konkade says. "We all have some well-earned time off coming up."

"Ah, who needs vacation?" I ask. "I was going to go the first week of April. But I'd have missed hanging out with you guys. And without me, you guys wouldn't have gotten anywhere on this case."

"La próxima vez que estés sola, ya sabes a quién llamar!" Martinez says to me with a big wink and his hand over his heart like he's picking up on me.

Big Tony gives him a dirty look and Martinez holds up his hands in surrender.

"I'm just kidding," he says laughing. "I keeeed. I keeeed."

Everyone at the table joins him. Except for me and Scalia. I don't have the energy to bust on Martinez right now. Doesn't mean I won't feel good enough to do so tomorrow.

"Kristen's right on one thing," Scalia says. "Before we start celebrating, we got to catch a serial killer."

"Woods can run, but he cannot hide," says Don, invoking one of the most tired and trite clichés in law enforcement.

Even as he says it, something strikes me wrong. It can't be Dell.

Dear God, help me figure out what you're trying to tell me.

———

I enter my apartment and immediately know something's wrong. It's absolutely spic and span with everything in its place. I'm sure Mom saw to that. I always keep a clean place, but that doesn't mean it's always tidy. But the order and stillness isn't what's got my antennae up. I haven't been as careful as I should in recent days and even though I still have police protection less than a hundred feet from my front door, I carefully and quietly de-holster my Beretta. I ease off the safety and bring it up to chest level with both hands.

I poke my head in and out of my kitchen and eating area. Nothing there. I walk in slowly and look under the table and in the broom closet anyway. I step back into my front hall. I creep up to the coat closet. I pull it open quickly and step back with drawn gun. Nothing. I repeat the process in my living room, my common bathroom, and my guest room. Still nothing.

My bedroom door is shut. I always leave it open. Maybe that's all that's bothering me. Of course, I wasn't the last one in the apartment. Maybe Mom or Kaylen pulled it shut before they left.

I now ponder my options. Continue searching my apartment so I can confirm nothing is wrong or go outside, ask two officers to come inside to help me finish checking everything out and when we don't find anything, let out a little embarrassed laugh, and explain to them that I'm just a little jittery since getting punched in the kidney and finding out my kind-of ex-boyfriend is a serial killer?

I turn the knob soundlessly and then push open the door hard enough that it slams into the wall stop. No one is hiding behind it. I keep my head on a swivel and check under the bed, in my small walk-in closet, in my tiny master bathroom, and even in the wardrobe that is probably just big enough to hold a person. Nothing. I look at my nightstand. The framed picture of me standing with Dad on the day I graduated from police academy, my uniform so neat and pressed, him in his dress blues and cap with braids on the bill, is missing. Weird.

Klarissa has said several times that she wants to come by and pick up some of my pictures and photo albums so she can have them scanned and saved electronically. Would she have just picked up that one picture and frame? I walk back into the living room. All my childhood photo albums are still lined up on the bottom row of my bookcase.

I walk back in my bedroom. I feel a chill and shudder. It has nothing to do with the weather. It's a gorgeous June afternoon, with temperatures in the low eighties. But something has caught my attention. My window is open a couple inches.

"Sure enough, someone came up that outside wall with a ladder and through your window," Konkade says.

It's quarter to five. Willingham and Reynolds are holding a press conference in forty-five minutes at city hall. The mayor, police chief, and a whole lot of other muckety mucks will be on the podium. Zaworski has been allotted two minutes—and not a second longer—for opening remarks. I heard Commander Czaka was expecting to speak and is not happy that it's Zaworski slated to be in front of the press.

Don and Martinez have the TV on WCI-TV in the living room. It's a house rule. Have to be loyal to family. Big Tony is directing operations with some uniformed officers outside. My security detail is about to be increased. The consensus is that I represent our best chance of bringing Dell in, whether it be taking his calls and talking him into turning himself in, or staying on the phone long enough for them to triangulate his location—or by serving as bait. They don't think he's through with me, either way.

My phone rings. Private number.

"Hi, Dell."

"Hi, Kristen."

"Where are you?"

"I can't tell you. You know I've got big troubles."

"I know. So why don't you come over and let's talk. Are you in Chicago, Dell?"

"C'mon. I'm not that dumb."

"Well, not coming in is not smart and I've always thought of you as a smart guy."

"It's interesting that now that you want something from me, you're incredibly attentive," he says with sadness. "I wish we could have talked like this before. You were always too preoccupied to really be there. Always multitasking and never doing any one thing all the way."

"It's been a tough couple of months, Dell. I'm listening now."

He pauses for a second, considering. "You know, I'm thirty-four years old and have never had a girlfriend for more than a couple of months. A lot of women think I'm great, because I'm okay-looking and

I spend a fair amount of money on them. But I was never good at relationships. Too many problems growing up. You were the first woman I really thought I could get to know. Do you know you were my significant other longer than any other woman in my life? Even if you didn't think of me the same way—I got it—that's still what you were to me."

Alarms are ringing in my head. If he isn't the Cutter Shark, he sure is sounding like him. I'll be known forever as a serial killer's significant other.

"I feel bad that I just didn't have the same feelings for you as you did for me, Dell. But I can't really force myself to feel something I don't, right?"

"I wonder if you feel anything at all."

I consider that and reject it, but answer, "You might be right," anyway.

He sighs. "It's good to hear you admit that."

I let him digest that a sec. I feel like a fisherman, allowing the hook to set in deep. "So when can we get your troubles sorted out? When are you going to come and talk to me?"

"I don't know. You won't really understand. Your family is perfect. And I wanted to be a part of that."

"What happened to your family, Dell?"

"It was bad. Dad left. Mom couldn't cope so she killed herself. On his way back to pick us up and take us to Loveland, of all names, my dad was killed in a car accident. We got passed around foster homes."

My antennae have sprung to attention and are sounding alarms. *Us. We.* "Dell, I thought you were an only child. And I didn't know your parents had died. I assumed they were still alive."

"How would you know? You never bothered to ask. I told Kaylen, Jimmy, your mom. But I waited for you to ask."

I close my eyes. I really can be a self-involved jerk sometimes.

"I figured you and your people knew by now. I have a brother."

"A brother. You have a brother?" My brain starts racing, all the missing pieces filling in gaps, like the last few pieces of a jigsaw puzzle.

"Yes. We got separated a couple years after my dad died. He was incredibly difficult. So mostly we grew up in different foster homes. I made out pretty good; he didn't. When I finally found him while I was in college, he was only seventeen, but he'd been in jail three times and countless juvenile homes. I put him in a nice place for troubled youth sponsored by a church I attended, and that seemed to help for a while, but when I tried to move him in with me and get him back in school—or at least help him find a job—he started disappearing for months at a time."

"When was the last time you saw him, Dell?"

"Six, I don't know, maybe seven months ago."

"Tell me right now; is he the guy we're looking for?"

There is a long enough pause that I wonder if he's hung up.

"I don't know for sure," he says quietly, "but I'm afraid he is."

I can't bring myself to say serial killer or Cutter Shark. But he knows and I know what we're talking about.

"What do you know for sure, Dell?"

"Not much. He emptied a bank account I keep for rainy days. It's not the first time. He went back to my place in Durango and stole some other stuff, too. He might not have thought of it as stealing, though. He thought of the place as his, which I wanted. I wanted him to feel like he had a home. Always. But I found some things on my office computer there that are disturbing."

"You haven't done anything bad or criminal yourself?" I ask Dell.

"Of course not. You really think I could?" Pain now etches his voice.

"You need to come in and help us right now, Dell. It's your only way out of this mess, and your brother's best path toward help. You have to come in."

"Let me think about it and call you back."

"Don't hang up, Dell."

"Kristen, I've got to. And you've got to understand. You have sisters. This is my brother we're talking about. I don't know for sure he's done anything wrong."

If he believed that, we wouldn't be having this conversation.

"Promise me you'll call back in the next hour. This is bad, Dell. And not just for your brother."

He hangs up before I can ask him what his brother's first name is. I whirl toward Don and Martinez, who are looking at me with wide eyes and stunned expressions. I was concentrating so hard I wasn't even aware they were listening.

I know the FBI has monitored the entire call from Washington, DC, but will whoever is listening know what to make of this—particularly in light of the fact that Dell is minutes away from being listed as the official Cutter Shark suspect to the world?

"We have to get to Willingham and Reynolds," I nearly shout. "They can't give Dell's name and picture to the press."

THE CHITOWNVLOGGER
JUNE 8, 5:55 P.M.

Johnson hit upload. Two minutes later he heard a ping indicating it was live. He decided to watch one more time.

—•—

"Welcome to the jungle, we take it day by day . . . "

A BAD CASE OF SUMMER TIME BLUES scrolls across the screen.

"We're going to keep this short and sweet, my admirers and enemies in Chicagoland and around the world. *Zdrah-stvooy*—that's 'hello' in Russian for all my fans in Moscow. Your ChiTownVlogger, the only reporter on the planet who has exclusive access to the Cutter Shark, has a direct message for Deputy Director Robert Willingham of the FBI and Police Commissioner Michael Fergosi of the Chicago Police Deparment.

"Just in case any cynics out there think I'm withholding information that could lead to the apprehension of the Shark—be assured I am a humanitarian before I am a reporter. Mayor Doyle is the master of whisper campaigns and, in an attempt to discredit my reports and take some of the heat off him and his cronies, I don't want him conducting one of his trademark smear jobs complaining that I'm sheltering a serial killer. Elections are only four months away. Of course he'll win, but he wants to win big to show an air of invincibility.

"What's the message I found in a bottle that washed up on the shore of Lake Michigan? There's good news and bad news. Which do you want first? I'll start with good news. The Cutter Shark plans to leave us in the near future. Our city will be safe once again—though not because of anything the combined forces of the CPD and FBI did.

"But here's the bad news. He's planning one more kill. He said he wanted to say a special good-bye to us. There is one other detail he sent me. I don't know how big of a deal this is. But he said nothing else will happen until summer. Not quite two weeks until you can move throughout our city with a feeling of relative safety.

"I can hear my critics already—and we know they mostly reside at city hall and the offices of what we commonly refer to as the 'mainstream media.' They will say that by going live I am jeopardizing the investigation and inciting a public panic.

"As is so often the case, they have missed the point. Airing this report won't change the Cutter Shark's plans. He wants the authorities to know what he is up to because he doesn't believe they can do anything about it. In medieval times they would say he has thrown down the gauntlet.

"As to public panic. Don't blame me. I'm just a private citizen. And if the police can't do any better than they have so far, I may join the stampede out of town!

"The jungle is heating up, ladies and gentlemen, boys and girls. Stop back often. It may be good news or bad news or both—but at least it's real news."

68

I had troubles getting online tonight so I couldn't download and print a copy of the *New York Times* crossword puzzle. I did find a copy of the large-print edition of *TV Guide* that my mom brought over earlier in the week. They publish a puzzle every week. The clues that didn't have anything to do with TV were way too easy. But most of the clues had to do with TV, and since I don't watch much, I was in trouble. I did get the three-letter word for a fuzzy, extraterrestrial, sitcom character right away. Alf.

At least I think so, even though I never connected any of the three letters with another word. Another day, another meeting.

Our task force meeting went a couple of hours. We met at city hall in a conference room a few doors away from the mayor's office, where Zaworski and Willingham were holed up with the politicians. The news conference that was called to announce a big break in the Cutter Shark case was cancelled. I can't believe how close they came to plastering Dell's name and face across the planet. As we waited, Don speculated they were working on damage control. I agreed with him.

The conference room was even nicer than the one we use at the regional office of the FBI in the State Building. An assistant to the mayor brought in a tray of glasses—they looked like real crystal—with the city's seal etched on the side. There was an ice bucket and a full assortment of soft drinks. She came back a few minutes later, pushing a cart with full coffee service. That's where most of us headed. Van Guten never moved, but nodded in the direction of the new group in from DC, and one of the FBI guys got her a small green bottle of San Pellegrino and a glass filled with ice cubes.

The brass walked in and Reynolds did most of the talking. He confirmed that Dell has a brother who was in and out of mental institutions from an early age. Willingham looks gray and weary. Maybe he got chewed out, too. He asked how everyone missed the brother. He saved his harshest glares for Reynolds and Van Guten. Blame is working its way down the food chain. Who is next? Reynolds, ever the cool customer, went on to explain that Dell's brother, Dean, grew up with a different last name than Woods in the course of getting volleyed around the foster care system and was essentially "lost." Van Guten announced she had run Dean's data through a series of psychological corollary tests she uses. She thinks Dean Pierre, his last known pseudonym, fits the bill for our Cutter Shark. More so than Dell.

I think we already have that figured out without your tests, I thought to myself.

"Our top priority is finding Dean Pierre," Reynolds continued. *Duh.*

He told us agents were being dispatched to Pierre's previous known cities as we spoke. His picture will be posted on every law enforcement bulletin board in the United States of America, including every port authority, to make sure he doesn't flee the country. Every cop in Chicago will be distributing his picture to shop owners, bartenders, waitresses, bank tellers, hotel and motel clerks, and anyone else who might remember seeing his face in the past year. The decision has been made not to officially put his face on TV or the newspapers yet—but that will happen within hours anyway. Someone from CPD will make a call to a friend at one of the stations and pictures will be smuggled to the outside world.

As we met, I looked at Dean's pictures from every angle I could turn my head. Dean and Dell are certainly not twins but I can see the family resemblance. Dean has lighter hair and is clearly the bigger of the two. His shoulders are wide enough that he could be a linebacker for the Bears. He has to lift weights. This is a guy who could have punched me in the kidneys and put me down in a hurry.

"Priority number two is Dell Woods," Reynolds said. I knew he wasn't the Cutter Shark, but no argument from me on that point. He has to come in and tell us everything he knows. If he won't, he needs to be brought in. Instructions have been given to all law enforcement agencies that it should be assumed that both Dell Woods and Dean Pierre are armed and dangerous. I don't think Dell is a threat to anyone but himself, but I understand that intentionally or not, he's been aiding and abetting a potential killer and he, too, must be approached with extreme caution. I feel bad for him in a whole new way.

But I was right. He's not the killer.

I am the obvious link to Dell, so my cell and home phones, my email and social networks—I only have fifteen friends on Facebook, which is embarrassing—will remain on live-access with federal agents both in DC and here in Chicago. After my parking lot incident, which everyone now assumes was Dean and not Dell—they are keeping a security detail assigned to me until the case is resolved. As boring as my life can be, I don't envy the mind-numbing nothingness that my babysitters have ahead of them.

How long will this go?

We watched the ChiTownVlogger's latest report on the Cutter Shark. Our killer is obviously using him to send us a message, and a tech crew is monitoring all the ChiTown Vlogger's communications to find out how—and the message is quite clear: the next murder will happen on June 21, the first official day of summer, or shortly thereafter. Unless he's smart and runs—we have his picture after all. Can we believe the message that his work is coming to a close in Chicago? He's short on his city death quota, but his pattern is so messed up, I doubt even someone as deranged as him is going to worry about symmetry and order. But if he's in the acceleration cycle Van Guten described, is he in enough control to wait? To leave?

The meeting raised more questions than answers.

I wonder again how we will know he is gone? How long will I need to watch my back? *Always and forever* I can hear Mr. Barry say.

As the meeting drew to a close, I asked the question that woke me up in the middle of the night: "If Grace Mills was Plan B, who do we think was Plan A?"

Everyone just stared at me. *Me?* "If it was me, I'd be dead," I said.

"We've talked about that," Blackshear said, "and have a couple ideas. Maybe something or someone interrupted him. Maybe he was just sending a warning then but didn't plan to kill you at that point—but does now. He did refer to his victim as 'special.' So taking out someone who has investigated him and who is under police protection would well qualify you as special."

———

I brush my teeth for the second time tonight. I shouldn't have eaten that oatmeal cookie from the batch Vanessa made for us. I use the bathroom—no pink in my pee, my new obsession—wash my hands, and pad to my bedroom. I check the windows and then walk through my entire apartment to make sure everything is closed and locked up. I am going to call Klarissa back when I lay down, but as I pull back the covers on my bed there is an envelope sitting on my pillow.

My skin crawls, and I glance around, although I know I'm alone. How in the heck did we miss that?

69

I put the call in to Konkade. Reynolds is the task force commander, but Konkade handles the details.

"Konkade here."

"Sergeant, this is Detective Conner."

"Good evening, Kristen. I'm so pleased you are calling me to wish me a good night's sleep. That is why you're calling isn't it?"

I sigh. He laughs.

"Didn't think so," he says. "I take it my wife is going to have to watch *Desperate Housewives* by herself tonight. What have we got?"

After explaining, I get off the phone and call Don.

Mom can't come to my apartment without doing some cleaning. *Thank you, Mom*, I think, now that my place has become the new task force headquarters.

Konkade's last instructions to me were not to touch anything. I was too tired to exercise my incredible powers of levitation, so I disobeyed his orders and put my tired rear end on the kitchen counter to wait.

Konkade called Bruce, the techie, but he was down at his mom's house in Kankakee, at least an hour and twenty minutes from my place, even with no traffic on a Sunday night, so Konkade called Jerome next. Jerome showed up to handle the evidence. I'm praying it's not a mushy card from my mom that she left on my pillow. I've never known her to refer to me as Detective—or misspell my first name. The envelope reads: *Detective Kirsten*. Maybe it's the barista from JavaStar. He writes "Kirsten" on the side of the cup almost every time.

Jerome is first on the scene—you know you're having a great week when your apartment is officially the center of a serial murder investigation not just once, but twice within forty-eight hours—and he lets me know he lives less than ten minutes away. I let him know that my mom had vacuumed and dusted after his last visit here, so he sure as heck won't find much in the way of evidence—or dirt. But he still puts on his miner's hardhat with a blue light and spends thirty minutes examining every square inch of my bed and bedroom.

By the time he comes out with the envelope held between a pair of rubber-tipped tweezers, the cavalry has arrived and my small place is packed. The brass has commandeered the kitchen and we working stiffs are sitting in my living room. I edge closer to the Formica counter that divides my kitchen and living space where Jerome has set up a light box. He.carefully lays the red envelope on it. Everyone has crowded in close, but I manage to muscle my way to Jerome's immediate right. Hey, it is my letter.

Actually it's a Hallmark card. Somebody cared enough to give the best. There's a picture of a red rose on the front panel. The inside has no printed message, just a couple lines scrawled in the same crooked letters that were on the envelope.

> You aren't bad, but not nearly as good as you think you are. I hope you haven't forgotten me already. We have unfinished business after all. Until then . . . think of me often.

"Someone find me a sample of Dean Pierre's handwriting," Reynolds orders.

Dean's decided to run. Please God. Don't let him get away.

June 15, 3:08 a.m.

I'm going to miss this city. Not.

After such an auspicious, promising start, nothing went as planned. That's never happened before. It still doesn't seem conceiveable.

What went wrong? Is it possible I made mistakes? Possibly. Okay . . . probably. But even my mistakes are evidence of my greatness. Despite living by no other man's code . . . for no other man's approval . . . for no god's, no nation's, no family's glory and honor but my own . . . If I confess to any shortcoming, it is that of kindness . . . I let down my carefully constructed defenses. Because of her. I must admit . . . I grew . . . I grew . . . fond of her.

I have worked hard to hone my craft, my art. This is not the end of what and who I am. I pledge to make a new beginning. I shall arise out of the ashes like a phoenix. I will be greater than even before.

Undoubtedly my strengths have also been my undoing here. Discipline. Work ethic. I have committed myself each day to the perfection of my body and my being, without break, for nigh on eight years now. I will stop judging myself harshly. After Friday night's ultimate act, I'll disappear for a time. Perhaps a respite is in order. I've never traveled abroad. I'd kind of like to visit Paris, but the currency exchange is murder. I just said "murder." Maybe that's an omen.

I hadn't really thought of it before. I could turn what feels like disappointment and defeat into a stunning victory. I could become the first international serial killer. I will give that serious consideration. Wouldn't that send the FBI into a frenzy? They'd have to bring in their Interpol pals.

The thought of it makes me smile.

But before I leave . . .

Kristen Conner. Beautiful. Accomplished. Intense. Great skin. She's good enough for Dell, but not good enough for me. Too messy. That's one reason I let her live—it would've been another kill I'd regret. I'm through with regrets. The other reason is that I know she will think long and hard about what she might have done to stop what's about to happen.

Kristen didn't prove to be my soulmate, as fun as it would be to tweak the Feds by taking one of their nearest and dearest. But then, almost by accident, I saw her sister. Articulate. Stunning. And never messy. Much better dresser. I followed her home from the other sister's house—the one with the cute daughter and bratty son—and found out where she lived. I strolled through her home while she was at work. I like her style. Much better than Kristen's. I realized Klarissa was my true soulmate. Kristen was just the warm-up band.

I couldn't have been happier when I found she was going to a different church than the rest of her family. As clingy as that brood is, it was almost as fortuitous of a break for me as when Kristen, my poor older brother's girlfriend, was assigned as one of the detectives on my case. I finally met Klarissa at that interminably boring Bible class she went to before the church service. I've worked that angle more than a few times, so Hallelujah, I know how to fit in. I wonder if the FBI has ever figured that one out.

I asked her to meet me for a cup of coffee. Nice and innocent. She said yes. I thought we had a pleasant time. But that's when she showed a cruel streak. I called her back for a real date and all she talked about was her ex-boyfriend—before saying no. No? To me? That was unacceptable. Hasn't she read the books that explain you have to let go and move on in life?

Then it got worse. She refused to go out with me . . . again and again and again. She flat out refused. I checked back nicely and she stopped taking my calls. I still can't believe it. Last time I looked in the mirror I saw a man that women are crazy about. I guess she's the crazy one. She wants a good Bible class? Well, her moment of truth and repentance is at hand.

I'll wait at her lovely home on Friday night as long as it takes until she returns . . . to me. I'm ready to get out of this stinky motel anyway. I can barely leave the room with my picture posted everywhere. Some skin bronzer, a much shorter haircut, some temporary tattoos, and a couple of biker outfits complete with wife-beater t-shirts should throw anyone off. But people are on edge.

I have just a few loose ends to tie up this week.

I am going to have to figure out a new revenue source. Big Brother has taken good care of me. I love manipulating his complex set of guilt inducers to get what I need. But he's moved things around on me. I can't get to the accounts I've accessed before. I think he's trying to cut me off.

Dell, Dell, Dell. I'm the one who cuts things off.

I was running so late for work this morning that I figured once I hit my cube and started working I'd never be able to break free to get a work out in. At first Soto wasn't going to let me into his gym because of my brief stay in the hospital, but when I told him I wanted to work the light and heavy punching bags he relented. All I really wanted to do was a soft spin on the recumbent bike, but that was never going to get me in the doors.

"Maybe you're going to start paying attention and figure out how to defend yourself," he said while taping my hands. "You shouldn't be in here but consider this a favor to your dad."

He crosses himself and says, "May his soul rest in peace. Good man. He had a heck of a punch, too. He was a real fighter. He and Big Tony. That was a team you didn't want breaking up your party. They could do the heavy lifting."

After finishing the tape he personally put me through the paces.

"Left cross! Left cross! Right straight! Again! Again! Again! Harder! Hands up and keep hitting. I said, *hands up*. You're about to get popped in the nose. Move and hit!"

I keep my hands up and keep hitting. Soto still doesn't seem to think my hands are up high enough.

"Don't stop. Hit! Hit! On your toes. On your toes. Dance, Kristen. Get off your heels and move. Get your hands up! If you're tired, quit and go home! Now hit!"

The only piece of exercise equipment that Soto likes better than a floor is the heavy punching bag. He likes the small speed bag, too, but he loves the big bag for building strength and upper body endurance. Go punch a bag for five minutes and you'll experience a profound and newfound wonder and appreciation for boxers. My arms are screaming for mercy and turning to Jell-O. I can taste bile in the back of my throat. My calves are burning. Even my butt feels like it's on fire.

"Don't quit! Don't quit! Kristen, get your hands up! This guy wants to break your nose. Hit! Mix it up. Cross, cross, straight, straight, left, right, right, left! Mix it up!"

Hearing him tell me to mix it up is a blast from the past. Dad kept a heavy bag hanging from the first-story floor supports that were open in the basement and he was always after me to change up my rhythm and sequence of punches. "Mix it up" was also a favorite of his from the sideline when I played travel soccer. About the time I really mastered my scissor step he was after me to work the helicopter spin. Dad was an interesting combination of laid-back and intense, of encouraging and in-your-face challenge.

As I walked toward the shower rooms, my legs and arms wobbly, Martinez exited the men's locker room. He gave a not-too-discreet up and down to my loose-fitting T-shirt and baggy running shorts, soaked through from perspiration, my hair a stringy tangled mess. He chuckled and gave a whistle.

"I know, I know," I said to him. I look awful.

"No, no. *Te ves bien. A quién tratas de impresionar además de mi?*"

I poke him in the chest with a forefinger and ask, "What'd you just say?"

Unfazed, he answers, "What do you think I said? I just wished you a lovely day. You've got to learn some Español if you want to live in this country."

I roll my eyes and laugh as he flexes for me. I head for the shower and he heads for the workout room. I'm pretty sure he didn't wish me a lovely day.

———

There's another sticky note on my computer screen when I get upstairs.

DEAR DETECTIVE KRISTEN—SOME GIRLS HAVE A WAY WITH THE GUYS. HOW MANY BOYFRIENDS CAN ONE DETECTIVE HAVE? I NEVER KNEW YOU WERE SO ROMANTIC. I GUESS THE LAST GUY WAS A REAL KILLER. PLEASE MAKE A LIST OF WHO'S LEFT FOR THE REST OF US!

The signature is a smiley face. I've had enough of the notes. I pluck it off the screen and stride out front to Shelly's desk.

"Did you put this on my screen?"

"What are you talking about?" she asks with a coy smile.

She looks over at Connie Davis, Zaworski's office manager, and winks. So it is her. I'm mad and I'm glaring and I can see some of her smug confidence starting to erode. She looks over at Davis for support, but Davis is suddenly very interested in her computer screen. Some of the other support staff and a few of the detectives peek over and around cubicles in our direction, suddenly curious.

"You know exactly what I'm talking about."

"You have no right to accuse me of anything," she says, her cheeks turning a crimson red.

"You know what, Shelly? Your job is to make this place run smoothly," I respond. Maybe you're the one posting the notes, maybe you're not. But if it's you, you better stop. If it's not you, you better find out who it is and make it stop. And I'm not jacking around with you. This stopped being funny the first time and it is a distraction on a case that is very important to the big boss. When the next note shows up in my cubicle, he's going to hear about how funny you think this is—he's ordered me to hand it over. I don't care if you or anyone else thinks I'm a snitch," I say extra loud so everyone else can hear. "Another thing, you want to write me up, go ahead and do it. In fact, I hope you do. Because I promise, I'm bringing your call logs during office hours with me to any hearing and it's going to get ugly."

Her mouth is wide open as I slam my fist on her desk and yell, "Don't jack with me!" Turning away, I bump her ceramic coffee cup and it falls to the floor and breaks. I ignore it and keep on walking toward my cubicle.

My hand is throbbing and I'm shaking as I log on and start working through emails. *Just do your work.* I send quick answers back and make notes on a separate sheet of paper to remember the bigger things.

I am in so much trouble. She's going to say she felt her personal safety was threatened. Internal Affairs is going to be paying me another visit.

I get to a message from Reynolds. Quick and to the point:

I'll be by your offices late afternoon. Let's go to dinner and talk.

Hmmm. Explaining to Van Guten's ex that I won't be having dinner with him tonight could take more than two minutes, so I just delete it.

The next email is from Klarissa. She lets me know she's going out with Warren tonight to talk through all the reasons they're not together. She goes on to say that she has a corporate dinner on Tuesday but that she wants to have dinner with me on Wednesday or Thursday. I'm glad she can fit me in.

Don pokes his head in my cubicle and asks if I'm ready.

"You bet," I answer. "For what?"

"Coffee. Let's talk. And it's my treat."

We walked to the JavaStar down the street. I assumed Don was going to chew me out for going off on Shelly. It never came up. He let me know Vanessa wants him to quit the cop job and to work with her selling real estate. Once the Shark business is finished, he says he's going to consider it. I'm numb as he talks. I don't make friends very easily. And Don is a friend.

I just lost it in the office today. And I might be losing my best friend on the force.

It's Friday night and I'm driving over to Jimmy and Kaylen's house. I'm working gears like Jeff Gordon at Taladega. I miss James and Kendra terribly. Between missing church and working overtime, I haven't seen them in two weeks. Or is it three? Time is blurring.

I wonder if Klarissa will be there. I'm still irritated with her. After making such a big deal about getting together and me not being there for her—blah blah—she stood me up for dinner last night. I know she's on air four to five nights a week and understand her schedule can change on the fly. A simple text to cancel would have been fine with me. She wanted to meet at Spiaggia on Michigan Avenue. I wasn't in the mood to head into the city in the first place and I was definitely not looking forward to spending a hundred bucks on a meal. She's a news reporter for the biggest local station in Chicago, landing quite a few commercials, and I'm a public servant—there is a difference in what we can afford. I don't begrudge her any lifestyle or cuisine that she wants, but she should be sensitive to my budget constraints.

Truth be told, I'm still not over the phone conversation when she referred to Patricia as "the drunk" and slammed my skills as a detective. We'd been doing so good. I guess too good to last. We're different cats. We'll always look at things differently. Even with her spending a night at my house we really haven't talked since that blowup other than to say we need to talk. So what's really bugging her? The dad situation? Probably. Is it Warren? She says no, but probably yes on that, too.

Jimmy picked up a giant deep-dish pizza from Giordano's and I ate three full pieces—no small feat for a man of any size, and simply amazing for a delicate young lady like myself. At least that's what Kaylen said. I'm going to run five miles in the morning. I may be under stress and Lloyd may think I'm too thin, but I haven't lost my appetite.

I plop between James and Kendra to watch the fourth Shrek DVD. I like the music. I love the tickling and cuddling, but James really does have a weird thing about sticking his feet in my face that gets irritating after a while. Plus you never know when he's going to hit you where it hurts when he starts roughhousing.

Jimmy is sitting on the floor in front of Kaylen and is rubbing her feet. I feel a pang of jealousy. James is sticking his feet in my face again and asking if they stink. Kendra is clutching her Kristen doll, the one with a far better figure than the real-life model, and stroking my hair. I sigh. No complaining. Life's not too bad. Not too bad at all.

Earlier Kaylen asked if I was up to coaching Kendra's soccer team in the fall.

"Please, Aunt Kristen," Kendra immediately chimed in.

How do you say no to that? I think the Snowflakes are going to take some people by surprise, come next season. Attila the Hun is probably already preparing for us. We handed his Lady Titans their only two losses of the season.

The phone rings. Jimmy gets up to answer while Shrek and the donkey fight some bad guys made up of fairy tale characters. There's no blood. Must be nice.

"Who was it?" Kaylen asks.

"Your mom. She's coming over."

Jimmy plops down on the couch beside Kaylen and kisses her on the head. He gives her slightly growing belly a tender caress as they wordlessly look each other in the eyes. Oh man. I am a loser when it comes to love.

———

Mom, Jimmy, Kaylen, and I are sitting at the table drinking coffee. The kids have gone upstairs to go to bed. They're not happy about it. James got a swat on the butt when he yelled, "Smell my feet!" as he tromped up the stairs. Sorry, buddy. You deserved that one.

They don't know how good they have it. I worked four fourteen-hour days Monday through Thursday and another twelve today. I would love to be heading upstairs for bed. Heck, I may jump in James's bottom bunk I'm so tired. The Cutter Shark has said his next kill won't be until summer. That's three hours away—though he didn't specify a time in summer. So what am I doing here? Not much less than I would have been doing in the office. The Shark and his brother have disappeared. Zaworski ordered us home to get some rest—and to be back in the office at seven sharp—but I couldn't help but notice he and Konkade were still on a phone conference with the FBI contingent across town when I left. I could hear Willingham's voice booming over the speakerphone. I assume Reynolds and Van Guten and a host of agents and staffers are there with him. Don had left but he's put in even more hours than me this week.

Who knows? Maybe tonight will go uneventfully. Mayor Doyle finally called a press conference and advised women to stay in tonight with all doors locked. I wonder how many false alarms will get called in to 911 the first time someone hears a creak in the house. It doesn't help that a bunch of bars are holding Cutter Shark parties. I heard a radio commercial for one promising free Bloody Marys to the first hundred women who showed up. The scary thing is, the place will be packed.

I think back to lunch at the Devil Dog. Our team was so excited when we finally had not just a lead, but a lead with a name and face to it. Okay, a couple names to it. Dean Pierre. Dean Jorgenson. Dean Woods. But the excitement was waning by Wednesday—and tempers were short and flaring yesterday. We could almost feel him in our grasp, but the trail went cold immediately. No sign of Dean—every motel and hotel front desk clerk in the city has been shown his picture. No sign of Dell either. He hasn't called me back. Is he more involved in this than I want to admit? At minimum he's seriously enabled his brother.

Mom had watched the end of the movie with us but kept asking questions about what things meant and what she had missed and kind of ruined the mood. How do you explain that Captain Hook wasn't really part of the story of the Three Pigs. Mom, you are confused, but I guess I have to keep you. It's about ten now and she looks up at me as if she just remembered something.

"You had dinner at Klarissa's house tonight. You must have left awfully quick."

"Ha ha," I answer. "Very funny. We were supposed to have dinner *last night*. She blew me off."

"She told me that. Not that she *blew you off* but that she had to cancel. She got assigned to do an interview with someone from the mayor's office, you know. But she said you two rescheduled for tonight. That's why she didn't come over with me when I called."

Mom has things mixed up in her mind. Again.

"And when did Klarissa tell you this?" I ask sarcastically.

"There's no need for that tone, Kristen."

"Sorry, Mom, but for some reason this story feels like Klarissa shifting blame for us not getting together my way. We made no dinner plans tonight."

"She wasn't blaming you for anything, Kristen. Are you sure you don't have things mixed up? Because you do have a lot on your mind these days with that awful Cutter Shark case. And you don't always listen as well as you should."

Even my mom is calling him the Cutter Shark?

"I guess it's possible, Mom, but I still suspect she got a better offer than rescheduling with me and didn't want to talk about it with you tonight. Her and Warren are talking again, you know."

Why did I say that? I promised I wouldn't.

"She told me," Mom and Kaylen say in unison. So much for having the inside skinny. I was probably the last to know.

Time to change the subject from Klarissa. I'm still a little mad at her. Jimmy wanders off to the bedroom with a book. Mom, Kaylen, and I chitchat another thirty minutes. I'm not really listening and my head is starting to bob as I almost fall asleep. I look at my watch. If I don't leave now I am going to end up sharing a room with James. I have to get some sleep. I yawn loudly, stand up and stretch—no pain in my lower back from the kidney shot anymore—and tell everyone I'm going to hit it. I go upstairs to say goodnight to James and Kendra. James is fast asleep. Kendra is about in la-la land too. She still has her Kristen doll held close in one arm. Her purple hippo that Dad gave her is in the other. I tell her I love her. I think she tells me she loves me back, but she's so sleepy, her words aren't clear.

I go back downstairs and give Mom and Kaylen a hug and kiss and head out the door. I press in the clutch with my left foot and fire up my Miata and shift into reverse. I back out of the driveway and shift into first to head up Oakmont Lane, across Belmont and up Clark toward my apartment.

I look in my rearview mirror and see headlights. I'm comforted and uncomfortable seeing them. My police escort is still on the job. I shake my head. How long will I have a security detail assigned to me? I've already told Zaworski he could cancel it, that I'm fine and can take care of myself. He and Willingham said absolutely not. But how long will that resolve last? I, too, have been forced to wonder if Dean has already fled town. If he has, does that mean I'm safe? He's never returned to any of his crime cities. But who is to say he won't break pattern? It's pretty broken already. I wonder again how close I was to being his victim.

Van Guten is convinced I would represent a prize victim for Dean; a dramatic flourish to express his superiority over his pursuers. Might be wishful thinking.

Nope. He's not gone. He isn't done. I can feel it. And he did say the next killing will be in summer. Less than two hours.

Dear God, please don't let him get away to start over somewhere else.

June 20, 10:05 p.m.

Now I kind of wish I wasn't leaving tomorrow. It's not been easy, but I think I've set the world to rights in the last few days.

Allen Johnson? No more self-aggrandizing ChiTownVlogger to clutter my story.

Carrie? I may not hold my big brother in high regard, but he is my brother. First Detective Conner dumped him. Then the stupid, giggling blonde cut him off. It was a bad rebound date for you, Dell. You deserve a lot better than her. She wasn't worthy of your attention or the full extent of my craft. So I just knocked on the door, pushed my way in, and broke her neck. That was quick—and different. Not satisfactory by any means, but interesting. That'll give the FBI something to chew on for a while.

Detective Conner? Sadly, the girl has too many sets of eyes watching her. Might be pressing my luck at the moment. I like to keep a neat pattern. But Chicago is such a mess I will stop back through sometime in the future to rearrange the pieces. I've always left kids out of my work. But maybe that little niece of hers would show the Conner family what happens when you mess with the Woods boys.

Today was pleasant and relaxed. Klarissa drove off in her shiny silver sports car at noon and I spent the rest of the afternoon in her place. I wish she'd been more considerate and stocked the refrigerator better for me. She got home later than I thought she would. But when she opened the door and saw me standing there, the look on her face was priceless. I wish I had had a camera to capture the moment.

She was terrified by the tattoos and stubble. She was petrified when she saw it was me behind the disguise.

I planned to go easy on her. I gave her just enough pentobarbital to keep her docile—but awake. Maybe I should have just done the deed then. But I sent the FBI and CPD a clear message that my next victim would be done the first day of summer. I want to leave town with them knowing who was in charge of this game, the whole time. So I have to wait until the clock strikes midnight to get started.

But now I'm not sure I should stay in her house any longer. Her mom called three times. What a meddler. I finally let Klarissa pick up and tell her mom she already had plans. And she did good. A sharp knife held against her throat made sure of that. I think it's funny she said she was with her sister. Can't wait for that to get back to Kristen, once Klarissa's dead.

But what now? I really think I need to move her. Where should we go? A hotel? I don't think I'll be recognized with my new look. But they'll want a credit card, and the cops will track it after they find her body. I don't know how long I'll need to use it once I hit the road.

I can't believe Dell has cut me off from my accounts. He and I'll need to chat about that.

No, a hotel room won't work. Hotels are too impersonal anyway. I want this to be special.

There is Carrie's apartment. She obviously doesn't need it anymore. But that might be even more risky than a hotel. Someone is going to start looking for her sometime and it could be tonight. The whole block where her apartment is located is mostly empty with DePaul out for the summer. Most of the primates have gone home. But no, still too many street lights and I might be seen carrying an unconscious news reporter into an apartment complex. And there is the matter that there is already a dead body in her apartment. That's not a pleasant thought.

There is Dell's place. I checked again this morning. The easy-to-spot unmarked police car hasn't been out front—or back—for two days. All the furniture is still there. And Dell is almost as neat, clean, and orderly as I am. Almost.

I think I've just come up with the obvious solution. Ah, yes. Perfect. It's a dark, quiet street. People lock their doors and mind their own business.

I wonder if Dell has ever felt my eyes on him? This isn't the first city I've followed him to. Sometimes he would stay too long in one location and I'd have to pack up and move on without him. But we've been together more than he knows.

Someday I'll thank him for what he did for me in Chicago. First he introduced me to Kristen. He didn't know he did, of course, but I saw her out with him. And that led me to Klarissa. My soulmate.

Time to get moving.

74

I pull into the parking lot of my apartment, find a spot close to my place, turn off the engine, and glance at my cell. I missed a couple of calls and have a text from Reynolds.

You ever going to talk to me again? Meet me for dinner. You can't stay mad forever. Let's talk.

I look at the time stamp. It came in about the time I was arriving at Jimmy and Kaylen's. Not tonight, Austin. And who are you to say how long I can stay mad?

Missed a call from Klarissa—so maybe she was going to invite me for dinner. Though I can't remember the last time I saw her cook. No message. Reynolds called before texting—no message from him either. Another missed call—and message—from a private number. Dell? Must have called while I was watching *Shrek*. I am tired. I haven't paid attention to anything tonight. Not good.

I feel guilty as I admit to myself that I am relieved. I don't want to listen to a message from Dell. I want to sleep. *It's game on, Kristen. Pay attention in case he calls back. Tired is irrelevant.*

I latch the top closed on my convertible and get out. I look up at a beautiful full moon. Summer is here but the temperature has dropped into the low seventies or upper sixties. A light breeze blows from Lake Michigan. It feels great.

My bodyguards pull up behind me and the passenger window

slides down. It is Carter, the buzzcut, riding shotgun. I don't recognize the driver. I'll meet him in the morning.

"I'll walk you upstairs, Detective," Carter says gallantly.

"I'll be fine."

"I'm sure you will. But I think I'll walk you up anyway."

"Captain's orders?"

"Yes ma'am."

He has been calling me ma'am all week. I know thirty is upon me, but come on, do I look like his mother?

"Carter?"

"Yes ma'am?"

"I am honored to be protected by a clean-cut, conscientious, and very polite all-American young man."

"Thank you, ma'am."

I sigh and continue. "But despite my admiration for a man with good manners, if you call me ma'am one more time I am going to—"

"Don't say it," he says laughing, his hand held up in the universal stop sign. "I am pretty polite but I didn't grow up in the South. Your, uh, partner, incentivized me to call you ma'am and let him know how long you would put up with it before saying anything."

"Incentivized?"

"Well, just a JavaStar card."

We're at the door. Oh, the things I want to say. Don is so dead. I just shake my head, give him a little half laugh and smile, and shut the door behind me.

I twist the dead bolt to the locked position and turn to head for my bedroom. A sheet of paper is folded and on the floor of my tiny foyer. Someone slid it under the door. If my downstairs neighbor is complaining about my workout routine again . . .

I bend over and pick it up. It's a take-out menu for a Chinese restaurant. I start to crumple it up to throw away but unfold it to make
sure nothing is on the back. There is.

A handwritten note from Dell.

I skim it and can barely breathe.

Oh God . . . what is going on?

June 20, 10:45 p.m.

*How in the world did he find me? Did Detective Conner rub off
on him? I can only wish. He would have matched her incompetence and not found me at such an awkward moment.*

*The Woods brothers are no dummies. Not bad Dell, not bad.
But why did you have to get involved and make a mess of things?
What were you thinking? What in the world did you think you
could do against me? Is that how you treat a brother? You just
barge into where he's working and interrupt what he's doing?
Have I ever done that to you? Of course not. That would be rude.
Unacceptable.*

*And then he had the audacity to insist I stop. Was he seri-
ous? I thought he was bright. I had hoped he would recognize
my genius. But in lieu of that, I would hope he had enough common sense to bow out gracefully, or at least appreciate what I'd
done for him. I am his brother after all. Doesn't blood count for
something? It does for me.*

He tried to talk me into turning myself in. Letting Klarissa go.

I don't need to do anything. I do as I will. And I finish what I start.

Klarissa was playing possum on me. Drugs must have faded while I dealt with Dell. I can't believe she hit me on the head with that vase and bit me. She has sharp teeth. I might need a rabies shot.

None of my girls have ever hurt me like that.

I'll have to show her that women aren't allowed to hurt me anymore.

She's sleeping quietly now. And soon she will enter the sleep of eternity.

I am frozen in place and time. What have I just read? Why didn't I see this coming?

The note from Dell read:

I hope someday you will forgive me. I swear to you, I never knew what he was doing. I should have come in and talked to you when you asked me to. I just didn't want to believe my brother was capable of such atrocities. He's had such bad luck in life, I wanted to know for myself what he was doing before pointing you in his direction.

I know I'm rationalizing. Here's what you really need to know.

I drove over to my townhome earlier this week. I didn't go in. I just wanted to see who was watching. I was expecting to see the police staking it out. Instead I saw Dean. That's when I knew he was probably involved in these murders. I followed him when he left. I can barely write these words. I know how much they are going to hurt you.

Dell knows where Klarissa lives. He drove to her street and watched her home for a couple hours. It was Wednesday. I lost him when he drove off, but I can't help but think she is his next victim. So I've been watching her home to protect her. I just haven't been able to bring myself to turn him in. But I finally came to my senses and realized I needed to let you know. When you didn't pick up tonight, I decided to drive over and tell you face-to-face. You weren't here so I'm leaving this note. I know it's inevitable so I'm ready to be interviewed by authorities. I just want you to be present and I want you to know what is happening first. That's why I didn't leave a message on your cell for the FBI to hear.

I hope you get this note soon.

I'm driving back over to Klarissa's home now.

I promise to keep her safe.

I'm sorry. Please find it in your heart to for-give me.

How in the world does Dell think he can protect Klarissa against a serial killer? What is wrong with him? And he thinks he can dictate that I'm there for his interviews? He's lost it.

I grab my Beretta from my handbag and drop it in the front pocket of my Under Armour jacket. I open the door, shut it with a bang, and run down the stairs. My eyes are scanning the parking lot for my protective detail as I hit the bottom of the stairs. Where did they park? I see them close to the entrance. I hop in my car, gun the engine, jam it in reverse, and lay down rubber driving over to them. Carter is out of the car, his hand held up to stop me. I roll down the window.

"Who's the best driver between you two?" I ask.

"Me," he answers. I remember him following me on the drive to Grace Mills' murder scene. He is good.

"Get ready to run some red lights and stay with me. And get your weapons locked and loaded. We've got a potential situation that includes the Cutter Shark."

His eyes get wide and he starts to ask a question. I interrupt with the first word still formed on his mouth. "I'm leaving right now. If you're coming, you better get in that car and start it up."

I've pulled out and am half a block away when I see the unmarked patrol car bounce out of the parking lot behind me in my rearview mirror. It's not quite eleven. I need to get over to Klarissa's now. Dell doesn't know what he's doing. I've got two pups to help me out. But I need the whole cavalry riding with me.

I hit Klarissa's number. This might not be the night he is going to strike. I can hope. But she still has to get out of there. I don't even get a ring. It goes straight into voice mail. I hit one to bypass the instructions and say to her, "Klarissa, listen carefully. You are not safe at your place. If you are home, you need to get out of there right now. But carefully. Turn off the lights. Do a quick outside scan. Then go out your back door if the coast is clear. I think that is probably best. Hit the alley and start running west. Call me when you're a couple blocks away and I'll pick you up."

Please be on the phone with someone else. Let that be the reason I got no ring. Please be safe.

I hit Don's number on speed dial.

"How are you, ma'am?" he asks with a chuckle.

"Don, do you have a piece of paper and something to write with?" I ask.

"Not in the mood for a joke?"

"Don, I'm on my way to Klarissa's. I need to give you her address. I need backup. Now!"

"What's going on, Conner?"

"Don, no time to talk. Don't ask me any questions. Call back after you get our team moving and I'll give you everything I know—which isn't much. But you've got to get things rolling now. The Cutter has targeted Klarissa. He may or may not be in the proximity of her place. Ditto with Dell. I need the ponies running now. But they have to come in silent and invisible. Got that?"

"Give me the address."

I repeat it twice and then hang up as he's trying to say something to me. I already know he's going to tell me to stand down until backup is present. He just needs to get the troops rolling and I need to handle whatever it is facing me at Klarissa's. I wish Dell would call me now. He was on his way to Klarissa's an hour ago. Call me, Dell. Tell me Klarissa is okay.

I call Klarissa's number again. It goes into voice mail immediately. Not good. Is she going to be there? She has to be. But if she is, is she still alive? I force that thought from my mind.

Dean, the Cutter Shark, has been neat and orderly his whole career of killing. Van Guten is right. He's unraveled—which is good for us catching him but not necessarily good for my sister right now. When he said his next victim was going to be at the beginning of summer, how literal was he being? The first day? The first official minute of summer—just an hour or so from now? He issued a challenge to us. But is his mind clear enough to follow through on it to the detail?

I downshift into second to slow down for a red light on Kenzie. I see a gap in the traffic flow, stomp on the accelerator, and run the red. I look in the rearview mirror and see that Carter didn't make it. I keep his number under a magnet on my refrigerator. He's called numerous times to announce visitors, but not much in the past week. I know his number is in my call log and I'm going to have to scroll down to find it.

I continue to weave in and out of traffic, one eye on the road, one on the tiny screen, and my mind everywhere. Van Guten said that the Cutter Shark's attack of me was a message to all law enforcement members on the case—letting them know who was in charge—but that it was also something personal. Why didn't I—why didn't any of us—think about my family's safety?

I think I'm close to finding Carter's number when my phone chirps and I hit the green button immediately, hoping Klarissa is calling me back to say she is on her way home from talking with Warren or a quick trip to the grocery store or anything else that has nothing to do with the Cutter Shark.

"Conner," I answer.

"Okay, what's happened, what's going on, KC?" Don asks.

"Do you have troops on the way to Klarissa's house?"

"I've been on the phone with Zaworski and Konkade. We've got a couple patrol cars on the way. No one is in the immediate neighborhood but the first should arrive within ten minutes. They're in the middle of a situation and are being told our deal takes precedence. Blackshear, Martinez, and Reynolds are all driving there, too. Reynolds is bringing his soldiers—not sure how many. I'm at least thirty minutes away. Not sure how far away the FBI guys and gals are. But we're coming en masse. Are you riding with your security detail?"

"Not exactly," I answer, looking in the rearview mirror for any sign of Carter.

"What's that mean?"

"They're following me over," I quickly say.

"Okay, good. Zaworski reminded me to tell you that you do nothing solo." I'll have no problem obeying—unless my sister is in imminent danger. "What did you get? What do we have waiting for us?"

"Dell slid a note under my apartment door, Don. He's picked up his brother's trail and knows he's been watching Klarissa."

"And he's known this how long?" Don asks in amazement.

"I'm not sure," I answer, "but he's either at Klarissa's or on his way over. He thinks he's going to protect her from his brother."

"What a fool!" he yells. "You sure he's on our side?"

"I think so," I respond, "but honestly, I don't know anything for sure, including the Cutter's whereabouts."

"And you think tonight is the night?"

"I don't think anything for sure. But it makes sense in light of his message through the ChiTownVlogger that the next murder would be summer."

"We need to bring in both of those boys tonight," he says.

"We need to make sure my sister is okay."

"It all goes together," he says. "How far away are you from her place?"

"Less than five." I am driving seventy-five and eighty on a road that has a speed limit of forty-five.

"Okay, you listen carefully, Kristen. I know it's your sister. But I am going to repeat what Zaworski said. Stand down and wait for backup. No freelancing. We don't need a double hostage situation." How about having a little confidence in your partner, Don? "I'll call you back in about five—let me give Zaworski and Reynolds a heads-up on the additional information. But you stay in your car until we get there. Understood?"

"I hear you," I say and hang up the phone. I'm getting close. I quickly thumb through the call log on my phone and find what I think is Carter's number. I hit the call button and he answers on the first ring.

"Detective Conner, I'm sorry but we've lost you," he says rapidly. "I just got off the phone with Sergeant Konkade and he gave us the address for your sister and we're flying low. But he wanted me to tell you to wait for us *outside* your sister's place until we arrive."

"Thanks, Carter."

My phone is already vibrating again. It's Konkade. No time to answer. I'm on Klarissa's street. I turn off my headlights and cruise slowly past her place. Lights are on downstairs. I try her cell again. She's still not answering. I park a block away and walk back toward her house on foot, keeping to the shadows on the opposite side of the street as much as possible. I watch her windows for any sign of movement and look at each car as I slide by. I don't know what kind of car Dell has now and there is no record of Dean picking up a rental in any of the names he uses. I don't see anyone watching—and none of the cars have a rental company sticker on the back.

I look at my watch. Maybe five more minutes for the first patrol car to arrive. Too long, I decide. I sprint across the street to her house. I know where she keeps her spare house key and jump the wrought-iron fence on the left side of her tiny front yard and head down the narrow brick walkway that separates her home from her neighbor's. I take a quick look at her garage. The door is closed, so I don't know if her car is there or not. On tiptoes I look inside a row of high windows. She never leaves doors unlocked, much less open. That's a big deal to her.

I freeze for just a second. I hear a voice tell me if I just walk away and go to my apartment and get in bed, everything will be fine; Klarissa will call me in the morning and say that she and Warren met up to talk about getting back together and argued until 4 a.m. We'll laugh at how I was worried about her and meet for coffee. We'll never argue again.

Move. Face whatever it is you have to face.

My heart is beating crazy fast. I force myself to breathe slowly. My fear is paralyzing me. It has grown in the pit of my stomach and is working its way up my chest and to my throat, threatening to suffocate me. I'm reminded of standing on a ledge, thirty feet above a

Smokey Mountains lake. We were on a family vacation when I was about fifteen. I was frozen in place on a small rocky perch for almost five minutes before absolutely forcing myself to dive into the air and into the deep, cool waters below.

God, let Klarissa be okay. And alone. Please. Kristen, move. Now!

On the back stoop, I push up the edge of the large, molded concrete flowerpot, feel around underneath, and find the key before letting the pot thud back to the ground. *Quietly!* I slip the key in the lock and turn the dead bolt silently, then wince as it makes a *thunk* sound. I open the back door and slip inside, thankful for no squeaky hinges.

I pull my Beretta from my pocket and hold it in front of me. Walking on the outside edges of my feet, I start looking around in the back two rooms on the first floor of her three-story town house, the kitchen and a small office. If she's here alone, I'm going to give her a heart attack. She's not in either room, and at quick glance, there's nothing out of place.

I quietly tread up the hall to the front rooms. I poke my head in the dining room. Nothing. I look in the formal living room.

That's where I find Dell.

June 20, 11:39 p.m.

I guess if someone outside sees us on the way to the door I'll just smile and tell them she had a little too much to drink tonight.

But I might not see everyone who sees us from inside. And the city is holding its breath. Change plans?

No chance.

I've changed plans enough in Chicago to last a lifetime. If you want the biscuit, you have to risk it. Dell used to say that to me when we were little. That makes me feel a little sad to think of us as little boys and now I've hurt him. But he did ask for it, trying to get in my way. Nope. No changes. It's almost time and this is the place.

I still wish I hadn't had to hurt Dell tonight. I think he might be my only living relation. He always tried to be nice to me. He visited me when I was a prisoner of the state. He got me out of the red brick monster that tried to devour me and into that church home. I wouldn't call it summer camp but it was definitely better than being behind the barbed-wire fence of the Colorado Institute for Troubled Youth. If you weren't troubled before you got there, you sure would be after you had stayed for a while. But not me. That's where I found myself, where I was set free. That's where I learned I was a man apart, a man of destiny.

Any desire I might have had for a relationship that falls within the social constraints of the masses died the day I was reborn. I knew I was beyond social constructs and traditions. But if I ever was to desire the kind of relationship others must settle for, it would be with her. She is my soulmate after all.

Maybe I will call 911 and get some help for Dell. No. That wouldn't be wise. Not enough distance between the front doors. I'm sorry brother, you are going to have fight this one on your own. I'll tell you what. You make it through this alive and I owe you one.

He's lost a lot of blood but he's alive," I explain to Konkade. Don patched me through to him with call forward. Konkade makes things happen faster than anyone else on the CPD, and he has already arrived back at the Second to coordinate actions.

"The ambulance will be there in next to no time. I think your backup is about to arrive, too. I'm sorry there were some delays. The closest squad car was involved in a domestic violence situation. But they'll be arriving any minute. So, Conner, I know it must be incredibly hard not knowing where your sister is, but don't move. We need you there to figure next action steps. We're going to find her with you."

I realize Konkade is yammering away to keep me on the phone. Zaworski suspects I'll bolt out the front door if I have any ideas on where Dean might have my sister. And he would be correct.

I hang up. Dell groans and tries to lift his head. I carefully cup a hand behind his neck and tell him to be still. His eyes are unfocused. "Help is on the way, Dell," I say. He has a gaping knife wound that draws a jagged line from his shoulder across his chest. The flow of blood is steady—the knife got an artery. I've pulled off my Under Armour sweat top and tied it around his chest to put as much pressure on the wound as I can. The flow has slowed to a trickle, but that's still enough to drain his life away.

I kneel over Dell and see his left temple is matted with blood, swollen and turning an angry purple shade. I look around and don't see a likely blunt object. Either Dean took it with him or more likely, after he knifed Dell, he kicked his brother in the head.

Dell opens his eyes and seems to focus on me, even as he labors to breathe. There's really only one question I need answered. "Where'd he take her, Dell?"

He clutches my hand and his eyes bore into me. His lips move, but no words come out. A red bubble pops from his lips. His eyes now seem to plead for me to understand something important.

"Hold on, Dell. Hear those sirens? They're coming to help you. But please tell me, where is Klarissa?"

He gurgles in an effort to speak. But his eyes are confused and filled with fear. They say *I don't know.*

His eyes close from the exertion and his breathing slows way down. For a second I think he might be dying in my arms, but then he opens his eyes again. He swallows, and then in a raspy breath says, "Kristen."

"Dell, you don't have to tell me you didn't know what your brother was doing. I know that already. Save your energy. Can you tell me where he's taken Klarissa?"

"I didn't know he was . . ."

Focus, Dell! I don't care.

"Where does Dean have Klarissa, Dell?"

"I swear I didn't know he was the . . ."

Dell's eyes shut again. Is this the final fade? I know I can't push him in this state, but every fiber in my being is screaming for him to shut up about his innocence and tell me something that will help. I want to shake him. I've got to get to my sister.

"Dell . . . Dell! You've *got* to help me. Do you have any idea where he has taken her?"

His eyes focus again and he battles to get words out, but they can't escape his lips. One corner of his mouth is turned up. Has he had a stroke? He turns from me and looks at the ground. I've lost him. I've lost Klarissa.

But then he starts moving his forefinger through the thin puddle of blood at his side. I watch as he writes one letter: *h*. Then another: *o*. And another: *m*.

"Home?" I whisper to Dell. His eyes go up and down in assent. "What home, Dell?" I ask.

Dell gulps and gasps for breath. More blood is pulsing from his wound and I put pressure on his armpit to slow the flow. I've got to let him rest, but I also need whatever else he knows. I pause, holding my breath. His eyes flicker and I think he's mouthing the word "my."

My? That's his. His home.

"Your home, Dell?"

His eyes move up and down. That's got to be a yes. And I have to move.

"Thank you," I say as a flood of sirens roars up. I dash to the front door and slam it open for two EMTs who have jumped out of an ambulance. One of them is Lloyd. Not as easy to recognize as he was a month ago. He's losing weight. Maybe it was my pep talk. I doubt it.

"Lloyd!" I bark.

He looks up at me in surprise. I'm wearing sweatpants and a sports bra and I'm covered in blood.

"Keep him alive."

I race down the steps before he can answer. The first uniformed officer looks like he is going to pull a gun on me. I realize my badge is still in my Under Armour top with Dell.

He blocks my way and says in a soothing but firm voice, "Excuse me, ma'am, let's step over by my car where we can talk. I need to ask you a few questions."

Before I can speak, a red-faced, out-of-breath Carter runs up, takes one look at me covered in blood, and says, "Have you been shot,

CUTS LIKE A KNIFE

Detective Conner?" He looks like he is going to be sick and his face color drains from bright red to pale white in an instant.

"Both of you, get your partners, get in your cars, and follow me," I nearly shout.

"What about the Cutter Shark?" the uniform asks me.

"He's not in there, but I know where he is."

I give him and Carter the address on North Dearborn. I tell Carter to have his partner drive and call the situation into Konkade while we are mobile. I sprint to my car and don't bother to check to make sure they leave with me. They know how to get there—and they are jammed up in the traffic around Klarissa's house.

Dell's house. I knew we weren't watching it full-time anymore—just spot-checks. I calculate in my head. It's twenty to thirty minutes from Klarissa's in heavy traffic; ten to fifteen minutes when the streets are reasonably deserted like now; maybe seven when you are pretty sure your sister is being held by a serial killer and you are willing to use sidewalks when necessary.

I zip across Wicker Park and then south through Old Town. I cut across Belmont and switch from Wells to Clark as I dart through late-night club traffic—most of it pedestrian at this point. So much for Mayor Doyle's instructions to stay in tonight. My engine is winding to its limits as I shift up and down the gear box.

I look in my rearview mirror. No sign of my squad cars. They'll get there soon enough.

Now I'm darting through traffic on Sheridan, still trying not to kill any drunks that are laughing and shouting at each other and reeling in the street. I cut over Addison and I'm on Dearborn. I'm three blocks away and still under seven minutes.

My phone is vibrating. I jab the green button with my thumb.

"Where you at, Don?"

"Close. We've been rerouted by Konkade. Everyone on task force is converging on Dell's house to meet you there."

"No sirens, right?"

"We're still running stealth. I'm in the car with Blackshear and Martinez now. No worries. We're all coming in with no lights or sirens so he won't know what hits him."

"Good. I need to get off now."

"Conner, backup is less than five minutes away. Sit tight, stand down, just stop. Listen for once."

"Don, I'm here now. I'm going in for Klarissa."

"Conner! Are you listening?"

I pull a fresh magazine from my glove compartment to put into my Beretta. Twenty rounds that will shoot almost as fast as any automatic. My scores on the shooting range are below average, but if there's half a shot and my sister is still in harm's way, I'm going to nail the mad dog right between his eyes. Honest to God I will.

I reach for my 9mm in the holster on the small of my back. No holster. No gun. It is in my Under Armour top. I slam the worthless magazine down in anger. *Mr. Barry, whatever you taught me, I need it now.*

I trot down the street and pick up speed. Forget the Beretta. I had to park almost two blocks away but I'm about there. My phone rings. Don. I hit the ignore button immediately. I'm two houses away and my phone emits the sonar ping. I look at the text message.

Do not go in alone. Direct orders. Zaworski!

This is distracting.

I pop the battery out and throw my phone in the bushes. I am alone and unarmed.

June 20, 11:57 p.m.

She's beautiful, but so thin. She's an angel. Though she was a bit naughty tonight.

I wanted her to be awake for our sweet good-bye, but I had to give her another 15 cc's of pentobarbital to help her behave herself. When you put the needle straight into the carotid artery, that stuff does its work fast. It worked on my sweet little filly as well as it does for equestrian vets.

I had planned to switch to Suxamethonium when we got here—no pain inhibitors. But she was more of a fighter than I anticipated and I had to give her the real knockout juice.

I dig my fingernails into my palms, watching her, frustrated that I might have given her a little too much. The minutes are ticking by. She needs to wake up. I don't want her to miss this.

Did she really think she could tell me she didn't want to see me?

Wake up, Angel. Wake up!

80

I stand before the house Dell rented—and recently abandoned. Two stories up and a half basement. Four steps up to a recessed front stoop with an impressive double door. I scan the face of the house. No lights on in the front rooms that I can see. I hop a fence in the side yard and run around back to the alleyway. No lights on in the basement or first floor. But I can see a sliver of light behind curtains in a back second-floor room that are not completely closed.

That's where he has her.

I carefully check the handle of the door next to the garage. Locked. Solid wood. Looks like metal bracing around the frame.

I dash back out front and jump the fence again to see if help has arrived. The street is silent. I bound up the five steps to the front door. The wrought-iron security door is unlocked. But I still am faced with two large oak doors with ornate carving and beveled-glass windows—but not big enough to fit through. I look at my watch. 11:58 p.m. I put my ear to the door. Not surprising, I can't hear a sound.

How am I going to get in? I'm not going to be able to do it silently. What happens then? Does he leave her and bolt? Does he kill her and bolt? Is she still alive?

If Dean, the Cutter Shark, is true to his word and waiting for summer to start—and if his watch isn't running fast—I have less than two minutes to get inside there.

God parted the Red Sea for Moses. All I need is for him to open the door for me.

June 20, 11:59 p.m.

Sometimes you've got to go old school to get the job done. It's amazing what a glass of ice water to the face does to interrupt one's sleep. My girl is awake at last.

Now why would she go and spoil the moment by calling me a nasty name?

Good girls shouldn't say bad words. Does she still not understand who is in charge?

I am forced to admit what I've tried to hide from myself. Our relationship isn't based on mutual respect and understanding. She really hasn't been a very good girl to me. Certainly no angel.

I like the way a metal edge looks against skin like hers.

I like that she's not so confident anymore—the way it makes her eyes go wide and pool up with tears. I don't like the red welt on her cheek. I didn't want to hit her. But she asked for it. She called me a dirty name. She needed to be punished.

11:59. A minute to go. No one would know the difference if I started a little early.

But I would know. And I want this to be right. So much has gone wrong in Chicago. I need this to be right.

And it will be.

The first-floor and basement windows are guarded by wrought-iron grills. I tug on each of them out front and all are secure. One minute to go. I am out-of-my-mind frustrated. I literally have a couple tears pop, not fall—pop—from the corners of my eyes. I guess I do cry. But only when I'm angry.

It's possible Klarissa is not even in the house with the Cutter Shark. I'm taking the word of a man who was on death's doorstep.

And the information he gave me came from a serial killer. Not the best witness. If that's the case, if Dean doesn't have her here, I can't save her. But I believe that Dell has pointed me in the right direction. I have no choice but to believe him. Because I can't believe I'm going to lose my sister.

Stop analyzing. The light is on. You know he has her in there.

If I don't get through this first door, knowing Klarissa is in here isn't going to matter. I have to get through this door and up a flight of stairs to the back of the house. I can't believe I left my Beretta behind. It would be so easy to blast off the door hinges with a round of bullets.

There are two large concrete planters on the front stoop with angels carved into them. I push both of them up to see if there's a key underneath. There isn't. I open the unlocked wrought-iron outer door and half scoot, half roll one of the planters on an awkward angle to hold it open. I pause and listen. Did that make too much noise?

I hear no sound inside and continue. I bend my knees and straighten my back and get the second planter cradled in my hands. I don't want to smash through the front door with all the noise it's going to make. But I have no choice.

Smashing in the front door it is.

June 21, 12:00 midnight

That's going to leave another bruise. Why not just hold still and make this easier for both of us? You're not cooperating like a good girl, Klarissa. And before this night is through, you are going to be a good girl. I deserve it. I demand it. And I will have it.

I'm going to help you. Help you find release. Closure.

Call out to God all you want. You aren't the first. Where you are, not even God can save you. And you can call for your sister all you want. What do you think she could do? I would break her like a twig. She thinks she's tough, but one punch from me and she went down easier than a house of cards.

Unless you want another shot of the sleepy medicine, time to hold still. You're only delaying the inevitable. You may not have plans this evening, but I've got to run!

Maybe this will help. I have a pretty good idea how proud you are of that face of yours.

Sorry to break it to you, sweetheart. People don't watch you do news because of your brains and articulation. They watch you because you have a pretty face. Maybe not so pretty now.

Now hold still!

I take two deep breaths and lift the planter to waist level—it has to weigh close to 300 pounds. My forearms are screaming. I torque my body so I am facing the street, get my body weight moving toward the building, rotate my torso, and swing the planter with all my weight behind it into the middle of the front doors with a crash.

I feel a pop in my right knee and pain shoots up and down my leg in a slow-motion moment of déjà vu that takes me back nine years to my last soccer game for NIU when I tore my ACL.

I feel woozy. Like I am about to faint.

Just keep moving. God, help me move.

June 21, 12:01 a.m.

You have got to be kidding me. What else can go wrong? It sounds like we have visitors, darling Klarissa. Just when I thought I had you all to myself.

I do find it frustrating that people won't leave me alone to do my work. That's all I asked for at this moment. To be left alone.

Sadly, Angel, our last time together is going to be rushed. Very rushed.

Adrenaline is an amazing gift from God. Not even the cortisone our team trainer used to shoot me with works like this. My knee feels no pain. I am sprinting up the stairs to the second floor. I know where he is and he knows I'm coming. I reach for my Beretta and discover it hasn't magically appeared. No matter. I can take him.

He's got a choice: fight or flight. I have a feeling he made up his mind long before this moment.

I'm at the top of the stairs. In the back of my mind, I know that my knee is shredded and will soon be weeping in agony. That doesn't worry me. A little voice is telling me that when the hand-to-hand combat starts, I won't be able to kick effectively, if at all. I may not weigh as much as the guys, but Soto says I pack a big punch. I hope he's right.

I stride down the narrow hallway to the back corner room. The key for me now is to not think but to just keep moving and let my training take over. There is no plan available other than a full assault on the bedroom door. Kick it in and be ready to attack anything that moves. Other than Klarissa.

Has not waiting for backup, for a full-blown SWAT team, encouraged the Shark to move faster? Maybe. But in the depths of my spirit I know that this is the only possible course of action if I am to save Klarissa.

I'm at the door and try to turn the knob. Locked. I take a step back, balance myself on my damaged right leg, and give an excruciating kick that buckles the door open.

I can only hope that my relatively quiet mad dash up the stairs gives me even a second of surprise to lash out first.

Hold on, Klarissa.

June 21, 12:02 a.m.

Only one set of steps. And they are light. Could it be? She came alone? If she did, then I will admit . . . not even I could have planned it so well. That would be too good to be true.

Sisters. A two-for-one bargain. Incredible.

Come on, Kristen, keep moving. To think I was ready to just settle for your sister before leaving town. But this is so much better. I get my sweet detective in the bargain too. I'm not going to get to express my full artistry—I'm sure the Keystone Kops are right behind her—but two in the hand is worth more than one in the bush. Ha ha.

Just a few more steps . . .

I don't have to guess where the Cutter Shark is as I hurl myself into the room. He is on top of me as I come through the shattered door. I have a split second to see his face and an eternity to take everything in. I even have time to agree that it must be possible to see your entire life pass before your eyes in the instant before death. He's not what I expected—and nothing like his pictures. He looks like a middle-aged skinhead with lots of tattoos.

Robert Frost's road poem flashes in my mind. Two roads diverged in the woods or snow or something. That seems quite apt for Dell and Dean. Whatever happened to them as boys, they definitely went different directions. The road I took, following my dad as a cop, means that for Dean and me, our roads have now converged.

The instant I kicked the door in, it bounced off the rubber stopper and Dean used the momentum of the door bouncing back to drive it at me and try to sandwich me in the doorway. The door whacks the right side of my body and my right arm. I'm pretty sure it broke my wrist. I'm very dependent on my right foot and hand, and that side of my body is now nearly out of commission. I spin away in agony, narrowly avoiding his roundhouse punch. I think of my dad taking me to the soccer field and having me kick left-footed goals over and over to build my power and aim. Thanks, Dad.

I hope there is some physical memory trace to help me now.

As he tackles me in a bear hug and both of us slam against a nightstand, the lamp crashes to the floor and we carom off the side of the bed and sprawl into the center of the spacious room. I catch a glimpse of Klarissa. She is tied to the bed with duct tape at her wrists and ankles. I see a flash of blood. Is she dead already? Am I too late? I want to scream. I focus and feel a supernatural energy to fight kick in. Adrenaline or God? Maybe both.

We grapple and roll and he ends up on top of me. He tries to pin me on my back but then reaches back to pull a knife from his belt. I spit in his face. He recoils and gives me just enough room to really arch my spine and put everything I have into a head butt. I catch him right on the bridge of the nose. It is with great satisfaction that I hear the cartilage splinter and see blood explode from his face.

He instinctively shoots both hands to cover his mangled nose and I am able to twist and scoot away on all fours. I thrust a donkey kick back in the direction of his head. I feel a nice solid thud on his jawbone with my left foot.

Enraged and bleeding he lunges at me from a crouch. He got the knife out fast and the blade is arcing sideways toward the center of my body. Half kneeling, I still get an arm up inside his trajectory and deflect his slash, while rolling away as hard as I possibly can. My wrist is definitely broken and I can hear more bones grinding from the force of his blow. The knife is already flashing toward me again and despite partially blocking it, I feel the blade cutting the flesh in my obliques. But I actually feel a surge of relief, knowing he missed my vitals and that the gash is going to be mostly superficial. What's another scar? Mom always tells me I should wear one-piece bathing suits. It crosses my mind she is going to get her wish. I get my left foot back up. Not enough room for a kick, but I push him away with it. We both stagger to our feet.

"You just love screwing things up, don't you?" he asks, panting and circling me. "I'm going to put an end to that."

He moves the knife in small circular movements in front of him. I take a step backward and then a second and third as he moves toward me.

What's left of the door is shut and I'm almost trapped against it. He lashes at my face and I duck under it. The momentum of his attack carries him forward as he jams the tip of the knife into the solid wood of the door frame. I watch his eyes widen from the effort to pull the blade free. I deliver a left-right combo, my broken right to his gut with little force, but my left hard to his mouth. He pulls the knife free and tries a quick back cut with it. I anticipate correctly and move to the side, landing a hard kidney punch. I hear him exhale sharply. But he counters with an elbow to my jaw and tries to grab my hair. I jump back and we are facing each other. I can hear a herd of loud footsteps on the floor below. He doesn't seem to notice. He has a crazed, bloody smile on his face. Blood is even bubbling between his teeth as he grins, reminding me of a . . . shark.

Help has arrived, but they won't get up here in time to save me. Whatever happens next is up to me. Problem is I'm physically shot. I can barely stand, much less move. Now it's me on the precipice between life and death. I've taken my sister's place. They'll get here in time to save her. I put her in harm's way, so it seems only right.

Ever the predator, he smells blood in the water and moves in for the kill.

Don't give up now.

I spin into an excruciating crouch and drive my left fist into his solar plexus with every ounce of power I have—Barry Soto would be proud. Dean seemed to be looking for a right and I mixed it up. I won't tell Mr. Barry it was from necessity.

Dean grunts and I hear a raspy wheeze as the air is knocked from his lungs from my blow. I dart forward. He has lowered the knife trying to catch his breath. I get halfway around him and manage to hook a finger in his eye socket with my thumb leveraged on the base of his already fractured nose. He screams and drops his knife, but still manages to lunge away, freeing himself from my grip. He recovers in a blink and comes at me low, but way too slow. I get both of my hands behind his head and pull forward as I drive my left knee forward into his already severely damaged face. But even as he falls back he drives his leg up and retaliates by nailing me in the crotch. I bend forward in pain, praying that nothing's broken down there. I may not want a husband just yet, but I know I want children someday.

Footsteps are pounding up the stairs. I have a chance. Now I'm simply trying to stay away from him. I'm panting, circling, bleeding, limping. Neither of us has a weapon. He bull-rushes me and grabs my hair to push me down and drives a sharp elbow into the middle of my upper back as I go down. The momentum is his, but I'm not through. I throw my head back and up, hoping to catch him on the nose again. I'll settle for the chin. I know the force of my head and his face meeting will hurt me as much as it does him, but I've got to get free. If he gets me to the floor again, I'm history. I connect with his chin and from the sound of grinding and twisting bone, I'm sure I've busted his jaw. I hope so, because I really am seeing stars and wobbling defenselessly on my feet with my back to him. He's too injured to finish me when he could have. But somehow we are both upright and facing off again. We look in each other's eyes. How am I going to attack him next? What do I have left that works?

His face is a twisted, tortured chunk of hamburger meat. He takes a faltering step forward, fists up, sneering. I bob to the right again and come back with a straight left to his already shattered jaw. He falls backward with a small grunt and lands flat on his back. He is out for the count. I barely stay on two feet and stare at his hands for any sign of movement. I then kick him as hard as I can in the side with my left foot, just in case he's playing possum. A couple of broken ribs will make any sudden motion just about impossible. But he doesn't even groan.

I still don't feel safe. My eyes never leave him as I stumble over to my sister. She is sobbing, but no tears are falling down her cheeks and she is not making a sound. She could be doing a pantomime in an old silent movie or posing for Edvard Munch's *Scream* painting. I look her in the eyes and they are absolutely empty. But she's alive.

We can worry about empty eyes tomorrow.

I pull her close and feel the pulse on her neck, which is strong and true. I try to rip the duct tape off her, but I'm too weak. I fall back on the bed beside her.

Don, Martinez, Blackshear, and Reynolds crash through the door, guns in two hands and safeties off, their eyes racing in every direction. The cavalry has arrived. My heroes. It's about time, you slackers. I don't have enough energy to say anything out loud. The battle's already won. I can relax now.

But instead I pass out.

89

June 22, Obituary Page, *Chicago Sentinel*

Allen (AJ) Johnson, 56, died at his home in Lombard, Illinois, on June 19. The cause of death was internal bleeding from knife wounds. Johnson was a longtime news anchor for WCI-TV and for the past six years produced his own news report that was distributed exclusively over the web. He was known as the ChiTownVlogger.

Johnson was the only child of Frank and Mary Johnson. He is a graduate of St. Michael the Archangel High School. He attended Lombard Junior College and the University of Illinois Chicago Circle Campus, where he studied public policy and journalism. While at UICCC, he was editor of the student newspaper and one of the first graduates of its school of journalism.

It is estimated that his ChiTownVlogger site received more than half a million hits every day. He was the second-to-last victim of serial killer Dean Woods, the man that Johnson dubbed the "Cutter Shark."

Johnson was a particularly vocal critic of Mayor Michael T. Doyle Jr. The mayor issued the following comment in a press release from City Hall: "Many people assumed that I disliked the ChiTownVlogger. Honestly, I found him entertaining. I always respected his willingness to engage in the issues confronting our city. We will miss his sense of humor, his wit, and his call to accountability."

According to Allen Bowker, professor emeritus at the McGill School of Journalism, Northwestern University: "The mainstream press dismissed the ChiTownVlogger for his brand of 'yellow journalism,' yet he was both admired and feared by the same people who criticized him. His popularity with Gen-X and younger residents of Chicago far outpaced the major newspapers and television and radio stations. His death will leave a hole in the fabric of Chicago's information and entertainment network."

Johnson was preceded in death by both parents. He is survived by a daughter, Rebecca Johnson, who is a graduate student at the University of Illinois.

90

I roomed with Kaylen until I was five years old. She turned ten that year and was awarded her very own room, including her own desk, which I thought was so cool and grown-up. She moved into what had previously been Klarissa's nursery. My dad wasn't the greatest at doing household projects, so Kaylen had to whine close to a year before he painted over Klarissa's bright pink baby room with a sunflower yellow. That was an ugly yellow. Klarissa turned three that year and moved into the twin bed next to mine. She never complained about losing her individual room status. I complained plenty.

"Kristen," Mom would say when my friends were over and she wouldn't leave us alone, "she just wants to be included. Can't you include her?"

It feels like old times right now. We're in day two of our hospital stay together at Northwestern Medical Center off Michigan Avenue. My right wrist is in a cast. They had to put titanium pins in there. They've put a brace on my right knee. MRIs confirmed that I have torn the same ACL that I did almost a decade ago playing soccer— and for good measure I got the MCL, too. The patella is broken as well, but it's more or less in one piece—a little more than a stress fracture. The orthopedic surgeon has assured me that rehab is going to be a lot worse this time around due to the interior tear and my age.

I think he looked happy telling me that.

With new developments in arthroscopic surgery I'm amazed at how quick the doctor thinks I will be up and on the go at 100 percent.

I would have gone home the morning after we—after I—nailed

the Cutter Shark, but the doctors insisted I stay in for observation after the trauma of two attacks in one week. Wouldn't have mattered; Klarissa was there, so I would have stayed in the hospital room with her, with or without an assigned bed.

I look over at her sleeping like an angel. How could anyone not want to include her? Was I always a brat? I reach over to give her hand a squeeze but they couldn't get our beds quite close enough for that. Both of us have to reach out to make contact. I guess that's what we've been trying to do these past four months. Really our whole lives.

She is heavily bandaged. They brought a plastic surgeon into the emergency room. The Shark slashed her three times and the doctor spent five hours sewing her up. I live in America and that means I love numbers. I asked how many stitches. He explained that they really don't do individual stitches anymore. Just one long thread per wound. I guess I looked disappointed so he said that in the old days it would have been close to 100 of them. Maybe 150.

I blink back tears from the corners of each eye. I still don't cry.

Y ou're a hero."

"Thanks, Don. You're a hero, too. Well, at least my hero. Against all instincts, you didn't shoot me when you *finally* showed up."

"You never let up, do you?" he asks.

"Would you still want to be my partner if I did?"

"I'm going to get back to you on that one."

I glare at him in mock anger.

"Good point," he corrects himself, thanks to a sharp elbow to the ribs by Vanessa. "What would life be like without you as my partner?"

He's not going to quit, is he? He may look like a real estate agent, but he's a cop at heart. Same as me.

Vanessa rolls her eyes, pushes him to the side, and comes over and hugs me. I'm in my recliner with an ice pack wrapped around my right knee. They didn't want to do my arthroscopic surgery within a few days of my night with the Cutter Shark because I would need both hands for crutches—and my right hand will be in a cast for a couple weeks. I insisted. I won't get to play in an adult fall soccer league this year, but I do want to be ready to coach my Snowflakes.

So they rigged an extra metal splint in the cast on my right wrist that allows me to endure the crutches. I had to sign a waiver promising I wouldn't sue the doctor and hospital if I have future troubles with my wrist. When Jeff and Patricia came by he said not to worry about it; in America you can't sign away your rights and he has friends who would represent me for free.

Kendra comes out of the spare bedroom where she's been playing with her Kristen doll. She wrapped the doll's wrist and knee in white medical tape. I think that's sweet. She motions for Veronika to come back and play with her. I guess Vanessa told Veronika that she had to hug me and say something nice before doing anything else, so she pushes in front of Don and Vanessa and gives me a hesitant hug and tells me she hopes I feel better soon. Then she scurries back to play dolls with Kendra.

Be gentle, Veronika. The Kristen doll isn't in too good of shape.

I love my work but I have to admit, it's pretty nice just hanging out for a couple weeks while getting paid. I've always felt guilty when not doing something, but my various aches and pains and medical accessories have assuaged all such feelings. I've had plenty of visitors, though, including the mayor, the chief of police, the deputy director of the FBI, and my local congressman—all at the same time. I'm guessing that allowed them to split costs on security. I've got a couple awards coming my way. Very cool.

Czaka showed up, but stayed out of the way.

I'm pretty sure Don is jealous. Extremely cool.

Jimmy and Kaylen are coming over tonight with Klarissa. She's going to move in with me indefinitely. She can't sleep. She needs her sister. I offered to move into her place, which is a whole lot bigger and nicer than mine. But it's not just being afraid of being alone that has Klarissa spooked since being held captive by a serial killer. The Cutter Shark, Dell's brother, spent time in her townhome. I think we're going to have to pack up the whole place for her and put it up for sale, because I don't think she'll ever step foot in there again.

There's a good chance Vanessa will be her real estate agent. Once she makes the sale I'm guessing Don is going to get a new watch—he's had a picture of a Breitling model that costs a couple thousand bucks tacked to the wall of his cubicle—and the cashmere fall-weight blazer he's been yammering about. He isn't going to stay jealous about anything shiny I get from the city for very long.

Dell is alive and got moved out of ICU yesterday. They've questioned him as hard as the doctors would allow. Barring any new information, he will not be charged with any crimes. Everything in his story of trying to be a good brother and not being aware of what Dean was really into has checked out.

I haven't visited him and don't plan to. Our story is done. I feel a small sense of gratitude that he almost died trying to save Klarissa's life.

But he was a big reason she almost got killed. My mom visits him every day, but I've made it clear that he isn't to be part of any family activities.

Dean lived. Broken ribs, nose (in multiple places), jaw, and cheek. He also had a severe concussion. Barry Soto is proud of me. The FBI is holding him in an unidentified high-security hospital. CPD nailed the Cutter Shark, but we will now find out any information on the interrogation, his recovery, trial plans, and anything else on a need-to-know basis. Oh, we and all other local law enforcement agencies that ever investigated the Shark are on call if the feds need anything.

Zaworski and the other CPD task force team members are furious and grumbling. I'm relieved to be done with him. I admit it. Van Guten and Reynolds will get a lot more information from him than we would.

———

"When are you going to make your decision?" I ask Don.

"I already have," he answers.

"And?"

Before he can answer, my front door opens with a bang. What in the world?

Martinez leads the way into my living room carrying a birthday cake with thirty candles burning brightly.

I guess Jimmy and Kaylen aren't coming over with Klarissa later. They are here now, along with my mom, Jeff and Patricia, Zaworski and his wife, and the rest of the task force and various family members. My apartment isn't made to host a group this size. No one seems to care. My neighbor is going to complain big time about the noise on his ceiling.

I blow out the candles and make a wish.

Not even Kendra can get me to tell what it was.

THE BEGINNING OF AUGUST

dog days of summer *pl.n.* The hot, sultry period of summer between early July and early September, when Sirius, the dog star, sets and rises with the sun.

A period of stagnation.

CAMBRIDGE DICTIONARY OF IDIOMATIC PHRASES

Aunt Kristen, can I see your scars?"

If it was anyone asking but James, I'd be tempted to shoot first and ask questions later. That's not really a threat with my shooting scores.

Chicago is having a record-setting August heat wave. I've been off my crutches three weeks, and even though I'm still moving slower than I would like, I feel wonderful. Even without Percocet.

I'm at Jimmy and Kaylen's for Sunday dinner with Mom, Klarissa, and the kids. I'm glad it's just us. I like the extra company that usually shows up, but sometimes just immediate family is nice. Kaylen has fed us barbecued brisket and I'm on my second helping. Nothing wrong with my appetite. Even Klarissa, my roommate the past six weeks, has wolfed down at least three medium-sized bites.

There are two outstanding mysteries following the Cutter Shark case. First, the case of the yellow Post-it notes. Shelly swears it wasn't her. She brought flowers from the department to me when I was in the hospital and wrote on a sticky note to prove she has a different handwriting than whoever really did it. I couldn't care less who wrote them.

The second mystery is, who left a Hallmark card on my pillow and stole the picture of me and Dad on my graduation day? The handwriting doesn't fit Dean Pierre. Timmy? The punk? My neighbor who thinks I make too much noise? I'm not sweating that either.

Maybe there's a third mystery. Why does God allow bad things to happen to good people? I have no answer, but I do care. So sometimes lying awake late at night I have doubts I never did before. Is it possible that doubt is an occupational hazard—or a natural development when you are employed as a detective?

I've just turned thirty, but I've already seen a lot of ugly things. I'm not complaining or feeling sorry for myself. My life has been full of blessings, and I'm experiencing a few of them right now.

Sitting around the table, watching the give-and-take, the banter, the talking, arguing, and laughter of a still grieving widow, a scarred beauty queen, a sweet preacher, a mother with two adorable children and a third on the way, all enjoying time together, I almost believe in God like I did back when I went to church camp as a schoolgirl.

My phone buzzes on my hip. I don't plan to answer, but look down and see it is from good old Austin Reynolds. I haven't talked to him since the night we nailed Dean Woods. How I feel about him is a mystery, too. We had only a few dates. But I did like him. He must have liked me too. He brought flowers to the hospital and camped out at my bedside a couple times. I pretended to be asleep every time he stopped in. I think there's a non-isolated activity stream in my life when it comes to guys. On impulse I push my chair back, stand up, push the green button, and walk into the kitchen before answering.

"Conner."

"Hold on a second," he says. "I have to sit down. I think I might faint. I can't believe Chicago's most beautiful detective picked up my call."

"Ha ha."

"Let me guess; it's Sunday dinner at Kaylen's house and there's a big crowd."

"You must not have me under surveillance. Only family is here."

"Sounds nice. I never did score an invite."

"You might be the lucky one. Didn't work out that well for the last guy I dated."

"You are always on your A game, Detective Conner."

"Listen, Austin, if you want to talk about us and what happened, I'm going to be honest and tell you I don't see the point. You're back to DC and I'm . . . here."

"You never do waste time getting to the heart of the matter. But hey, I didn't call about us."

"Okay, what's up?" Did I sound disappointed? Am I disappointed?

"I'm actually calling for Willingham. He thinks you are the 'bomb' —his word, not mine. He wants you in DC tonight to work with us on a training program called TAR by yesterday."

"TAR?"

"Terrorist Attack Readiness. We are developing a program that filters to local law enforcement, and we think you'd be great to help us think through how local law enforcement can best digest information."

"I'm in rehab for my knee and wrist."

"First couple weeks are classroom only. Plus, we've got the best rehab center in the world. It's 200 yards from where you'll be staying."

"Did you remind Willingham that, number one, I already have a job and, number two, I'm still on paid disability leave?"

"I did. But he's pretty direct himself. He's already called your mayor and police commissioner and they said if you agree, you're free to work with us on a temporary assignment—and still keep your temporary disability pay. We'll pay you, too. Not full entry-level salary, but more than you're making. Double dipping wouldn't be too bad for a while, right? And if you find you like the work, there may be a chance at a longer consulting contract or permanent job offer."

My head is spinning as he tells me to get packed and head for the United Airlines counter at O'Hare where there is a first-class ticket will be waiting with my name on it to whisk me to Washington Reagan. He's pretty confident I'm going to say yes. I say nothing, but he presses on. He tells me to pick up some cash, grab a cab, and go to the Marriott Marquis by the White House, where there's a prepaid room reserved in my name. I'll meet an FBI staffer and receive a packet of complete instructions in the morning at the JavaStar on K Street, and then head to the FBI training grounds in Fairfax for five weeks.

Just a little over a month. I'd be back in time for Kendra's soccer season.

I wander back into the dining room in a daze. Mom is holding court as I bend over and hug Kendra and James close to me, planting a big kiss on their cheeks. James protests and makes some retching sounds. Jimmy gives him the look and he stops immediately. I even get a kiss on the cheek.

"I think we should drive over to the Indiana Dunes for a family day at the beach," my mom says, looking up at me. "You remember when we used to do that when you three were just little girls? Your dad loved it."

I'm overwhelmed for a moment, certain that this room holds just about all the people I love most in the world, and I'd never want to be anywhere else. Do I have it in me to leave? Even for a month?

I've hugged everyone and said my "I love you's." Mom is sniffling. Klarissa is, too, but she's been the most adamant about me packing a suitcase and catching the flight. She's gonna move from my place to Mom's house. *Dear Lord, help her. She's going to need it.* Thanks to her fab plastic surgeon, her scars are healing nicely, but I know there are more inside.

I didn't mention to anyone that Reynolds said this could turn into a job offer.

But I can't deny I'm excited. I've never flown first class. I've actually only flown three times in my life.

Can't remember what poet said, "Parting is such sweet sorrow."

He was soft-peddling it. It cuts like a knife.

M. K. Gilroy is a veteran publishing executive who has also authored, compiled, or ghostwritten numerous books that have landed on various bestseller lists. *Cuts Like a Knife*, his debut novel, is quickly garnering critical acclaim. www.mkgilroy.com.

WORTHY
PUBLISHING

IF YOU LIKED THIS BOOK . . .

- Tell your friends by going to: http://www.cutslikeaknife.org and clicking "LIKE"

    - Share the video book trailer by posting it on your Facebook page

    - Head over to our Facebook page, click "LIKE" and post a comment regarding what you enjoyed about the book

    - Tweet "I recommend reading #CutsLikeAKnife by @markgilroy @Worthypub"

- Hashtag: #CutsLikeAKnife

- Subscribe to our newsletter by going to http://worthy publishing.com/about/subscribe.php

WORTHY PUBLISHING
FACEBOOK PAGE

WORTHY PUBLISHING
WEBSITE